White Mountains

Brown River

Red River

White
Demesnes

Lattice

Vampires

East Pole

Blue
Demesnes

Red
Demesnes

Werewolves

Trolls

Mound Folk

Brown
Demesnes

PHAZE

PHAZE DOUBT

PHAZE
DOUBT

Piers Anthony

An Ace/Putnam Book
Published by G. P. Putnam's Sons
New York

An Ace/Putnam Book
Published by G. P. Putnam's Sons
Publishers Since 1838
200 Madison Avenue
New York, NY 10016

Library of Congress Cataloging-in-Publication Data

Anthon y, Piers.
  Phaze doubt/Piers Anthony.
    p. cm.—(The Apprentice adept series)
  "An Ace/Putnam book."
    I. Title. II. Series: Anthony, Piers. Apprentice adept series.
PS3551.N73P4   1990   89-24249 CIP
813'.54—dc20
ISBN 0-399-13529-4

Printed in the United States of America

1   2   3   4   5   6   7   8   9   10

This book has been printed on acid-free paper.
∞

Contents

PHAZE DOUBT

1

Lysander

Lysander found his assigned seat in the shuttle as it commenced slow acceleration. The spaceship had been a liner, with individual cabins for each passenger, but the planetary shuttle was cramped in the manner of an atmospheric transport. Well, he was used to tight quarters, after his time in the laboratory.

He hesitated, glancing at the young human woman in the adjacent seat. She was in the process of getting out of her dress by working it up past her legs and buttocks. "Please, excuse me, if it is not an imposition—"

She looked up at him, pausing in her labor. She had short curly black hair and dark brown pupils, in those respects almost matching him. But what was coming into view below didn't match. "Am I embarrassing you?" she inquired brightly.

"No, I am most interested. Your form strikes me as pulchritudinous."

She blinked. "What?"

Evidently he had used the wrong term. "Of aesthetic outline. Comely. Subject to admiration. Incitive of sexual ambition."

She smiled. "Attractive?"

"Yes, thank you. That must be the operative term."

"You're not from this neighborhood," she remarked.

"This is a perceptive observation. Indeed I am not. But you—you are a native of the upcoming planet?"

"Yes. In a manner. I'm a serf. We don't wear clothing."

"Now I understand. I read the handbook. I will be a serf too, to earn what I need to be recognized as an independent individual. But would you be willing to exchange seats? I have little experience of planetfall and would like to gaze out the window."

"Oh, of course. I've seen it before." She got up and stepped to the center aisle, her dress remaining halfway up. Lysander took the seat she had occupied. Then she lifted her dress the rest of the way off, over her head, leaving only pink bra and panties. She was a well-endowed female, quite appealing in that limited outfit. She folded the dress carefully and took the outer seat.

"Thank you," Lysander said. "May I introduce myself? I am Lysander, from Planet Grenadier. I am a specialist in robot feedback circuitry."

"Alyc," she responded. "That's A-L-Y-C, not ALICE. We serfs have little of our own except our names. I'm assistant whatever for Citizen Blue. Not in your class, I guess."

"Class?"

"I'm not educated like you. I just help with housework and cooking and whatever, as I said. I never got beyond regular schooling."

He smiled. "There may be a misunderstanding. I did not have schooling. I am an android."

She stared at him momentarily, startled. "You're joking!"

"My humor is limited, as it is in all my kind. My body was generated in the laboratory."

"But androids are, well, not smart. You don't talk at all like that!"

"Perhaps that is because my brain is fully organic. It was taken from a living creature and implanted in the android body, in the manner of a cyborg. I was pre-educated in the laboratory, so my only challenge was learning to use the body."

"That's fascinating!" she said. "I never heard of an android cyborg!"

"So as you understand, I am not in your class, not being a proper man. I have existed in this form only two years."

She was gazing at him with increasing interest. "You haven't had social experience on your own world?"

"I am not entirely certain what you mean. I am conversant with the appropriate modes for eating, eliminating, sleeping—"

"Man/woman," she said. "Interaction."

"I have been instructed on the mechanism for copulation."

Alyc laughed. "Dating. Dancing. Kissing."

"The mechanisms for relating the local calendar to current events, or—" He saw by her expression that he was not reflecting her intent. "I suspect not."

"Would you like to start with me? I mean, until you get into things in Phaze?"

"Phase? To be in phase, or out of phase?"

She laughed again. "Phaze. With a z. The magic part of Proton."

"Magic? I think I must misunderstand."

"So you don't know about that. Well, I guess they haven't bruited it about, offplanet. You'll see. But what I meant was whether you would like to be my boyfriend, until you find a girl of your intellect?"

"But you are full human!" he protested. "My indoctrination is specific about the perils of miscegenation. I am obliged to inform any human person of my status as quasi-human."

She turned earnestly to him. "I am a serf. And you will be too. We're all equal, on Proton: humans, robots, cyborgs, androids, and aliens. All naked, too; will you be able to handle that?"

He frowned. "The social—the types interact? I assumed that the social interaction was confined android to android, and man to woman, in practice."

"You are a man, Lysander, as I'm sure I can show you. The only forbidden interaction is disobedience to a Citizen. Of course serfs don't normally marry, but they do have relationships. So—" She looked at him questioningly.

"In that case, yes, I would like to be your social friend. As I remarked, your physique is attractive."

"Oh, I'm so pleased!" she exclaimed. "I'm sure it will be very nice, the little time it lasts."

"These affiliations are of limited duration?"

"With me they are. You see, I like smart men, and I can attract them at first, but they always leave me for smarter women."

"I apologize in advance for doing that."

She started to laugh, but changed her mind, remembering that he wasn't much for humor. "Well, let's make it count." She leaned over to kiss him.

"Secure belts for landing." It was the shuttle announcer system, giving warning of higher acceleration. The vessel had been accelerating at just under one gee throughout, backward, its jets toward the planet. In this manner it had reduced the momentum it had started with at the ship. But now it had to make planetfall, and that would require more than one gee.

"Never fails," Alyc said. "Just when things get interesting." She kissed him quickly and settled back into her seat, fishing for her harness.

Lysander heeded the directive, and snapped his own seat harness about his humanoid body, glancing around as he did so. The other passengers were all humanoid, most of them seeming to be fully human beings, some seeming to be robots. This was hardly surprising, since Proton was a human colony; few creatures of planets other than Earth found it compatible. Gravity, atmosphere, diurnal cycle, light intensity, and temperature range closely matched those of the colonizing planet.

"Is it all right if I watch the approach?" he asked. "I am of course interested in what you propose, but you will remain, while the vision of the landing will be fleeting."

"Of course it's all right," she said, after a slight hesitation. "I'll just hold your hand, meanwhile."

Lysander peered out of the old-fashioned porthole. They were approaching the planet obliquely, and he had an excellent view of it. He was indeed fascinated by it.

The odd thing about Planet Proton was that its South Pole pointed directly toward its sun, always. Most planets in most systems rotated in the planes of their ecliptics, so that their equators were warmest and their poles coldest. Some were skew, so that their poles were alternately heated as they proceeded through their years. But Proton acted as if it were on a fixed axle extending from the star, in seeming defiance of the laws of physics.

The acceleration increased. Gee rose to about 1.5. His right hand felt odd. He tore his eyes away from the porthole and looked at it.

Alyc was holding his arm to her bosom and kissing his hand. It was warmth of her breath on his fingers that had distracted him. Relieved that it was nothing serious—sometimes this body reacted in odd ways to stress, and 1.5 gee was a type of stress—he returned his gaze to the porthole.

What Lysander found hard to figure was how the planet maintained a regular day-night cycle. With the sunlight coming always toward the South Pole, there should be no changes; the southern hemisphere should always be day, the northern hemisphere night. Yet that was not the case. The planet acted as if the light were turned at right angles, and it cast its night shadow to the side. The manual indicated that scientists had never been able to agree exactly how this was possible, but it was so. The prevailing theory of the moment was that the planet acted with respect to light like a black hole, bending the light ninety degrees without affecting anything else. This left formidable questions unanswered, but was the best that offered. Apparently no competent local study had been undertaken to resolve the mystery.

Then the shuttle changed orientation. The planet seemed to swing back and out of sight. They were coming down to the surface. There was nothing of interest to be seen now.

Alyc still had his hand. She was licking it. Lysander tried to remember whether this was normal procedure, but found no applicable facet. He had to assume that it was within tolerance for the species.

Alyc saw him looking. "I'm sorry," she said. "High-gee makes me nervous." She removed her mouth, but did not let go of his hand.

A stress reaction. He filed the information in a facet. Others might have different mechanisms of coping. Still, it was possible that it was not the mere availability of more intelligent companions that caused males to leave this woman.

The gee increased. Then there was a bump, and the gee reverted to one. They were down.

Alyc relaxed. She released Lysander's hand. "I feel so much safer on solid land," she said. "Low-gee or high-gee just—" She shrugged. Then she touched the center of the bra, and it separated and fell away. "We might as well wait for the others to clear," she said, nodding her head at the people now stepping into the aisle.

Lysander noted that a number of the others had done as Alyc had, and were now naked. They carried their clothing bundled under their arms. They seemed to have no luggage.

Alyc drew up her legs, bending the knees. In a moment she had worked the panties off. "You might as well strip here," she said. "That way, they'll think you're a returning serf, like me, and you won't have to go through the indoctrination routine."

Lysander nodded. He preferred to avoid attention. He started to get out of his clothes, awkwardly, in the seat.

Alyc jumped to help him. Her hands touched his body caressingly, not shying away from the genital region.

"I am not certain this is wise," he said.

"Oh, no, it's better to strip now," she assured him.

"The presence of your hands is causing a reaction," he explained.

"Oh, that's right—you're new here. You think naked is sexy!"

"I was under that impression. Am I mistaken?"

"Yes, here. Serfs aren't sexy, they're dull. We really have to work at it to get sexy. Clothing helps a lot; I got so heated up the first time I went offplanet—" She shrugged again. "But I know it's the other way around, with you. I can take care of it, though. Just get naked so I can—"

He realized that she intended to proceed to a sexual engagement. Human interest in the act declined after it had been indulged. But he foresaw points of awkwardness, because he understood that such an act was normally done in a private place, and would attract some attention if done publicly. Also, his inexperience was likely to contribute to miscues. It would be better to avoid it at this time.

However, he did not wish to walk out of the ship in an obvious state of sexual excitement; that too might attract attention.

He would have to draw on his true nature to turn it off. "I think I am adapting to the culture," he said. "Allow me a moment."

"If you wish." She seemed disappointed.

He reverted to his core facet. Now he saw things as he would if in his natural body, rather than as the humanoid body did. He opened the two eye segments available and looked at the woman.

She was completely repulsive. A mat of long fur sprouted from the top and rear of her head to dangle around the auditory flaps and the jaw bone, tufts of it coiling of their own accord. Her breathing orifice projected, and her eyes were rounded and set in sockets. Assorted white teeth showed within the peeling gash of her sustenance intake orifice. Substantial bags of flesh hung against her front. She had two massive upper limbs and a bifurcate base.

He shut off the eyes; the awful vision was too strong. If he allowed it to go further, he would be unable to function in this alien society, and therefore unable to pursue his mission.

He stood and quickly completed the disrobing. He had no sexual interest in the female now. He hoped he would be able to damp down the vision of her fleshy nature when the time came, as it inevitably would, to indulge in the way she preferred.

"I guess you did adapt," Alyc said. "Well, maybe some other time.

It isn't too good in a shuttle, anyway, I think." She evidently would
have been glad to make a trial of it, however.

"Yes. Now I must enter the city and seek employment."

"You don't have a job yet?" she asked.

"I understand that employment is inevitable. Was I required to
achieve it before coming?"

"Oh, no! I just thought maybe you had been brought in for your
expertise. A special assignment."

"No, I merely wish to achieve a suitable situation, in a culture that
accepts androids more readily than does my own."

"Then maybe you can apply for work with Citizen Blue!" she exclaimed, delighted. "He's a good employer, really he is! He's very
generous. Most Citizens don't allow their serfs offplanet until their
terms are up and they *have* to go, forever, but he let me travel."

Lysander frowned, though this was exactly what he wished.
"Wouldn't that be a conflict of interest?"

She was preceding him down the aisle, her fleshy posterior shifting
its masses in ways that threatened to alienate him again. He focused
his two eyes on her face as it turned halfway back toward him. "Conflict?" she asked, perplexed.

"If you and I are to have an association, wouldn't that disallow
employment by the same Citizen?"

She laughed, as she so readily did. "No way! Citizens don't care
about serf interactions. Just so long as they do what they're told. The
only trouble is when a Citizen wants a serf-girl for sex and doesn't
want anyone else using her. But Blue isn't like that; he's true to his
wife, as he has been for twenty years."

"She must be a remarkable woman."

"She's a robot. They have a son." She paused, waiting for his reaction.

He made it, as they left the shuttle and passed into the interior
chamber of the spaceport. "A robot had a son?"

"The son's a robot too," she explained. "Her name is Sheen, and
his is Mach. Mach-Sheen, Machine, you see; it's sort of a pun, only
nobody laughs. And he's married to an alien female, and they have a
daughter, Nepe. Only it's more complicated than that."

"I think that's as complicated as I can assimilate," Lysander said
ruefully. He glanced around the large chamber. Sure enough, only
the clothed parties were being challenged; the naked ones were ig-

nored. "So you believe that Citizen Blue might employ me, if he has use for my abilities?"

"He sure might!" she said enthusiastically. "I can ask him for you!"

"Is this normal procedure? I understand that I should register for employment, and that if I did not obtain it within three days I would be summarily dismissed from the planet. I admit this is a concern."

"You register, but Blue will ask for you, if I ask him, maybe," she said.

"In that case, by all means ask him," Lysander agreed.

"Oh, this is working out so well!" she said, taking his hand and holding it as they walked side by side.

Lysander was coming to understand better why Alyc's liaisons tended to be brief. She was quite open, and perhaps possessive, offering her wares too rapidly, so that her store was quickly exhausted. But this was extremely convenient now. He had received instruction in the laboratory, but had no direct experience, so her forward attitude enabled him to learn quickly without a great risk of error.

She brought him to a registration desk at the spaceport. "Check in here, and they'll give you a three-day permit," she explained. "Then I'll take you to Blue."

He approached the desk. "May I register for employment?"

The naked woman behind the desk glanced at him, bored. "Name and planet of origin?"

"Lysander of Grenadier."

She glanced at a terminal screen. "Right. Android. Your specialties are games and computer circuitry. Put your eyes to the window."

She had a detail wrong, but it seemed expedient to let it pass. He was trained in robotic feedback circuitry, which related to programming rather than hardware.

There was a panel with a scanning window. He put his face to it, knowing that the scanner would record his retinal patterns and match them to those of his listed identity. Such identification could be counterfeited only by the replacement of the eyeballs, which was more trouble than the average intruder would care to undertake. Androids were standarized in many respects, including the immune system, so they could take eyeball transplants more readily than full humans could. But all android retinal patterns were registered, so unless the paperwork was in order, a transplant was useless for any purpose other than correcting a defect in vision.

"Are you familiar with local protocol?" the woman asked as he stepped away from the window. The scan had checked, of course.

"I believe so. I go naked, address every Citizen as sir, and do what I'm told."

"There are details. Are you aware, for example, that magic is operative here?"

"Prestidigitation is a game skill I have developed. It will be interesting to compare local techniques."

The woman's mouth turned wry. "This is more than that. Perhaps you should take the indoctrination course."

"I'm helping him," Alyc put in. "I'm Alyc, employee of Citizen Blue. May I call the Citizen now?"

"If you wish." The woman turned a videophone screen toward her.

"Alyc calling Citizen Blue," she said to the screen.

The clerk's eyebrow elevated. "You expect him to answer you direct?"

A woman's face appeared on the screen. Her eyes were green and her hair brown, fading to bleached strands at her shoulders. The lines about her face and neck indicated that she was not young, but she remained beautiful. "You're back, Alyc!" she said with evident pleasure. "Was it a good trip?"

"Yes, Sheen. But funny wearing clothes. I'm glad to be back. Could —could I talk to the Citizen, please?"

The clerk made a tiny shake of her head at this audacity. It was obvious that smart serfs did not push their luck like this.

A man's face came on the screen. There was no question of his age; he was at least in his fifties, but his eyes were alert. The collar of a shirt was visible at the base of the picture; he was clothed, therefore a Citizen. "Yes, Alyc."

The clerk's jaw dropped slightly. She turned away.

"Sir, I met a man on the ship back, and maybe you could hire him."

The Citizen's countenance quirked in what was becoming to Lysander a familiar expression in those who spoke to Alyc: the one assumed when dealing with a child or harmless animal that had intruded on the carpet. "Perhaps. Who is he?"

"Lysander. He knows about computers and games. I thought—"

"He is present?"

"Right here, sir," she said eagerly, moving aside so that the Citizen could look at Lysander.

Blue nodded. "No promise, Alyc. But bring him here."

"Oh, thank you, sir!" she exclaimed, actually jumping in her excitement. But the Citizen's glance at Lysander, as the image faded on the screen, was disconcertingly sharp. This was going to be far more chancy than the registration had been!

Alyc led him out of the spaceport to a public transport car. It was half filled with naked humanoids, with a few machines of various configurations. All the human beings were in good health, none fat; it was obvious that the governing Citizens did not encourage overindulgence. In fact, this seemed to be a well-run planet.

"About magic," Lysander said. "What did the clerk mean about that? You mentioned it on the shuttle but did not clarify your reference."

"About a year ago the frames merged," Alyc said brightly. "Citizen Blue did it, to stop the Contrary Citizens from taking over and ruining everything. That was just before I came here, so I don't know how it was before, but it certainly is nice now. Anyway, science works, and magic works. It's a lot of fun."

"My education, as I said, was programmed. My brain was in effect force-fed with the language of this planet and the general nature of the galaxy, and the necessary skills of survival were inculcated. Perhaps I missed something. Magic is generally known as a fraud, something that can not possibly operate as claimed. It is nonsensical by definition. Therefore I wish to know what is meant by the term here, as it can not be what I mean by it."

She smiled knowingly. "Brother, have you got a learning experience coming!"

"You propose to show me actual magic?"

"Well, not me personally. It's mostly only those who have been here a long time who can do it, especially the mergees. But I'm sure—"

"Mergees?"

"Oh, this gets complicated! You see, there were these two frames, Proton and Phaze—with the z, remember?—and they were sort of separated, and in one science worked and in the other magic worked. The people, a lot of them were the same, I mean people in Proton had other selves in Phaze, who did magic. But then they merged, and all the people merged too, and now they—well, wait till you meet Mach/Bane and Fleta/Agape!"

"MacBane and Fleta who?"

"They—you won't believe me until you see it. Meanwhile, just take my word: there's magic here now, because the lands merged too. But they say a lot of it only works once, so they don't do it much, except for the natural shape changing."

"I will take your word," Lysander said, hoping she did not catch the cynicism. She had not seemed crazy before! In due course they arrived at the section of the city that housed Citizen Blue's estate. Lysander was surprised to find it ordinary; there was no ostentation. His respect for the Citizen grew, and his dismay; he was not at all sure he could fool this man.

"You look nervous," Alyc remarked. "I know how it is; I was so scared when I first came here I thought I'd do something in my pants—and I didn't have any. But Blue is just great; you'll like him."

Lysander doubted it.

"And we can be together," she continued cheerily. "I can show you around everywhere. Blue does that; he lets newcomers break in easy."

That was more appealing. The longer he had before he had to get serious about his mission, the better it would be.

He assumed that they would be admitted to some outer chamber, where the Citizen would interview him by video. This was not the case. They were ushered instead into the main apartment, where Citizen Blue and Sheen stood waiting.

Sheen stepped forward and hugged Alyc as if she were a dear friend. Sheen was a robot, but this was hardly apparent; she seemed as womanly as it was possible to be.

"Did you have a nice visit home, dear?" Sheen inquired.

"Yes!" Alyc agreed with her customary vigor. "Mom told me I needed to eat more, I was thin as a reed!" This was laughable; she was about as well fleshed as she could be without sacrificing sex appeal.

"Don't listen to her," Sheen said, smiling. "Men prefer thin. Speaking of which—this is your new young man?" Her eyes turned to Lysander.

"Yes—as of an hour past," Lysander said. "She has been helping me get adapted."

"She does that," Sheen agreed. She turned back to Alyc. "Let's go get reacquainted with Agnes. The men may want to talk."

The two naked women walked to another room, leaving Lysander with the Citizen. Citizen Blue was a tiny man, a head shorter than average, though not so small as to be a dwarf. He wore an open shirt and casual trousers, with slipper-type shoes. On any other humanoid planet he would have been dismissed as a man of no consequence. Here the clothing made him a figure of stature.

Yet even if Blue had been naked, his bearing would have set him apart. The man had power, and it seemed to imbue him with a presence that was not to be ignored. Lysander presumed that this was typical of Citizens in general, but perhaps especially of this one, because he knew that Blue was not just any Citizen. He was *the* Citizen—the leading figure of the planet. That was why his ready accessibility was surprising. Surely there were bodyguards watching, or killer laser beams oriented on the visitor; the Citizen would not leave himself open to the mischief of a stranger.

"Sit down, Lysander," Blue said, and took a seat himself.

Lysander sat opposite, in one of the simple plastic chairs. This was no social visit; it was an employment interview. It was also, more critically, a test. If Blue had any notion of Lysander's true mission—

"Your meeting with Alyc was no coincidence," the Citizen said.

And there it was, already. "No, sir," Lysander agreed.

"Please explain."

"I have special training. My planet—the authorities there—wish to upgrade their computer technology, especially with regard to self-willed robots. They feel that solid experience with advanced systems should help. When they discovered that a servant of a family including two self-willed robots was returning to Proton, they felt the opportunity was too good to be allowed to pass. So they arranged for me to be seated beside that servant, who was known to be friendly to handsome men."

"And you were created handsome," Blue said.

"Yes, sir. My body is android, crafted on ideal humanoid lines. My brain is animal, so that I do not suffer the typical dysfunction of androids."

"You are using Alyc as an avenue to employment here?"

"No, sir. That is, the intent was to befriend her, and so have better access to those who are in a position to guarantee my employment in my specialty. It was known that you support your employees, so if you felt her situation would be improved by my retention as a serf on this planet, you would arrange it. But actual employment *by* you—"

"She surprised you by being too helpful," Blue said.

"Yes, sir."

"Your background checks out. We can use you. But I take exception to the mechanism of your acquaintance with Alyc. She is vulnerable to exploitation, especially by a male such as yourself. She wears her heart on her sleeve, as one of our ancient sayings puts it, but she is not an unworthy person. What are your intentions toward her?"

"I have no present emotional commitment, sir. If you direct me to disassociate with her, I will do so."

"I do not make directives of that nature."

"Then I would prefer to explore the association she proffers, sir. I am inexperienced in social and sexual interactions, as I was crafted two years ago and have spent the majority of my awareness in training. I believe she could show me much I lack."

"And when you have had that experience?"

"She has informed me that her associations are generally brief, because men come to prefer more intelligent women. My interest is in my specialty rather than in any social situation. I see no reason to break with her unless that is her preference."

"These things are not necessarily predictable," the Citizen said. "I loved a human woman, but later lost that love, and associated with Sheen instead. If your interest changes, you should do as you wish. I only ask that you give Alyc a fair chance, and if you have occasion to change women, that you set her down gently."

"I shall do that, sir."

"Then go and tour the planet," Blue said. "Alyc will show you the landmarks. Familiarize yourself with our conventions before settling down to your specialty."

"But sir, with all due respect, I have only three days to find employment. If I squander it—"

Blue silenced him with a slightly elevated hand. "I apologize, Lysander. I thought you understood. You have been registered as my employee. My suggestion was in the nature of a directive."

Lysander stared at him, for the moment too surprised to speak.

The Citizen smiled. "You are new here. That is why you need to familiarize yourself with our culture. Let me anticipate Alyc with this one caution: when a Citizen speaks to you, take him literally. Never protest the case, unless you are sure you know something he doesn't which might affect the case. In all other circumstances, simply ignore a Citizen, except to stay out of his way."

"I apologize for transgressing, sir," Lysander said, embarrassed.

"And don't apologize to a Citizen; that presumes sufficient status to make it meaningful."

"Yes, sir," Lysander said, embarrassed again.

"And do not speak at all unless he requires it of you."

Lysander was silent.

Blue laughed. "There is no offense, Lysander. Merely a demonstration. Come, we shall join the ladies." He got up, and Lysander immediately stood also.

Blue glanced at him. "Did I tell you to stand?"

"No, sir," Lysander said hastily, sitting down again.

"But it was implied. I invited you to join the ladies, which you would find awkward to do if you remained seated. But if you stood merely because I did, you were in error."

Lysander stood again, silently. He suspected he was flushing the full length of his body.

Blue clapped him on the shoulder. "A few days with Alyc will enable you to get everything straight. But your specialty may attract the interest of other Citizens, or I may contact you myself in that period, and I would not want to be embarrassed by having an employee who seemed uncertain of relevant protocol. I can not say I approve of all the details of our system, but others do, and that makes appearances important. Do you understand?"

"Yes, sir."

"Exactly." Blue showed the way to the other room.

An older maid was serving a beverage at a table. "This is Agnes, maid and friend," Blue said. "In the absence of myself and my wife, she is the ranking figure of this household, and you will honor any request she makes of you."

Lysander nodded to Agnes, but did not speak. They took places at the table.

Alyc glanced at the Citizen as if wanting to say something. Blue nodded. "Sir, Lysander doesn't believe in magic."

The Citizen frowned. "And you had the audacity to associate with him?"

Sheen smiled. Lysander, taking his cue from her, smiled also.

"Yes, sir," Alyc said, abashed. "I thought maybe—"

"This sounds like a job for my granddaughter," Blue said.

"Yes, sir."

"You can spare him for an hour?"

"Yes, sir!" Alyc said, happy.

"But you know he will never be the same, once Nepe finishes with him."

"Don't tease her, dear," Sheen reproved Blue. He smiled. It was obvious that Alyc was quite satisfied to be teased by this man.

The Citizen nodded to Agnes, who left the room. Then they settled down to their beverage, which turned out to be pseudo-wine. This had the flavor and texture of something vintage, but no alcoholic content. Lysander was interested to see that Sheen drank it too. She was the perfect woman, machine though she was.

Lysander saw a problem on the horizon. These were likeable people, and he liked them. That was apt to be awkward, when he had to act.

2
Magic

The Citizen's granddaughter Nepe showed up before they finished their wine. She was a little girl, nine years old, naked in the serf manner, with flouncing brown hair covering her ears. She dashed up to Citizen Blue for a hug, her hair flying out with a vigor of her motion, then spied the visitor and abruptly turned formal. "You summoned me, sir?"

"I have hired Lysander," Blue said, indicating him. "He does not believe in magic."

Slowly the girl's head turned toward Lysander. She smiled impishly. "We shall have to do something about that," she said, with an odd certainty.

"Go with Nepe," the Citizen said to Lysander.

Without a word, Lysander got up and approached the child. She extended her hand, and he reached out to take it—and paused, startled.

Her arm terminated in a mass of squirming tentacles.

Oh—she was a shape changer. There were several galactic species that could change their forms, and some of them were surely represented here. If this was the nature of the "magic," he need have little concern.

He took the "hand" without flinching, knowing that it was someone's notion of a joke or an initiation.

Suddenly they were standing in a field. Pleasant gray clouds drifted overhead, and sunlight brightened the waving grass. There was no evidence that the rays of the sun were bent at right angles; they seemed to descend from almost overhead, this being midday. But this amounted to an optical illusion. Just as a person saw the reflection in a mirror as an extension of the local scene beyond the mirror, he saw the sun where it seemed to belong. It was actually at right angles, to the south.

"You hungry, Lysander?" the child inquired in a different voice.

He glanced sharply down. He was now holding the hand of a boy! A tousle-headed lad clothed in black jacket and trousers, with blue socks and sneakers.

Oh: the girl had shape-changed again, forming her body surface into the appearance of clothing and quite possibly the semblance of masculinity beneath it. Still no magic. However, the abrupt change of scene still mystified him. How had that effect been arranged?

But he had to play the game. He affected unconcern. "Yes, actually. Is there suitable food here?"

"There's a melon tree not far off, but it's guarded by a dragon."

"I'd like to see this dragon," Lysander said. Indeed, he was curious about what the child would come up with next. He had to concede that this was an excellent demonstration.

"I'll give you a ride. But you'd better put on some clothing. Outside the domes it's Phaze now."

Suddenly Lysander was clothed. Shirt, trousers, shoes—everything. It had happened like magic.

Uh-oh. The child was still trying to trick him.

There was a musical honk. He looked—and saw a horse standing beside him. No, not a horse—a unicorn, with a long spiraled horn set in its forehead. Where was Nepe?

The animal honked again, gesturing with its horn toward its own back. Actually it was male, and the honk came from the horn itself, sounding like a woodwind instrument. If this was a simulation, as seemed to be the case, it was a clever one!

Well, he would continue to play along. He stepped toward the animal. "I'm not much at riding," he said. He had ridden horses, as it was an aspect of his gameplaying practice, but those had been tame and trained. He feared this creature was neither. He was also used to a saddle; bareback was more of a challenge. But if that was the way it was, so be it.

He grabbed a handful of mane and jumped, swinging a leg up and over. He half expected to get dumped as the animal bolted, but it remained still. Only when he was securely mounted did it move, and then carefully, so that he had no trouble keeping his seat.

The unicorn picked up speed, going into a trot. Then it played music through its horn: an actual melody. Lysander hung on and listened, amazed. He was unable to ascertain how such special effects were being accomplished.

They approached a grove of trees. Sure enough, one of them bore huge fruit that looked like melons—and there was a monstrous winged serpent snoozing around its base. The creature woke and hissed at them, sending up a cloud of smoke.

Lysander realized that such a creature could readily be mocked up with plastic and pseudoflesh, but the heat of its breath would still be dangerous. "Maybe I'll pass on the melon," he said.

The unicorn shrugged. Then it sprouted huge wings, pumped them, leaped, and became airborne. Lysander clung to its back, alarmed. The ground was now receding at an astonishing rate. Magic? It was getting difficult to doubt!

They approached a purple mountain. The thing was literally purple, even at close range; the foliage of the trees had a purplish cast. He had seen a map of Proton on which was marked PURPLE MOUNTAINS, but he had assumed that was figurative.

A gross bird launched from a tall tree. It flew up to intercept the flying unicorn. Lysander tried to judge what kind it was. He knew most of the Earth types that would have been brought here with the human colonists, but this ungainly thing with the huge head and dangling tresses—

It was a harpy! A mythical creature, part vulture and part human woman. No such creature existed, and even if it did, it would hardly be able to fly, any more than the unicorn could. The dynamics were all wrong.

Magic? It was a good show!

"Sheer off! Sheer off, imbecile!" the harpy screeched. "Think I want a 'corn in my tree?"

The unicorn sounded a brief melody. The harpy listened. "Oh. Sorry, Flach," she screeched. "I should have recognized thee. I were looking at the handsome man. Well, land at the foot and we'll talk."

The unicorn descended, and in a moment came to a four-point landing at the base of the tree. Lysander dismounted, and the boy reappeared. Then the harpy came down and landed somewhat clumsily on the ground beside them. Her face and breasts were young, but her wings and talons destroyed any attractiveness she might have had for a human man.

Then she changed form, and became a young woman, tall and slender. Her face was the same, and probably her bosom, which was now covered by a feathery gown. "Well, what brings you here, Flach?" she inquired.

"This be Lysander," the boy said. "He believes not in magic."

The woman eyed him speculatively. "New to this planet?" she inquired.

Lysander nodded. "I arrived about an hour ago. I admit to being confused."

"Hi. I'm Echo. My better half is Oche." She extended her hand.

He took it. "I don't wish to be impolite, but it has been my understanding that there is no such thing as magic."

She nodded. "So Flach is showing you. That figures."

"Actually, a little girl was showing me. I am not certain what—" He broke off, for now Nepe was standing before him, dressed in a pinafore, her wild hair neatly braided.

"It's hard to get used to, at first," Echo said. "I didn't believe, until the frames merged, and then I had one hell of an adjustment to make. How would you like to turn into a harpy without warning?"

"I would find that awkward," Lysander agreed.

"You bet! But you have it easy, because you're not native, so you didn't have to merge with your opposite."

"You and the harpy are the same individual?"

"Just as Flach and Nepe are," Echo said. "You see, when there were two frames, one was science, the other magic, and long-term residents were represented in both. When they merged, so did the folk, and I'm telling you, it was carnage for a time! But now most of us have made the adjustment. When we go into the domes, we strip down and are serfs; outside we're in Phaze. Then we dress and speak in the Phaze manner, and do whatever magic we can. It's a pretty good combination, actually."

"I don't wish to impose, but would you object to providing more evidence? Could you, for example, change forms if I were holding you?"

She eyed him again. "That's the neatest come-on line I've heard yet! Sure, hold me, handsome." She stepped into his arms and kissed him.

He closed his arms around her, less interested in the kiss than in the mechanism of the change. He held her firmly—and then found himself with an armful of feathers. She had become the harpy, her lips still touching his. He was so surprised he let go.

She fell away, and had to flap her wings to recover before she hit the ground. "Thou didst drop me, thou dork!" she screeched. There was the tinkle of Nepe's laughter.

If this wasn't supernatural, it was a device beyond his reckoning. Echo had felt every inch the human woman—and she had been within his grasp as she changed.

"Let me try again," he said. He squatted, and grabbed her two bird legs. "Change back."

Abruptly he was holding on to one knee and one thigh. Both were definitely human.

"Satisfied?" Nepe asked. "Or do you want to squeeze her gams some more?"

Hastily he let go, though his human orientation was returning, and he found the legs interesting. "If it isn't magic, it's beyond me," he confessed.

"It's science," Echo said. "I'm a cyborg. See, my body's inanimate." She opened her robe, exposing her breasts. She touched the right one, and it swung out from her torso to reveal a hollow cavity instead of mammary glands. "But Oche, she's magic, all right."

"I'll take thee to the wolves," Flach said, having changed without notice.

"Wolves? I'd rather not."

But the lad was determined. "Take my hand; I'll conjure thee to the Pack."

With resignation, Lysander reached for the hand. "Come see me some time when you're not busy, handsome," Echo said. "I work for Citizen Powell, when I'm on duty in Proton. You?"

"Citizen Blue," he said.

"You're lucky!"

Then his hand made contact—and the scene changed.

They stood at the edge of a lovely valley whose flower-specked expanse led down to a small meandering stream. A herd of horses were grazing, guarded by a single stallion pacing the perimeter. Horses? No, unicorns; each had its horn, and the colors were beyond anything seen on ordinary equines.

The stallion galloped up. He had a bright blue coat and red "socks" on his hind legs. As he moved, he played music on his horn, sounding very like a mellow saxophone.

The unicorn who had carried Lysander reappeared. This one had a black coat and blue hind socks, seeming to have a family resemblance to the stallion. He played a return melody, his flutelike theme prettily counterpointing the saxophone.

Then both animals became human, the change like the flick of an image on a computer screen. The boy was familiar, but the man was not. He had black hair and a black suit, with blue socks, and was of mature age. He looked tough.

The man eyed Lysander. "My grand-nephew tells me that thou be a new employee of Blue, and that thou hast difficulty assimilating our culture."

"Correct. I had understood that magic was mainly illusion."

"Flach will happily demonstrate magical illusion!" the man said. As he spoke, a disembodied eye appeared in the air behind him, the white of it grotesquely veined. A second eye formed beside it, and the two focused on Lysander. Slowly the right one winked. "But not now," the man said sternly, without turning. The eyes vanished. "I suspect thy best course be to assume that what thou seest be valid, until thou dost become convinced. Ignorance be lethal, here."

"I believe that, sir."

The man frowned. "Oh, aye, thou seest me clothed, so dost assume I be a Citizen. Nay, in Phaze there be no Citizens. When the mergence came, we had to compromise in a number o' ways, because some folk were merged and others had no other selves, and the status o' selves could be different in the frames. So—" He paused. "Be I confusing you?"

"Yes," Lysander admitted.

The unicorn reappeared, and blew a loud note. Immediately there was the sweet tinkle of bells, and a mare broke from the Herd. Her coat was a deep red verging on purple, and her mane rippled iridescently. She was an astonishing and beautiful creature.

Then she became a blue heron, and flew toward them. Soon she landed, becoming a unicorn as her feet touched ground. She tinkled her bells again questioningly—but the sound was actually from her horn.

The stallion played another brief melody. The mare's head angled so that one eye could orient on Lysander.

"Go with Belle," Flach said. "Great-Uncle Clip wants to talk with me."

"You mean, ride her?"

"If thou dost wish," the boy said. "Oh—she will explain about the mergence."

"But I can't understand bells!"

"Now thou canst," Flach said.

Lysander chose not to argue. He presumed there was some point to all this. His job was to go along, learning what he needed to. Certainly what he was experiencing was amazing, and the surprises showed no signs of abating.

He approached the beautiful mare. Up close he saw that she was old, like the stallion; flecks of gray showed in her hide. "May I ride you, Belle?" he asked.

Her bell sounded. "Aye."

"Thank you." He climbed on her back.

Then he did a doubletake. "I understood you!" he exclaimed.

She laughed with the pealing of bells. "Flach did it. He be the Unicorn Adept. We o' the Herd be proud o' him." She started walking, leaving the man and boy behind.

"Unicorn Adept?"

The bells tinkled again, melodiously. "Clip asked me to clarify our system for thee." These were not her precise words; rather, he was translating the sounds into his own sentences, as he was coming to understand the dialect of Phaze. It didn't matter; he understood her perfectly. It was apparent that any further effort to resist acceptance of magic was likely to be futile; it was the readiest explanation for what was going on. "There were two frames, one magic, the other science. We unicorns lived in magic Phaze, while the Citizens and serfs lived in science Proton, in their domes, because they had polluted all the air and ruined the land. Many o' us had other selves, but we could cross oe'r not."

"Let me see whether I understand," he said. "You were a unicorn, and some person in Proton was the same as you?"

"Nay, some mare," she tinkled. "I have no human form; it were not one I chose. We unicorns can usually learn two other forms, and I chose the heron and the cat. Clip chose man and hawk. So we trot together, and we fly together, but when I go to Proton with him he be a man and I be a horse. But I like it there not, so I remain out on the range."

"The frames merged, and now the domes are Proton, and the outside land is Phaze?"

"Aye, by agreement. So when a Citizen steps outside, he assumes his Phaze form. If he be Adept, he has great power, but most o' them be just ordinary folk. So the Proton folk mostly stay in their domes, and we Phaze folk remain mostly outside. Many o' us have no opposite selves anyway, so it be easier. Things really changed not much, after the mergence settled down, except that the Adept Stile gained power."

"Who?"

"The Adepts be the ones with much magic. They be mostly human, but the Red Adept be a troll, and the Unicorn Adept be part unicorn. The Blue Adept always supported the unicorns, and the werewolves and vampires, so—"

"But you named a Stile Adept."

"He were the Blue Adept, but he changed selves with Stile, and now he be Citizen Blue, and Stile be the Adept."

"Oh—so Nepe's grandfather—"

"Aye," she tinkled. "Clip's sister Neysa had a filly, Fleta, who mated with Blue's son Mach, the rovot—"

"What?"

"In Proton there be rovots," she tinkled patiently. "Like golems, only made o' metal. Nepe be their child, so she be—"

"Wait! Wait! I'm all confused. I thought the frames were separate. How could a unicorn filly mate with a robot? Even if it were possible physically, they were in opposite frames!"

"Mach crossed o'er, and took Bane's body, here, and loved Fleta. Their child be Flach. Bane crossed to Proton, and took Mach's body, and married Agape the alien, and their child be Nepe. But when the mergence came—"

"They became the same!" Lysander exclaimed, the light dawning. "Stile and Blue are the same, and their sons are the same, and their grandchildren! But—" He broke off, troubled by another aspect.

"One child be male and one be female," she tinkled, understanding. "We believed it not either, but it be so. That unbelief were critical in Stile's victory."

"Just what was this victory? How did it relate to the merging of the frames?"

"The Adverse Adepts were gaining power, and were in league with the Contrary Citizens, and the Purple Adept sought to kill Stile and assume power. But Blue summoned the Platinum Flute, and Clef to play it, and they piped the frames together. Blue and Stile merged and liked each other, and Fleta and Agape liked each other, and Flach and Nepe, for all were good folk. But the bad Adepts and Citizens were mean folk, each out for himself alone, not sharing power, and they could stand their other selves not, and fell in torment struggling with themselves. By the time they came to accommodation with their opposites, the good folk were firmly in power. Now it be verging on the golden age, for Stile and Blue be reconciled with their sons Mach and Bane and their grandchildren Flach and Nepe, and all value the land and creatures. Ne'er again will evil govern either frame."

"But how can magic work here, when it is unknown in the rest of the galaxy?"

"It be the Phazite," she tinkled. "The magic rock 'neath the mountains. It be the source o' magic and energy. The bad Citizens were mining it, and selling it, and depleting it, so our magic were less. They cared for our welfare not, any more than they did for the air they spoiled before. But Stile and Blue stopped them, and now little rock goes out."

"This rock provides magic *and* energy?"

"Aye. The Proton ships use it and the rovots and 'chines, and it be best in the galaxy. The Citizens were getting much wealth, but we were fading." She made a merry serenade of bells. "No more!"

Abruptly she halted. "What's the matter?" Lysander asked.

"A goblin, spying on us!" she tinkled. "Do thou dismount; needs must I drive him out."

Lysander quickly got off. Then she was a black panther, bounding into the brush.

There was a swirl of motion, and something like a little man leaped up and dodged behind a tree. The panther circled the tree, but evidently the goblin was gone.

The big cat came back. The beautiful unicorn reappeared. "They have no business here," she tinkled indignantly. "These be 'Corn Demesnes."

Evidently so. Lysander remounted, and they continued on around the grazing herd. By the time they returned to the boy and stallion, the two had evidently finished their conversation. Indeed, the unicorn was grazing again, and the lad was playing with tiny clouds, making the black one chase the white one in crazy patterns just above the ground. When the two collided, there was a crack of thunder, and flare of lightning, and a bucket of water drenched the soil.

The boy became the unicorn. "We thank thee for thy help, Belle," Flach piped politely. Lysander seemed to understand all music talk now, and he knew he wasn't imagining it.

"Welcome, Adept," Belle tinkled. "It be fun to rehearse the history. Tell the Lady we miss her."

"Aye, I'll nag her!" the boy said zestfully, reappearing. "Or I will," the girl Nepe added. The changes seemed instant; Lysander could detect no transition. What else could it be but magic?

Then Nepe extended her hand. Lysander took it, knowing what was coming.

Sure enough, the scene changed. They were standing at the edge of a forest clearing where a number of wolves were lying. The wolves jumped up, smelling the intrusion—and beside Lysander was another wolf. "Tear him not, brothers!" Flach growled, this form of communication also now comprehensible. "I be showing him magic at Blue's behest."

A wolf approached Lysander—and abruptly became a woman. She was of indeterminate human age, no young innocent but also not old. "For thee, Flach, we honor this. But canst be sure he be worthy?"

"I thank thee, Bukisaho," Flach said. "He be new to Phaze, and Blue wants him broken in. I know no more than this, and that he be named Lysander."

"Thy human names be e'er strange," she said. "I would second-guess Blue not, but mayhap thou shouldst include the Adept Tania on thy tour."

"Aye, excellent notion, bitch!" the boy exclaimed, startling Lysander.

The woman, noting his reaction, laughed—and so did the surrounding wolves, in their way. "Aye, he be new!" the woman agreed.

A young wolf appeared at the fringe of the camp. "Sirelmoba!" Flach cried, spying it.

The wolf charged him, leaped into the air with teeth bared—and became a girl about his age, smacking into the boy with her mouth against his for an extremely solid kiss. Her hair was dark, like his, as were her furry jacket and skirt; she could have been his sister, but obviously wasn't.

After an intense moment, she drew back her head but not her

body. The two might be children, but they looked much like lovers, Lysander thought. "O Barel, it be but days but it feels like years!" the girl said. "I feel my age drawing nigh, any year now; be thou ready when I be!"

"But once we mate, we part!" he protested. "I be in no hurry for that, Sirel."

"We will part not, only turn to friendship."

He nodded. "Aye. Still, I be not rushed."

"I will make thee rush, when my heat come," she promised.

They *were* like lovers! They were talking of mating!

"This be Lysander," Flach said, turning to him as the girl released him. "He be a new serf for Blue."

"Pleased to meet thee, Lysan," the girl said. "Thou hast no Phaze form?"

"No Phaze form," Lysander agreed.

"Then I assume mine other form, to greet thee," Sirel said—and abruptly a wheeled machine sat in her place. "I am Troubot, the trouble-shooting robot," it said via a speaker. "I love Nepe, but I fear my love is vain."

"Oh, I don't know," Nepe said, appearing, naked as she had been in the dome. "But unless you want to put on a humanoid body like Daddy's—"

The wolf-girl reappeared. "It be more fun being a bitch."

Bitch: a female dog or wolf. Now Lysander had it straight.

"I must on," Flach said. The changes were so quick and natural that it seemed pointless to try to track them. "We be going to see Tania."

Sirel frowned cutely. "Thou knowest I like thee not with that woman." The way she said it, "woman" sounded the way "bitch" did away from Phaze.

"Dost forget she played the Flute, that we might beat the e'il Adepts?" Flach inquired, smiling.

"Nay, I forget that not, neither her power."

"Which she would waste not on me," he retorted.

Sirelmoba relented. "Aye, why waste anything on thee!"

He made a grab for her, but she turned wolf again and glided away. Flach turned wolf himself, and growled after her, then reappeared as the boy. "Come, Lysan," he said, extending his hand.

Lysander took it—and they were at the base of another section of the Purple Mountains. Partway up was a pleasant cottage, with a thatched roof and plaster walls. An easy path led up to it.

"If I may inquire," Lysander said cautiously, "what is significant about the Adept Tania?"

"She has the power o' the Evil Eye," Flach explained as they walked up the path. "When her brother were the Tan Adept, and sought to destroy what Grandpa Blue had wrought, she fought for us, and helped us prevail, and now she be the Adept while Tan be prisoner."

"But why should I see her? I am of no significance."

The lad glanced at him with a disturbing hint of understanding. "Blue takes serfs not for naught, and sends them to Phaze not for naught. Least does he put us"—Nepe flashed momentarily, showing that he meant the combination—"in charge of such, e'en for an hour, without reason. It be our task not merely to show thee magic, but to fathom thy nature. Tania will do that."

"Fathom my nature? I'm an android!"

"But what is thy mind, Lysan? Thinkst thou to step into the Blue Demesnes unchallenged? An thou be sent to assassinate Blue, needs must we know it early."

"I'm no assassin!" Lysander protested, appalled.

"An we take thy word on that, be we smart?"

"I see your point. So Tania will know? What is she, a mind reader?"

"Not exactly. She will compel thee with her Eye, which be not truly e'il now, and thou willst tell thy nature."

Lysander felt a chill. If the woman could do that, he was lost! But perhaps it was a bluff. What could a child know, after all?

They completed the ascent to the cottage. Flach knocked on the door. "Adepts, this be Flach! I bring a serf from Proton-frame."

The door opened. A beautiful woman of about thirty stood within, in a tan dress. Her hair was tan, and her eyes too. Suddenly the significance of the name registered. Tan, Tania. The color was a badge.

"Welcome, Flach," she said, smiling. "We be e'er pleased to see thee, and any thou dost bring." She glanced at Lysander—and he felt another chill. Her eyes abruptly seemed larger, and intense, as though capable of hideous power. "Come in." She stepped back to give them access.

Inside was a pleasant room with a picture-window view of the mountainside and open field beyond. There was also a man, somewhat older than Tania, bespectacled and of slight build, though healthy. Lysander realized that he must have qualities that didn't show, to be the companion of such a woman.

Flach performed the introductions. "This be Lysander, new serf o' Blue, from offplanet. This be the Adept Clef."

Clef walked forward to shake hands. "Welcome to Phaze, Lysander. What brings you here?"

Was there any point in telling his story? But he realized that all he could do was bluff it out. "I am an android, trained in games and computer feedback circuitry. I hope to achieve both pleasure and information during my tenure here, and money too, so as to be a person of account on my home planet when I return."

"Yes, I remember my own tenure as a serf," Clef said. "When I washed out in the game, I thought to depart Proton, never to return. But Stile showed me Phaze, and later Tania brought me back." He went to the woman and put his arm around her affectionately. She turned immediately and kissed him with an eagerness reminiscent of that of Alyc. But she was no Alyc; what was it that made Clef a figure to compel her devotion?

"Methought Tania could test Lysander, to be assured of his constancy," Flach said. "We like strangers not around Blue."

Again Tania glanced at Lysander. She shifted subtly. "Why not put him on a lie detector?" she asked.

"If he's an assassin," Nepe said, "he would be trained to fake through that. But he can't fake you, Citizen."

Lysander realized that Tania had shifted to her Proton form, which was evidently the same as her Phaze form. So she was also a Citizen! That meant that she had enormous power, if she chose to exercise it, despite her rustic residence.

"You know my wife does not like to use her power carelessly," Clef said. "She can orient on a given subject only once."

"Gee, I forgot," Nepe said, abashed. "I was thinking it was like the weres or 'corns, always there."

"Always there for a new subject," Clef said. "If there is any chance that Stile might want him checked at a later date, we should wait on that. But perhaps I can be of service, instead."

"Would you, dear?" Tania asked, evidently relieved.

"For you, anything," Clef said. He seemed to be speaking literally. He walked across the room and fetched an instrument from a shelf.

Lysander wasn't sure whether to feel relief or increased concern. These people obviously intended to check him out—but how did they propose to do it? Nepe was right: no lie detector would betray him; he had been manufactured to be resistant to the human signals such machines interpreted. Only a direct mind probe could fathom his truth, and his masters had not anticipated that on this planet. In immediate retrospect, he realized that he had blundered in accepting employment directly with Citizen Blue; of course the man was careful about his associates, being the leading figure of the planet! Had Lysander sought employment with a lesser Citizen, he should have passed unnoticed. He had asked for trouble, and now was getting it.

The instrument turned out to be a shining silver flute. No, not silver—platinum. This was the Platinum Flute the unicorn Belle had mentioned, that Clef had played to merge the frames. That had seemed like mythology, but now it seemed literal. But what could a flute really do?

"Sit down," Tania said, indicating chairs and taking one herself. "It's always such a pleasure to hear him play."

"Aye," Flach agreed. "Ne'er heard I the like!"

Lysander did not anticipate pleasure. If the Flute really could somehow fathom his mind, it would be the end of him. Yet maybe it was illusion or bluff.

Clef played. It was immediately evident that he was an expert flautist; the music was sure and sweet. But how could mere music verify whether a man was an assassin? Of course that was not the case with Lysander; he was merely a counterinsurgency agent, who would kill only at need. He liked Citizen Blue and his family, and would do his best to avoid doing them harm, so long as his mission was fairly accomplished. Still, the premature exposure of his mission would be fatal to it and probably himself.

The music intensified. Lysander felt it orienting on him, entering him, drawing him out of himself. It was as if he were floating up and looking down at his body and the bodies of the others. But he wasn't dying, he was relaxing; it was pleasant. He would be satisfied to float forever on this magical music!

But if they had intended to make him talk about his true mission, they had failed. He felt no compulsion at all to talk about anything, merely to float and reflect. So he could relax, until the Hectare came. Then—he would see.

The music ended. Lysander thought it had been only a minute or two, but the sun seemed to have jumped forward in the sky beyond the picture window. It had been at least an hour. That music was potent!

The others were silent as Clef put away his flute. They seemed to be recovering from the effect of it, just as he was.

"Did I pass inspection?" he inquired, trying to be light.

Clef turned to him. "I suspect you are the one we want. It is fortunate that Citizen Blue hired you."

"For work on circuit feedback?"

"There is a prophecy that a great trial will come to our culture, that can be ameliorated only by a particular person, a newcomer to the planet. We have been watching for promising arrivals. The music suggests that you qualify. I hope it is correct."

"A prophecy?" Lysander asked, surprised again. "A magical prediction?"

"You might call it that. Actually, prophecies are more difficult to assimilate, as they are often vague about details, and considerable interpretation is needed. But they are always correct in the end. If you are the one, you will be invaluable to us."

Lysander spread his hands. "Somehow that seems like more than I should be credited with. I'm really not a planet-saving type."

"Perhaps." Clef shrugged as if unconcerned. "It was pleasant to play again, at any rate."

"It were fun to listen!" Flach said. Then Nepe appeared. "But I guess we better go on back to Grandpa Blue." She extended her hand to Lysander.

He took it, relieved that he had gotten through their test. Evidently the magic had oriented on his special mission, but not clarified its nature. Save the culture? Not by their definition! He was on the other side.

He blinked. They were back in Citizen Blue's apartment, all naked except for the Citizen, and Alyc was there, gazing at him expectantly. "Yes, I now believe in magic," he said, forestalling her. "This little lady showed me quite a world!"

3
Decision

After polite dialogue of the adult kind, Citizen Blue packed Lysander off with Alyc for the familiarization tour of Proton. But he held Nepe with the tiniest indication of a finger. She faded back, but did not depart. She had known it would be thus.

When things were clear, the Citizen held a brief meeting with Sheen, Agnes the maid, and Nepe. "Verdict?" he asked Nepe.

"Clef piped out his soul, and says he may be the one."

Blue nodded. "I thought that might be the case. His arrival was too pat. How much is Clef sure of?"

Nepe shrugged. "He didn't say, because 'Sander was there. Just that there's a prophecy, and he might qualify as the special person we want to help us get through the bad time."

Agnes snorted. "Special person! The man's an enemy agent!"

"If he is the one," the Citizen said. "And *if* he is the one, we desperately need him. I don't think Clef would have mentioned the prophecy if he wasn't fairly sure."

"He may be sure the man is an enemy," Sheen said, "but not that he is the one we need."

Blue nodded. "It would be premature to take action at this time. But at least we can use this as a focus for our investigation. I shall arrange to keep him occupied with the Game Computer."

Sheen pursed her lips in exactly the fashion of a living woman. "But if he is versed in computer circuitry—"

"Have no fear, my love; he will not have access to the circuitry. The Oracle will divert him cleverly enough. Meanwhile, we shall be taking his measure, and discover perhaps in exactly what way he may be useful to our effort."

Sheen nodded, satisfied. If the Oracle was working on this, there would be no errors.

Blue glanced at Nepe. "You and Nessie know what to do."

Nepe nodded. So did Agnes.

"We shall cover for you as required," Blue concluded. "Otherwise, you're on your own. Project Phaze Doubt depends on you."

She laughed, though she knew it wasn't funny. "Phased out by a little girl!"

He smiled. "Don't get cute, amoeba face. We love you, and want you to succeed."

How true that was! She would keep her doubt to herself, and do her utmost to complete her mission. She could not afford to dwell on its immense responsibility; she would tackle one step at a time.

Nepe went up and embraced her grandfather, than her grandmother. "Nessie will update me," she said, wiping away a tear.

"And so will we, while we can," the Citizen said. "Until Alyc turns us in."

Another laugh bubbled up in Nepe, despite the gravity of the situation. "Maybe she'll turn *him* in too!"

"Maybe," Blue said, smiling.

Then Nepe took Agnes' hand. "Follow my lead, Grandam."

The woman nodded. Nepe changed to Flach and conjured the two of them to a vacant chamber across the city. There she reverted to Nepe-form, and melted into a pool of protoplasm. Agnes, who was Nepe's mother's elder portion, melted with her. Soon the two Moebites were flowing across the floor, and into a disused drain channel.

I don't think anyone's watching, Nepe thought, her direct contact with a creature of her species making communication possible, though they were not telepathic. It was simply a matter of tangential nerve signals. *But we don't know how many other spies there are, or when the invasion's coming, so we have to be careful.*

Agreed.

This leads outside, near a horse range. Flach'll be a horsefly, till we get to Clef.

Just don't bite me!

Nepe sent a peal of laughter that jarred loose the contact.

They flowed out of the pipe and settled on the ground. It had been seeded after the mergence, but the grass had not yet filled in completely near the dome.

Nepe shaped herself back into girl form, hiding against the wall, then became Flach, who would have had trouble dealing with puddle form. The mutability of the Moeba complemented that of the Adept, each able to change in ways the other could not. They found it best to assume human form at the exchange platform, to avoid miscues.

Flach became the horsefly. He buzzed up, looking around with his multifaceted eyes. There were horses grazing not far off, attended only by a mobile watering station.

He buzzed down to Agnes. He touched her briefly and sheered off.

She was more facile than he in the change, having had more experience. She went directly from pooled protoplasm to unicorn, standing in the shadow, where her black hide helped her fade out. She had white socks on her hind legs, and a spiraled horn. She was Neysa, the Adept Stile's longtime companion, and perhaps the one who knew Flach best.

Flach flew down to light on her head, between the ears. She walked beside the wall until the site of their emergence from it was not clear, then turned outward. She put her head down to take a bite of grass, so that the watering robot would see the outline of a grazing horse. After a moment she moved on, keeping her horn angled away from the machine.

In this manner she worked her way to the fringe of the seeded turf. Then she stepped out onto the natural ground of Phaze, and quickly lost herself in the higher bushes growing there. Once she was fully clear of the dome of Hardom, she worked into a trot, moving at moderate speed westward, then southwest, toward the great Purple Mountain Range. If anyone saw her now, she was just one more unicorn traveling her own course, like so many who ranged out from the Herd to find choice foraging.

As afternoon closed they came to the mountains. Flach remained in fly form, taking no chances. Even if it wasn't necessary right now, it was good policy for the future.

As they neared the residence of Clef and Tania, Flach buzzed off Neysa's head, and she assumed her third form: a firefly. As horsefly and firefly, they buzzed up to the cottage. They flew to the picture window, and Flach banged against it several times, making a noise.

In a moment Tania spied him. She nodded, and opened a smaller window. The two flew in, lighted on the floor, and assumed their human forms.

"We were expecting you," Clef said, joining them.

"I be glad to see thee here, our past differences done," Tania said separately to Neysa.

"Thou didst shame me into forgiving my filly," Neysa responded to her.

"Because I loved Bane—and Fleta," Tania said. "Before Clef came, and fulfilled my life."

"It was mutual," Clef said. "Now I suspect you want my full report on the visitor."

"Grandpa Blue has put us on alert," Nepe said, taking over from Flach. She was better at talking, and at Proton matters. "But he needs to know more before he acts."

"I am as yet not adept, as it were, at reading souls," Clef said. "But there is no doubt in my mind that Lysander is a hostile agent. He appears to mean no personal ill to us, but his loyalty is to a foreign power. When that power strikes, he will support it."

"Yes, Grandpa Blue is investigating his origin. He'll find out who 'Sander works for. But since the prophecy says that only the right one can save us, that won't be enough. We have to know if he's *the* one."

"Exactly," Clef said. "The difficulty is that Lysander doesn't know the answer himself. That is why I mentioned the prophecy. I hoped to elicit some reaction that would clarify the matter. But there seemed to be only perplexity."

"Exactly what is the prophecy, and what does it say?" Tania inquired. "I had not heard of it before."

"Trool came across it in the Book of Magic," Clef said. "He had seen it before, but it wasn't relevant to the immediacies of prior situations, and there is so much in that book that he ignored it. But when we merged the frames, he remembered, and spoke of it to a few of us. We did not bruit it further about, not wishing to alarm others. But suddenly its relevance is manifest. The wording is simple, just two sentences: 'When frames merge, comes a time of great trial. Only one alien to the culture and opposed can save it—an he choose.' We interpret that to mean that an enemy will attack, and that a member of the enemy force can help us prevail, if we can convince him to do it."

"It could be a female," Tania pointed out.

Clef shrugged. "Yes, of course. But from offplanet, and not conversant with our ways. So we are considering Lysander, who represents an alien force. I think we dare not assume he is *not* the one. If other prospects appear, we must consider them too."

"Like Alyc," Nepe said.

"Yes," he said. "And any other foreign agent. If we were to eliminate any one of them, we might doom ourselves. But Alyc is human, and has adapted well to the culture, so we doubt it is her. Lysander, in contrast, is an extremely sophisticated android. I would like very much to know what kind of brain he has. When I piped out his soul, the part that associated with the body was ordinary, but the part that was the brain, and therefore the mind, was as strange as I have seen. Certainly it is alien! So Lysander seems to be a far more likely candidate."

"If he choose," Tania said. "I might make him choose."

"You could compel him to do our bidding, dear," Clef said. "But that might also destroy his usefulness. I suspect we will need his full understanding and cooperation, which would be another matter. Also, if his mind is truly alien, you might have difficulty exerting your magic on him."

She nodded, appreciating the point. "Then perhaps it is better to give him reason to support our culture. Suppose he fell in love with one of our women?"

"That has been known to achieve remarkable things in the past," Clef said with a bit of a smile.

"When my father Mach loved the unicorn filly Fleta," Flach said, "all Phaze and Proton changed."

"And when I loved Bane, I changed too," Tania said. "I know the power of love, even that which be not returned! But can an alien thing love similarly?"

"Lysander is schooled to emulate human ways," Clef said. "His reactions here were normal. Unless his core personality is unable to love, I think he should be normal in that respect also."

"Then methinks we needs must find him a woman," she said.

"He has a woman: Alyc," Nepe said.

Neysa snorted.

Tania turned her great eyes on Nepe. "Thou knowest we must link him to one o' our own."

"I guess so," Nepe agreed. "Maybe the enemy's using Alyc to keep him in line."

"I would tend to doubt that," Clef said. "The most effective spies I should think would be those who do not know the identities of the others. That way, if one is discovered, he can not give away the presence of the others. I think the presence of two in Citizen Blue's household must be coincidence—or, if not, their true natures must still be concealed from each other. So they would be unlikely to discuss the details of their conspiracy. However, if they did, Blue would soon know of it."

"But while they are together, we can't put one of our own with him," Tania said.

"Alyc has a short attention span with men," Nepe said. "Her romances seldom last longer than two or three weeks."

"Even that might be too long," Clef said. "We need time to work on him."

"Choose a woman, and introduce her to him," Tania said. "Then she'll be there when he breaks from Alyc. She may even take him from Alyc."

"Thou tookst Bane not from Agape," Flach said, a trifle smugly. He knew that Tania had had four years to try, and hadn't made a dent. Instead, she had lost her own heart to Bane, until Clef won her with his magic music.

"Thy sires were one hell of a lot better men than Lysander," Tania said. "Lysander I could take, an I wished."

"You may have to, if our ploy fails," Clef murmured. "That's why I prevented you from using your power on him at this time. It may be needed more critically later."

Tania made a face. "I will do what I needs must do, but I loathe the prospect. Thou be not the first I loved, but thou surely be the last."

"So what woman?" Nepe asked. "A nice wolf bitch? Some of them are sexier than human women. Ask Flach."

Flach took over, embarrassed. "She be always teasing me about that. I want just to mate with my Promised, Sirelmoba, an we come of age. But Nepe be right: meseen what a bitch can do with a grown man, an she choose."

"But an she be a dog in Proton, that be no good," Tania pointed out.

"Brown is close to the wolves," Clef said. "She should know which ones have suitable analogues."

"*I* know," Flach said, annoyed. "I be closer than any!"

"Of course thou dost be," Tania said. "Clef be gone from Phaze then. Who dost thou recommend?"

Now Flach was taken aback. "Actually, they be all Promised or mated, in my Pack."

"So we might as well ask Brown," she said.

He had to yield. "Aye." He looked at Neysa, who had been mostly silent, as was her wont. "But mayhap my turn to move us?"

Neysa was never keen on Adept magic, but respected it in her grandchild. She nodded, knowing that his way would be both faster and less obvious.

Flach took her hand, and conjured them both to the Brown Demesnes. A given spell could work only once, but he had devised so many variants for conjuration that this was no limitation. They landed in the massive wooden castle, in a private chamber reserved for just such events. Flach knocked rhythmically against a panel, signaling their presence.

Soon a wooden golem tramped to the door. The Brown Adept could make them in the perfect image and manner of living folk, but around the castle she didn't bother. This one was obviously inanimate, despite its activity. "Who comes?" it demanded.

"Flach and Grandam," Flach said.

"Then follow me." The thing about-faced and led them down the hall.

The Brown Adept awaited them in the main chamber. She was a somewhat spare woman with clipped brown hair, much the color of the wood she worked with. "Ah, Flach!" she exclaimed. "And Neysa! It be good to see thee, mare!" Neysa was now in human form, but of course Brown knew her. They had been friends for thirty years, ever since Stile had met Brown when she was ten.

"We come from Clef," Flach said. "Can anyone hear?"

"Mayhap," Brown said. "I have, as thou dost know, two prisoners. They be under geis nor to harm me neither to escape, but their magic be not entirely stifled."

"Mayhap I can make a privacy spell," Flach said. "But first should I make sure where they be."

"It be near their feeding time," Brown said. "Come see them while I do it."

They followed her to the kitchen, where a golem chef had prepared a platter. "Thou dost feed them well," Flach remarked, smelling the aroma. "Pumpkinseed pie!"

"My garden be fertilized with unicorn manure," Brown replied. "From it comes the very best pumpkinseeds, so many I can do naught but bake. It were unkind to share not."

"Then share with me!" Flach said eagerly.

"Aye, lad, and gladly," she agreed. "Canst stay the night?"

"I fear not," he said. "But we can eat while we talk, E'en my grandam likes pumpkinseed pie!" He glanced at Neysa, who did not protest. It was a taste they shared.

A golem carried the platter. They followed it to the cellar, where the prisoners were housed. There were no bars, but that didn't matter; there were stout golem guards who could not be corrupted, and who never slept.

The chambers were surprisingly pleasant. It was a well-organized suite, with curtains and cushions and pictures on the wall. One of them was a magic window which showed scenes of Phaze as desired: the unicorn range, ogre dens, ocean shore, or mountains. Flach had never understood why the Brown Adept had volunteered to house the prisoners; perhaps she had been the only one able to handle this chore. Flach's grandfather had not wished to kill them, though they deserved death; but they could not be allowed to run loose. So they were confined, and a geis suppressed their magic, and they were here for the duration.

The prisoners were ready in the main chamber. They were the Purple Adept and the Tan Adept, also being Citizen Purple and Citizen Tan, Tania's brother. Actually their titles had been stripped; Tania had assumed her brother's status, and the Purple Demesnes were vacant. But their magic remained; were it not for the geis, they would be extremely dangerous men.

Both stood as the party entered. "Good evening, Adept," Purple said. He wore a modest purple robe, and was clean and neat. He was by no means a handsome man, but might be called portly. Tan, on the other hand, was in the vigor of his life, so like his twin sister in appearance and talent that it was eerie. Flach had hated both Tan and Tania, until Tania changed sides and rendered the vital help that enabled Stile/Blue to win.

"Good evening, Purple," Brown said briefly. "Good evening, Tan. Are you in satisfactory form?"

"Excellent form, Adept," Tan said. "We thank thee for thy excellent care."

The golem set down the platter. "Then I will leave you to it," Brown said. "I have company."

"So we note," Purple said, glancing at Flach. "Mayst thou prosper, Adept."

Flach didn't really like being called Adept, but it was true: he had magic enough to qualify. "Thank thee, Purple."

Tan turned his hypnotic eyes on Neysa. "And still spry, mare," he remarked. Neysa did not bother to answer.

They departed the prison section. "Now I have them placed," Flach said, "I can set my privacy spell. They be demoted, but they be Adepts yet, in magic, else such care were not needed."

"Nay," Neysa said. "Needs must we go on immediately."

Flach turned to her in surprise. "But Grandam, the pie!"

"It be excellent pie, an I do say so myself," Brown said. "There be no need to rush on. I welcome the company."

"Remembered I aught," Neysa said.

Flach was perplexed and dismayed. He knew better than to naysay his grandam, though he was Adept and she was not. He would have to give up the pie.

"Have I given offense?" Brown asked, a hysterical edge sounding in her voice. "Neysa, please, I apologize—"

Neysa stopped and took Brown by the hands. "I have known thee long," she said. "I will return alone. Needs must I now see my grand-foal to Trool. There be no offense." It was a singularly long speech, for her.

"Thou willst return," Brown said. It sounded like a prayer.

"Aye." Neysa took Flach's hand. "On, Flach," she said, squeezing his fingers in a way he recognized. She was serious, and would brook no delay.

He conjured them to the Red Demesnes, a similar chamber in Trool's castle. He broached her on it immediately. "Grandam—"

"Aught be amiss," Neysa said. "Needs must I fathom it, ere secrets be told. Conjure me back to Brown, and excuse me to Red. Say naught o' this."

"But Trool be—"

"To other than him," she amended. "Send me."

Baffled, he conjured her back. Then he knocked on the closed chamber door, to let Trool know of his arrival.

In a moment, lovely Suchevane was there. "Ah, Flach," she said, hugging him. He always liked that, for she was not only the prettiest woman of her age, she was one of the nicest. "Come join us at sup; we have pumpkinseed pie."

"We lucked out!" Nepe exclaimed, taking over.

Suchevane conducted Nepe downstairs to the dining hall. There was Trool the Troll, now the Red Adept, and his son Alien. Trool lifted a finger, and abruptly Nepe was clothed in a fluffy dress. "Oh—thanks," she said. "I forgot!"

For normally it was Nepe who visited this household, because Alien was sweet on her and she liked the attention. Originally it had been Alien's Proton alternate, 'Corn, who had the feeling, but it had spread to both.

The pie was served, but between mouthfuls Nepe made their mission known. It did not matter that Suchevane and Alien were present; this whole family was to be trusted.

"So thou dost need a mistress to corrupt an enemy agent," Trool said. "Methinks that be not much in our line."

Alien chuckled. "But an I grow up, I'll need me a mistress," he said, leering at Nepe.

Nepe stuck out her tongue at him. "This is all adult stuff I don't understand," she said. "I'm just carrying the word."

Suchevane choked over her tomato juice, which she drank because of the color. "All thy experience emulating Troubot in Proton-frame, and thou dost ken naught?"

Nepe glanced at her with obviously faked innocence. "Won't wash?" For Troubot, in that period, had carried the most intimate messages between Citizens, including those setting up sexual liaisons between Citizen Purple and Tania's sexy secretary Tsetse. Troubot could hardly have been innocent of the ways of sex, since the robot also monitored the ongoing activities.

But the memory gave her a notion. "Tsetse! She's anybody's mistress!"

"She be *old!*" Alien protested. "Thirty, at least!"

"Twenty-nine plus a few months," Suchevane said. "Just younger than Tania—and me."

Alien shut up, knowing when to quit.

"However," Suchevane continued, "I fear she would be ill for this purpose, for other reasons. She be a singleton—no Phaze opposite, no merging. She worked in Proton not long enough before the mergence. Best we choose one firmly rooted in both cultures."

Trool nodded agreement. His alternate had been Citizen Troal, and Suchevane's had been the Bat Girl. They preferred the Phaze mode, but both knew Proton well and maintained their places in it.

"Also, Tsetse's bisexual," Nepe said. "She can make it with any man, but she prefers women. So scratch that."

"Let me check the Book," Trool said, getting up.

"May I come too?" Nepe asked, gulping down her last mouthful of pie and getting up.

The Adept shrugged. "An thou dost wish."

"I'll take thy seconds!" Alien warned her.

Nepe hesitated just long enough, then resumed her motion. "It's fattening anyway."

In Trool's private chamber, where he kept the phenomenal Book of Magic, the compendium of the most potent spells of Phaze, Flach took over. "There be a problem, mayhap, Adept."

"Aye, so methought when Neysa left thee here," Trool said.

"We were on our mission, and about to inquire of Brown, when Grandam hustled me here instead," Flach said. "This be not her way."

"She recognized a problem with Brown she knew not of before," Trool said. "She realized that thy mission were not best bruited there."

"Thou knowest?" Flach asked, not really surprised. Trool was the most versatile of the Adepts, and he made it his business to keep informed. "What be the problem?"

"It were not kind to say it," Trool said. "But methinks Neysa be correct: until it be abated, say naught to Brown."

"But Brown be no traitor!"

"Aye. But why burden her with more when she has much already? Question thy grandam naught on this; she be sworn to privacy, and it bear not on thy mission."

Flach did not like being excluded from anything, but realized that he could not debate the matter with Trool and Neysa. "Then canst find a woman for 'Sander?"

"Aye. There be a vamp seems suitable. Winsome, committed, and between men."

Flach was gratified. Trool of course related well to the vampire community, being married to one of their number. His presence had protected the local Flock from molestation by goblins and, yes, trolls. "Who be she?"

"Jodabyle, age twenty in man years. In Proton she be named Jod'e, of android persuasion."

"Android! And he be android!"

"Aye. So it seem a fair match."

"Willst tell her his nature?"

"Nay. She must be innocent—but loyal."

"But an she love him, and he betray her, what o' her?"

"What o' Phaze?" Trool asked in return.

Flach nodded. If this ploy failed, their entire planet might be doomed. The happiness of one person became incidental. "I follow. But I like it not."

"Thou dost now appreciate the ugliness o' the choice o' the lesser evil."

"Aye." Flach brooded a moment, then got practical. "How may she be introduced to him?"

"We shall arrange a coincidental meeting. Till things sour with his present lady friend, that be the extent o' it."

"What now for me? I know not when Grandam will return."

"Remain here, an thou wishest," Trool said, closing the Book. "Alien likes thy company, and Nepe's too."

"But needs must I update Grandpa Blue."

"Nay, best that thou remain clear 'o him till this be done, that thy travels yield little hint o' our effort. We know not how many spies o' the enemy be among us."

"Dost know the enemy?"

"Aye. It be an alien galactic species called the Hectare. They may move within the month."

"But if we know—"

"They possess enormous power. We can oppose them not."

"But with magic—"

Trool shook his head. "We would take such losses as to make it not worthwhile, including mayhap our planet itself. They could destroy it from afar, gi'ing us ne'er a chance. We needs must depend on the prophecy. All our leading figures will be prisoner, we think not maltreated, but helpless to oppose the invader."

Flach realized that if Trool said it, it had to be true. "Then this mission with the woman be most important."

"Aye. And thy freedom be vital too. Surrender to them not."

"I have more part in this?" Flach asked, surprised.

"Aye. We depend much on thee, in both thy forms. More I may not say."

They left the chamber. Flach, troubled, let Nepe take over. He knew why Trool was not telling him more: so he could not betray others who might be part of it, if he got caught. Just as the vamp-girl would not be told her role. At least it meant that the elders were doing what they could.

Nepe behaved in a childlike manner, except when she flirted with Alien, pretending that all was well. But she knew it wasn't. Her sleep that night was uneasy. How bad was it going to be, if all the major figures of the planet were to be taken captive? And what had bothered Neysa so much that she had interrupted even this mission to talk to Brown alone? Trool said it did not affect Nepe or Flach's own mission, but she wasn't sure. Anything their grandam took seriously affected them.

4
Shame

Neysa arrived back at the Brown Demesnes, in the same chamber as before. She knocked on the wall, signaling her return, and waited. In a moment Brown was there.

"I thank thee for coming back so soon," Brown said. "I be distraught for lack o' company."

"Needs must we talk alone," Neysa said. "I fear that can not be here, near the Adepts."

"Aye. They be under geis, but they hear."

"Will thy castle keep, in thine absence?"

"A few hours."

"Then march us to my Herd."

"Aye." They walked to the front storage chamber of the castle, where assorted wooden golems stood idle. "Franken," Brown said.

A huge and spectacularly ugly golem stirred. It was in the likeness of an ancient Earth monster said to have been crafted in a laboratory. The name was a misnomer, because it was the doctor, not the monster, who had been called Frankenstein, but for this offhand use it sufficed.

Franken picked Brown up. Neysa assumed her firefly form and flew up to perch on the golem's head. Franken tramped out of the castle, faced the setting sun, and proceeded at cruising velocity. That was faster than a unicorn could run, because the golem was big and indefatigable. The landscape passed at a horrendous rate. To Neysa, perched on the head and hunching down to avoid the rush of wind, it seemed most like an image in Agnes' mind: that of an airplane flying low over the terrain, coming in for a landing at a dome. Such machines were fewer now, because of the concern about pollution; less wasteful means were employed to travel. But Agnes had been in Proton during the old days, and ridden such machines many times. She remembered.

At dusk they reached the spot where the Herd was grazing. Clip charged up, but recognized the golem and relaxed. Neysa flew down, assumed her natural form, and conferred with her brother in horn talk.

"Brown and I needs must converse in private for a time."

"Graze in the center; none will hear."

"Our thanks to thee, sibling."

"There be an ill wind coming."

"Aye."

She trotted back to the golem, now waiting like the wooden statue it was. She assumed human form. "Walk with me within the Herd," she told Brown. "Magic penetrates not there, an we will it not."

Brown dismounted. They walked among the unicorns, who ignored them, each grazing a particular section. In the center was a broad area, already grazed.

"Thou dost be pensive, and the prisoners be flip," Neysa said. "Be the geis slipping?"

"Nay, it be tight," Brown said. "They can harm me not."

"But there be aught. I felt it as we arrived, and when I saw them, I knew. Thy straight be dire. Willst tell me?"

"Mayhap I will harm myself."

Neysa shook her head, unpleasantly perplexed. "At their behest? How can that be?"

"Willst make oath o' silence?"

"Be it that bad?"

"Not to thee, mayhap."

"I make the oath." And from her proceeded a tiny ripple, barely visible in the twilight, but significant: the splash of truth.

"Then will I tell thee what may please thee not," Brown said. "It be with relief I tell, for the secret consumes me. Yet, an thou have patience, needs must I tell it mine own way."

"Then ride me while I graze," Neysa said. "My patience be endless then." She assumed her natural form.

Brown mounted her, and began to talk. Neysa listened, and let her mind clothe the narration with the details she knew. It was a tale that should have amazed her, yet somehow did not, for it answered much that would have puzzled her had she thought to ponder it.

Brown was a child of eight when she ran away from home. That was not her name then, but her name didn't matter. It wasn't because her mother beat her; all the children of her village were beaten as a matter of policy. It wasn't that she often went hungry; that too was common, when the goblins raided the village stores. It wasn't that her father intended to betroth her to a fat merchant's son; that was a satisfactory placement as such things went. It could have been that the gang of boys was making her take off her clothes and do things with them she neither understood nor enjoyed; but that happened to any girl they caught; and hardly a girl escaped at least one such session before she came of age to marry. Some had been caught many times, because their houses were beyond the lighted fringe of the village, and the boys lurked in ambush. Some even claimed to like it, though Brown suspected they were merely covering the hurt with bravado. Brown made no bones about not liking it, but it didn't matter; if they caught her, they did it. She had become canny, so had been caught only three times. She often walked home through the woods, because she liked the trees, and the trees liked her. When the boys tried to ambush her there, a tree would arrange to snap a dropped branch under one of their feet, alerting her. Then she would reroute, and avoid them, and if they set out in direct pursuit she would shinny up a tree, knowing how to do it without getting scratched. If they tried to climb after her, they would snag seemingly by accident on the twig stubs and thorns, and the tree-ants would bite them. The trees were her friends, and the trees were not the boys' friends; that made all the difference.

No, none of these things drove her out. It was when she started making things from the wood of the trees that the trouble came. Because she liked trees, she liked wood, and the trees did not mind if she took their deadwood and worked with it. She made herself a doll from an old curly knot, and it kept her company at night; they told each other stories. She fashioned a pretend dog from a twisted fragment of a stump whose roots projected like legs and a tail. She had always wanted a dog, but never had one. So she adjusted the legs, and used charcoal to paint fur, and affixed old buttons for eyes, and wooden pegs for ears, and splinters for teeth, and she had her pet. She named it Woodruff.

It was when she started taking Woodruff for walks that the trouble began. The boys ambushed her, and Woodruff growled them off. When that got around, her father got nervous. He tried to throw the dog out, but it hid under the bed and growled. He used a broom to push it out, and kicked the dog, and Woodruff bit him on the leg. So he smashed it to pieces with the axe. Brown came home from lessons and found the sundered pieces. That was when she ran away, blinded by tears, taking only her doll.

But it was evening when she left, and night in the forest. The trees did not seem nearly as friendly at night, and it was cold. Her strait, as Neysa was later to put it, was dire. She had either to return home and take her punishment, which would be horrendous, or continue on, and perhaps perish in the wilderness. She could hear big animals prowling, and was terrified.

The animals were wolves, who ranged these parts and did not get along with the villagers. But they were werewolves, and Brown was obviously a child in distress. A bitch changed to human form and took her in. When they learned that Brown had run away and would die rather than go back to the village, because her brute father had killed her pet dog, the other wolves became more friendly. But though they could succor her for a night or two, they could not keep her. She was not a were, and would not be able to hunt with the Pack. Their leader, Kurrelgyre, was in exile because he had refused to slay his aging sire in the werewolf way, and things were in disarray already.

But there was someone who might be able to take her in. He was the Brown Adept, who lived in a wooden castle not far off. "Adept!" she cried, terrified anew. Everyone knew how terrible the Adepts were.

The wolves assured her that this one was kind to animals, as was the Blue Adept. He would not hurt her, and if she did not want to stay, he might help her go to the Blue Adept, who they understood had a beautiful and kind wife, the Lady Blue.

The huge golems were a forbidding sight, but they let the bitch and girl pass. The Brown Adept was a gnarled old man, his long brown beard turning white. "But I don't know the first thing about taking care of a child!" he protested.

Brown, catching on that he was a woodworker, turned positive. "I can feed myself, if there be food," she said. "I will be not much bother, honest, if thou dost mind not my playing with thy wood dolls."

Wood dolls? The golems were huge and ugly, a sight to frighten any normal child. The Brown Adept reconsidered. Perhaps he could let her stay for a few days.

That was the start of a friendship that quickly became an apprenticeship. The Brown Adept recognized in the child the talent to work magically with wood. He had no family and there was no one to take his place. He had thought that his Demesnes would simply fade away after his death; now he saw that they could continue. He showed the girl how to fashion the wooden golems, the way their bodies were pegged together so that they could move without falling apart. He showed her how to supervise the existing golems in their foraging for the proper kinds of wood. No live tree was ever taken, but a freshly dead one was harvested as soon as possible, so that the wood would not rot.

Soon she made another wooden dog—only instead of adapting this one from a gnarled stump, she made it from solid wood, with strong and jointed legs. He showed her how to make the dog heel at her command, so that it would not bite anyone unless she told it to. As for her doll—that had been his first clue that she had the necessary talent, because it had taken him years to make his golems talk, yet she had done it with her first one.

It was a great time, for a year. But the Adept was old and growing older. He had been hanging on to his health with the help of amulets he had traded from the Red Adept, but even these could not keep him going forever. "I am going to die," he told her. "Thou must be the Brown Adept. Do not let others know I be gone, until thou hast grown into thy full strength, else they may try to destroy these Demesnes in thy weakness."

"But I be not ready!" she protested tearfully. "Thou must live longer, Grandpa Brown!" For so she called him now, having adopted him in lieu of the family she had thrown away.

"Alas, I can not," he told her. "But this I needs must say: thou has made my last year a delight, and banished my loneliness. For that I thank thee, lovely child."

"Thou has been good to me too!" she said. "Ne'er didst thou beat me or starve me or do to me what the village louts did."

"An I had known o' those things, I would have sent my golems into the village to slay those evil folk," he said, grimacing.

"Grandpa Brown, I beg thee, leave me not!"

He squeezed her firm little hand in his worn brown hand. "It were not my choice, O sweet girl." Then he died.

She wept. Then she told a big golem to take him out and bury him under the garden. It was the onset of her Adept status—and her awful loneliness, which he had unwittingly bequeathed to her.

She had her doll and dog and the other golems for company, but none of them were alive. She did not dare let it be known that the old Adept was gone, for fear of an attack by others, as he had warned her. She didn't even tell the werewolves, though they were her friends; she pretended she was merely running errands for her master, who was busy making more golems. She managed, but she wasn't happy.

So it was for a year. She learned to make and handle the golems better, but knew she had more to learn. She longed for living company, but even when she dealt with others, trading golems for food and other staples (in the name of her master), she never got personal. She didn't dare.

Then the Blue Adept raided her Demesnes. At first she was afraid of him, and tried to drive him out, but he destroyed her defenses with his magic and had her at his mercy. But then he turned out to be a nice person, and helped her. He had somehow thought that *she* was a bad Adept who had attacked him, because one of the golems had been fashioned in his likeness and tried to take his place. He was a very small man who called himself Stile, and he was even newer as an Adept than she was. He had a small unicorn with him, the first she had met up close, and she was nice too. Her horn sounded like a harmonica, and her music was wonderful.

"And that were the onset o' our friendship, Neysa," she said. "Thirty years gone. Much has it meant to me."

Neysa, grazing, blew an affirmative note. She remembered their meeting, but had never heard it from Brown's point of view before.

"I were just ten then, but suddenly I knew love," Brown continued. "I loved the Adept Stile, but kept it secret, knowing it were laughable. He had the Lady Blue."

"I loved him too," Neysa said in horn talk. "And I an animal."

"Child and animal—how could we compete?" Brown asked rhetorically, and Neysa agreed.

Stile went on about his business, in due course destroying the Red Adept, who had killed his other self. In those days only a person who had lost his otherframe self could cross between the frames; that was why Stile had been able to cross from Proton. Then Stile became a Citizen in Proton, and the Contrary Citizens opposed him, as well as the Adverse Adepts. Brown of course helped him all she could. She would have done anything for him, but he treated her with perfect courtesy like the child she was, never knowing her love. Finally he saved the frames from the depredations of the bad Citizens and Adepts by separating Phaze from Proton. He restored the body of his other self, the original Blue Adept, and made ready to return to Proton and to the robot lady Sheen, who loved him (of course!) but whom he did not love. (How could he love any other, with the Lady Blue? How well they all understood!) Here it was that Brown betrayed him in her fashion. She had temporary access to the great Book of Magic, and made a spell to reverse things so that it was Blue who went to Proton, and Stile who stayed in Phaze, where he longed to be.

There, separated, the frames remained, for about twenty years, until Stile's son Bane exchanged places with his other self, the robot Mach. That set off a complicated sequence, and renewed the warfare between Citizens and Adepts, as the bad ones tried to grab power. After most of another decade, Stile went the opposite route: he summoned the Adept Clef, and the Platinum Flute, and they merged the frames.

But in the long quiet periods between Adept wars, Brown remained alone. She no longer had to hide the loss of her predecessor, and she mastered the control of the golems, but her life was mostly empty. For now she found that isolation was not just a temporary state; it was standard for Adepts. Those few who were married were extremely fortunate; the others existed in increasing private bitterness, for all normal folk were afraid of them.

With reason. After the third assassination attempt against her, Brown knew better than to trust any stranger even slightly. She associated only with other Adepts, whom she mostly detested, and with the werewolves of the local Pack. They, at least, could be trusted. But that did not mean they were close. They were invariably polite and accommodating, but they had their own lives and commitments, and she realized that she was imposing when she visited them too often.

Then she broke her foot. It was a stupid accident with a golem. She had had it carry her to the Red Adept's castle—Stile had arranged to install Trool the Troll in those Demesnes, and to her surprise the troll turned out to be an excellent Adept and excellent man—so that they could make arrangements for further exchanges of magic that benefited both. But on her return trip the golem had stumbled and fallen, and her foot had been caught. She had needed healing and assistance, and had to go to the wolves for it.

They had helped, of course. They assigned a bitch to care for her and manage the castle under her direction, until she mended. This was Lycandi, fifteen years old, the same as Brown. The bitch was nice enough, and attractive enough in both her wolf and woman states, but was something of an outcast because she had rejected first mating and never achieved the final syllable of her name. This was probably why she had been assigned to this chore: she would hardly be missed from the Pack.

The healing of the foot was slow, but Lycandi was patient. Indeed, it became evident that the bitch liked this assignment, for here there was no pressure on her to do what she chose not to. They talked, and Brown learned the bitch's concern.

A werewolf was not considered mature until he or she indulged in a first, ritual mating, and exchanged syllables with the partner in that mating: the Promised. Thereafter those two would never mate with each other again; each would find another to pair with. Lycandi had come into her first heat two years before, and had received offers from several wolves, but had turned them down. In the ensuing time she had steadfastly refused to mate, though it locked her into juvenile status.

"But why not, 'Candi?" Brown asked. "It be a simple thing to do. I were not able to fend off the village boys e'en when a child, while thou—"

"Didst thou like it, when they forced thee?" 'Candi asked sharply.

"Nay. I hated it. But—"

"I, too."

"But that were because they were louts. Were it the Adept Stile who sought me, or e'en a handsome wolf in man form—"

"I like not wolves *or* men, that way."

"But surely the mating urge, the companionship—"

"Companionship, aye, and mayhap the urge. But not with wolves."

"Then with a human man. That may count not toward the completion o' thy name, but I have heard they can be fine temporary lovers."

"Why didst thou not take such a lover, then?"

"I can trust no human man. Three tried to kill me."

'Candi nodded. "Thou hast reason, then. Me, I wish no lover, nor man neither wolf. That be my shame."

Brown was amazed. "But an thou hast the urge—"

"Any bitch would tear my throat out."

Brown stared at her. "A bitch . . ."

She saw the bitch, in her girl form, sitting beside her, suffering. She reached out to comfort her, then drew hastily away lest she be misunderstood, then moved again. Something in her own life was coalescing, a mystery she had not fathomed before.

"Wouldst settle for one who were no bitch?" she whispered.

Lycandi gazed at her, her eyes wet. "Thou—Adept—"

"And woman." Brown caught her shoulder and drew her in.

Then they were together, kissing, their tears mixing. Brown had never imagined love of this nature, but now she discovered what it offered. The ambushes of the boys had soured her on males in a way she hadn't fathomed, and the assassination attempts had soured her on adult males. Now she realized that it was more than that. She had loved Stile, in part, because he was unavailable; he would never seek sex with her. The violence of the male, the urgency, the cruel brevity—this was not to her taste. But this, gentle, sensitive, understanding of her nature, with a female . . .

And so they were lovers. Lycandi did not depart when Brown's foot healed; she became servant and guardian, and Brown paid a wage to her Pack, for the loss of one of their members. Neither of them ever stated the true nature of their association to any outsider, for neither the wolf nor the human cultures would have accepted it. The problem of companionship had been solved, for them both.

But in time Lycandi had sickened with an intractable distemper that sometimes affected wolves. Magic could ameliorate it only so far. Two years ago she died, and Brown was alone again.

The horror of her isolation closed in on her once more, not one whit abated because she was now a mature woman. She missed her lover, and grieved for her, but that would gradually pass. The lack of companionship would not. Brown saw no end to that other than death.

That was why she had volunteered to host the two Adept prison-

ers. She wanted nothing of them as men, and she had no sympathy
for their plight. Both were evil men who deserved death. But Stile
had been loath to kill unnecessarily, so had spared them. Trool had
bound them with the geis, but only an Adept could be sure of keeping
them out of mischief. So she had done the other Adepts a favor, and
garnered a bit of company for herself. For whatever else these men
were not, and no matter how much she despised them, they were
human presences. That was a quarter loaf, but far better than none.

At first the men had been barely aware of her or their surroundings.
The mergence which had put the Purple Adept into the same body
as Citizen Purple, and the same for the Tan Adept and Citizen, had
set off a struggle for mastery of those hosts. They were selfish, un-
feeling men; neither of their aspects was accustomed to considering
the wishes of any other party. That was why the good Citizens and
Adepts had taken over after the mergence: they were able to get
along better with others and themselves.

But gradually the evil men came to rough terms with themselves.
Perhaps they had set up a system of alternating days, giving each self
his turn in control. Perhaps some other device. The effect was that
they began to take an interest in their surroundings, and their de-
meanor and manner improved.

They began to talk with Brown. At first they cursed her as a foul
captor who would one day be tortured to death. She responded by
letting the golems handle them, remaining clear herself. The golems
were immune to insult, having no feelings. The men soon enough
saw the futility of their effort, and apologized and promised to be
more civil. Brown resumed personal attendance, and the two were as
good as their word, being meticulously polite. It was as though they
were guests, and she the hostess; they thanked her for her hospitality.
It was of course insincere, but even the semblance of appreciation
was better than nothing, for them as well as for her.

Gradually this changed. The appreciation seemed to become more
sincere. Tan especially was attentive to her. He complimented her
not only on the food, but on her dress and then on her person. Finally
she realized what he was up to, her understanding perhaps delayed
by her revulsion of the notion: he was attempting to seduce her.

So was Purple. But there was no evident conflict between the men.
They were operating in tandem, the one giving way to the other.
One was a good decade older than Brown, the other a decade

younger; they would settle for whichever type she preferred. Their object was not sex, though evidently they would not object to it if the opportunity offered, but power: they wanted to corrupt her away from her commitment as prison guard. If they could make her love one of them, they might prevail on her to release them. That would only be part of their effort, for the geis would remain on them; only the Red Adept could remove that. They would remain unable to use their magic for any hostile purpose, or to harm any other person physically. But once they were free, they would set about nullifying the geis, probably with the same determination. Maybe they would find a way to sneak into the Red Demesnes and look at the Book of Magic, finding the spell that held them, and its antidote. Maybe they intended to persuade her to send a golem to steal the Book, so that they could gain complete power.

She was bitterly amused, once her outrage subsided. They were trying to seduce a woman whose romantic interest was not in men! Since they were unable to use any kind of force, even verbal, because of the geis, their chances of success were nil. But sober consideration caused her to realize that she had two excellent reasons for concealing her immunity. First, the last thing she wanted was for these enemies to discover her private nature, which she had kept secret from all but her lover Lycandi for so many years. She would be mortified to have that exposed! Second, even though she had no use for either man, she appreciated their civility and attention far better than she appreciated their anger and discourtesy. She could at least pretend she had some company worth having. Her need was for the semblance of companionship, not romance, but if she had to pretend susceptibility to the latter to achieve the former, that was better than the alternative.

So she responded guardedly to their overtures. She was courteous to both, but paid slightly more attention to Purple, not because she found him more attractive, but because she found him less attractive. Tan, even under the geis, was dangerous; his eyes could work no evil now, but looked as if they could, and sometimes illusion was a significant part of magic. Also, his twin sister Tania, now the wife of the Adept Clef, was quite another matter; had that lovely woman approached Brown with amorous intent, Brown would have been lost in an instant. Tan resembled his sister as closely as was possible without a change of sex; it was easy to picture him clean-shaven, with his hair grown long, as Tania. Therefore she guarded herself from him, and favored Purple, who was fat and ugly and totally devoid of appeal for her.

The equanimity with which Tan accepted this loss of favor confirmed his motive: had his suit been real, he would have been jealous. Given his choice of women, a forty-year-old spinster would have been the very last he would take. Purple, older, seemed more practical: any woman would do in a pinch. He would gladly have an affair with her—and as gladly drop her the moment he was free. She felt far more at ease with that attitude, ironically.

But as the months passed in this subtle game, she came to appreciate another hazard. She was playing coy, as befitted one who was not supposed to be corrupted. But she did not care to overdo it, lest they catch on that there was more to her diffidence than mere duty. In the process of judging her calls, she realized that she might have to choose at some point between actually succumbing to a sexual encounter she did not want, or betraying her secret. Which would it be? If she actually lay with Purple, she would have to school her revulsion not to show, and her secret would be safe, for men could not conceive of a woman preferring anything other than sex with them, once it was tried. But she would feel absolutely filthy and ashamed. Could it be worth it? She was in horrible doubt.

The men were prisoners, and powerless. But if they learned her nature, they would speak of it to others. This she would be unable to prevent, for periodically other Adepts did come to make sure that all was under control here. This was the one nonmagical, nonphysical way they could hurt her—and they surely would do so, if it suited their purpose. Could she bear the shame?

She seemed doomed to shame, either way. The matter pressed on her awareness, day and night. She dreamed of fat Purple coming down on her body, saying, "Do this, bitch-lover, else I tell!" He might tell anyway, if he caught on that she wasn't enjoying it in the fashion of other women.

At this point in her dilemma Neysa and Flach visited. Brown's relief at seeing them was immense. All the loneliness of her situation abated—and returned with added force with their departure, though it was temporary. She needed advice from a friend, desperately.

"And now, if friend thou still dost be," she concluded, "I lay on thee the burden o' advice: what needs must be my course?"

Neysa, grazing as if unaffected by the narration, controlled the welter of her emotions. Her friend Brown—a woman's woman? Desperately lonely, all these years? How could she, Neysa, have missed the signs?

They had to move those prisoners elsewhere! Yet if they did, thus abruptly, Purple and Tan might realize why. Also, where could they be moved? How could Neysa ask for this, without giving reason? She could not give reason, for she had given her oath of secrecy, which she would not abridge. And if she found some other pretext to move them out, what then of Brown, thrown into complete isolation again?

Then she caught a glimmer of a notion. She played a warning note on her horn, to advise Brown to dismount. Then she changed to woman form. "Methinks thou dost need out o' this mess. An a need come for golems, many golems in a far corner, made from the wood there, thou couldst be called away, and some other put in charge o' thy Demesnes for the interim."

"But Neysa—" Brown protested.

"I would break not mine oath! I would find other way to justify the project."

"But what I needs must know—"

"No word o' thy shame! It will be hidden."

Brown paused. Then she nodded. "I thank thee, Neysa. An thou canst do that, my concern be eased."

They walked back to the standing golem. Soon they were on their way back to the wooden castle, charging along under the starry sky.

Once Brown was safely home, Neysa set out for the Red Demesnes afoot, where she knew Flach would remain until she rejoined him. She ran well in her natural form, but not as fast as in her youth. Still, it was a pleasure; she had always liked to run. She remembered the old years, with Stile, and her hopeless love for him, never spoken. Later her filly-foal Fleta had done what Neysa had not dared do, and had openly loved a man. In late retrospect, Neysa could not say that was wrong. Sometimes secret love was better in the open.

And what of Brown's secret love? The bitch Lycandi was dead, but the love she had indoctrinated Brown with remained. Neysa would help Brown win free of the trap the Adepts had put her into, but how could she free her from her secret shame? "No word o' thy shame," she had promised, and Brown had paused, then thanked her.

Why had there been that pause?

Neysa was not the cleverest of unicorns, and age was not improving her mind, but she normally figured things out in time. It was as if Brown had not been entirely satisfied with Neysa's response. But it had been hard to be reassuring, when the shock of her discovery of Brown's nature was new.

Then it came to her. Brown had wanted to know how *she* felt, and whether her friendship had suffered because of the revelation. And Neysa had answered without meaning to: "No word o' thy shame." Brown had hoped she could speak without sacrificing their friendship, and had been disappointed.

Yet now, too late, regretting what she had said, Neysa could not deny its truth. A curtain had dropped down between the two of them. How could true friendship survive the knowledge of what Brown was?

5

Game

Lysander had to admit it was interesting. The child Nepe, who was also Flach, had shown him magic; Alyc was showing him science, and the things of the science frame. Most of the naked serfs were working, but many had free time, and they populated the lounges and the Game Annex. Since food and sex were free, their main entertainment seemed to be competitive games. That of course was a major interest for Lysander, too, but he hesitated to push it, lest Alyc be uninterested. His first job was to cement his relationship with her, so as to remain in Citizen Blue's favor.

But after they ate—there were machines that dispensed anything desired that was healthy—and covered the premises, there wasn't much to do. It was night, and though the halls had no closing, he was tiring. "I have had a long day," he said. "It started on board a spaceship, and included an outdoor tour that had me talking to a unicorn, and now an indoor tour that has shown me more naked people than I thought existed. Is it possible to sleep?"

"The Citizen allocated a chamber for you," she said. "But if you would like to join me in mine . . ."

He considered. Her incomplete sentence was evidently an ellipsis, and that meant that something significant had been omitted for his consideration. His preliminary briefing had made clear that whatever else occurred, when a man spent the night with an unrelated woman without other company, he was expected to indulge in copulation with her. If he did not wish to do so, he did not stay with her. His effort to dampen his reaction to her sexual attributes had been effective, and he had no inclination to get into human sex with her at this time. His brief handling of the harpy/cyborg's legs had evoked temporary interest there, perhaps because Echo was a stranger; that was not the case with Alyc. But if he declined, she might be hurt or suspicious.

Perhaps he could talk his way out of it, this night. "I am new to this culture, and fear giving offense. I think I am not at this time ready for anything other than a night of sleep. May I decline the sharing of your residence without upsetting you?"

"Well, sure, of course," she said, evidently disgruntled. "I mean, you don't have to do anything you don't want to, unless a Citizen says to. I just thought—" She broke off, shrugging.

This wasn't being easy. "I understand—please correct me if I am mistaken—that a man does not stay with a woman unless he copulates with her. I think I would like to do that with you, when I am less tired. So I feel I should not seek the pleasure of your company under false pretense."

She was studiously gazing away from him, but she peeked. "You mean it's not that you aren't interested?"

He was getting it right! "By no means! It's that where I come from, some experiences are best reserved for ideal conditions, rather than being squandered when things are imperfect."

She thought about that, and it was evident that the longer she thought, the better she liked it. "Then, maybe, would you like to stay with me, and just sleep?"

"Why that would be very nice, if it is not an imposition."

"Right this way!" She strode for home at a brisk rate.

Lysander followed, making a perceptual adjustment. He had abolished any sexual inclination by visualizing her as she was. That had to be modified now. So he schooled himself to see her as a human male would, blocking out his natural perception. For example, the way her plush buttocks flexed as she walked was supposed to be interesting and sexually appealing. A human male, contemplating that at length, was supposed to become sexually aroused, so that his copulatory member expanded—

Oops. Hastily he cut off the focus; obviously he had it right. He stared over her head, hoping that none of the other serfs had noticed. But it was evident that they had, and were amused. Well, amusement was harmless.

Alyc's private chamber was pleasant enough. She had a body-cleaning alcove, a video screen, and a foam bed. "Clean up and lie down," she told him. "I'll watch the show."

Lysander stepped into the alcove, while Alyc lay on her bed and watched the screen. There was some kind of entertainment program on, resounding with people slipping and falling, getting whacked on their posteriors, and loudly protesting indignities. Alyc laughed, evidently enjoying it. He would have to study her reactions, so as to key in the normal human pattern. There was much his training had not properly prepared him for.

He had assumed that the cleaning alcove would employ sonics, but this seemed not to. Instead there were handles whose purpose was opaque. This, too, had been omitted from his training: the details of variations of human hygienic devices. He hesitated just to turn the handles, lest he misuse the equipment.

"Excuse me," he said. "I don't wish to interrupt your entertainment, but I am unfamiliar with this mechanism."

"They don't have showers on Planet Grenadier?" she asked, surprised.

"They have sonic cleaners. Do you mean you clean with water?"

"Sure," she said, bouncing off the bed. "Why not? It's recycled. You turn on the water here—" She reached past him to work a handle. Water blasted down from the ceiling, startling him. It was hot, but not unpleasantly so. "And soap here." She worked another handle, and got a handful of foam. "Then you just spread it on and rinse it off, like this." She smeared the foam on his chest.

"But you are also getting wet!" he protested.

"Well, I need to get clean too. Do you mind?"

"Of course not. It is your chamber. But—"

"You can soap me, then." She guided his hand to the foam spout, and he got a handful of the frothy stuff.

He smeared it on her shoulders and back and breasts, and she covered him similarly, while the water descended on them both. She reached around him to massage his back, in the process pressing in close and slippery. His hands slid down to the same buttocks he had contemplated before. They had been visually intriguing; now they were tactilely intriguing.

"Is it permissible to reconsider?" he inquired.

"It's too late to skip the shower!" she cried, laughing.

"About indulging in copulatory activity. It occurs to me that this occasion might after all be suitable."

"I thought it might," she murmured, satisfied. Then she reached up and hauled in his head for a wet and steamy kiss.

Belatedly he realized that this had been her intent throughout. She was an expressive, open woman, and she liked full interaction. She had known the human condition better than he; not only was their sexual encounter feasible, it was quite positive. His reservations about the human form faded away; this was a human body, and this activity was natural for it.

Finally, both clean and sated, they emerged to lie on her bed and watch the show. He followed her cues, and began laughing when she did. Soon enough his mind followed, and he found himself genuinely enjoying it.

In due course they slept. But he woke in the night, discovering that she was stroking his body. There was a certain art to it, and before long it occurred to him that another episode of sexual interaction might be appropriate. So it turned out to be.

In the morning she woke him again, kissing him and rubbing her body against his suggestively. She was evidently interested in yet another copulatory encounter. "About this time, most men begin to get tired of me," she said. "Are you tired?"

"Not yet," he said. He regarded this as excellent experience.

Later in the day she showed him how actually to play the game. "There are these consoles," she explained, approaching one. "We stand on opposite sides, and it has a grid. Or it used to, before the mergence. Now sometimes it does and sometimes it doesn't."

"The rules have changed?"

"Not exactly. I mean, the grids shift a little each year, and sometimes the numbers are down the side, and new games get added and old ones subtracted, but that's routine. But now it's really different. Maybe I can show you."

Perplexed, he stood opposite her. Before him was a screen, on which was a diagram.

PRIMARY GRID

	1. PHYSICAL	2. MENTAL	3. CHANCE	4. ART
A. NAKED				
B. TOOL				
C. MACHINE				
D. ANIMAL				

"Ah, I believe I follow," he said. Actually, he had been trained in this type of grid, and knew it well, but he preferred to let her have the pleasure of showing him. It might even turn out that she would have some pleasant surprises for him, as she had during the night. It would take a phenomenal effort to convince himself that she was an unappealing creature, physically, now that he had indulged in the human copulatory ritual. She did seem to feel that there was something special about this game. "One person selects a number, and the other a letter, and where the two intersect defines the nature of the game to be played. Or am I mistaken?"

"Not exactly," she repeated. "I mean, that's how it's played, yes, only sometimes it doesn't work. You'll see, maybe."

"Then let's play it," he said. He saw that the numbers were highlighted for him, so he touched 3. CHANCE. She would have no chance against him in any ordinary game, so this was the only fair way, as it largely negated skill.

"I'm choosing A. NAKED," she said, touching her screen.

"But are you supposed to tell me? I thought the point was that the choices are hidden until the result is manifest." Indeed, that was the essence of gaming: the hidden strategy and counterstrategy.

"Well—"

She broke off, and he saw why. Instead of highlighting the 3A box, the screen was flashing words. SOME TALK OF ALEXANDER, AND SOME OF HERCULES; OF HECTOR AND LYSANDER, AND SUCH GREAT NAMES AS THESE. GOOD MORNING, LYSANDER! HAVE YOU MADE ANY RECENT CONQUESTS?

He looked over the console at Alyc. "This is a joke?" he asked, uncertain whether to laugh.

"Not exactly," she said. Her cheeks showed a becoming hint of a flush. "I mean, I didn't do it. It's the Game Computer."

"The computer recognizes me?" But obviously it did, using the ubiquitous sensors of Proton. It was already talking again.

LYSANDER: NAVAL AND MILITARY COMMANDER OF SPARTA, WHO ENDED THE PELOPONNESIAN WAR IN 405 B.C. BY DESTROYING THE ATHENIAN FLEET AND REDUCING ATHENS TO A SECOND-RATE POWER.

"I am no military commander!" Lysander protested. But he wondered: could the computer know of his true mission?

LYSANDER: A CHARACTER IN SHAKESPEARE'S *MIDSUM-*

MER NIGHT'S DREAM WHO FALLS IN LOVE WITH HERMIA, WHO FLEES WITH HIM TO THE WOODS IN ORDER TO AVOID MARRIAGE TO HER FATHER'S CHOICE OF MEN. HAVE YOU TAKEN A WOMAN TO THE WOODS, LYSANDER?

"Well, actually she took me," he said. "Her name was Belle, and she was a unicorn. She spoke to me musically on her horn, telling me of the recent history of the planet and the mating of 'rovots' and the unwelcomeness of goblins. But she had no human form."

YOU ARE PLAYING CAT AND MOUSE WITH ME, LYSANDER. THEREFORE I GIVE YOU THE GAME OF FOX AND GEESE. DO YOU KNOW IT? A pattern appeared, showing thirty-three dark circles arranged in lines of three and seven.

"I know it. But this is not the type of game we selected."

IT IS CLOSE ENOUGH. REPORT TO THE GAME CHAMBER SHOWN BY THE BLUE LINE. A line appeared on the floor, leading away from the console.

"See?" Alyc asked. "It does what it wants. It won't let us play any game but the one it chooses for us."

"Intriguing. Do you think the magic affected it?"

"It must have. Now it's a self-willed machine."

"Well, let's see what it's like. Do you prefer to be the fox or the geese?"

"I have no choice. It marked you the fox."

"Oh. I hadn't noticed. Very well, I'll play the fox. You have played the game before?"

"Yes, it's fun, the way it's set up. Only I don't like the way other women cut in."

"Women cut in? Are we talking about the same game? This should be a board, with marbles—"

"You'll see."

Something was definitely askew. Lysander shut up and followed the blue line.

The chamber was larger than necessary for a table and board game; indeed, neither was there. Instead there were rows of human-sized neuter mannequins standing as if ready to march to war.

"I think we have the wrong room," Lysander said.

"No we don't. It's a life-sized game. Those are the geese, and you're the fox."

"But in the game, the fox tries to jump the geese and remove them, while the geese try to block in the fox so it can't move."

"See, the places are there," she said, pointing to the floor. Sure enough, it was laid out in the game pattern—and each mannequin was standing in a circle. "You don't literally jump the geese, you just touch each one so she gets off the board and you step beyond her. It's the same, only larger."

"She? Those mannequins are neuter."

"No they aren't." She stepped up to the center of the forward line, which had one blank circle. As she did so, things changed. Suddenly all the mannequins were clothed in frilly dresses that were padded to make them look female, and all had wigs that contributed to the effect. So did Alyc—and in the dress and wig, she looked astonishingly like the others. Rather, they all looked like her. It was a transformation that seemed almost magical.

Almost? Now he knew that magic was literal, here; it could indeed be involved. "But you're in clothing! I thought only Citizens—"

"In the games it's okay. It's costuming. But we would never go like this outside!"

He nodded. Special license for costumes made sense. It also gave serfs a chance to act out whatever fantasies they might have. He was coming to appreciate why the Game Annex was so popular among those who might not otherwise have been game-minded. It represented therapy on unspecified levels.

"Now play," Alyc said. "You move first."

Lysander saw that there were instructions playing on the screen, for any who happened not to be conversant with the details of the game. He discovered that this was the archaic version: thirteen geese, and moves were allowed in any direction, including slantwise. He had not played that variant, but could adapt readily enough.

He stepped to the board, before the ladies. Abruptly he became clothed himself, in a fine coat of brown fur, reminiscent of a wealthy fox. The coat was real; he felt its pleasant heft. Now, zeroed in, he stepped diagonally toward the geese. He knew he was at a disadvantage; the geese could win every time, if played correctly. That was why the archaic form had given way to the modern form, where the geese could move only forward or sideways, while the fox was unrestrained. But the moves could be tricky, and Alyc was not the brightest person, so he should be able to win anyway. Not that winning was important, in this instance; he was just letting Alyc show him around.

He had taken his turn. Now she took hers. She could not jump him or attack him; she could only try to box him in. But she had thirteen pieces, and as few as six could box him, if the position was right, and eight otherwise. So he had to eliminate a sufficient number of geese to make her win impossible. If he got her down to five, that was it; she could not claim a draw by skulking along the sides. A draw was possible if both players were conservative; that, again, was reason to modify the old form of the game.

It was odd, seeing thirteen women just like Alyc. She had remarked that clothing was a sexual turn-on for serfs, instead of nudity; already he was coming to accept that. Alyc nude was an interesting figure of a woman, as he had come to appreciate during the night. But Alyc clothed was exciting. When she walked, the dress swung about her legs and accented her hips, making the legs seem more shapely and hinting at further marvels beyond. The bodice nominally covered the bosom, but somehow showed a fair amount and made the remainder intriguing. The woman was now twice as appealing as she had been before.

In fact, all the women were appealing. The mannequins had assumed the mannerisms of life. Each was breathing and blinking, and a girlish tremor went through any one of them he looked at. In fact, they were warm and soft, as he discovered when he tagged one for removal; he had caught her unflanked and "jumped" her. She gazed at him with muted hurt and walked sadly off the board, making him feel guilty—and she was only a mannequin. There *had* to be magic!

Alyc was not a skilled player, as he had suspected, and he won the game handily. The last one he removed from the board was her; he had almost lost track as the positions changed during the game. It had been an experience quite different from what he had anticipated.

The mannequins lost their clothing and returned to their immobility. Lysander and Alyc became as they were, naked serfs. The whole thing was a bit hard to believe.

They were about to depart the chamber, when another serf woman stepped up. "I wish to challenge the winner," she said.

Lysander looked at her. She was spectacular, with golden hair, deep green eyes, and a figure that made Alyc's look somewhat dumpy. "Is that permitted? We were assigned this game by the computer."

"It is permitted if there is no other assignment for the chamber," the woman said. "Let me introduce myself. I am Jod'e, android; I work for Citizen Troal."

"I am Lysander, android, working for Citizen Blue," he said. "This is Alyc, who also works for Citizen Blue. She is showing me around, and I'm not sure—"

"It's the custom," Alyc said with disgust. "They can cut in if they want to, and you have to play a challenger one game."

He sympathized with Alyc's annoyance. Apparently a handsome new serf was fair game for the sharks. It surely was worse when the new serf was a shapely woman. But he did not want to make a scene. "One game, then," he said shortly.

"A variant," Jod'e said. "I will be a goose. You must kiss each goose you jump, and if you jump me without recognizing me, I win regardless of the position."

He looked at Alyc. "A variant?"

"She challenged you," Alyc said grimly. "You can insist on the same rules as the prior game. But usually a serf goes along. It's all supposed to be fun, after all."

Lysander was not pleased. He was a spy, true, and his loyalty was not to this planet. But apart from that, his sense of fair play was straight. It was a matter of honor, a concept which was ingrained in the Hectare brain. He had made a commitment to Alyc, and he did not care to abridge it. Jod'e was trying to lure away Alyc's boyfriend, and that seemed less than right at this stage. Evidently this sort of thing had happened before, and Alyc was used to it, but he did not like being a party to it. Let his association with Alyc run its natural course; if later they agreed to break it up, then he was fair game for predatory women. Also, Alyc was a useful contact with Citizen Blue, so he had reason to remain with her.

Well, he would play the game. But the interloper would get nothing from it. "I agree," he said. "Your variant."

Jod'e smiled. It was a phenomenal smile, crafted to impress, and he was impressed. At the same time he wondered why she was making this effort to vamp him. Was it just because he was here? Or to spite Alyc? But Jod'e seemed not to know Alyc, or to have known of Lysander before seeing him at this game. Was she a shark who simply took whatever offered and threw it away when finished?

Jod'e stepped into the key circle, and the mannequins walked to their places. The transformation occurred again. This time all looked like Jod'e, and a stunning collection it was. Every one of them was a vision of delight.

"Turn your back a moment, while I shuffle," Jod'e said.

He turned away. When he turned back, the assembly looked the same—but he knew that Jod'e had switched places with one of the mannequins, so that he could not identify her by location. He thought it would be easy to pick her out from among the mannequins, but discovered it was not; he did not know her as well as Alyc, and there was nothing to distinguish her. Those mannequins were amazing!

He made his move, and a figure made the counter. He saw right away that Jod'e was a more experienced player than Alyc, and knew how to press her advantage. Now he wondered how the figures knew when and where to move; there was no separate player giving directions, because she was right there among them, as silent as they. He would have to ask Alyc about that, later; there was indeed more to this game than he had thought.

They maneuvered, each side taking turns. Then he got a chance to trap and jump one of the figures. He suspected that Jod'e had done it deliberately, for she had played flawlessly until then. True to the new rule, he kissed the doomed figure.

She felt exactly like a woman. Her lips were warm and soft, and he felt the tickle of the breath through her nose. Her breasts pressed against him enticingly. He let a hand slip down behind her, out of Alyc's view, and squeezed a buttock through the cloth; it felt exactly like living flesh. This must be the real Jod'e, presented because she wanted to kiss him. But he had already seen amazing things, when there was magic, and there had to be magic here; how could he be sure it was her?

So he pressed in with his fingers, not only squeezing the buttock but feeling as far as he could into the cleft between buttocks. How far could a neuter mannequin emulate a living woman? It still felt real. He hooked a finger, giving a slow, personal goose, no pun. How long could a living woman keep from reacting to this impertinence? Alas, he found evidence neither way; she seemed to be perfect, physically, and she didn't react.

But he could delay his decision, and announce his guess when the game ended. So he released her, and she walked to the side, off the board.

The play continued. The geese had been reduced by one, but there were still more than enough to barricade him against the side, and he was hard-pressed. Then another opportunity offered, and he stepped up to kiss another figure off the board. He came in slowly, looking down into the decolletage of her dress, to see whether the padding that made the figure look female was visible. What was there was visible, but it wasn't padding; the dress covered a very firm pair of heaving breasts, with an extremely nice cleavage. He pressed against that bosom as he kissed her, and it still felt genuine. If this were not the real woman, he was up against a much stiffer challenge than he had realized.

He released her without a word, and she walked away to join the other. The two of them stood motionless at the side, now seeming much more like dummies, despite their costumes.

There were more moves, and still he was hard-pressed. Then a third opportunity came, and he took it. He was now far more intrigued by the riddle of identity than about the game itself. There had to be some way to tell!

This time he placed himself so that his body blocked most of hers from the view of Alyc, and as he bent to kiss her lips the fingers of his right hand gathered in the back of her dress until he hauled up the hem and was able to get in underneath. Slowly kissing her, he reached into her cleft and felt most intimately. She wore no panties; the costuming was only external. He explored until he found the aperture he sought: damp and hot. She definitely had the equipment of a living woman.

Yet so had the other two, as far as he had been able to ascertain. Could the magic have made the mannequin alive, just for the game? Or was it illusion, so detailed that it was complete? She had tolerated his exploration with the patience of the inanimate; she never flinched or reacted in any way. He was inclined to believe that all three were mannequins, because of their lack of reaction, but he wasn't sure. He released her, and she joined the others.

On the fourth one he tried a deep kiss. He opened his mouth on hers, and forced his tongue between her lips. He met her tongue, completely human and ready, matching his, move for move. This *had* to be real—yet maybe not. If magic could transform a boy into a unicorn, why couldn't it give a mannequin a functioning mouth? Or an anatomically correct cleft? Or were the mannequins fashioned as complete android women who seemed lifeless between games, but could animate their bodies for the game? Still, he had seen them without breasts before the game started, yet now they all had them.

He let her go too. As far as he could tell, all of them were complete, and were in every way alive. Yet they could not be. He was baffled.

Desperate, he tried one more thing, when she gave him his chance at the fifth one. He moved to kiss her, but instead of meeting her lips squarely he caught her lower lip between his lips, sucked it into his mouth, and bit it. If he tasted blood—

"Mmmph!" she protested, jerking back. "You win, you guano!" Then she became a large bat, and flew away.

Astonished, he stared after her. "A—a—" he stammered.

"A vamp-girl," Alyc said. "How clever of you to figure that out! She had me fooled; I thought she was a werebitch."

"But I—" It was still too much to grasp.

"A vamp can't handle blood, even her own," Alyc continued. "I mean, they eat it only for very special ceremonies, and it sends them into frenzy. She had to get out of here before she went wild."

"But they all seemed alive!" he said. "I was just guessing; I didn't know that was the one. I couldn't tell them apart at all!"

Alyc smiled. "Then you lucked out! She pulled a double whammy on you. They were *all* her."

"But they were all different!"

"No, I saw what was happening, because I was outside the game. She used magic all right, but just on you. To make you think you were taking five different figures, when it was really the same one each time. That's pretty easy magic, for Phaze folk, if they work at it. Each time, you kissed her, and then one of the dummies walked off, and you thought it was the same. I was so mad! But I couldn't say anything. I just had to hope you would see through the trick, and make her pay—and you sure did, Lysander, you sure did! That was a stroke of genius!"

"It was luck more than genius," he confessed. "I was trying to test for the real one, but every one of them seemed so authentic. You mean I kissed the real one five times?"

"Yes. I was getting good and jealous, but you know I was laughing too. When you goosed the goose—!"

So she had seen enough to figure it out. But she was laughing, and he laughed with her. "And she had to stand there and take it, so as not to give herself away. I thought it was a dummy I was goosing!"

"Maybe it was," she said cheerfully. "Then when you bit her—oh, Lysander, I was worried, but you sure came through. Let's go back to my room and you can do it all to me, except the biting."

"Good enough!" he agreed. He was getting good at schooling himself not to react sexually in public, but now that he realized what he had been doing to a real woman, the notion was getting ahead of him. "Hurry!"

They ran down the halls. Soon they got to her chamber, where they proceeded to passionate sex without bothering with the preliminaries.

After that, things were quieter. He played other games with Alyc, and enjoyed her frequent sexual favors. There was much to be said for enthusiasm!

He saw Jod'e again, and she did not seem to hold his bite against him. "You beat me," she said. "I thought I had you beaten, but you turned the ploy. I have to respect that." She did not make any further move on him, but he encountered her often enough, because her off-shift was the same as his. He would have been quite intrigued by her, had it not been for his prior association with Alyc, and Jod'e's too-bold opening move with the game.

He got into the work that Citizen Blue had for him. Blue was trying to fathom exactly what had gone wrong with the Game Computer; he suspected that the arrival of magic in Proton had infected the computer and given it full self-awareness. Even the self-willed machines were not usually independent; they had awareness and desire, but were satisfied to honor the existing order. The Citizen's son Mach had been special—and now it seemed the Game Computer was, too.

But the Game Computer was complex and canny. It seemed to have borrowed something from the Oracle, which was a self-willed machine whose ultimate motives were at best uncertain. Lysander needed to learn more about both of these, because both were integral to the functioning of the planetary society, and could generate significant problems for the occupying force after the conquest. He asked to see the source code for the game-grid program, but it seemed that this was sealed off, to prevent any possible cheating. He had to figure it out from the field, as it were.

He played game after game, exhausting Alyc's patience. "You're a gameoholic!" she complained.

"You have me dead to rights," he confessed. "But at least I am working for Citizen Blue while I indulge my fell appetite. I am searching for some pattern that will offer an insight into the change in the Game Computer. It isn't in the circuitry; it has to be in some interaction between the program and the magic of Phaze. Something that makes the machine not only conscious, but independent. I think it must be a tricky kind of feedback—"

"Yes, yes, I know; your specialty. Let's make love."

"That is an attractive counteroffer," he said. He had learned the code terms: "making love" meant copulation.

They retired to her chamber. He had by this time lasted longer with Alyc than any of her prior boyfriends, and he knew why: he wanted no disruption in his relation with Citizen Blue's household. That was the center of the governance of the planet, and the likely center of any resistance to the conquest. As long as he remained with Alyc, that association was secure. But it was also true that once he had attuned himself to the sexual activity of the human body, it was a pleasant enough diversion. Serfs were treated to eliminate any chance of disease or conception, so sex was free. Those who wished to marry and have offspring had to petition their employers, who might or might not grant them the treatment that enabled conception. Neither Lysander nor Alyc (or, as the Phaze forms would put it, nor Lysander neither Alyc) wanted that, so were content with the normal indulgence. Actually he, as an android, was infertile anyway. So if she wanted it twice a day, he was satisfied to oblige. He gave all other women short shrift, which further pleased Alyc.

Thus his life settled in, for a month—until the investment.

6
Hectare

It happened with stunning swiftness. Lysander and Alyc were in the Game Annex, between games, about to punch a beverage from the food dispenser. Jod'e approached. "May I join you?" she inquired, politely enough.

Alyc, having long since ascertained that Lysander had no sexual interest in Jod'e, was amenable to her company. It served to show every serf on the premises that she, Alyc, had nothing to fear from even the most beautiful competition. Jod'e had more of a taste for games than Alyc did, so often played them with Lysander, whose interest was insatiable. So the three of them were about to drink— when the announcement blared from all the speakers.

"This is Citizen Blue. An alien fleet has surrounded the planet without warning. It has the capacity to destroy all life and industry here. We have no choice but to yield to superior force. Hold your places for the announcement by the Coordinator of the Hectare."

Jod'e stared at them, astonished. "Can this be a joke?"

"No joke," Alyc said. Her face was assuming a more serious mien, unsurprising in the circumstance.

After a moment a harsh, computer simulated voice spoke.

"The Planet Proton is within the sector controlled by Alliance forces. Investment by the Hectare is proceeding. The following personnel will report to the central concourse for internment: all Citizens, Adepts, and government functionaries. If in doubt, report. Any eligible personnel who fail to report will be declared surplus. All interested in serving the new regime in a supervisory capacity report to the Game Annex. All others will proceed about normal business until directed otherwise. There will be minimal disruption."

"Report for internment?" Jod'e said. There was a murmur all around; the other serfs were as amazed and confused.

"Exactly," Alyc said. Now her bearing had changed completely; she was no longer the enthusiastic, slightly low intellect serf. "I am an agent of the Hectare, sent to perform advance reconnaissance. I will identify all the members of the leading Citizen's household and family and see that they are apprehended. I advise you, Jod'e, to volunteer for service in the new regime; the Hectare will find compatible use for all who do volunteer."

Jod'e shook her head. "I am amazed! I never figured you for a traitor, Alyc! I'm not about to become one myself. I'll take my chances with the old order."

Alyc shrugged. "As you wish." She turned to Lysander. "But you, I am sure, are more sensible. You have expertise that the Hectare can use as readily as the Citizens could; the Hectare are game fanatics, and will want to correct the Game Computer malfunction promptly. I can guarantee you an excellent position—and it hardly needs clarifying that you will remain my paramour."

Lysander was astonished. He had never imagined that Alyc could be a Hectare agent! But she was not the type of agent he was. His duty required a response she would neither understand nor appreciate.

"I'm sorry," he said. "It's been fun with you, Alyc. But though I have been here only a month, I have come to respect this culture for what it is, and I shall not betray it to any alien usurper." That was an outright lie, required by his mission. But what followed was the truth. "Had I known you were an enemy agent, I would have turned you in at the outset. You fooled me, and I am disgusted."

"The Hectare do not employ incompetent agents," she said. "The longer you take to change you mind, the less advantageous it will be for you."

"I'll take that chance," he said, rising from the table.

Jod'e rose with him. "I think we had better vacate the premises quickly," she said.

"It will make no difference," Alyc said. "If the Hectare want either of you, they will find you and take you. But it will be better for those who volunteer."

Why was she so sure? She was correct that the first and most sincere volunteers would be treated best; she, as one of the very earliest, would have her pick of lovers, so she didn't need him. But she acted as if he himself would be rounded up immediately, when that was obviously impractical. Lysander didn't have time to ponder; he wanted to get well away from her and this region. Already the serfs were milling, as the majority sought to get out before they were mistaken for volunteers.

He did not look at Alyc again. He had been true to her, but in a devious fashion he felt she had not been true to him. This was a foolish sentimentality, for she had offered him a good position in the new order. He had evidently assimilated more of the local culture than he realized.

Lysander and Jod'e joined the throng crowding toward the nearest exit. "I don't like this," he muttered. "Suddenly there's an alien take-over, and we're supposed to cooperate?" He was saying what he knew was on the minds of most serfs, testing her for reaction. It had oc-curred to him that Jod'e had been conveniently close—indeed, had been close to him throughout. Had she known this was coming? If so, what was her purpose?

"She worked for Citizen Blue," Jod'e said. "It won't be safe for you to go there. I can help you get outside."

The jostling crowd gave them better privacy than could be had elsewhere. "Why? Why should you bother with me?"

"I've been trying to make a play for you throughout!" she said. "Now's my chance."

"I don't buy that. You're beautiful. You don't need me. You know I'm no changeling. I can't convert to bat form and fly away with you. If I go outside, I'll just be a liability to you. Make your own break; I doubt they'll want you. But Alyc may feel she has a score to settle with me."

"Women do not judge on appearance alone."

"You've been interested in me, but not because of any encourage-ment I gave you. I'm not messing with you at all unless I know your real interest. I've already been betrayed by one girlfriend!" This was not precisely the case, but his mission required him to say it.

She glanced at him sidelong. "Oho! You think I'm another foreign agent?"

"You could be. Exactly why did you come after me?"

They had squeezed out the Annex gate and were now in the concourse. Lysander didn't want to be there, either, though he saw no Citizens.

"Crowd's thinning," Jod'e said. "Can't talk here."

"Yes we can," he said. He grabbed her arm and swung her into an alcove. He embraced her and put his mouth against her left ear. "Tell me."

"How clever," she murmured, her mouth beside his own ear. "You tell me you don't want my love by getting fresh with me. I remember a similar technique in that first Fox and Geese game."

"Never again, if you don't stop stalling!"

"Very well. Citizen Troal sent me."

"Troal! Your employer. Isn't he close to Blue?"

"Very. And we vamps are close to the Adept Trool."

"Does this have anything to do with the prophecy that Clef told me about?"

"Prophecy?"

She didn't know about that? "Never mind. So Troal sent you to me as a favor to Blue?"

"Yes, I believe so. You had better kiss me or do something with your hands; someone's looking."

He slid his hands down her back. He remembered their first encounter, of which she had mischievously reminded him, when he had explored her torso so intimately, thinking it was a mannequin. The memory excited him now; she did have a perfect body. "Why, when I was already dating Alyc?"

"Maybe they knew what she was." She shifted against him, bringing more of that body into play.

Suddenly it made sense. If Blue had known Alyc's mission, he would not have said so. He would have sought quiet ways to nullify it. If he really believed that Lysander had a key role to play in the support of the planet, he would have tried to protect him from subversion by an enemy agent. So he could have arranged to send an attractive counteragent in. Unfortunately, Lysander had misunderstood the ploy.

"You don't know why Blue might care about my corruption?" he asked, his hands stroking memory-familiar contours.

"No. My guess is that he really wanted the Game Computer fixed, and not for the aliens."

He decided she was to be trusted, partly because she didn't seem to know any more than a pawn in a chess game would know about the motives of the king. "Then let's get out of here."

"I know a way out," Jod'e said. "Then maybe we can get Phaze help. The aliens may not know much about magic."

Surely true, for he had been quite unprepared for it. He separated from her and started down the concourse—and stopped.

"Serves you right, lover," Jod'e said, laughing. For he had gotten too involved in their diversionary activity, and his masculine member had responded.

But Alyc had shown him how to handle that. "Run; I'll chase."

She took off, and he pursued her with evident amorous intent. But such was the distraction of the other serfs that they paid no attention, this time. By the time Jod'e brought him to the exit she knew, his ardor had subsided.

They crouched by a machine service entrance. "Must wait for a robot," she said. "Then walk out in its shadow, so the scanner doesn't catch the human form. I'll turn bat and perch on you."

"Just don't do anything on my shoulder," he muttered.

She laughed again. "Speaking of which—did Alyc scratch you, when?"

"When what?"

"Some women get very excited, when. They can claw a man's back."

"No, she's not that type. No scratches. Why should you care?"

"I felt a bandage on your back, when I was stroking you."

"A bandage? I have no bandage!"

"Yes you do. A flesh-colored tape. Effectively invisible; if I hadn't been touching you, I wouldn't have known. Here, feel." She took his hand, twisted his arm behind his back, and brought his fingers to the place. It was at the most difficult part for him to reach alone.

Now he felt it: a smooth section that was not his own skin. "She must have put it on me, when—I mean, there was a lot of physical activity, and she liked to touch me in the night."

"I suspect she had some reason to touch you," she remarked with the hint of a smirk. "Want me to take it off?"

"Yes. No. It could be—" He was abruptly angry, as the realization came. "An identifier. Something an enemy agent would use to mark someone."

"Then you had better get it off!"

"No. These things—I understand they can be used as beacons. To show where a person is. I don't want her to know I've caught on."

"But how can I sneak you out, then?"

He sighed. "You can't. Maybe you had better leave me; I think I'm dangerous for you."

"But if the aliens want you that bad, you shouldn't be allowed to fall into their hands."

"It's probably just Alyc who wants me that badly. I doubt the aliens care."

She nodded. "She wants to hold on to you. Maybe she anticipated your reaction to the invasion, so made sure she could find you. If she's truly their agent, they may give her what she wants. It would be a perquisite of the office."

"Yes. I liked her, and I didn't like you trying to cut in. But now—" Again the irony: he was a spy for the Hectare himself, but had to argue the case of the opposition—and found himself believing it. His respect for Alyc had plummeted the moment he learned her nature. Now Jod'e was far more intriguing, and not merely because she represented a prospective route to the core of the true resistance that would be forming. She had been sent at the behest of Citizen Blue, so even if she didn't know why, she would be able to make contact with the organization he needed to infiltrate. But she was also a true patriot for her culture, and that integrity of motive was appealing. Her beauty hardly diminished the effect.

"Me too," she said. "You were just an assignment, but you are becoming a person."

"Thanks." He regretted that the loyalty she saw in him wasn't genuine. "But we're in a bind. If she claims me, she'll make sure that you are in no position to get near me, now that we have declared ourselves united in opposition to this invasion. Now that I have taken notice of you. You can't afford to associate with me." This was a deeper truth than she could know at this point.

"But I can't let you be taken by the enemy!" she protested. "If the Citizens knew the invasion was coming, and wanted to protect you from it, then it's my job to do that."

"But you can't help me. You might as well save yourself—by disassociating with me."

"And betray my employer? My culture?" She turned to face him, putting her arms around him. "Lysander, you took some liberties with me, when I was pretending to be a mannequin. Now I'm going to take one with you." She drew him into her, her arms reaching around him.

He yielded to her, because he expected to send her on her way in a moment. It was true: he had handled her about as intimately as it was possible to do, short of all-out sexual engagement. If she wanted a kiss in return—

Her fingernails scraped across his back. They caught in the tape. They ripped it off. "Now we make our break!" she said. "The tape stays here; we go to Phaze!" She threw the bit of tape away.

"You bitch!" he said, half admiringly.

"Nay, I be no werebitch," she said. "I be a vamp. Now tread in the shadow o' yon rovot, Lysan, and I will guide thee out." She became a bat, and leaped to perch on his hand.

Lysander found himself committed. He could not say it was wrong. He had simply wanted to spare her from being implicated in his break, and from being subsequently betrayed by him. But he had also known that she would not desert him, because she was as committed to her mission as he was to his.

The machine she had indicated was a walk-brusher, evidently going out to clean the walk to a garden at the edge of the dome. He ducked down and ran beside it, letting it shield him from the lens-eye that covered this exit. The machine ignored him; it was equipped only to do its job, not to inspect its surroundings.

The bat in his hand peered to the right. Lysander went that way, finding an offshoot from the main path. He ran through dwarf palms down to a tiny artificial stream that originated in a fountain. Then on into the channel of the stream, which turned out to be stone, not mud. Then he waded through a small pool and scrambled over a decorative wall.

Beyond was the wild vegetation of Phaze; they were now beyond the dome environment. The bat flew up, evidently searching for something. Lysander ducked down beside a tree whose leaves were in the shape of floppy stars, waiting for Jod'e to complete her reconnaissance.

Then he heard hoofbeats. He looked—and spied an old horse trotting toward him. The bat was on its back.

Clear enough! He stepped out as the horse arrived. It was a mare with a dark, almost reddish coat. He got on her back, and she turned and headed directly away from the dome.

The problem with this was that they were exposed. Anyone who looked would be able to see them. But maybe nobody would care about a man riding a horse.

Then the horse changed. Now a shining spiraled horn projected from her forehead, and her mane was iridescent. Her coat had deepened into a deep purplish red.

"Belle!" he exclaimed.

There was a tinkle of assent. Then she picked up speed.

He hung on. Bareback riding was not his favorite mode, and the unicorn had more power than a horse might. They were zooming through the high grass at a dizzying pace.

He discovered something as the run continued. Belle was getting hot, but she wasn't sweating. Instead she was dissipating the heat in her breath, which was turning fiery, and her hooves, which were throwing off sparks. So that was how unicorns cooled themselves!

Something caught his eye. It was a shadow in the shape of a disk. Oh-oh. He craned his neck and saw the origin: a small Proton flyer. The pursuit was on, already!

Belle dodged to the side, seeking the cover of a copse. But the flyer angled to intercept them, and it was much faster than any animal could be.

"They'll use stun rays!" Lysander cried. "Change and scatter! They'll only go after me!" He flung himself off the unicorn, taking a trained fall and rolling through the brush.

They changed and scattered, but not the way he had intended. While he ran for the cover of the trees, the bat headed straight for the flyer. The unicorn became a heron and also flew for the flyer.

The bat lighted on the top of the flyer. Then it was the woman again, her weight bearing the machine down. But it wasn't enough; the flyer remained aloft.

Until the heron landed on it—and returned to unicorn form. Now the flyer crunched down to the ground.

Lysander was amazed, but not reassured. "Get away from that thing!" he cried. "It can send the rays in any direction, or detonate a stun bomb—"

Too late. There was a dull explosion, and a burst of radiation from the machine. Jod'e and Belle collapsed, and then Lysander, who was farther out and hit with less intensity, but still unable to escape it. He saw the ground advancing toward his head.

It seemed only an instant, but the sun had moved; it had been about an hour. Lysander woke to find a second, much larger flyer beside the first. A trainer robot was before him, its treads flattening the grass. "Identity?" it demanded.

Lysander knew that his retinal patterns would give him away soon enough anyway; there was no point in trying to give a false name. "Lysander. I work for Citizen Blue."

"Confirmed. The identities of your companions?"

Were their patterns on file? Jod'e's yes, but maybe not Belle's. He might be able to help the unicorn go free. "Jod'e, employee of Citizen Troal. The mare has no human identity; she's just a steed."

"A unicorn steed," the machine said. "They will be registered too." It turned its lenses on Belle. "Stand, mare." A beam touched her.

Belle, freed from the effect of the stun beam, climbed to her feet. She stood, uncertain what more to do.

The machine ground toward her. Suddenly another beam speared out. There was a sizzle, and a puff of smoke.

Belle screamed almost in the manner of a woman. She leaped up, but could not escape the pain. She had been burned on the flank. It was evident that though her hooves were adapted to heat, her hide was not.

She hit the ground running. In a moment she was far across the field.

"Why did you do that?" Jod'e demanded of the machine. "There was no call for—"

"All human forms will be registered by retinal pattern," the machine said. "All animals will be branded. None will escape identification."

"Branded!" Lysander exclaimed. But there was no more he could say; the deed was done, and he didn't want to get Belle into any more trouble. It was better if they thought of her as only an animal.

"Enter the craft," the machine said.

Jod'e hesitated. "Do it," Lysander said. "We have seen that the invaders—or whoever is giving the orders now—have no compassion. They will stun us again if we don't obey."

She nodded. She knew it was true. They climbed into the flyer. There was barely room for the two of them, and none for the robot it had brought.

The panel closed. The flyer jerked aloft. They clung to each other to shield themselves from the buffeting.

"You can change form," Lysander murmured in her ear. "Fly away. You've done all you could."

"They know my identity," she reminded him. "They'd only search me out, and punish anyone who helped me."

He was silent. It was true. She was probably in for it, because she had tried to help him escape, and Alyc wouldn't like that.

"I should have agreed to serve the Hectare," he said. "And walked out when I had a chance."

"I'm glad you didn't." She leaned forward and kissed him. "We'll both pay for this break, as Belle did, but at least we tried."

He kissed her back. "As romances go, this has been extremely brief. But if both of us should later find ourselves free . . ."

"Agreed," she said. "Maybe this is just a temporary occupation, and the invaders will move on to another planet."

"Somehow I fear not." And such was his identification with his role that he felt real regret. He knew that the occupation was to be permanent. The Hectare needed the planet's supply of Protonite, which was the finest known compact energy source, and they regarded the game setup as ideal for relaxation. They would desert the planet only when there was nothing remaining to make it worthwhile to exploit.

But his private requirement was clear: he had to escape the captivity of the Hectare and seek sanctuary with the native resistance movement. Once he had fathomed its nature and had identified all the key personnel, he would betray it to the authorities, and the planet would be secure. He was sure that there was such a movement; there always was. If the Citizens had known that Alyc was a Hectare agent and left her alone, it could only have been because they were hiding their true effort. Jod'e might have led him there, but they had been intercepted too soon.

That was surely Alyc's fault. It was another irony that she had unwittingly allowed her personal desire to interfere with the larger plan of her true employer, the Hectare. If the resistance movement made mischief because the counteragent was nullified by a superficial agent—but it was his job to see that that did not happen. He had special training which would enable him to escape, but he would avoid drawing on that as long as he could, to maintain the semblance of untrained loyalty to the native culture.

Meanwhile he was truly regretful that he would be unable to have a fling with Jod'e. Alyc had been entertaining, in the human fashion, but Jod'e would have been delightful.

"I think I have fallen in love with you, this past hour," Jod'e said.

"If you have, banish the notion!" he said, alarmed. "They could use it against you by threatening me!"

"Yes, that would be the way of the despot," she agreed.

"But had things been otherwise, I think I could have returned the sentiment," he said, kissing her again. That was probably true, if some very large allowances were made.

The flyer landed at the dome. A disciplinary robot was waiting for them. It herded them to a cell in the holding section adjacent to the spaceport, where fired serfs were normally held until deportation was arranged. There was a bunk and shower and video screen, and that was all.

"They left us together?" Jod'e said, surprised. "This is a cell for one."

"Three conjectures," Lysander said. "One: this is only temporary, until they dispose of us shortly. Two: no one told the machine otherwise, so it dumped its load in the nearest cell. Three: they are so crowded with new detainees that they have to jam us in double."

"Four," she said. "They want to give us a chance to talk together, so they can listen and learn what we were doing out there. Five: the thing you said."

He nodded. He had warned her how one of them could be made to do what the captors wanted, if the other was threatened. Both her conjectures seemed good. Still, he was glad to be with her.

How should they play it? The moment Alyc received news of their capture, she would act. She knew the situation. So was there any point in pretending indifference to each other? Maybe a romantic motive would be better than a political one, as far as the Hectare were concerned.

He sat on the bed. "I think they don't care about us, other than to ascertain whether there is any political significance to our attempted flight," he said. "Since our association is romantic rather than political, we have no need to hide it."

Her lips pursed appreciatively. "And we may not have much time together."

She took three steps and plumped down on his lap, evidently intending to make their time count. He embraced her, finding her body just as intriguing as he had found Alyc's. The nakedness of serfdom was asexual; it was the expression of sexual interest that made a woman appealing. He knew that Jod'e was a bat, in one of her aspects, but it didn't matter; he had seen how genuine the mixedbreed folk of this society were. Had Jod'e been a full android, she would have been stupid; it was her vampire aspect that lent her both wit and sex appeal. He himself was a type of crossbreed, with his superior brain in an android body.

She grabbed his head and bent hers down to kiss him fiercely. His hands roamed as they had during the game of Fox and Geese, but this time there was no question about the nature of her body. "I wish we had understood each other better before," he said, his pulse racing.

She lifted her head, then brought his face into her bosom. That was a move Alyc had lacked, and it electrified him. He no longer cared what other types of creatures they both might be; body to body was what counted at the moment.

The cell door opened. "Sure enough."

Both Jod'e and Lysander jumped. It was Alyc!

Well, did it matter? He had broken with Alyc when she revealed herself as a traitor to the planet. Jod'e was next in line.

"I don't suppose I could trust you anyway now," Alyc said to him.

"I was true to you, until you were false to Proton," Lysander replied. "If Jod'e had sided with the invaders, I'd have dropped her too. But she declared herself before I did."

Alyc considered. "Very well. Have your fling. I shall see what can be done to make you both useful to the new order." She stepped out of the cell, and the door slid closed.

"I don't like the sound of that," Jod'e said.

"She's jealous," he agreed. "She can probably have me gelded and you put on permanent scullery duty."

"But will the invaders support her, if it's too much trouble?"

"Probably not. Her job is done. She has betrayed those who befriended her. But if she should find a way to continue being useful to the invaders, they might humor her."

"So this may remain our only opportunity," she said. "But if it's all the same to you, the joy seems to have been deflated."

"Yes." He released her, and she got off his lap.

She turned on the video and tuned it to the news channel. They were abruptly locked into ongoing developments.

In the course of the rest of the day, and into the night, they absorbed reports of the landing and takeover by the Hectare. The investment of the planet, as they called it. There were human agents throughout, and these were handling the reorganization. Any Citizens who had not promptly reported to the concourse had been quickly hunted down by robots. The Hectare had evidently concentrated on the robot centers, and taken them over at the outset. But the real reason it was so easy was that the alien spaceships orbited the planet, and periodically blasted small craters out of the landscape, just to show how readily it could be done. Any such blast at a dome would burn thousands. Open resistance was pointless.

One item disgusted them both: the freeing of the two renegade Adepts, Purple and Tan. Lysander had not seen either directly, but had learned their history. They had been part of the Adverse Adept group that had tried to seize power from Citizen Blue (or the Adept Stile), and then they had betrayed even their own side and tried to become dictators. They had deserved execution, but Citizen Blue had been lenient. Now they were free and the loyal Brown Adept was prisoner, under house arrest in her castle. So the evil were being uplifted, and the good cast down. Lysander was a hidden agent for the Hectare, but this was hard to stomach.

What had happened to Tania, the beautiful woman Lysander had met, and her husband Clef? There was no report on them. Probably they had been driven into hiding. Lysander hoped that when he penetrated the heart of the resistance movement that they were not there; he did not want to have to be the one to betray them.

Finally, tiring of the dreary news, Lysander and Jod'e lay on the bunk. They had considered taking turns on it, but decided that if they were to be punished for being lovers, they might as well act like lovers. So they stretched out together, intending to sleep, but got interested so decided to make love—and then fell asleep before getting to it.

All next day they remained confined, with only each other and the video screen for company. A portable food dispensing machine was brought periodically so that they could select their meals, but they saw no living person or even a humanoid robot. They did hear faint sounds in adjacent chambers, and realized that the premises were indeed crowded. Any new regime had many enemies to contend with, and prison or the equivalent was about the only resort until they were all sorted out.

"If they get too crowded, they may have to let us go," Lysander said. "After all, we haven't done anything, and we're hardly a threat to them."

"Let's hope," she agreed. Then, curious, she assumed bat form and flitted out when the mealbot came, flying back unnoticed before it finished serving. "Jammed," she reported. "They're going to have to move us out soon."

But it wasn't until the following day that they were taken out. A guard machine escorted them to the main hall, where a small cargo transport waited. They climbed in and a sliding panel sealed them in. Then they suffered a fast, rough ride through the city transport system.

When the transporter stopped, they were at the entrance to an attractive estate. In fact, it was that of Citizen Tan; Lysander saw the marking at the entrance.

Indeed, Citizen Tan was there: Tania's brother, not only freed from confinement but restored to his former status. No need to inquire what had happened to Tania; she must have been interned with the other true Citizens. The Hectare had acted with startling precision and speed to secure their base. The capture of Lysander himself had probably been just one of hundreds of such missions proceeding simultaneously. The Hectare were old hands at planetary subjugation; they allowed no leeway for problems.

They entered the main chamber—and Jod'e's breath hissed in with shock. A monster stood there.

Lysander blinked and reconsidered. Monster? That was a Hectare! It stood somewhat above the height of a human being, with monstrous multifaceted eyes at the top, many stout little caterpillar feet at the base, and a hairlike greenish mantle covering much of the torso. A perfect specimen of its species. He, Lysander, had become so acclimatized to the human state that he had seen the creature through human perception.

It was probably well that he had done so, for his muted reaction would have been noted. A Hectare saw everything in its vicinity; that was the ability of the eyes. Each facet was individually lensed and controlled, an entire separate eye, and any several could focus on a particular object and perceive it with complete acuity. He had reacted normally, and so had not given himself away. For it was as important that the local Hectare not know his nature and mission as that the natives not know. That way, nothing could give him away.

The man stepped forward. He wore a headdress that looked like nothing so much as a squirming mass of little tentacles. "Serfs, meet your master," he said. "This is the representative of the Hectare, whose private identity is irrelevant for you. You will henceforth obey any creature of this type as you would a Citizen, implicitly. However, the Hectare will normally work through intermediaries such as myself, identified by Hectare caps, whom you will also obey without question. Early examples will be made of any who cause difficulty."

He frowned. "Indeed, the two of you, together with an errant unicorn, did cause minor mischief. The male is desired by one of our collaborators, and the female aided him in an attempted break. Examples shall therefore be made of you—but not unpleasant ones, for you. Each of you shall become the love slave of a collaborator. Do you find that appealing?"

There was no answer. Tan made a signal, and rays lanced down to sting both Lysander's and Jod'e's bare feet. Both jumped back with exclamations of pain.

"When questioned, you will answer," Tan said.

"I find that appalling," Lysander said quickly. His mind was racing. If Tan had the same power of the Evil Eye that Tania had, that meant he could look into the face of a person and compel that person to do anything he wished. Lysander was probably proof against such suasion, because he had been well prepared as a counterresistance agent, but if he showed that, Tan would know his nature, and his secret would be compromised. He had to avoid Tan's effort.

"So do I," Jod'e said.

Tan looked at her, his eyes narrowing appreciatively. "You have the vamp aspect, and you are extremely comely. You could have an excellent situation, if you cared to serve the Hectare."

"I am loyal to the old order," she said.

"And you, Lysander," Tan said. "You are an expert gamesman, and you have training in computer feedback circuitry. You too could have an excellent situation."

"I prefer not," Lysander said.

"The two of you are lovers?"

"Yes," Lysander answered. They had not actually made love, but they would have soon enough, and wanted to. The cell's spy lens would have recorded their start in that direction, before Alyc interrupted it.

"Let me make something plain to you both. The Hectare power is absolute. It will remain here indefinitely, until the planet has been exploited to the point that it is no longer worthwhile. You can not change that. But you can affect your own lives. If you join the Hectare, and give loyal service, you will be rewarded with an excellent life. If you do not, you will serve the Hectare anyway, but your position will be less advantageous for yourselves. You may make your choice now."

Both shook their heads no.

"You are lovers," Tan said. "Agree to serve, and you may remain so. You will work together, and your free time will be your own. You will work in your specialties, and not be asked to do anything against your consciences. This is a good offer."

Lysander looked at Jod'e. "I think you should accept. I believe it is as he says."

She turned to him. "Are you going to accept?"

"No."

"Then I could not be your lover, because they would not grant you your wish."

"This is true," Tan said. "The reward for the cooperation of the two of you is yourselves. If one does not join, you will have lovers, but not each other."

"I did not intend to accept anyway," Jod'e said. "The most I could agree to is not to work against the bug-eyes if I am released. But I would never collaborate with them against the true culture of this world."

"There will be a penalty for the pejorative term," Tan said.

"Then I might as well make it clear that they will always be bug-eyed monsters to me. BEMs, exactly as in the old stories."

The Hectare made no reaction.

"This has gone far enough," Tan said. "Your penalty for failing to cooperate is to be compelled to be the love slave of a collaborator, as I mentioned before. Your penalty for the crass remark is to become my personal love slave. Does this appeal to you?"

"The prospect revolts me," she said.

Tan's aspect changed subtly. Lysander realized that the man had shifted to his Phaze identity. "Do thou look at me, vamp."

She turned her face away from him.

A stun beam came down from the ceiling, evidently set at partial intensity. Jod'e slumped but did not fall.

Tan reached out and turned her head toward him. She was unable to resist. He stared into her eyes. "Thou dost be mine," he murmured.

The beam shut off. Jod'e recovered. "Aye," she said.

"Thou mayst kiss me."

Lysander had expected either extreme reluctance, or a carefully faked effort. He was dismayed at what actually happened.

Jod'e flung her arms around Tan and kissed him passionately. "O thank thee, beloved!" she breathed.

Tan did not respond in kind. "Now kiss Lysander," he said.

Jod'e froze. Then her head turned toward Lysander. "Needs must I?"

"I wish to demonstrate that thy orientation be completely changed. Kiss him."

She grimaced. "An I must, I must," she said with resignation. "I hate him not, but it be thee, sir, I long for." She stepped up to Lysander and kissed him fleetingly on the cheek.

"That be not sufficient," Tan said sternly. "Yield to him." He looked directly at Lysander, and his eyes seemed huge. "And thou, Lysan— I compel thee not, yet. But take her in thine arms and do with her as thou wouldst. Make her respond to thee."

It was a challenge Lysander was glad to accept. He enfolded Jod'e and held her close for the kiss.

Her body was stiff, and her lips mushy. Either she was a consummate actress, or she had no interest in his attention. She gave him no private signal. She merely tolerated his touch. As soon as he released her, she stepped back toward Tan, her stiffness fading.

"She be thine no longer," Tan said to Lysander. "I can use my power but once on a gi'en person, but it be permanent. I would spare myself the effort on thee. Thou hast lost thy love, but canst still achieve a worthwhile position an thou accept allegiance now."

Lysander was impressed. He didn't think Jod'e was pretending. But his mission prevented him from collaborating with the puppet government the Hectare was setting up. "No."

"Then needs must I prepare thee for Alyc, as she asked," Tan said. "Face me."

Lysander had delayed as long as he could. He had to act. He turned his face slowly toward Tan—then leaped for the Hectare.

He passed right through the creature—as he had expected. It was a holo image, not a physical presence. The Hectare were careful about personal exposure; only when they were quite sure of their company did they risk it.

But beyond the image was a decorative vase he had spied before. He swept it up, turned, and hurled it with precise aim at the lens complex in the ceiling. The vase smashed—and so did the lens. Now he could not be stunned from above.

He leaped back and grabbed Jod'e. He put a nerve hold on her shoulder. She stiffened, realizing that she was helpless; any effort to break free would be prohibitively painful. "Do not move," he ordered Tan.

The man was not directly facing him, and remained in that orientation. "Thou canst hurt her, but thou canst compel me not," Tan said. "In a moment will I turn and compel thee with mine Eye. I suggest thou dost desist before thou bringst upon thyself a type of punishment thou willst find really distasteful."

But Lysander was already backing toward the exit panel. He kept his head behind Jod'e's so that the Adept could not get a bead on him.

Tan stalked him. Whatever else might be said against the man, he was neither coward nor fool; he was yielding nothing. He was moving slowly but purposefully, closing the distance between them.

"You wouldn't have bonded this woman to you if you didn't desire her," Lysander said as his back touched the panel. "You wouldn't want her hurt."

"I want thee hurt not either," Tan said evenly. "In a moment thou willst be as loyal to the new order as she."

Lysander squeezed the nerve in Jod'e's shoulder. She screamed. Tan stopped advancing.

But Lysander wasn't merely stalling for time; that was pointless. With his free hand he was tapping on the panel. He knew a way to make it open, if the Hectare had been true to form. Hectare, experienced at planetary subjugation, never left things entirely in the hands of the natives; they made sure at the outset that ultimate control was in the tentacles of the nearest Hectare. That meant rekeying the locks—all locks—to be responsive to Hectare hidden codes. One of the standard codes was auditory: a pattern of taps that few others could duplicate if any knew of their existence. Because Lysander's brain was Hectare, he knew and could perform the cadences.

With one bare heel he tapped with one changing pattern. With his knuckle he tapped with another. As the two converged, interrelating, the Hectare code overrode the ordinary mechanism, and the panel slide open.

Lysander stepped back, hauling Jod'e with him. He saw Tan's mouth open with amazement. The man had not known of this device, of course; he was merely a quisling, used without being trusted. Then the panel slid back, separating them.

Now he was out—but where was he to go? They were among serfs who were hurrying on their errands. The pursuit would commence in seconds. What was he to do with Jod'e?

That turned out to be easy. "Now you're free," he told her. "Follow me; he'll be out in a moment." He let her go, and started down the hall.

"He's here!" Jod'e cried, not trying to run. "He's getting away!"

Lysander came to an intersecting hall and ducked into it. He could not try to conceal himself as another serf; all the serfs here would be checked. He couldn't run far; the halls would be closed off any moment. The chances of any ordinary serf escaping capture were approximately nil.

But he was not an ordinary serf. He jumped to a private door panel and did a quick double tapping. It opened and he stepped in—just as the rumble of the larger hall-sealer panels commenced. All the serfs in that section of the hall were trapped, and would not be freed until their identities were verified.

He was in another Citizen residence, but it was empty. Its owner would have been interned. He ran through to the kitchen, where the food-delivery apparatus was, and the waste-disposal mechanism. He did not need to use the code tapping here; the conduits were not locked. He climbed onto a garbage cart and touched its Go button.

In a moment he was zooming through the nether pipes of the city, heading for one of the central processing stations. When the cart slowed, approaching the first sorting stop, he jumped off, surprising the robot. "An error in classification," he told it. "I will correct it." The machine would not question a human voice of authority.

He got on the machine trundleway and walked to the human section. From there he exited to the main network of halls. He had escaped, for now; since the bit of beacon tape was gone from his back, they would have to do a citywide search to run him down.

They would do that, of course. No dictatorial government could tolerate dissent. But it would be awkward for them, because they would not want to disrupt the ongoing flow of business, and would not want to admit that any serf *could* give either a Citizen or a Hectare the slip. The Hectare whose image he had seen would not tell Tan about the code; it would keep that secret, realizing that Lysander was something unusual. Tan would just have to assume there was a defect in the door panel that had released Lysander by chance.

As for Jod'e: he had tested her, and verified what he feared. Tan's Evil Eye had been effective, and she was now his creature. Had she been faking it, she would have run with Lysander; instead she had sounded the alarm the moment she was able. That had made no practical difference, but had shown him that it was pointless to be further concerned about her.

Perhaps it was for the best. Jod'e would probably be well treated. Had she fled with him, and had they made good their escape from the city this time, she would have lived the life of a fugitive. Eventually he would have betrayed her to the Hectare, along with the people of the resistance movement. It was kinder to have her taken now. He would let others know that it had not been voluntary, and they would respect her.

But it surely would have been nice to be with her for the interval of his penetration of the resistance movement. He had adapted so well to his human body that its delights had become his delights. Loving her, and being loved by her—how he wished that could have been true, for a time. As it was, he had lost his second woman.

But now he had not only to escape the city, but to make contact with the resistance. That meant he needed help to escape: the help of someone who had the appropriate contacts. He had no idea who that might be. This was the trickiest part of his effort. If one of them did not contact him, before the net closed on him, his mission would be cut short prematurely. No, the Hectare would not let him go; they had no tolerance for ineffective agents. His best fate if captured would be a return to Tan for the Evil Eye, and then assignment to Alyc as her love slave. If the Eye wasn't effective, or if Alyc no longer desired him, they would simply melt him down for protoplasm.

He walked along the passage, back toward the concourse. He had to expose himself to as many serfs as he could, hoping that one of them would know how he had tried to escape, and would be looking for him. Any decent resistance network would have ways of keeping abreast of the news, and would know of the business with Tan. They would know that speed was of the essence.

Someone caught his arm. Lysander jumped, in a purely human reaction; he had been lost in his thoughts, which was another human trait. It was a woman, with feathery brown hair and black eyes. " 'Sander!" she said. "Remember me?"

In a moment he made the connection. "The harpy!" He had met her briefly, when little Flach had become a winged unicorn and flown him to the Purple Mountains. Actually, the cyborg, in her Proton form.

"You seemed interested in my legs, as I recall," she said.

He had been trying to verify the nature of her form changing, by holding on to her as she shifted. "They were good legs." Despite their being metal and plastic, crafted to emulate living legs. On this planet, it was practically impossible to tell emulation from living flesh.

"I hear you're in trouble."

"You understate the case."

"Will you trust me?"

"That depends whom you serve."

"Citizen Powell."

Not the Hectare. She must be his contact! "Yes."

"This way." She turned and led him through the thronging serfs.

7

Bomb

Nepe, in the form of a serf boy, was running an errand for one of the quislings. She had planted this identity long ago, and had used it before, just keeping her hand in; no computer check would cast doubt on it.

She was sad that Grandpa Blue had had to report for internment, but understood how it was. The spy Alyc had tagged him and all his family and associates; any who tried to skip out would have been pursued. Of course Blue could have avoided capture, but to what point? They would only have chased him until they got him, and meanwhile started imprisoning, torturing, and murdering his associates to encourage him to cooperate. He preferred to avoid that.

So Blue had reported in, and so had Red and Brown, and the former Adverse Adepts: Yellow with her power over animals, Orange with his plants, Translucent with his water magic, and White with her glyphs. Purple and Tan had been freed, and had immediately joined the other side. But five had not: Clef (Tania no longer counted, since Tan had taken back the title of Adept), Black with his lines, Green with his fire, Robot (Flach's father), and Flach himself, the Unicorn Adept. So of fourteen now-recognized Adepts, seven were captive, two collaborated, and five were hiding.

Nepe knew why the Robot Adept hid: he had taken the Book of Magic, and if he had not been the strongest Adept before—no one was certain whether that honor belonged to the Red Adept—he surely was now. The Book of Magic was the ultimate compendium of enchantments, and could make anyone Adept in short order. It had to be kept out of the hands of the likes of Purple and Tan, if Phaze was to have any chance at all to throw off the Hectare yoke. So the Robot would hide the Book, and if it ever came to the point where the enemy was going to get it, he would destroy it instead.

Nepe also knew why she hid: she was the most elusive creature on the planet, and served as the messenger for the resistance to the invader. She and Flach had had a lot of experience in hiding, and so were natural for the role.

Clef was hiding in order to protect the other single most valuable thing of Phaze: the Platinum Flute. It had been crafted by the Platinum Elves, and yielded by them only for the most serious reason: to save Phaze. When Clef had played it the first time, the frames of Proton and Phaze had been drawn together and temporarily overlapped and then hurled apart, enabling Blue to take over in Proton and Stile in Phaze. When he had played it the second time, the frames had been permanently merged, a year ago, again enabling the good forces to overcome the evil forces, when all seemed lost.

Now, suddenly, the planet was in trouble again, and it seemed that nothing but the Flute could rescue it. But even that seemed too little, for the Hectare were already in control. The Flute had done its job twice; there seemed to be nothing else it could do. But it represented hope, and had to be kept safe. So Clef was doing that, and as long as Clef and the Flute remained out of enemy power, that faint hope remained.

But why had the two other Adepts hidden? They had been associated with the wrong side before, and never evinced much political interest anyway. Were they merely ornery, or were they up to something?

Nepe's thoughts were interrupted by Echo. She had found Lysander! They had known the man was somewhere in the dome, and that he was in trouble because he had refused to join the enemy, but he had turned out to be surprisingly good at hiding. They needed him, because of the prophecy. Nepe wasn't sure she believed the prophecy, or that Lysander was the one it referred to, but Mach had said to rescue him if possible, and she was trying to do that.

She knew that Echo would not have brought him if he wasn't ready to go. As the two approached, Nepe turned and fell in beside them. "Look for a group of three," she said. "Man, woman, and boy."

"Who is this?" Lysander demanded suspiciously.

"Who do you think, unbeliever?" she replied without looking directly at him.

"There," Echo said, gesturing to three serfs walking the other way. "They're not a group, but—"

"Turn and close on them."

They did so, and in a moment were following the others. Nepe turned over the body to Flach, who did not have to pretend being male. He murmured some doggerel verse in a singsong: "Make those front three like he, thee, and me."

The appearance of the three serfs changed. Now the man resembled Lysander, and the woman Echo, while the boy looked like Nepe in boy form.

Flach spread his hands, holding his companions back. They slowed, letting the mimic-three separate from them. The mimic-boy crossed away from the man and woman, going his own course, but it didn't matter; it had simply been easier to do the magic on them as a close group.

In a moment Flach guided them into a side passage where fewer serfs walked. When it seemed likely that no one was looking, he uttered another singsong verse: "Take the rest to Oche's nest." He willed the implementation, and the two vanished.

Flach walked on, watching for anyone watching him. None seemed to be, but he didn't trust that. He would wait. He turned the body back to Nepe, who was better at Proton matters.

What would Lysander think, when he found himself back under the harpy's tree? Nepe wondered. He had just been betrayed by two girlfriends; would he be suspicious of the third? For that was what Echo would be. They had chosen Jod'e for him, but the Tan Adept had gotten her. They had to write her off, as Mach put it. They had feared they would have to write Lysander off too, but somehow he had escaped. The word was that he had banged against the door panel, and it had opened. Tan must have been furious at that malfunction at that critical time! But maybe the prophecy had known that Lysander would squeak through.

But it was more likely that he had simply drawn on his enemy knowledge to *make* that door open, seemingly by accident. That confirmed that Tan didn't know Lysander's nature. Interesting: the Hectare didn't trust Tan either! They were merely using him, and when he was of no further use to them, they would dispose of him.

But Lysander was dangerous. If it weren't for the prophecy, they would never have brought him in. Suppose he *wasn't* the one? Then they were probably lost already, because the prophecy didn't say there *would* be one, only that only such a person, alien to the culture and opposed to it, *could* save it. There might be no such person, or they might have the wrong one, or they might have the right one and he would choose not to save them. It seemed exceedingly chancy.

Chancy—yet their only hope. So she had rescued Lysander, the enemy agent, and Echo would be his woman. Echo didn't know the truth; she was likely to have a severe disappointment coming up. But if that happened, they would all be lost. If it didn't, he would save them, and their gamble would have paid off. So Echo would do her best to make Lysander happy, exactly as Jod'e would have, so that when it came to the point of decision, he would be more likely to choose for Phaze instead of for the Hectare.

Meanwhile, she had to check in with others. Satisfied that she was not observed, she ducked into a service niche. "Nepe," she murmured. "Admit."

A panel slid aside. She climbed into the rear service area, and the panel closed behind her. The self-willed machines were maintaining a low profile, hoping to escape the notice of the Hectare, but they cooperated with Nepe. That was part of her situation; she had lived among them for years, and her father was one of them, and her grandmother. They trusted her, though her actual flesh was alien.

"Mach," she said, stepping into a baggage transport cart.

The cart began to move. Nepe focused on her body, changing it slowly from human boy to machine. Flach could change in an instant, but he had to use a different spell each time, so he didn't waste it. Nepe was slower, but she could do the same form a thousand times if she had to. So she did most of the changing, when it wasn't an emergency.

She was ready by the time the cart brought her to her father. Actually he was Flach's father, but it was all complicated, and both Mach and Bane were really fathers to both Flach and Nepe now, since the mergence, and maybe before. She rolled out on small wheels, a spot bag handler.

She rolled up to the larger machine. Mach was in humanoid form, unloading suitcases from a baggage compartment near the airport. Without hesitation he dumped a bag on her, then picked up two suitcases and strode away down the hall. She followed, heeling like a trained canine. The conquest of the planet was fresh, but care was being taken not to disrupt the tourist trade. Many tourists, in fact, didn't realize that a hostile occupation was in progress. They would not be bothered as long as they didn't interfere.

"Mission accomplished," she reported on the machine frequency. Communication of many types and many levels was required to run the complicated society of Proton, and this had not changed with the advent of magic. Anyone in authority could listen in on the machine frequency, but there was little point to it, and there were thousands of exchanges of information going on simultaneously throughout the city. Each machine had limited range, to allow the use of the same frequencies without much interference.

"Tsetse is being assigned to Brown," Mach replied. "Investigate."

Nepe detoured into a side hall and rolled up to a disposal unit. Her bag was a dummy. She had the unit take it in, and then herself.

Soon she was connected to the command network. *Troubot—status of Tsetse,* she sent.

In a moment a message came back: *Order just in. Guidebot to take her to Brown Demesnes.*

By whose order?

Citizen Purple.

The renegade Citizen! That meant that some sort of mischief was afoot. Yet what would Purple's interest be in the Brown Adept? She was harmless to the Hectare, now that she was under house arrest.

Could this relate to Grandam Neysa's odd behavior, when she had hustled Flach from that wooden castle? Well, maybe Nepe could satisfy her curiosity while performing her investigation.

Assign me.

Done. Reach this location ASAP. City coordinates followed.

Nepe disconnected and got moving. Troubot would do anything for her, even if it weren't business. As she caught a machine transport and zoomed to the address, she reflected briefly on that.

Troubot was a machine she had associated with for years. She considered him male, and he considered her female. He was in love with her. That might have seemed ludicrous to anyone offplanet, but it was feasible on Proton, where the self-willed machines could have feelings. But in Phaze, Troubot became Sirelmoba, the pretty little bitch who was Flach's Promised. There, the sexes were reversed. But for years it had been assumed that alternate selves had to be of the same sex, and almost always they were. Why was it different here?

She had pondered this before, many times, but could come to only one conclusion: the sexes *did* match, either male to male or female to female. The only exceptions were when one of the selves was neutral. Troubot was neutral, because a machine had no inherent sex. Troubot thought of himself as male, so he was male, but there was nothing else to substantiate it. Nepe's father Mach (technically, Bane in Mach's body) thought of himself as male, so he was male. Her Grandmother Sheen thought of herself as female, and indeed she looked and acted female. But all were in essence neuter machines. All could be set up with other bodies and other programming and be of opposite sex. So there really wasn't a change of sex, just a change of perception.

Nepe herself, like her mother Agape, was also neutral in essence. Her living component was Moebite, whose species was sexless, but assumed sexual identities when visiting other planets, in deference to the prevailing standard. So she, like the machines, simply assumed a sex, and remained with it because she preferred it. So when she became Flach it wasn't any true sex change, only an apparent one. He was male and she was neuter, technically.

Yet it certainly *felt* different!

She reached the location. A gray-eyed, silvery-haired serf woman of about thirty sat in a shipment station. The hair was no sign of decline; it had been permanently tinted. She was an extremely pretty woman despite being past the flush of youth. This was Tsetse, formerly Tania's obliging receptionist, then Citizen Purple's mistress. Beautiful, complaisant, and not unduly smart: she had been ideal for her positions.

Nepe had known Tsetse for five years, and privately liked her. The woman was fundamentally innocent, amenable to whatever was required of her. But since she was now Purple's serf, if no longer his mistress (he knew her age), she was not to be trusted. It was important that Tsetse never suspect Nepe's identity.

"Guidebot for serf Tsetse," Nepe said through her speaker grille.

The woman stood. "Here." She looked nervous, and her eyes were a bit puffy. She had evidently been crying.

"Follow." Nepe rolled down the hall at a comfortable walking pace. There were many means of transport, but serfs typically walked unless the distance was far or their assignments were urgent; that was why the halls were usually filled. Normally a serf did not rate a machine guide, but if the mission was important it could happen. Anything could happen at the whim of a Citizen, of course, and that was evidently the case with those who served the new masters. It was also possible that the assignment of a guide was a reminder to a perhaps reluctant serf that the directive was to be obeyed without question.

Since Tsetse was the most docile of serfs, why was such a reminder considered to be in order? She should simply have been given the order to report to her assignment at a given hour, and left to find her own way there. All transport was free for serfs, on the presumption that they were serving the interests of their employers, and directories of routes were available at convenient locations. She could have gone alone.

The woman was evidently unhappy. Had there been a falling-out? Yet this was hardly a punitive assignment. The Adept Brown was a good woman. For many years she had had a werewolf servant whom she had treated well. She would surely treat Tsetse well.

But there was another mystery. Purple had been Brown's prisoner, and now she was his. Why should he not only allow her to keep her residence, but assign a pleasant servant to her? Purple had never been noted for generosity to anyone.

Nepe rolled up to the airport entrance. "I'm going out?" Tsetse asked forlornly.

"Yes," Nepe answered, as any machine would. Suddenly she had her answer: Tsetse didn't know where she was going! That was why she needed the guide—and why she was afraid. She thought she was being punished for some infraction!

Nepe pondered briefly, and decided to take a risk. It might even lead to valuable input. She overstepped the nature of a normal guide-bot and volunteered information. "To the residence of the former Brown Adept in Phaze."

Tsetse pounced on the news with pitiful hunger. "To be his servant there?" She thought Purple had taken over the Brown Demesnes.

"To be *her* servant there."

"Oh, if only it's so!" Tsetse breathed, the tension going out of her.

Nepe was glad she had spoken. Tsetse might not be much intellectually, but she didn't deserve unkind treatment. Purple was a hard master who evidently used her and abused her without concern for her feelings. He could have told her where she was going, but perhaps had preferred to make her suffer. This was true to his form.

Nepe led the way to a seat on the small airplane available. There were no other passengers. "Brown Demesnes," she told the control panel, and the plane started moving. Its flight would be coordinated with others, controlled from the ground. They were merely passengers.

"But why should I be assigned to the Brown Adept?" Tsetse asked. "The Purple Adept doesn't even like her!"

That was exactly what Nepe was wondering. But she was in no position to hold a dialogue on the subject, lest she betray her nature. She did not respond.

The flight was a short one, and soon the plane came down in a field beside the wooden castle. Brown had a Proton identity, but her Phaze identity was dominant, and her Proton self had effectively disappeared during the mergence.

The plane stopped. They got out. The plane took off without them. They were left in the field, gazing at the castle.

A wooden golem came out and approached them. "Who are you?" it asked.

"This is Tsetse, assigned here by Citizen Purple," Nepe said. "I guided her here, and now am stranded." Indeed, Purple had cared no more for the convenience of the machine than for that of the serf.

"Follow." The golem turned and marched back toward the castle.

"I can not," Nepe called, for her little wheels were useless here.

The golem turned again, strode back, bent, and heaved her up. It carried her awkwardly, but with the unyielding strength of wood. It made again for the castle, with Tsetse following.

The Brown Adept met them at the front door. "What be thy purpose here?" she inquired somewhat grimly of Tsetse.

"I am to be your servant," Tsetse replied, surprised.

"I know naught o' this." She glanced at Nepe, who had been set on the floor. "What be thy transmittal orders?"

"To guide the serf Tsetse to the Brown Demesnes," Nepe replied. They had assumed she was to be a servant; it wasn't specified in the order.

Brown looked again at Tsetse. "Thou dost work for Purple?"

"For Tania, then for Purple," Tsetse said. "I will do good work for you, if you give me a chance."

Brown was still for a moment, evidently struck by the woman's eagerness. It seemed that neither party had been told about this assignment. "What type o' work didst thou do for them?"

"I was Tania's receptionist, and whatever. For Purple, whatever."

"What dost thou mean, whatever?" Brown asked sharply.

Tsetse looked down, ashamed to answer.

Then Brown caught on. "Purple had thee for sexual purpose?"

"Yes, for a time."

"And Tania too?"

"Yes," Tsetse whispered. "When she had no man."

"And thou hadst no choice, being a serf," Brown said. "I understand. There will be not such coercion here."

"I didn't mind, really," Tsetse said. "Tania treated me well."

"And Purple?"

Tsetse was silent.

Brown put an arm around her. "My dear, mine authority be diminished, since the invasion. I remain here only by the sufferance o' mine enemies, and I know not how long that will be. But thou needst have no fear o' me during that interim."

"Thank you, sir," Tsetse said, trying to stifle her tears of relief.

"Nay, not sir. I be an Adept, a Citizen not, and in any e'ent my power now be scant. Come, we shall get to know each other. But first needs must we clothe thee; this be not Proton, and thy fair form will be chilled in the drafts."

"But what of me?" Nepe asked. She did not want to get stranded here; she had other business to do.

Brown glanced at her thoughtfully. "Go to my storage chamber until thy service be needed again."

Nepe headed into the castle and down the hall, making her way to the chamber where the wooden golems stayed when not animated. The matter remained curious. She still had no hint why Purple, who cared little for the welfare of any other person, had sent a pleasant woman like Tsetse to work with Brown. Why did he allow Brown to have even the semblance of freedom? It was obvious that neither woman knew the answer, and Nepe didn't either. She hoped Mach could make some sense of it. But she didn't dare send a message from here; Purple was surely monitoring whatever happened at this castle.

She moved back to the darkest recess of the storage chamber. Then she changed slowly back to human form. There was no activity.

The two women were probably comparing life histories. Nepe was sure it was lonely here, and the company of another woman would be a blessing to Brown. But that only heightened the mystery: Purple could have sent anyone to watch Brown: a harridan or a cruel man or a machine. He had sent possibly the most compatible person available. That was completely unlike him. Why hadn't he simply had her locked in a cell?

When her change was complete, she shifted to Flach. He became a flea and jumped through a crack in the wall, working his way outside. When he got there, he became a small snake and slithered through the grass away from the castle. Only when he was well clear did he conjure himself directly to Hardom, where he returned the body to Nepe.

She wasted no time contacting Mach, joining him again on the baggage route so they could talk. "Report on Brown: Tsetse assigned as servant, unknown to either Brown or Tsetse. Mysterious act of generosity on Purple's part. He let her keep her Demesnes, too."

"Do the two women get along?" he asked.

"Yes, well."

"Then Purple means to use Tsetse as a lever against Brown. She will have to serve the Hectare."

"Brown wouldn't do that!" Nepe protested.

"She will have to. How did you exit?"

"I asked Brown what of me, and she looked at me and told me to go to the storage chamber. So I did, and sneaked out from there. No one saw me."

"How did you know where the storage chamber was?"

"Silly! I've been there many times before!"

"But you were supposed to be a Proton guidebot."

Now it sank in. "I shouldn't have known! The machine shouldn't have known!"

"Which means Brown caught on to your identity."

"But she wouldn't give me away!"

"I'm afraid she would, Nepe, now."

"But why? She's on our side!"

"She is being blackmailed."

"What?"

"Her sexual preference is for women. Trool knew, but kept his counsel until he realized that Purple and Tan were catching on. Then he told me. Neysa was going to help her, but the invasion came too soon. Now they are forcing her to cooperate with the Hectare, lest her secret be publicized."

"But who cares what she likes?" Nepe demanded. "She's not the only one! Tsetse—" Then it came clear. *"That's* why Purp sent her! To—"

"To make clear that he knows her secret, and will not only keep it, but give her a lover—if she cooperates," Mach said. "Carrot and stick. She can keep her Demesnes and nominal freedom, and have a truly lovely and obliging woman—or she can suffer the humiliation of exposure and unkind imprisonment. Rape by males would no doubt be part of that punishment. She is a good woman, but sensitive and alone. She can not withstand that combination."

"But do the rest of you really care? I mean, you tied in with an alien blob and a unicorn; what do you care about who she cares about?"

"Nothing. We can accept her as she is. But she can't believe that. Had we realized how it would be used against her, we would have made our position plain before the Hectare investment. But of course most of us simply didn't know. She was once smitten with Stile; we had not questioned beyond that. We should have."

"Grandam Neysa—that's why she hurried us on," Nepe said. "Why she went back. Maybe she told Brown it was all right."

"Neysa is conservative. It took her almost ten years to accept Fleta's relationship with me."

"So she wouldn't go for it," Nepe said. "So Brown thinks that's how we all think!"

"It is an irony of the situation. We were distracted by the coming conquest, and didn't realize how this would relate."

"So Brown will tell on me, because she has to. I wish I hadn't given myself away! What do we do now?"

"We shall have to move quickly, before the golems stake out the Poles."

Nepe was baffled. "What are you saying?"

"Something I preferred not to, before. We have set two counter-ploys in motion. One is the Magic Bomb which Black and Green have made."

"The what?"

"Its detonation will destroy the planet and all on it. So if we lose, we will take the Hectare with us. But we prefer not to lose."

Nepe was daunted by the horror of the notion. "I had no idea!"

"We preferred to shield you from that sort of reality," he replied. "But it is time for you to know, so that you understand the importance of your own role."

"But I'm just a messenger!"

"Your messages are critical. You will have three, and you dare fail in none. Soon all of us will be captive except you. Here is the message capsule. Do not attempt the second until the first is done, or the third until the second is done."

"I'll try," she said. "But—"

"I have erased my own knowledge of the plan," he said. "I was the only one who knew the full course. Now none of us can betray it to the enemy. I can only say that its details will be completely surprising. If you are caught, destroy the capsule without reading it."

"But then we will all be destroyed!" she protested. "By the Magic Bomb!"

He cracked a small smile. "Get offplanet if you can."

"But Daddy—"

"You are on your own, alien flesh." It was an endearment he used on her, referring to her Moebite ancestry. "On your way, and do not communicate with me again."

She knew he meant it. She scooted away from him, the weight of the planet suddenly on her little shoulders. They were playing what in the game was known as hard ball.

When she was safely alone, she activated the capsule for the first message. It was simple: GO TO NORTH POLE.

That was all. She waited, hoping that there would be some explanation, but was disappointed.

She pondered it, her mind whirling. Tsetse had been delivered to Brown, and suddenly to save the planet Nepe had to go to the North Pole! How could she make sense of that?

Well, she could make a little piece of sense of it. Brown now understood what was at stake for her. Brown had also caught on to Nepe's presence. That meant that the enemy would be on her trail. But maybe not immediately. Brown might take a few hours to realize what she had to do, and Purple might have trouble tracing Nepe after that, even with magic. So maybe there would be no pursuit. But the Hectare might have devices that no one else knew about, that could sniff out even a magic trail, with a little advice from an Adept. So they couldn't take a chance. So Mach had given Nepe the full dose, on the assumption that they would trace him down though her, and take him out of the game. He could not afford to assume otherwise.

So before she went to the North Pole, she had better mask her trail. But quickly, because she didn't know how much they already knew. Mach had said they might have Brown's golems stake out the Poles. What did the Poles have to do with all this? Probably the answer was in the Book of Magic, which Mach had taken somewhere. He must have hidden it where it wouldn't be found by the enemy, because with it they could overcome anything any Adept tried.

Where would that Book be? Where else: the North Pole! So if she went there and got it, maybe she could use it to do whatever else was needed.

Nepe moved about within the city, crisscrossing her trail so that it would be excruciatingly difficult for anyone to track her by any normal means. She was good at hiding, as good as any creature could be, but there remained that lurking doubt: if Brown had told immediately, and Purple had put a magic tracker on her, that would be impossible to shake by physical means. So she might be wasting her time here.

Still, Flach was experienced at magical hiding, and he could do his best to nullify that tracker spell. So after she was done here, she would turn it over to him, and he would complete the job.

It all seemed reasonably simple. But she very much feared it wasn't.

8
North

Flach put together such a combination of moves and transformations that he doubted that anyone or anything could untangle them. He even assumed bug forms and spied on any Hectare that were outside of their antiseptic chambers. All seemed quiet, apart from the grim business of the takeover itself.

In the course of this, Flach got a fair notion of what the Hectare were doing. They were setting up to exploit the resources of the planet. Crews were being assembled to cut the greatest forests for exportable lumber. That would destroy the environment, and many wild and magical creatures would die. It had been exactly that type of ruinous exploitation that had ruined Proton before, so that life was possible only within the force-field domes, with all else a noxious desert. Other crews were to mine out all the remaining Protonite. That would destroy the magic, leaving the planet completely mundane. What would happen to the starving, magic-gelded creatures? It looked very much as if their flesh would be melted down for protoplasm banks.

Mach was right: it was better that the planet be destroyed, than that the Hectare have their way with it.

The Hectare themselves were true bug-eyed monsters; indeed, the serfs and ordinary folk of Phaze had instantly named them BEMs. It seemed that there were two or more major alliances in the galaxy, one of which was the humanoid. Proton had once been in the humanoid sector, but the pattern of colonization had in due course left it stranded with a few others in alien territory. So there was no hope

of rescue by human forces; it would be too costly for them to pene-
trate this deep with sufficient force to accomplish anything—and even
if they did, the Hectare might simply destroy the planet rather than
give it up. So Proton was on its own—just as any alien planets were
on their own when they had the misfortune to find themselves within
human territory.

The Hectare themselves were simply one of a number of species
in their alliance. They were the closest, so on them had fallen the
chore of exploiting the planet. They had not bothered before, but
when it became evident that it had magic now, they had moved it up
on their schedule. It wasn't that they understood magic, but it made
the planet intriguing. It was about as easy to take over the planet as
to investigate it, so they moved in.

The Hectare of course didn't think of themselves as bug-eyed monsters, or even as monsters. They thought of human beings as asym-
metric few-limbed worm segments. A Hectare was symmetrical,
having no front or back or left or right; its eyes surveyed the entire
hemisphere (the flat ground and dome of space above it) simultaneously. Its tentacles circled its body like a mantle, and its tread-feet
took it immediately in any direction. Flach could appreciate their
point of view, though a Hectare remained a BEM to him. According
to Nepe, planets colonized by nonhumanoid creatures that found
themselves in the human sector of the galaxy were being exploited
and reduced just as savagely; there was no special virtue in being
human, when it came to galactic power tides. On such planets, the
horrible menace was FTS—few tentacled slugs, or human beings.
Her sympathy was with the natives, there.

Once Flach was satisfied that there was no pursuit, he started on
his mission. He could not go directly to the North Pole, for several
reasons. Other planets, he understood, were hot at their equators and
cold at either north or south poles; nothing was said about their east
and west poles, oddly. But Phaze (and Proton) was hottest at the
South Pole and coldest at the North Pole. A trip to the south would
be difficult because of the constantly burning heat; a trip north was
a similar problem, because of the intense cold. If he conjured himself
directly there, he would freeze before he could do anything, unless
he was all bundled up or invoked a protective spell. But that was
academic, because he couldn't conjure himself there. His magic was
operative mainly within the "normal" range of Phaze, roughly between

the White and Purple mountain ranges. Beyond that, the hostile magic of the demons interfered. He might be able to learn snow magic, as his Grandfather Stile had, but that would take time and practice. To the south, below the Purple Mountains, it would probably be all right; as far as he knew, nothing but dragons dwelt there, and they didn't interfere with magic. But the more potent exercises of magic made larger splashes, similar to those of emotional commitment, that could be detected by others. With the Purple Adept searching for him, a self-conjuration of that magnitude would be folly; Purple would zero right in on it. That was why he had kept his maneuvering small-scale so far; each splash was below the threshold detectable from a distance.

So he would have to make his way to the White Mountains by a series of small conjurations, or by swift physical travel. Once there he would have to enlist the aid of the snow demons, and travel physically the rest of the way to the Pole. Then he would have to see what offered; the message hadn't told him what he would find there, probably so as not to give it away to the enemy. He didn't expect the trip to be fun, but it had to be done.

He started out. He assumed his unicorn form, which he could do without any splash of magic, because it was natural; he was half unicorn. He was privately proud of his pretty blue hind socks and glistening black coat. As he trotted, he played his horn to the cadence of his hooves; this enhanced the pleasure of the motion. A unicorn could trot for a long time to its own music, because there was magic in music, and it restored much of the energy expended by the body. Nepe said his horn sounded like the science instrument called the recorder, which was a woodwind related to the flute; it was blown from the end instead of the side, and had a mellower tone. The folk of the science frame tended to classify things in their own terms. His dam Fleta could play two or three notes at once, making duets with herself; that was unusual. He wished he could run with her now, or with his Grandam Neysa, sharing harmonies. Fleta was captive of the Hectare, and Neysa was playing dumb animal so as to be ignored by them. They were depending on him to save the world—or to let it be destroyed.

As night came he assumed his bat form, and used sound to track his course north. He snapped up night bugs as they offered, for though he had magically assumed the form, it didn't fly by magic. It needed food energy. What he ate as a bat would sustain him in his other forms too, if he consumed enough. Since he could feed without pausing in this form, it behooved him to stuff himself for the next day. He was not a natural bat; he had adopted it as an alternate form, completing the normal unicorn roster of three. Thus this one also was neutral, because it was the unicorn way, and would not make a splash. The nonsplash forms were repeatable, while individual magic was not. Once a unique spell was done, it was finished; if the same thing needed to be done again, it had to be by a different spell. So even Adepts were careful not to waste magic. Fortunately, human ingenuity could devise many spells, so the limitation normally didn't squeeze.

He had mastered other forms, however, extending his unicorn range. Grandpa Stile had trained him for this, making him the Unicorn Adept. This ability had enabled him to hide from the Adverse Adepts for four years, making a critical difference in the contest for control of Phaze. Now he hoped it made a similar difference, in this contest for the survival of Phaze.

As dawn approached, he shifted to wolf form, and ranged on through the diminishing forestland. He was making excellent time, but he was tiring, for all the forms required rest and sleep eventually. He hoped the ice demons were hospitable, so that he could get some rest there.

Being in wolf form reminded him of his Promised, Sirelmoba. What a fine little bitch she was! He almost wished he had not made the commitment to her, because once they came of age and mated, they would separate and never mate with each other again. If he had taken some other bitch as his Promised, and exchanged name syllables with her, then he would have been free to establish a permanent liaison with Sirel. But of course he wouldn't have come to know her so well then. The wolf way was a good way, but sometimes hard. And, he had to remind himself, he was not really a wolf; he had joined the Pack when in hiding, but he was more truly a unicorn, or a man.

Finally the great White Mountains loomed beyond the scrub. Now he was glad he was moving rapidly, because even in his furry wolf guise he would have had some trouble with the cold here. Natural wolves got acclimatized, but he had spent his life in the temperate zone and was soft. Also, he lacked his full growth. In the necessary alignment of things, the unicorns and werewolves and vampire bats lived the same ages as humans; a nine-year-old human boy was as young in proportion as a 'corn or wolf or bat. It had been a job, carrying Lysan! He had had to use supplementary magic to lighten the load.

He came to the base of the mountains. Grandpa Stile had told him of one of the tribes of snow demons he had come to know, because he had played chess against the demon champion, Icebeard. Even demons loved good games! They had been on opposite sides in the Adept struggle, but demons did not take human altercations too seriously. In any event, they should all be on the same side now: the side of Phaze.

He found the pass leading to the demon caves. He started up, his paws feeling the ice. Soon he would have to change to boy form and invoke a spell of warmth.

A snow demon appeared, and roared a windy challenge. "Away, wolf, ere I bury thee!" It was no bluff; the creature could set off a snowslide in a moment.

"I be friend!" Flach called in growl-talk. Not all creatures understood all languages, but there was some interaction between wolves and snow demons. With magic he could do for himself what he had done for Lysan: make their languages compatible.

"Demons have no friends!" The demon made ready to start the slide.

"I be grandpup to Adept Stile, come to see Icebeard."

The demon paused. That name was known here. "Prove it."

Flach assumed his unicorn form, then his boy form. He made a minor conjuration of clothing, lest he freeze. "Dost see the semblance?" For he did have a family resemblance to his grandfather, one he had cultivated from pride.

"Aye," the demon said grudgingly. "An thou dost be faking it, we shall make o' thee a statue o' snow."

"As would be proper," Flach agreed.

The demon led him on into a cave farther up the pass. Soon he stood before the demon chief, who was a fearsome figure. He was made entirely of ice, with wild icicles for hair and of course matted ice for a beard. He gazed coldly at Flach. "Thou claimest to be the 'Corn Adept?" he demanded, his breath a freezing fog.

"Aye. An thou wishest, I will perform small magic."

"Why small? An thou dost be he, thou canst make big magic."

"And have our enemy spy my location," Flach replied. "That were not kind to thee or me."

Icebeard considered. "Dost play chess?"

Flach laughed. "Aye! But I be far from Grandpa's league—or thine."

That was a good answer. "What willst thou here?"

"Knowest thou o' the Hectare?"

"Word reaches e'en the hinter. Thou hast dealings with them?"

Here was the crux. If the demons had sided with the enemy, he would have to risk strong magic to escape. "Aye. I be dealing to destroy them."

The demon chief smiled. "Then we be together, this time. We ha' no joy in aliens who would mine out our mounts."

"Aye, I hoped so," Flach said, relieved. "My sire the Rovot Adept opposes them, and hides the Book o' Magic."

"We remember the Rovot—and Fleta 'Corn, a mare one could learn to like." That was strong language, from those who liked no one. Flach's dam had evidently made a considerable impression.

"Stile be their captive, and most o'er Adepts. Mayhap I alone can implement our defense."

"And needst our aid?"

"Aye."

"Shallst have it, 'Corn. What needst?"

Just like that! Demons evidently wasted no time pondering. "Needs must I go to the North Pole."

Icebeard was taken aback. "That be one hard haul. I would trust not my cold bones there. The weather be mean."

"Aye, I fear I can make it not alone."

"But my daughter be full o' the flush o' youth. She will lead thee there, with picked guard."

"My thanks to thee, chief o' demons!" Flach said gratefully. A demon squad could handle anything short of Adept magic—and they would not encounter that near the Pole.

"But a caution," Icebeard said. "My cub be impetuous, and my guards be virile. Needs must a man's presence keep them in check."

"I be but boy," Flach protested. "An I not be the only one remaining, this task were ne'er mine."

"Thou dost be Adept," Icebeard reminded him. "Canst do magic we wot not, an we oppose thee not."

"Aye—but an I invoke it, the traitor Purple be on my tail. I can risk but small spells."

"Illusion be but small."

Flach gazed at him, catching on. "Make myself seem older? Maybe twice mine age o' nine?"

Icebeard nodded. "My cub be twenty. That be close enough. She will show the way. An a guard show interest in her, do thou step between."

Flach was daunted. "I know not if I—"

"Do thou fashion a seeming o' robust strength and brief temper. That, plus mine orders, suffice."

Maybe it would. Flach realized that it would have to be risked, if he was to get to the Pole. "I will try, Chief."

"Mayhap soon I find suitable match for her. But an she fall for a mere guard, that be complicated."

Flach could appreciate that. Each group had its own conventions about romance and marriage, and violation of them could be perilous. Flach knew the wolf conventions, and was catching on to the human ones, thanks to Nepe's information. Icebeard wanted his daughter emotionally uncommitted until there was a good marriage lined up for her. Naturally there was no worry about a relationship with a warm-bodied man; any closeness would freeze him or melt her. There was even less concern about a nine-year-old child. The chief might be taking advantage of Flach's mission to keep his daughter safely out of temptation until he completed his arrangements for her.

This could be good for Flach, too. Any demon help would be good, but because Icebeard valued his daughter, these would be picked guards, able to handle just about any threat. That, plus Flach's minor magic, should get them through in good order.

"Methinks it will take thee a day to get the party organized," Flach said. "I be tired from my trek here—"

"Didst not conjure thyself close?"

"Nay, that be strong magic. I came by land, running day and night and day."

Icebeard snapped his icy fingers, and a demon female appeared. She was stooped, and her hair was a curtain of icicles, but she was human rather than beastly in general configuration. "Take him to a secure chamber and watch him sleep," the chief told her.

The woman walked to Flach, picked him up, and carried him out of the room. She was taking the order literally, and taking him as she would a block of ice. He had to do a quick spot spell to prevent their contact from doing each harm.

She bore him to a bubble of air deep in the glacier and dumped him down on a bed of snow. Again he did spot magic to make the interface proper: now the snow seemed like warm feathers, and did not melt under him. He stretched out, ready to sleep for twelve hours.

The demoness stood there, gazing down at him. Time passed, and she did not move. Then he realized what it was: she was watching him sleep, literally.

So be it. He would surely be safe, this way. He closed his eyes and slept.

Next day, refreshed, he conjured some bread to eat, found a crevice for natural functions, and went to see what had developed in the interim.

Icebeard had been busy. A troop of ten stout snow demons had been assembled, and a similar number of demon dogs, also made of ice. Several were to be harnessed to a sled, and the others would range out around the group, guarding it. They were to travel in style.

"Adept!"

He turned. It was a petite young demoness, not greatly taller than himself. He was surprised; he had thought all demons, of any type, were ugly, hideous, or grotesque, but she was a perfect figure of a woman molded from ice. "Aye," he said.

"I be Icedora, but thou mayst call me Icy," she said, her voice like the crystalline tinkle of glass dangles. "That be spelled with a *c*, not a *k*, for I be not Iky!"

"I can see that," he said, awed even at his age in the spectacle of her frozen splendor.

"We be traveling together, methinks."

Icebeard's daughter! He realized he shouldn't have been surprised. The demon chief had said she was twenty, which was adult, and that he was trying to set up her marriage, but he had neglected to say she was beautiful by any standard. "Aye," he said after a moment. "I be Flach."

"I met thy dam, the 'corn," she said. "I were but thine age then, but she were beautiful."

Flach hesitated, not knowing the appropriate response. *Icy's the same!* Nepe prompted him.

"No more so than thee," Flach said.

Icy smiled, and that confirmed the compliment, for her smile made her seem almost warm. "Methinks we shall get along well enough," she said.

Told you! Nepe put in. *Way to a woman's heart is flattery.*

So it seemed. He would try to remember that, for the time when it might count for him. "That should be nice. Who rides the sled?"

"Thou—and I. So we had better get along well!"

"Aye." He looked around, to make sure that no other demons were listening. "Thy father says I must pretend to be older, so I will make a spell o' illusion. But thou must remember I be but a child."

"Aye. But thou dost be distressingly hot. Canst make thyself comfortably cool?"

"Aye. I will seem cold, but will not be cold. I will not melt thee, and thou willst not freeze me."

"I be glad o' that!" she said, laughing. "We folk associate not much with thy folk, because o' their oppressive heat. An they e'er change their ways, all will be cool."

"Aye," he agreed, not caring to argue the point.

On the following day they started off. Flach had generated an illusion that doubled his age, so that he looked and sounded eighteen instead of nine. He seemed larger and heavier, but he retained the strength and mind of his true age. His image moved exactly as he did, magnified appropriately. He was rather proud of the spell; he had never done this before.

Icebeard looked him over and cracked a slow smile. "An that not fade in thy sleep, it be suitable."

"It will remain till I counter it," Flach assured him. "My spells fade slow. But an I have to do a man's work, I needs must use magic to amplify my strength."

"Nonesuch be required. The story be this: my daughter has a mission to the Pole, and thou too, to help her complete it. Thou willst tell her what needs must be done, and she will tell the guards. The dogs will not attack thee." He paused, then lowered his voice. "Canst tell me what thy business be at the Pole?"

"I know it not, only that I must go," Flach said, appreciating why he had not been told. He could not blab the secret to anyone. "I hope to discover why when I get there. Then mayhap it will be known to all."

"Mayhap," the demon chief agreed, disappointed. "Come, needs must I introduce thee to my cub, lest she mistake thee for other."

"I met her yesterday," Flach said.

"In this form?"

"Nay, in mine own."

"Then the introduction be needful."

He had a point. Flach now looked completely different. He had the aspect of a powerful young man. He hoped he would be this solid and handsome when he really did grow up!

Icy was evidently impressed when she saw him. "I knew not that warm ones could be so rugged!" she exclaimed, eying him in a way that made him uncomfortable.

You should be! the inner voice that was Nepe told him. *That's one hot snow demoness! She's going to find out just what is possible, before this trip is done.* She formed a mental image of wolves sniffing tails, then making ready to mate.

Flach shrugged. Nothing was possible, of course.

They got on the sledge, which was shaped to allow them to sit comfortably side by side, their backs supported by the supplies behind and their legs moderately bent in front. Icy took the reins. "Mush!" she cried, and the dogs took off.

But they were high on a mountain slope. The sledge careered down and to the side, skidding toward a drop-off. "Yiii!" Flach cried, grabbing on for dear life.

The sledge turned just before the ledge and zoomed along its edge. Flach hung on, afraid to look down into its dark depths. They seemed about to bounce off the snow and tumble right off the mountain.

"Well, now," Icy said, her frozen breath tickling his ear. Flach opened his eyes.

She was what he had grabbed on to! Hastily he let go, steeling himself to sit upright and ignore the horrendous scene just beyond the sled, and the breathtaking one on it.

The demons skiing behind laughed. So did the racing guard dogs. So, in a moment, did the harnessed dogs. They had done it on purpose, to make him react.

Flach relaxed. If they were so sure of their footing and Icy's safety, he might as well be sure too. They surely knew every inch of these mountain slopes, and could handle them precisely. They had had their fun with him, but he would keep his nerve better from now on.

Soon they were beyond the mountains and heading north across a relatively flat plain. The dogs ran indefatigably, and the skiing demons kept the pace. It quickly got dull.

"Dost know any good games?" Icy asked with a toss of her ice tresses. "We have long to ride."

"Well, there be tag—"

"And which o' us gets off and runs to do that?" she inquired archly.

"It were a stupid notion," he admitted. "I could conjure cards—"

"I have played e'ery game there be for cards!" she said crossly. "A chief's daughter has much time on her hands."

There's one she hasn't played, I'll bet, Nepe thought. *I don't know what it's called, but I remember how it goes.*

Flash conjured a deck of playing cards. "Mayhap I have one thou hast not."

"Willst bet on't?"

"Bet what?"

"Consequences."

Flach wasn't sure he trusted this. "What consequences?"

She shrugged. "I'll decide, after I win."

"Suppose I win?"

"Then the consequence be thine to decide, for me."

"I have a mission to accomplish. I can't be diverted to—"

"Innocent tasks," she said. "Like saying 'I be a warm ogre bottom!' or mayhap standing on the sledge and sunning the guards."

"Sunning?"

"Mayhap thy kind calls it mooning."

This was beginning to sound like the kind of challenge a person of his generation couldn't turn down. "An thou dost lose the bet, I define a consequence for thee?" he said, making quite sure.

"Aye. So long as it be harmless and delay our travel not."

This creature is dangerous! Nepe warned admiringly. *But you better accept her challenge, or she'll come up with worse.*

"Agreed," Flach said. "The bet be whether I have a card game thou hast ne'er played before."

"Aye. Name it."

"I can't name it. But—"

"Then thou dost lose!" she exclaimed.

"Nay, that be not the bet!" he protested. "I need not name it, only describe it. An it be a good game thou has played not before, I win."

She reconsidered. "Aye, that be fair. Describe it."

Drawing on Nepe's information, he described it: "Several can play, or only two. The dealer lays down cards according to a secret rule, and first to guess that rule becomes dealer."

She considered. "I ne'er heard o' it," she confessed. "But be it a real game? Who wins it, who loses? How be points scored?"

"The dealer wins, long's he holds his place. It be like king o' the hill: the one atop wins till he loses. But we could play for points an thou wishest: each wrong guess be the dealer's point."

"But the dealer gets all the points!" she protested.

"Aye, but the players can become dealer by guessing right, and get points. When the game end, belike one be ahead."

"Aye," she said, considering it. "I like this game. Thou dost win the bet. What wouldst thou make my consequence?"

Flach was tempted to make her sun the guards, but lacked the nerve. "Let's play the game, and this be my first point."

She looked at him. "Thou dost be generous, Flach. I would have gi'en thee worse."

"I lost my nerve," he admitted.

She laughed. "I like thee, warm one! I will not make thee do aught onerous."

"An thou dost win."

"Ne'er fear, I will win," she said confidently. "I be not Adept, but I be sharp at card games."

Flach marveled at her certainty. Though his own experience with the Proton Game was slight, Nepe had played it often, and her expertise was his to draw on now that they were merged. Also, he had played games with his adopted sibling wolves, among which guessing games were prominent because they could be indulged while running together through brush in quest of game (the other kind). In short, despite his youth, he regarded himself as a good competitor, quick with his wits. Could this sheltered snow girl be the same?

He shuffled the cards. They were plastic, able to withstand both his heat and her cold. "Wouldst be dealer first?"

"Nay," she said. "How couldst thou have the first point, and thou not be dealer? Lay me out."

He glanced at her, unsure of her terminology. She had undone her ice coat, evidently feeling too warm, and had her feather-ice sweater open to view. It was a remarkably shapely sweater, rather like a contour map with two perfectly rounded mountains.

"Some cards," she clarified, laughing so that the mountains shook. Well she knew the nature of his confusion and his distraction.

When I grow up, I'm going to practice to make my sweater move like that! Nepe thought enviously.

That helped clarify things for Flach. He had found that sweater oddly intriguing, but hadn't quite realized why. No doubt when he became the age he had made himself appear to be, he would have no trouble realizing why. Apparently there was a greater correspondence between the interests of demons and men than he had appreciated.

"Then thou must shuffle," he said. "That be standard, to assure I cheat not."

She laughed so hard that her sweater threatened to ripple apart and hurl the mountains into limbo. "Thou fool! Canst be serious?"

"Aye, serious," he said, annoyed. "Needs must the game be played fair."

"Willst bet on that?" she asked, suppressing a chortle.

"Aye! I would not cheat!"

She calmed down enough to face him directly, but the mountains still quivered with merry aftershocks. "This be no random dealing, Flach," she said. "This be cards laid down by secret rules. How canst thou have a rule, an thou deal randomly—'less random be thy rule?"

Ooops! She had caught him in an embarrassing blunder. Even his simulated aspect blushed. "Thy point," he admitted.

Her head darted forward, and she kissed him on the cheek. The magic of the illusion was such that her cold lips scored on his own flesh, though it was not quite where the flesh of the older youth seemed. "But I like thine honesty," she said. "Thy foolishness becomes thee."

That made him blush worse. He tried to ignore it. "Now must I put the cards back in order," he said.

"Easy, Adept!" she said, taking the deck from him. "Make us a table—a sheet o' ice will do—and I will play a game o' clock solitaire."

"But a game will just mix them up more!" he protested. "And what be this about a clock? Time be not o' the essence."

She shook her head wonderingly. "I had thought it to be dull, shepherding a boy into the bleak. Methinks I forget the joys o' na-ïveté. Watch—nay, no pun!—and learn, lad."

He conjured the sheet of ice she wanted, and they laid it across their laps. His woolly clothing and protective spell prevented his heat from melting it, and her body would only freeze it colder, so it was an excellent table. She put the cards down in a circular pattern of twelve piles, and a thirteenth pile in the center. "This be the clock," she announced. "North be twelve, south be six, and the rest in order. An I complete the numbers before the center, I win—but that be seldom."

"One chance in thirteen," he remarked.

"How cle'er o' thee to figure it!" she said, smiling. He knew she was teasing him, but he felt a surge of pleasure. *She's mistress of her trade,* Nepe thought appreciatively.

She lifted the top card in the center pile. It was an ace. She put that face up under the 1 pile just right of the 12 pile, and lifted the top card of that pile. This was a 6, so she put that under the 6 pile, and took its top card.

So it went, from pile to pile, each one showing the way to the next. Icy's snow-white hands flashed cleverly from pile to pile, placing and lifting cards so quickly it was hard to follow. Obviously she had played this game many times before—and many others. She had spoken truly about her experience in this regard.

The first king showed up, and went to the center. Later another, and a third. Then the first of the circle to reach all four cards appeared: the 3 pile. Then, after only a few more moves, the fourth king.

"Hot lava!" she swore. "I be lost ere I have more than one hour on the clock! That be a bad omen."

"I hope not!" Flach said. Omens were serious things.

She shrugged, and again the mountains moved. "Mayhap not. They say lucky at cards, unlucky in love, and I have e'er been luckiest at cards. An my luck turn, my father may find a good demon for me."

"He can find not a demon for one as fair as thou?" Flach asked, surprised. "Be appearance not the first thing men seek?"

"Aye." Her hands resumed their motion, as she lifted the top card on the 12 stack and continued the placements. That card was an 8, and the next a 10. "Many be eager enough, but it seems I have a curse." The 8 pile was completed, then the 2's, and the 4's.

"A curse? It be not apparent to me."

Her quick hands brought up the fourth queen for the 12 pile. "Fire! Lost again." For the 9's and 11's remained incomplete. She took one from the 11's, and in a moment all the piles were done. Then she picked them up: the four aces, four 2's, and so on. The deck was in numerical order. "An thou needst suit order, I can play a game for that," she said.

"Nay, this be good enough," he said, taking the cards. "But what be this curse on thee?"

"Let me see those," she said suddenly, taking them back and turning the pack over. "I ne'er looked at the backs! This be one o' the fairy folk!" For the picture was of a winged girl in gauzy green, flying up to pick foliage.

"Aye. I met her when I was a wolf, so put her on my cards. It were when I was in hiding."

"Thou wast hiding?"

"From the Adverse Adepts, four years."

"And they found thee not?"

"They found me after those years. Then it were difficult, till Stile merged the frames."

"But were thy sire and dam not on our side? My father taught the Rovot Adept to play chess."

"Aye. I hid from him, till he searched me out."

"Thou didst have a difficult life," she said sympathetically.

"Nay, it were a good life, only not with my parents. But why dost thou turn aside the subject when I ask about thy curse?"

" 'Cause it be my shame," she said. "An thou beat me at cards, thou canst make me tell thee for consequence."

That seemed fair enough. He picked out the 10 of hearts and laid it down. "When thou dost think o' the rule, make thy guess," he said. "It must be apparent within four cards, 'less thou preferest other. An thou guess wrong, my point. An thou not guess it in eight cards, my point."

"Aye. Lay thy four."

He put down the 4 of clubs, the jack of diamonds, and the 5 of spades.

"That be not enough to define the rule," she said. "An I guess a rule that fits, but it be not thine, what then?"

"I tell thee nay, but no penalty. Otherwise it become cumbersome for two. An several play, bad guesses help others to win, so players be cautious. But with two, there be no urgency to guess, so it can be the whole deck before a guess." He was getting this from Nepe. "So I put limits, but thou canst protest them."

"Nay, no protest. Thy rule be change color and diminish by six, in circular fashion. Mayhap also repeat not suit till all be used, but that were not certain."

She had nailed it with alarming accuracy. Flach handed the deck to her.

"My deal be same's thine," she said, not taking up the four cards. "But my rule other."

Flach studied the cards with new interest. "Two-digit number alternating with one-digit number," he said.

"Nay. No penalty."

"Lay more cards."

She put down the 9 of spades, the 3 of spades, the 6 of clubs, and the 8 of clubs.

Flach stared at the cards. The colors no longer alternated, and the numbers no longer descended. There was no consistent pattern of odd and even. He had to admit he was stumped.

"Third card be odd," she said.

"But the third, fourth, fifth, and sixth cards are odd!" he protested.

"Not odd in total, odd in being different from the first three," she explained. "See: each has two symbols in top row, till the third, with one. Then two, two, and one."

He looked, and it was so. She had looked at the cards in a different way, and been more original than he. "Thy point," he conceded.

They played again. She dealt the 8 of hearts, 11 of spades, 5 of clubs, and 4 of clubs. When he was baffled, she dealt out the 9 of diamonds, the ace of diamonds, 7 of diamonds, and 6 of diamonds.

He was unable to get it. "Alphabetic," she explained.

"But the ace should be first!"

"That be the one, as in one, two, three et cetera."

He admitted defeat.

So it went. Icy was immensely more talented than he, in this game. By the time they were ready to camp for the night, he was hopelessly behind on points. Any penalties she had in mind for him were hers to dictate.

"How camest thou so apt in cards?" he asked ruefully.

"My sire be chess champ o' demons, and but for thy grandpa, o' all Phaze," she said. "From him do I inherit a memory and grasp o' numbers and positions. None beat me at such."

"Mayhap that be thy curse!" he exclaimed. "Demons like not to be beaten by demoness."

She shook her head. "Thinkst I know that not? Were thou a prospective match, thou wouldst ne'er discover so helpless a female, in anything relating to male's domain."

It seemed she did know what she was doing. She didn't need to worry about beating him, as he was in no way a prospect for her. It was foolish, he knew, but he almost regretted that.

They ate supper while riding. Flach conjured cold sandwiches and cold milk for himself, not wishing to upset her by having hot food, and she ate ice cream from her own store. After a while his milk froze, so they traded, and she chewed on it while he had some of her ice cream. If a person was what she ate, he could see why she was sweet.

The demon guards went hunting on the move. They skied down ice rabbits and killed them with ice spears. They fired ice arrows up at ice geese and brought them down. This frozen realm was full of life, when a person knew what to look for. Perhaps the magic that protected him from the cold, and shielded Icy from his heat, also facilitated his perception of the nature of this region. It was far more interesting than he had supposed. Now he saw that there were ice plants, too, ranging from cut-glass blades of grass to snow trees.

"I fear I be losing my touch," Icy remarked. "Thine eyes be straying across the landscape." She inhaled. "Dost spy elevations more symmetrical than mine?"

"Thou wouldst not tease me so, an thou knew not mine age," he accused her.

"Aye," she agreed, satisfied.

The dogs drew up at a bit of an outcropping of ice, perhaps a glacier that had gotten lost. To the west dark clouds were surging, blotting out the chilly sunset. "There will be nice weather tonight," Icy observed. "But methinks thou willst prefer to be under co'er."

"Aye. Snow and ice be not as appealing to me as to thee."

She smiled obscurely. "Mayhap we shall see."

The demon guards unpacked a tent made of stitched snow, and stretched it over great long icicles that made fine poles. Icy crawled in, beckoning Flach to follow. She brought out an ice lamp whose central crystal radiated cold blue light, just enough to illuminate the interior.

"There be not enough snow for two beds," she said, brushing the snow into a central pile. "Thou willst have to share with me."

"I can make a small spell to make mine own—" he started.

"Nay, that were pointless," she said, removing her coat. "Thy spell will stop thy heat from melting the snow."

"Aye, but—"

"And I like thy company," she continued, pulling off her fine sweater. "I like not sleeping alone, anyway."

"But—"

"Get thy clothes off," she said, stepping out of her layered ice skirt. "Dost want to soil clean snow?"

"But I need my clothes to keep warm!"

"Nay, thy spell protects thee," she said, removing her scant undergarments and hanging them neatly on an ice hook. Her body was now innocent of apparel, and resembled a glass and alabaster statue animated by the Brown Adept as a lovely golem.

"But a man be supposed not to sleep beside a woman not o' his family," he protested.

"But thou dost be no man, but a child. Thinkst thou my memory be so brief?"

"E'en so, it be not right to be naked together."

"So? Were that the way it be with thine o'er self in Proton-frame?"

She had him as handily outflanked as she had on the card game. Nakedness was the norm in the other frame. Of course Nepe was used to it, but he couldn't turn the body over to her, because she lacked the magic to confine its heat.

Defeated, he undressed. He was tired, and did need the sleep, and the snow did look very soft and fluffy. Though he was clothed with illusion, his apparel seemed to fit the larger body as well as it fitted him, and when he doffed it his apparent body was as naked as his real one, in a more manly manner.

Icy lay on the bed. "Didst say thou was with a Pack?" she inquired.

"Aye. They were kind to me."

"Then thou hadst a Promised bitch?"

"Aye. When we come of age, will we will mate, and go our ways."

Icy spread her legs. They were as marvelously rounded and symmetrical as her upper features. "Methinks I will show thee how to do it, so thou dost know, when."

I knew it! Nepe thought. *I saw it coming!*

How do I get out o' it? he thought desperately.

Why bother? It's good information. I'm learning things from her like mad!

Fat lot o' help thou dost be! he retorted. Aloud, to Icy, he said: "I thank thee for thy consideration, but methinks I had better sleep."

"Dost remember our card games?" she inquired, stretching her nicely proportioned arms languorously.

"Aye. But—" Then he caught her drift. "Consequences!"

"Bright lad! Thou dost owe me a mountain o' them! Come, Flach, I will hurt thee not. I want only to play with thee."

"But why? I be o' no interest to thee!"

"Because," she said seriously, "an I practice with thee, and find what works, mayhap I can surmount my curse and nab a good match o' my own kind."

"Tell me thy curse, and mayhap I can make a spell to abate it," he offered hopefully.

"Come to my arms, and I will tell thee, though I owe thee not."

Flach got down on the bed beside her. She turned over, caught his shoulder and rolled him into her. She was amazingly pleasant to lie against. His spell served as a barrier against heat leakage, so that neither could hurt the other, but it allowed all other aspects of touch to register. It enabled him to catch a tactile glimpse of what grown folk found in each other, physically.

"Four times have suitors come my father deemed worthy," she said. She took a breath, and her softness pressed caressingly against him. "Each were eager to be close to me. But each were stricken at the moment he sought to do with me as I would do with thee. Two died, one went lunatic, and one be yet in coma. Now the suitors be nay so eager, and I fear the onset o' being an old demoness. It be the curse, that strikes down any who would love me."

"I checked thee for malign influence when I met thee," Flach said, trying to focus on his words instead of on her breathing. "That be no distrust o' thee, but 'cause my mission be dire, and I fear bad magic 'gainst me. There be no curse on thee I can fathom, Icy."

"Kind of thee to say so, Adept," she said. "But then what struck those suitors?

"Mayhap I can fathom that. I should be proof 'gainst it, 'cause o' my magic, youth, and not being thy kind." He hoped; that sounded like a dreadful curse, and the qualities he had named were barely protecting him from her wiles. If the curse turned out to be stronger than her blessings, even his magic might not be enough, since he did not want to make a big splash. "Exactly how did it happen?"

"When I get a demon close," she said, "and I kiss him like this"— she kissed him on the mouth, and if her prior kiss on his cheek had been pleasant, this was so much more so as to resemble Adept magic instead of minor peasant spells to ward off flies. "And I squeeze him like this"—she pressed him in to the length of her body, and the length of his body responded with such a warm surge of feeling that he feared it would break across the protective spell. "And I whisper in his handsome frozen ear an endearment." She put her lips to his ear, and breathed, "I love thee," and though he knew it was merely a demonstration, his heart seemed to swell and burst with responding passion. To love such a woman! What could anything else matter, after that?

"Oh!" she squeaked, horrified.

Flach rolled away and scrambled to his feet, afraid of what had happened. Sure enough, there was a melted streak the length of her beautiful body. His burgeoning heat had broken through and touched her, horribly.

"O, Icy, I be sorry!" he said. "I will make magic to mend thee!"

"The pain be awful," she gasped. "An thou canst—"

"The burn dispel, and make her well," he singsonged, willing the healing power. This was stronger magic than he liked to use, but he felt guilty for hurting her, and had to make it right.

A small cloud of freezing vapor appeared, and coalesced against her body. The meltline disappeared. Icy relaxed.

"Ah, thy magic be profound!" she said. "The burn be gone as it never were. I thank thee, I thank thee!"

"Nay, it were my fault I hurt thee. Thy kiss, thine embrace, thy words, they heated me so it burst through the spell, and I harmed thee awfully. I beg thy forgiveness, lovely creature!"

"Nay, apologize not to me!" she exclaimed, sitting up. "I led thee to it, with my foolish game. I tried to make thee hot, as I made the others—"

She broke off, staring. Flach came to the same realization. "The heat!" he exclaimed. "I be warm, but I be but a child. An thou couldst do that to me, what couldst thou do to a grown man?"

"Well, they be o' ice, like me—"

"But an they heated, *they* could melt!" he said. "That be no curse— that be o'erabundance o' passion!"

"But such ne'er happ'd before to demonesses!" she protested.

"There was ne'er a snow creature nor as lovely neither passionate as thee before!"

"Aye," she breathed, appreciating the validity of his observation. "Then love be my curse."

"But now the cause be known, can we mute it," he said. "Needs must I merely put a spell on thee to cap the intensity o' thy effect on others. Then canst thou love freely and safely."

"Safe love," she agreed, delighting in the concept. "Canst do it to me now?"

Even in her innocent expressions, she's sexy! Nepe noted jealously.

"Aye." Flach pondered briefly, then singsonged: "Let the lady's love be cool, not hot; his passion be but half she's got." As verse it was nothing, but his concept was true: any male approaching her would find his ardor muted to about fifty per cent, which should be survivable. At the very least it would slow things, and give her time to choke down her intensity if she saw the male becoming uncomfortable.

"But I feel not different," she said.

"The effect be on thy lover, not thee," he explained.

"Needs must I verify this," she decided. "Come here, Adept."

Oops. *And you thought you'd gotten out of it!* Nepe laughed.

Well, there were worse fates. Flach lay down beside her again, on the bed of snow. "Mayhap I should increase the power o' my barrier spell," he said. "I want not to melt thee again."

"An thy magic work, no need," she pointed out. "Thou willst not heat enough to break through. We have found that the same passion which melted demons caused thee to melt me; an thou no longer melt me, nor will they melt. That be the test. I want to damp them not down more than be needful."

He had to concede it was a fair test. Too much damping would be deleterious to her romance.

She took hold of him again and pressed him close. He felt as if he were aging several years: good, manly ones. She kissed him. He felt as if he were floating through a golden radiance of delight. She touched her ice-perfect lips to his ear and whispered, "I love thee, Adept, for the favor thou has done me." He felt as if he were floating through a golden radiance of delight.

What? That was the *last* feeling! What about his heart swelling and bursting with responding passion?

It's the feeling-cap, dummy! Nepe reminded him.

Oh. Of course. "I think thou dost be wonderful," he told Icy. "But that be the limit."

"Be that so?" she inquired, feeling challenged. "Mayhap I can show thee a thing or two." She rolled him over on top of her, spread her legs, and wrapped them around his hips. The legs were evidently the two things she was showing him. She inhaled, causing his body to be lifted by cushions. That made two more things. She kissed him in a way he had not realized was possible. That was two more things, her lips, more amazing than either of the prior sets. "Where be thy limit now?" she whispered.

"I be floating on golden clouds," he said. "And gazing at a hea'en I long to reach, but can not. I love thee, demoness, but can feel only the part o' it. I beg thee, tease me not further, lest I find ne'er in the rest o' my life the like!"

"Then I be proof 'gainst heating my man!" she exclaimed, delighted. "An this not heat thee, naught will!" She flexed her legs a bit, and took another breath, and squeezed him miraculously tight yet gentle, sending him for a ride on another golden cloud.

"Aye," he agreed sadly. "Naught will. But had I been the man I look, methinks not e'en the spell would have stopped me from melting thee to a puddle."

"For sure, Adept," she agreed, pleased. She let him go, and he rolled over onto his own side of the snow with mixed emotions. "But the demon I take will be ice, and his heart will melt not. He will be reduced to the performance le'el o' a demon's way with an ordinary demoness."

"Aye," Flach agreed. "Dost that abate the onus o' all my consequences?"

"Aye, Adept!" she agreed. "But I ne'er meant to make thee pay them; it were but fancy."

He had suspected as much. Still, it was a relief. "Thank thee, Icy. Methinks I will e'er regret I were not made a snow demon."

"That be but natural," she pointed out. "Now needs must we sleep, for the morrow we meet the Pole."

He had almost forgotten his mission, in the intrigue of his dialogue with the demoness. "Aye," he said, and closed his eyes.

But it was a while before he was able to make his way down from the golden cloud to the more ordinary bed of snow, and sleep.

* * *

The guard demons had to dig them out in the morning, for the storm had buried their tent in snow. Icy sat up and stretched and breathed the horrendously cold air that rushed in as the tunnel reached the tent entrance.

Flach saw the shoveler-demon staring. "Icy, thy clothing," he murmured "Dost not want thy guards melting before we reach the Pole."

"To be sure!" she agreed, delighted, and got up to fetch her clothing. Actually his warning was not well taken, because she could no longer cause males to heat enough to melt. But he was mindful of her father's caution; Flach's grown image was to discourage the demons from getting ideas about a woman who was intended for demonly princes, not guards.

"And thou too, lover," Icy said mischievously, glancing back at him.

Now Flach remembered that he was naked too, and that he had the semblance of a grown man. The guard demons could draw only one conclusion about what had gone on in the tent during the night. They would be wrong in detail, but perhaps not in principle. Had he been older, and colder . . .

He got up and dressed. Then they exited the tent, the demons gazing jealously at Flach, and got on the sledge. They had their breakfasts while zooming on toward the Pole. They played card games, and she skunked him continually. The consequences she demanded were always the same: she would wait till a guard was looking, then make Flach kiss her on the cheek or, sometimes, the lips, while she feigned reluctance. To the demons it would seem as if Flach were the one winning, and demanding the kisses from her. She wanted the world to know that she had made a conquest, and that the man had not died. All true, as far as it went. He wished it could be more than a mere game to her, and more than an impossible dream to him. He had understood the principle of mating, but had never before properly appreciated the intense lure of it, or the utter fascination a woman could represent for a man. Already he knew that it would take a very special woman to fulfill the longings Icy had seeded in him. Would there be any such, when he grew up?

"There it be!" she abruptly exclaimed.

Flach looked, surprised. There in the middle of the plain was a pole sticking in the snow. It was disappointingly simple, a mere column of ice with spiral ridges down its length. The oddest thing was that it was half in shadow. They drew up to it and halted.

"What now?" Icy inquired. "I realize that thy mission must seem a paltry thing, after my love, but surely thou dost have aught to do here?"

The guard demons fidgeted at this seeming confirmation of their suspicions. The demoness was truly enjoying herself.

The problem was that Flach had no idea what to do. The message had simply told him to come here. What now, indeed?

He walked over to the Pole. He touched it.

Immediately the Pole rose. A circular panel of ice came up, revealing a hole beneath. There were stairs going down.

"A cave 'neath the Pole!" Icy exclaimed, delighted. "Ne'er suspected I this!"

Neither had Flach. But rather than seem uncertain, he squatted, ready to climb down the first big step. There had to be something for him in here.

I don't like this, Nepe thought.

"Adept, ne'er would I gainsay thee, since thou mastered me," Icy said timidly, for the guards were close by, nervously watching the hole as if afraid a fire-breathing dragon might put its head out. "But I intuit some mischief."

Flach shrugged as if indifferent to mischief. "Dost think my mission takes me not here?" he asked.

"I fear it as I fear a fire lake," she said. "It be not hostile, yet it be deadly. O my love, go not into that hole!"

She exaggerated her sentiment, of course, but underneath she did have some concern. He was glad to accept the pretext for caution. "I will humor thee by being most careful," he said gruffly. The guards nodded; this was the way to handle a beautiful woman with foolish notions.

He peered into the hole, his eyes adjusting to its darkness. Now he saw a rope stretched along the stairs, going down out of sight. Its upper end terminated in a loop. A trap for his foot? Would it close about his ankle and haul him roughly into the depths?

"Willst humor me just a trifle more, my hero?" Icy inquired submissively. He was coming to appreciate just how docile a woman could make herself seem, when she chose. Nepe was making avid notes. "Let me drop aught inside, to see what stirs."

"What could stir, here at the Pole?" he asked, hoping she had an answer.

"I know not, great one," she confessed prettily. "But thou hast beaten me so badly at cards, requiring only kisses as penalties, which in truth be not burdensome at all when they be thine—" Here she paused to bat her fine ice eyelashes at him adoringly. "I feel I must repay thee by in some way ensuring that thy bold foot slip not on those dire steps leading I know not where."

"As thou wishest," he said generously. Her worry was infectious; *was* there some threat there? Then why would his father send him here without warning?

Icy took a handful of snow and dropped it into the center of the hole. It powdered down, drifting slightly in the breeze, half of it bright in the daylight, half fading in the shadow that cut across the Pole. But as it passed ground level, it slowed and then halted.

They stared at it. The trailing fluff continued down, but the leading snow was hovering in place, not landing on the highest step.

Flach peered closely at the phenomenon. "It be moving down, but slowly," he said. "I pose this as a riddle for thee, fair one: what be the meaning o' this?" He hoped she had an answer!

"I thank thee for this chance to try my skill at what thou has already fathomed," she said contritely. "Methinks this be a slowspell, that harms not who enters it, but slows him down so that what seems ten minutes to him be an hour outside, mayhap more. An thou go in there, we could wait long 'fore thou dost emerge." She raised her great eyes to him. "My love, I doubt I can wait that long for thee!"

That's one clever doxie! Nepe thought. *A slowspell! She must be right.*

"And how wouldst thou have me accomplish my purpose within, timid demoness, an thou be so impatient for my return?" Flach asked sternly. This was a game he could get to like!

"Why, methinks I would have thee pull on the cord," she said. "And bring out what lies within to thee, here in normal time."

Flach stared at the loop at the end of the rope. Not a trap, but a pull-cord! That made perfect sense!

"Well, needs must we try it," he said. "Methinks thine answer be apt."

Icy downcast her eyes and made a snowy flush: a mirror-gloss formed on her alabaster complexion. How visibly she appreciated the compliment from the master! He knew it was only a game to her, but he couldn't help feeling masterly.

That creature could give lessons to any warm female in the business! Nepe thought, awed. *No wonder she melted males!*

Flach reached down to grab the loop. His hand moved swiftly until it reached the region of the slow-falling snow; then it slowed. He felt no different, however; if he hadn't been watching, he would not have realized that the slowdown had occurred.

But though his hand was slow, his arm was above, in normal time. He shoved it down, and the hand had to go. Thus he was able to pass the snow and reach the loop, thanks to his leverage. But when he closed his fingers on it, they failed to respond. They *seemed* to flex normally, but he could see that nothing was actually happening. They would react in their own good time—which seemed inordinately slow.

But he didn't have to wait. Her fingers were partly curled already. He moved his body and arm, the hand at the end seeming like a fixed hook, and scraped it across the rope so that the fingers caught in the loop. Then he hauled his hand up, and the rope came with it. In a moment his hand was back in normal time, instantly clenching on the rope, and the loop was in his possession.

But what was on the other end? He saw that the loop was actually part of a continuous cord, the two ends of it twining about each other to make the larger rope. No chance of this coming loose! He hauled on it, and the rope came out, not heavy.

Then it went taut. Flach hauled harder, and it came. By the feel of it there was some kind of animal on the other end, walking forward as it was hauled along. But why would he have been sent here to fetch an animal?

Flach kept hauling, hand over hand. Then the animal came slowly into view.

It was man! In fact, it was the Black Adept! Flach immediately recognized the black cloak and boots. The man had been on the other side in the war of Adepts, but had been fair by his definition. He was made of the line, or the line was made of him; Flach had never quite gotten it clear.

He had been sent here to rescue this man? There had to be a reason! "Icy, caution the demons to make no hostile move," he murmured. "This be the Black Adept, and he be not good to cross."

"Aye," she said, gesturing to the guards, who promptly retreated. All creatures of Phaze had respect for Adepts, having learned it by hard lessons over the decades. Flach's magic was less potent here, but he was an inexperienced child; the older Adepts would be as dangerous here as elsewhere.

Flach finally hauled the Adept out. It wasn't by muscle so much as guidance; the man was walking to magnify the tugs of the rope. Soon he stood beside the Pole.

"Adept, I be the so-called Unicorn Adept," Flach said, somewhat nervously. "We met once—"

"Aye," the man said, having no trouble recognizing him despite Flach's added years. It was often that way, with Adepts, who knew each other instinctively. "When thou wast prisoner o' Translucent, on his ancient isle."

"Aye. I was sent here, but I know not why. This be Icy, the daughter o' Chief Icebeard, who guided me here."

The Adept nodded briefly to Icy. "Thou hast done well, fair creature," he said.

Icy, evidently in awe and fear of the Black Adept, flushed with a truer mirror-shine than before. "My pleasure, Adept," she said doubtfully.

"Retreat, ere Green emerge," Black said.

Icy fled. Black turned and hauled on his own rope, which connected to him like a tail. In a moment a ball of fire emerged from the hole. Once this was in the open air, it coalesced into the form of a stout man in green. Flach recognized him too: the Green Adept.

"We thank thee for thy promptness," Green told Flach. "It were a slow trek out, on our own, though time seemed normal to us within."

"The Rovot Adept sent me, but he told me not why," Flach said, amazed at this development. "Canst tell me?"

"Aye, lad," Green said. "We set the Magic Bomb."

"Under the Pole?" Flach asked, amazed again.

"Aye. Know this, lad: an the main ploy fail, the Bomb will destroy all. We detonate it now."

As Green spoke, Black jerked on his line, and it came out of the hole. Evidently the cord had attached to something.

"Now?" Flach asked, appalled.

"Aye. But it be in slow time, so will break not free for six weeks. That be time enough, an thou perform as well thine other tasks as this one."

"An I do that, thou willst turn it off?"

Green laughed. "Nay, lad! It can be turned off not. It be in process o' explosion. None can approach it."

"But then—"

"This be what thy sire told thee not, lest the enemy learn and come 'fore we were done: thine other two missions will save Phaze, yea e'en from this. Take care thou dost complete them, lad, lest we all perish."

"But I don't know what—"

"Nor do we, lad. But the Book o' Magic and the Oracle hatched the plot, and thou be the one to implement it. Now listen well: the part o' Black and Green be done. We made and triggered and placed the Bomb. We be now expendable. We shall guard and hide thee so thou canst proceed about thy next mission. Check it not till thou dost be back in the pleasant latitude. Concern thyself not for us; merely see that thou be not caught."

"But—"

"The enemy has traced thee, lad, but knows not what we do here. There will be an ambush at the White Mountains. When I signal thee, do thou assume a form none will suspect, and leave us to our fate. We will co'er for thee. Dost understand?"

Flach's head was spinning. But it made sense, if what Green told him was true. He had to avoid capture, so that he could fulfill the remaining two directives on the message capsule. "Aye," he said bravely.

Flach rode the sledge back, seated beside Icy as before. The Black Adept donned a white cape of snow and skied behind, seeming to have no problem with the cold. Perhaps that was because Green, in the form of another fireball, rode with him. It was a strange procession, but no stranger than the discoveries Flach was making.

"Canst tell me what be o' such import that three Adepts join in it?" Icy inquired. "My female curiosity be about to melt me!"

There seemed to be no harm in the news now. "We have a dire plot to save Phaze from the Hectare," he said. "An it succeed, we all be free." He decided not to tell her the alternative.

"Aye, methought it be aught like that," she said. "Meanwhile, howe'er that turn out, I will be fore'er thankful to thee for curing my curse."

"Thou didst help me much," he said. "When I grow up, I will have an awful time finding a creature as wonderful as thou." He had mentioned this before, but realized that it bore repeating, because she was even nicer to him when complimented. It also happened to be true. Her father Icebeard was one of the finest chess players of the planet; Icy took after him in being one of the most attractive females of the planet. It was obvious that both worked very hard at their specialities.

"Aye," she agreed complacently. Then she leaned over and kissed him, granting the reward he had hoped for.

When they camped for the evening, the two other Adepts remained apart, evidently able to fend for themselves. Flach shared the tent again with Icy. She did not try to seduce him this time; she merely embraced him and slept. It was about the finest sleep he could imagine. He was quite smitten with her, despite the formidable differences between them; she knew this, and was satisfied. She liked to win, in love as well as cards, and was generous in victory.

On the second day, approaching the White Mountains, trouble came. Geysers of hot gas erupted from the snow, appearing randomly. One formed near a guard, and the demon had barely time to scream before he melted.

"O my love, our geyser enemy be striking!" Icy cried, terrified. "We must away, 'fore it destroy us all!"

But already the gas vents were behind them; there was no sure way out. Flach, after his association with the snow demons, well appreciated the horror of this threat. Heat was their deadliest enemy. The icedogs were whimpering and milling about, seeking comfort close to the sledge. But he didn't know how to stop the gas. Had he known about this threat in advance, he could have devised a suitable spell to counter it, but now he couldn't think of anything.

The Black Adept skied up on his black-line skis. "Do thou do it now!" he called to Flach.

Flach realized that he was referring to the transformation Green had spoken of. He sang his spell: "In co'er o' fog, exchange with dog."

Vapor appeared, hiding him. Suddenly he was in the form of one of the icedogs—and the dog was in the form of the man Flach had appeared to be. The dog was bound by the form, unable to leave the sledge—but it was a good place to be, next to Icy.

Then the green fireball sailed up and exploded. Light blinded them all. But in a moment, as Flach and the demons and dogs blinked back their sight, the hot gas vents were gone. Green, the Adept of fire, had taken charge and suppressed them.

"Go on through!" the Black Adept called. "Before the jets resume!"

Icy called to the milling dogs, and they re-formed their lines and forged forward. Flach was one of the loose dogs, running beside the sledge. He saw Icy speak to the man-image beside her, then her surprise as she realized that something had changed, for the image barked in response.

Icy, absolutely no dummy, glanced across at Flach. He nodded his head. She nodded hers, catching on. She pursed her lips in a farewell kiss. Then she turned back to the figure on the sledge, treating it as a companion, while Flach ranged outward as if searching for new threats to guard against. He was glad she understood; with two other Adepts along, and an ambush awaiting them, she knew that he had to hide again. Perhaps he had been foolish to let her know about his change of form, but he thought she would help cover for him, and he didn't want her believing that he was captured with the others. It was his hope that beneath her humor and games she really did care for him a little. That hope would sustain him for a long time.

The group went to the White Mountains—and the ambush was sprung. Icy had just directed the dogs to skirt a bank of fog, because she did not trust fog in this cold. It might be natural ice-fog, or it might be more hot venting. But before they could clear it, it abruptly expanded, and armed men stepped out of it, forming a semicircle around the sledge. This might be the realm of magic, and the demons might be made of ice, but they knew immediately that they were helpless before this enemy. The men were armed with flame-throwers, the most deadly mundane weapon here.

The Purple Adept stepped out of the fog. "We have tracked you three, and now have you. An any resist, we shall torch the snow demons here and take him anyway; we have set a spell to snare any who try to use magic to flee. What shall it be?"

"Thinkst to employ my specialty 'gainst me?" the Green Adept said scornfully. "I can douse those flames, or turn them against thee."

"An thou dost, thy family pay," Purple said evenly. "And thine, Junior Adept," he added, looking at the figure beside Icy. "We have all in tow." He looked at the Black Adept. "And we can cut thy line: a Hectare missile be oriented on thy castle. But the Hectare be indifferent, and will harm none not who resist them not."

"Thou dost come too late," Black said. "We have planted the Magic Bomb where none can retrieve it."

"About that we shall see," Purple said. "Now, submit yourselves to Hectare power, and it be done."

Green shrugged. "Methinks this be not the end o' this." But the two Adepts went with Purple. Now a Hectare saucer-ship came into view within the fog. This trap had been thorough!

When the two of them, and the man-figure beside Icy, stood with Purple, the snow demons were freed. "Go, maid o' ice, and tell thy folk to associate not again with enemies o' the power that be," Purple cried.

The harnessed dogs scrambled away, hauling the sledge, and the loose ones ranged beyond them, resuming their guard duty. Flach knew he had escaped; by the time Purple discovered his error, it would be too late to do anything about it. He was just one dog, coming into the mountains where thousands were, and no snow demon would betray him.

He hoped Icy did well in her quest for a suitable match. He rather thought she would, now.

9

Play

The Brown Adept knew it was further folly, but she was quite taken with Tsetse. The woman was beautiful and obliging, and made a perfect servant and companion. Perfect except for the fact that she was a creature of Citizen Purple's, his former mistress and surely still his spy. It would be her job to watch Brown and report on any deviance. So she could not be trusted.

Yet what did it matter? Purple had finally fathomed Brown's secret, and required her cooperation with the Hectare invaders on pain of the revelation of that shame. His cynical ploy of assigning a woman who had been the mistress of both a man and a woman demonstrated his complete contempt for Brown. He was happy to facilitate her shame, binding her yet more closely to his fell cause. Brown understood this, but was helpless against it.

Tsetse herself was innocent, being genuinely relieved to have a compatible assignment instead of whatever other horror Purple might have visited on her. She wanted very much to stay here at the Brown Demesnes, and eagerly did anything Brown asked. There really wasn't much that needed doing, other than going into Proton to check the affairs of Citizen Brown, who of course wasn't a Citizen any more. She much preferred the isolation of the wooden castle. So Tsetse's availability for that was nice. If she reported to Purple at the same time, what of it? Brown had never been under any illusion on that score.

But Tsetse as a companion was a temptation it was hard to resist. Tsetse knew the ways of love with either sex, but preferred female. She had made it clear that such a thing would be no sacrifice at all. What was Brown to do?

For days she had stewed over this question, appreciating the horrific nicety of the trap Purple had set for her. If she got friendly with Tsetse, then Tsetse would become a hostage in a way that Brown could not. One Adept could not truly hurt another by magic; some inherent magic in the position of Adept seemed to nullify their efforts against each other. Brown had kept Purple and Tan prisoner, but had not tried to hurt them; now Purple had reversed the ploy, and was making no direct move against her. Of course the Hectare could have her killed, but it was already evident that they preferred to use native talent when they could, and that Purple had promised them to obtain her cooperation. So Purple was working on her—and if she made it too plain that he was getting nowhere, then the Hectare might do it their way.

Brown did not want to die, but neither did she want to betray her friends. She did not know which way she would go, if put to a straight choice between those alternatives. She could only hope it would not come to that. But that hope had never been great, and was diminishing as she saw how methodically the Hectare were consolidating their hold on the planet. Already all but five Adepts were captive, and the hunt was on for those. Clef they would not catch, but the others . . .

Tsetse hurried up, looking elegant in the temporary robe Brown had given her. "Brown, there's something in the storeroom!" she exclaimed. "I heard it!" She used her native speech, and Brown used hers, and there was no problem between them on that score.

"Surely not," Brown said in a businesslike manner. "But needs must we check it." She hoped it was a certain thing, but did not feel free to speak of it. She walked to the golem storeroom with Tsetse.

Inside were the inactive golems, and the guidebot that had brought Tsetse here. "Thou dost see, all be in order," she said. "It must have been a mouse. They do get in, and I have not the heart to trap them."

"But it sounded like a machine!" Tsetse protested. "I heard it from outside, and it frightened me."

"Well, there be one machine here; I had forgotten." That was a lie, but a necessary one. "The guidebot that brought thee here; perhaps it were restless."

"Maybe you should send it back," Tsetse said doubtfully.

"Yes, surely I should! Unfortunately I have no ready conveyance for it, unless I have a large golem carry it." She reflected briefly. "Yes, that may indeed be best. Why dost thou not go and fix us something to eat, while I ready a suitable golem?"

"Certainly!" Tsetse agreed readily, and hurried off.

Brown walked around the chamber, looking at golems. Then she came to the guidebot as if to check its size. "Why didst thou return?" she inquired quietly.

"Mach said you did not betray me," the machine replied as quietly. "Though you did recognize me."

"Of course I betrayed thee not, thou darling child! Thou knowest I support thy grandfather, as I always have."

"But Purp will make you," Nepe said. "I know how."

Brown stiffened. "Thou knowest?"

"I must ask you to do something awful," Nepe said, retaining her form as the guidebot. "My father asks."

"*What* dost thou know?" Brown demanded, hoping it was something else.

"Brown, not all of us are conservative like Grandam Neysa. We don't care how you live; we know you're a good person. But we need your help, and you can do it if you can stand to. It would really make a difference."

Brown realized that the child did know. "What dost thou want?"

"Do what Purp wants."

"What?" Brown was horrified.

"Go with Tsetse. Let him blackmail you. Do whatever he says. But don't tell on me."

"Betray thy grandfather—to help thee?" Brown asked, appalled.

"Brown, they've nabbed Black and Green, but their mission was accomplished. The Adepts covered for Flach, so we could escape. Now it's just Mach and me, and he'll give himself up to save me. But we need your help to get Purp out of the way."

"Thou'rt going after Purple?" Brown asked, amazed.

"In a way. I'd like to wipe him out, but we can't afford to waste our effort doing that. So we're just going to punish him a little, and keep him occupied."

"What dost thou need from me?" Brown asked grimly.

"Take Tsetse with you when you go to the game."

"What game?"

"The one Purp has to play against the Hectare."

Brown was astonished. "I understand not!"

"We're going to throw off the Hectare, and soon, but it's a plot so tricky that none of us knows the whole. All I really know is that I have three messages, and I must do what they tell me. I have done one. The second tells me to do something more complicated, and that's what I'm doing now. I need to sneak a person in past the Hectare alerts to fetch something, and this is the best way I can figure to do it. So it won't be Tsetse with you, really, it will be this other. Don't tell, and when Tsetse disappears, cover for her. She'll be back. Do this, and I will accomplish my second task. If I get through all three, Phaze can be saved, I think. If I can't, then it will be very bad. Will you help me?"

"O' course I will, dear! But how canst thou know the Purple Adept will—"

"You go with him to his game, and help him all you can, and take Tsetse along and don't let on about her. I can't tell you more, Brown, because if this doesn't work I'll have to try some other way, and you mustn't know anything that would hurt us."

Brown spread her hands. "As thou sayest, dear. But it makes not much sense to me."

"It should happen within the hour," Nepe said. "He's coming here to put the screws to you. Now you know what to do."

"An thou be sure—"

"Almost sure," Nepe admitted.

Brown had mixed feelings. She was appalled by the notion of going along with Purple, and worried about Nepe, whom she had known as Flach, but relieved that she no longer had to choose between life and culture. She could yield to the enemy, yet not betray Phaze! If what the child said was true. And though Nepe was a child, she was a remarkably special one, and surely to be trusted.

"'I put mine honor in thy hands," she said. "I will do as thou dost ask. May it save Phaze!"

"Thanks, Brown!" the seeming machine said. "And oh, don't tell Tsetse. She must hide, and not know why, until you return."

"Aye, child." Then Brown left, closing the door behind her, so that the room would not be disturbed.

She shared the meal with Tsetse. Now that her mind was somewhat at rest, she was able to consider the woman more subjectively. Tsetse was beautiful and docile; it would be easy to love her. Now, perhaps, it was time.

"I have a matter o' some caution to broach to thee, trusting I give not offense," Brown said.

"Have I done something wrong?" Tsetse asked, immediately worried.

"Nay, woman! My concern be this: I have by choice no man in my life, but that be not because I be without passion. It be that I prefer mine own gender. I find thee attractive, and would know thee better, an the notion not disturb thee."

"It doesn't disturb me!" Tsetse said, and her relief was obviously genuine.

"Yet thou dost prefer employment here, so mayhap dost feel not free to speak thy true mind. I would not seek to play on that to—"

"I've had both men and women," Tsetse said. "But pleasure only with women. I think you're a great woman!"

"Yet I be concerned. I ask thee to take time to consider, and if thou dost conclude against, I will have no onus against thee. I be minded to send thee on a day-long trip to fetch wood, and if thou dost not reconsider by thy return, we may talk further."

"I don't need—"

"But *I* need, Tsetse," Brown said. "I am athwart a conflict o' interest, and needs must give thee time."

"Yes, of course," the woman said, always amenable. "I'll go immediately."

"The golems know the route, and carry supplies. Thou willst be safe and comfortable. Thou has only to see that they load good wood; they choose not well alone."

"I'll do that!" Tsetse was eager to prove herself.

"Methinks Franken be good to lead the party," Brown said. "He be used to carrying me in his knapsack, and will carry thee in comfort. He will obey thee when thou dost call his name, and keep thee safe. An a dragon attack, say 'Franken, save me,' and he will do it. But thou must speak always literally, for he be not smart."

"Yes," Tsetse said, less eager but ready.

Within the hour, woman and golems were gone. The large golems hauled a wagon for the wood, and Tsetse rode in Franken's knapsack. There were four hauler golems, and four guard golems; she would be safe enough. There was a magic tent on the wagon, that she knew how to invoke for the night's repose. Tsetse might not really like being alone with the golems, but it was something she needed to learn if she was to be genuinely useful, and the mission was a valid one.

Not long thereafter, a small aircraft arrived. It was Citizen Purple, as Nepe had predicted. Probably the child had gotten hold of a divination, so that she had known the timing. It had been a fairly near thing.

Purple strode into the castle as if he owned it—which was close enough to the fact now. He wore the ludicrous tentacle-cap of Hectare service. "Have you considered your situation, Brown?" he inquired brusquely. He was in his Citizen aspect, which meant he wouldn't be using magic. That was a small relief, for a magic check could have spotted the golem party, and it would have been awkward if he realized that Tsetse seemed to be in two places at once.

"At length," she confessed. "Thou has power now, and canst make my life difficult an I not cooperate with thee."

"And comfortable if you do cooperate," he said. "Look, woman, I don't ask you to renounce your heritage. Just put your golems at our disposal, and swear that you will not allow them to harm any person or thing associated with the Hectare. I know your word is good."

"I can keep my castle and my privacy?" she asked. There was more to that question than showed, as they both knew. She wanted assurance that her shame would not be advertised.

"Yes. You will answer only to me, and the Hectare, who are not concerned with personal details."

"My golems I can pledge, but my heart not. I will do what thou sayest, and the golems will obey, but I will betray not my friends."

"Soon enough there will be none loose to betray."

"And Tsetse—"

"She's yours as long as the golems are ours."

"And that be the whole o' it?"

"Almost." He waggled a fat finger at her. "You were a temperate keeper, when Tan and I were your prisoners. But then you were honor-bound to keep us, not to harm us. Now you are not. I want your word that you will obey me personally, and seek no physical or magical harm to me. I know you don't like me, but you will never try to lead me into harm, or refuse to help me if I am in peril."

Brown reflected. Nepe had said they were going to punish Purple, but not actually to hurt him, and in any event that was not Brown's doing. If she saw that Purple was actually being hurt, she would have to try to help him. That seemed to be an appropriate compromise. "An thou keep thy word to me, I will keep mine to thee," she said. "I will obey thee and seek not to lead thee to harm, but an thou come to it by device other than mine, it will grieve me not."

"Agreed. Now I have assignments for your golems. I want a complement set to the North Pole to ensure that no other person or creature has access to it."

"The North Pole!" she exclaimed, surprised. "There *be* no such Pole!"

"There is in Proton. Now there are four. Can your golems get there and remain functional?"

"If there be no fire."

"Snow, not fire."

"Then they can go. I will send a complement. But I must advise thee that golems be not smart; they will prevent thy forces also from approaching it."

"Understood. Do it."

"That be the extent o' mine obligation?"

"For the moment, Brown." He got up to go.

There was a beep. Purple brought out a holo cube and set it on the table. "Purple," he said, evidently acknowledging a call.

A three-dimensional image formed above the cube. Brown's breath stopped. It was a Hectare, one of the bug-eyed invaders. She had shielded herself from such contact, trying to pretend the creatures didn't exist, but here one was virtually in her castle.

The thing's tentacles writhed, rippling around what could be its neck section, and there was a faint, unpleasant keening. They spoke by rubbing short tentacles together, she had heard, producing mostly ultrasonic whistles that the human ear could not fathom if it were able to hear them at all. Evidently it was so, for in a moment the translation started.

"I am pleased to accept your invitation to game," the thing was saying. "A studio is being reserved. Be there with your second in ninety-four minutes." The image faded out.

Purple's mouth hung open. He looked as though he had received a death sentence. This communication had evidently come as a complete surprise to him.

Then he gathered his wits. "Do you know what this means, Brown?"

"I knew not e'en the invaders played games!" she protested. "Thou didst ask to play with it?"

He stared at her. "You don't know that the Hectare not only play, they bet? That they are compulsive gamers who play for keeps?"

She returned his gaze blankly. "I know as little o' them as I can."

"Then you shall learn!" he said grimly. "Make yourself ready, woman; you shall be my second."

"Thy second? I know not how—"

"My adviser, my supporter. You will do your best to see that I win that game."

Suddenly she remembered what Nepe had said: that Citizen Purple would play a game with a Hectare, and that she should go with him, and take the mock Tsetse. How had the child managed this? But she had no time to wonder; she had to do it. "I agreed to do thy bidding, Purple, but must warn thee that I know naught o' seconding or the game, and may be o' little use to thee. I may help thee best by urging thee to obtain a more competent second." Absolutely true!

Purple fixed her with an abruptly steely eye. "Do you know what the Hectare do to losers?"

"Nay. I—"

"They cut off the loser's hand."

She stared at him, speechless.

"That is to ensure that no native throws a game to a Hectare. There is no penalty for winning, and no loss to the Hectare for losing, other than its bets. They're not really good at the game yet, being unused to our conventions, so they often do lose. But they are getting better. They're not stupid, and they do not forget a ploy that defeats them. It's like Phaze magic: it won't work twice. So I have no certainty of winning."

"But then why didst thou challenge—"

"I didn't challenge!" he shouted. "But the Hectare evidently thinks I did, so I'm stuck for it. Now, woman, understand this: you will be my second, and you will see that I win. Because if I lose, *you* lose. Do you understand me?"

Brown didn't need to ask how she would lose. Her secret was on the line. She would have to do her very best to help him to win. Which was exactly what Nepe had told her to do. She had for the sake of integrity urged him not to use her; now her course was clear.

"Aye," she said slowly. "But let me bring Tsetse."

"To remind you what you're fighting for?" He shrugged. "Bring her, then. But be ready in ten minutes. I'll be at my plane." He swept out.

Flustered, Brown went to the storeroom. She opened the door—and paused, astonished.

Tsetse stood there, absolutely authentic. Brown knew it wasn't her, but the likeness was so good that it was hard to believe. "Thou needs must come—" she said, faltering as the surprise continued to percolate.

"Yes, of course, Brown," the woman said in Tsetse's voice. "Whatever you say."

Did the woman stand a little taller than before, and was she heavier? Brown peered closely at her, to see whether she had been magnified a size, but could detect nothing. This emulation would readily pass inspection. But how had they managed it?

She decided to treat the emulation exactly as if she were Tsetse, so that there could be no slip. "Something has come up. We must leave for Proton immediately with Citizen Purple. I am to assist him in a game against a Hectare."

"A game against a Hectare!" Tsetse exclaimed, wide-eyed. "But don't they make natives—?"

"Aye. Needs must we help Purple win. Now come."

Tsetse followed her obediently. They went out to the waiting airplane.

"You can keep your clothing, Brown, but she's a serf," Purple reminded her as he climbed into the pilot's seat.

"Remove thy apparel," Brown told Tsetse. "Thou canst have it back when we return."

The woman struggled out of her gown, in the confines of the plane. Brown helped her. She still seemed completely real, and even her struggle to get out of the robe was authentic. Her breasts shook and her hair got disordered. But when Brown's hand touched her body, she found that it was a good deal more solid than it looked.

Illusion! That was the secret! The other person was larger, but looked the same. There should be no problem as long as no one actually touched her.

Purple was taxiing around, getting aligned for the takeoff. By the time Tsetse was bare, the plane had gotten up speed. Purple, concentrating on his piloting, had paid no attention to Tsetse. That was just as well, since he would have caught on instantly had he touched her. He had after all had an affair with her. This remained chancy business!

Soon they reached the Hardom dome, and landed. A Citizen transport was waiting for them. They entered the chamber, and it moved into the hidden transport network of the city.

Purple touched a console. "Replay my engagement to play a game with the Hectare," he snapped.

A wall became a screen. It was as if they were looking through a picture window to a larger room. There was Citizen Purple, exactly as now, speaking from the screen of a phone. "I crave the honor of engaging my Hectare supervisor in a game," the figure said politely. "I feel this would benefit our mutual understanding. Of course there is no obligation, if you have other business, and I apologize for intruding on your time."

That was it. The inset screen clock showed that this call had been made just about the time Purple was arriving at the Brown Demesnes. It was an obvious frame—to those who knew what he had actually been doing.

Brown, true to her agreement, said what she could. "Someone somehow emulated thee, Purple. But that was when thou wast talking with me, as I will attest. If thou dost explain to the Hectare, maybe—"

"Too late for that. Once the Hectare accepted the challenge, that was that. I'm hoist. But once I catch the perpetrator . . ."

"Methinks only Mach could do it."

"The tech for the call, yes, Mach/Bane," he agreed, pronouncing the names as if they were one name, appropriately. "But the emulation, that would be Flach/Nepe. I've tangled with that brat before, and she's more dangerous than any of the rest. I told the Hectare, nail her first, but they didn't understand. Now she's getting me back." He glanced at Brown. "I know you're on the other side, but this need be no secret. I've got a healthy respect for that one, and if I don't kill her, she'll kill me. But you have made a deal, and you will not allow her to attack me through you."

"I made the deal with thee," Brown agreed. "But that extends not to betraying those who support Phaze."

"Don't quibble, woman. If you know where the brat is hiding, you won't tell me. But if you know the brat is about to do me harm, you will protect me from it. She shall not use you to harm me."

Brown realized that Nepe had set up the bogus challenge to the Hectare before approaching Brown. In fact, she had probably recorded it, and then her father had sent it at the critical moment. Nepe was using Brown to fight the invaders in some devious way, not to harm Purple directly. But if Purple lost the game, he would be harmed, and Brown would have some share of blame for that, because she was cooperating with Nepe. It was a devious situation, ethically, but as she saw it, she had to make sure that Purple won the game. "Aye."

"I am sure you have had contact with her," Purple continued. "Your castle is being watched, but of course she can get around that. It will be thoroughly searched during your absence. But as long as you honor the deal, no harm will come to you. Your chances of inadvertently betraying her are as good as they are of helping her. I figure that balances it out."

"Aye." She was developing a grudging respect for Purple. He was an unscrupulous and personally loathsome person, but he had made it possible for her to retain her loyalty and life-style while helping him. It was a more generous deal than she might have expected. She knew that Nepe understood that no direct attack on Purple could be tolerated now, however tempting it might be; if such a thing occurred, Brown would be obliged to betray Nepe to the enemy. Perhaps Purple, whose mind was as devious as any, was hoping for that.

The transporter stopped, and the door opened. They were at the Game Annex, about fifteen minutes early.

"Where is the game studio?" Purple demanded of the nearest serf.

"I will lead you there, sir," the serf replied. "You are expected."

"My second and her maid are also to be admitted."

"The Hectare has arranged it, sir," the man said as he led the way.

Indeed, the Hectare was ready. It stood within the studio, huge and grotesque, its myriad eye facets glinting. Brown did her best to mask the revulsion she felt at its proximity.

"Sir, this is my second, the Brown Adept, and her maid Tsetse," Purple said.

A man stepped forward. It was Citizen Tan, wearing his tentacle-cap. "I am the Hectare's second," he said. "What the hell are you doing, Purple?"

"A frame," Purple said darkly. "We need better security on the phone system."

Tan nodded. "The brat—and maybe serf Lysander, who has computer circuitry skills. I want that one myself." Then he turned to the Hectare. "Sir, Purple is ready when you are."

The Hectare walked to the console, in its fashion: dozens of fat little tentacles or feet or caterpillar treads buzzed it along quite adequately. There was a chirrup, and the translator spoke. "We shall indulge the Game Computer."

"Of course, sir," Purple said, moving to take his place on the other side of the console. He did not look easy, for it was known that the computer could be pixyish in its selections, and if it had a grudge against Purple, he would be finished. Brown hoped it had no grudge.

The Hectare extended a tentacle and touched its side of the console. Then Purple nodded to Brown. "As my second, how would you recommend I play?"

"Thou canst consult openly?" she asked, surprised.

"Yes, the Hectare permits this. It can overhear, of course. What shall I select?"

"But the Game Computer won't give you what you select!" she said, shifting into her Proton self, because that one was better conversant with the rules of technology.

"It might. So I had better choose well."

She saw that he had the numbers: Physical, Mental, Chance, and Art. "Avoid Chance," she said. "And I think avoid Physical, because it might steer it into a contest where tentacles are a decisive advantage. As for Mental—that too is chancy. So it should be Art, where the human interpretations probably still prevail."

"Good idea." He touched the fourth column.

Words flowed across the screen. SO FATSO WANTS TO WAX ARTISTIC, AND THE BEM WANTS TO PLAY WITH MACHINES. VERY WELL, THIS TIME I SHALL HUMOR BOTH. YOU SHALL BECOME ARTISTS OF THE STAGE, WITH HUMANOID ROBOTS AS ACTORS. SINCE YOU BOTH ARE ARTISTIC CRETINS, I WILL MAKE THE SETTING CRETAN. BEHOLD: THE PALACE OF KNOSSOS, 1550 B.C., WHOSE LABYRINTHINE PASSAGES AND CHAMBERS ARE AN EXCELLENT SETTING FOR A MYSTERY.

The chamber darkened and expanded, assuming the likeness of a great stone castle or palace whose hard walls were brightly painted and whose massive columns were both cylindrical and block-shaped. The pillars were slightly larger at the top than the bottom, enhancing the seeming scale of the building. The thing was a monument to the grandeur of a bygone age that stunned Brown. She knew that much of this representation had to be holographic, for there was no room within the Game Annex for it, but still it was awesome.

Now the Game Computer spoke through its speakers, its voice sounding artificial to only that degree it chose to indicate its origin. "The king has suffered an indisposition, and it has been determined that an attempt was made to poison him. Fortunately he consumed only a trace of the tainted food before his food-taster succumbed, so ceased immediately, and survived. It was determined that the poison was in the dates, and six residents of the palace had access to those dates in the prior day. These are therefore the six suspects. One of them is the guilty party, and will be proffered to the Minotaur for whatever pleasure the bullheaded brute cares to take before it consumes the person. It should be an excellent show, as the Minotaur has been restless lately, tossing his horns about. That is to say, horny. Three suspects will be with each player, and each player will make the case against one or more of the suspects of the other player. The victor will be the one who succeeds in condemning an opposing suspect. Choose your suspects."

A curtain lifted on a stage that had not been evident before. On it stood an assortment of humanoid robots garbed in the costumes of the time: men with belts and codpieces, otherwise naked, and women with multitiered skirts and breast-baring boleros. Older men wore robes over their briefs, and older women shawls that were allowed to cover their open bodices. All were barefooted. Behind them, a great fresco showed a young man and a young woman engaged in the dangerous sport of bull-leaping, a prominent activity of the day. At the borders were pictures of ornate double axes, religiously significant.

Citizen Purple looked at the prospects. "Take first choice, sir," he suggested to the Hectare. "I will settle for first move."

The Hectare moved to the stage. Its tentacles extended and took hold of a lovely damsel whose skirt layers alternated colors: red, blue, white, and tan. Her black hair was bound with chains and beads, combs, and a band above the forehead. One lock passed before the ear to dangle down the side of her face. The Hectare lifted her high and carried her to the center of the set. "So BEMs *do* lust after femmes," Tsetse murmured. "I don't care to watch this." She backed away, and in a moment was out the door. No one challenged her; if anyone other than Brown noticed her departure, that person didn't care.

The girl-figure came alive. "Put me down, you monster!" she exclaimed, kicking her feet. She spoke in contemporary Proton dialect, not the ancient Cretan language; the Game Computer could go only so far.

The Hectare put her down. If it felt any affront, it did not show it. Brown realized that the creature was alien to human culture, and did not understand human ways or reactions, and probably would not have cared had it grasped them.

Purple glanced at Brown. "What for me?"

"Chances should be even if you match with a similar suspect," Brown said. "That may be safest, until we know the Hectare's strategy."

"Umph," he agreed, gazing intently at the young women. He had always had extreme interest in the female human form, Brown remembered; his activities in that respect were notorious. He might want to choose three young women, even though he knew they were only robots. Robots could perform almost any task as well as living folk, and all he cared about was the form and the obedience.

Purple made his selection: a woman whose skirt bands alternated gold with blue, and whose bare breasts were especially robust; they fairly burst out of her bolero. Her hair was styled like that of the first woman, with her dark front tresses trailing down beside her bosom. She wore three separate necklaces of differing sizes, so that one fit close about the column of her neck, a second hung lower, and the third dangled across the upper curvature of her breasts and down between them. "You, cutie."

The figure animated, and stepped down from the stage, now exactly resembling a living woman. She came to stand near Purple, expectantly.

The Hectare chose a young man. He looked athletic, perhaps being one of the bull-leapers, but his waist was so slender, and cinched yet more narrowly by the belt, that from behind he could have been mistaken for a woman. He wore a pointed cap, but no beads in his hair, which trailed almost to his waist, with a single strand behind each ear.

"Match him?" Purple inquired. He seemed determined to have Brown's input at every stage, so that if he lost the game, she could not avoid implication.

But Brown was beginning to work out a possible plot for this play. "No. Choose parents for the girl."

Purple shrugged, and chose a stout older man that vaguely resembled himself.

The Hectare chose a second young man. Now its cast consisted of three youths, two male and one female.

Purple selected an older woman who, Brown realized with dismay, could be likened to herself, if allowance was made for the different costume and hair style. Her breasts made the mandatory appearance, but were modest, and the shawl was a blessing. She had an apron hanging from her waist that overlaid several of the tiers of the skirt, which reached all the way to the floor.

Now Purple's complement consisted of the elder couple and the young woman.

"You will have five minutes to consult with your seconds privately and establish your strategies," the Game Computer said. "Then Citizen Purple will make the first statement: why he believes one of the Hectare's players is guilty of attempting to poison the king. I will serve as referee, but a selected audience who does not know the identities of the players will make the decision as to the victory."

They withdrew to separate private chambers for their strategy consultations. Their chamber was in keeping with the set: it resembled the architecture of ancient Crete, with a stone floor and a flower mural on the walls. The Game Computer must have been working on this set for some time, crafting every aspect of the illusion, and had drawn on it when opportunity offered. The onset of magic in Proton had evidently brought creativity to the computer. But Brown couldn't help responding to the setting; she found herself longing for that culture, four thousand years before, on the distant planet of Earth. She felt the nostalgia of the loss of those artistic folk, perhaps foreshadowing the loss of her contemporary culture. Had the barbarian Greeks overrun Crete and exploited its resources and made of it a secondary or tertiary power—as the barbarian Hectare were about to do with Phaze? Perhaps, but they had been assisted by a volcano, whose horrendous detonation had smashed apart the lovely palaces and buried them in ash. Phaze lacked that excuse.

"Now what are you thinking of, woman, with your family group?" Purple demanded.

Brown was jolted back to the unpleasant reality: she was helping a man she detested to save his hide. She had to succeed, or she would pay a price that horrified her. "A family group would be unlikely to seek harm to the king," she said. "These must be nobles of the palace, favored by the king, and their lovely highborn daughter can be a prospective match for one of the king's sons. They would want the king to prosper, and his son after him."

Purple nodded. "But the Hectare will make the case that the no-bleman wanted to take over the throne himself, bypassing the mid-dleman."

"Yes, that's an obvious target. So we must prepare a defense, while working out an offense of more devious nature, that may catch the Hectare by surprise and lead to its disadvantage. Your devious mind should be able to craft such an attack. Let me work out the family defense, while you work out the attack."

"My devious mind," he said. "I would take that as a compliment, if I didn't know you."

"I agreed to help you," she retorted. "I never agreed to like you."

"And you will do the one, and not the other," he agreed. "I would rather have an honest enemy in my camp than a dishonest friend. This is why I chose you, apart from your propinquity."

She nodded. Purple was awful in every way except cunning. Cer-tainly she was more to be trusted than his ally Tan. His choice of her for his second made sense despite her lack of experience with the game. He had had to make a decision quickly, and it would have taken precious time to run down someone else, while she had been right there. Nepe must have figured on that. Still, Nepe was a nervy player herself.

She gazed at the wall and pondered the play-family situation. Fa-ther, mother, daughter, father accused of poisoning the king in order to assume the throne. By the rules of this contest, she was sure, any statement made by a player had to be taken at face value; if the Hectare said the father was next in line for the throne, then it would be so, and they would have to find a way to nullify that motive without denying the connection. They could do that at the outset, as Purple had the first statement, but that would be purely defensive. If they said that the father was unrelated, merely a good friend of the king's, who had no motive to do him harm, the Hectare might merely modify the charge: the father was doing it *because* he had no personal ambition, and would be unsuspected; he had a secret reason to pro-mote a third party, who had promised him a much better position. That would be hard to refute, and the effort would keep them on the defensive, a bad position to be in. So the answer must be in the attack: keep the heat on the other side, so that it could not attack the father.

She was discovering that her mind was attuning nicely to this challenge, despite her lack of experience. Perhaps it was the fascination of the setting, whose appeal made her truly want to participate.

"Time," the Game Computer announced.

"Go for the attack!" Brown said hurriedly. "Never let up! I'm not sure of our defense."

"My own conclusion," he said.

They passed through the decorated stone door and reentered the main chamber. The Hectare and Citizen Tan emerged from an opposite chamber.

Now it occurred to Brown that the layout of the palace could be significant; a person could establish an alibi by showing that he was nowhere near the kitchen at the time the dates were poisoned. No, the suspects had already been determined, so must have had access. Still, the complicated network of the palace might figure in some other way; she would keep that in mind.

"We are gathered here in the South Anteroom to determine the truth," the Game Computer said. "The scenes will be reenacted as described. Players will take turns addressing particular actors. Citizen Purple will make the opening statement."

"I address the maiden in the multicolored dress," Purple said. As he spoke, that one animated, looking at him. "She is the sister of that young man." He pointed to the narrow-waisted man Brown thought of as the bull-leaper. "She is in love with her brother's friend, there." He indicated the other young man. The young woman walked to the young man and embraced him, dramatizing their love. They made a pretty couple. "She wanted to marry him, but the king wanted her for a concubine." The couple broke, and the woman gazed with evident dismay offstage, where presumably the king was beckoning. "So, in order to protect his sister, the brother tried to poison—"

"Objection!" Tan cried. "He is charging an unaddressed player."

"Sustained," the Game Computer said. "Statement must be limited to the addressed player."

Purple scowled, and Brown, sharing his situation, understood. The rule should have been clarified beforehand. "Still, you can establish the motive by implication," she murmured.

Purple nodded. "Correction: the young woman knew that the king desired her for a concubine, and that this would ruin her chance to marry her beloved, so she pleaded with her brother to do something to ease her case." The young woman approached the man designated

as her brother, and gestured animatedly as she faced him: her pleading. "She knew he would do whatever it took." She looked confident.

Brown considered it a good attack. The Hectare could hardly afford
to ignore it; even if a motive were established for some other player,
that brotherly love would be persuasive. It was also a good animation.
She knew that the setting was largely illusion, and that the characters
were robots, but everything looked real and alive, and it was easy to
suspend disbelief. The drama was coming alive for her.

The Hectare consulted briefly with his second, then made some
squeaks. "I address the brother," the translator said. The indicated
young man animated. "It is true that he loves his sister, but his loyalty
to his king is paramount. He would do anything to promote the welfare of his sister that does not conflict with his honor. So though she
begged him to help her, and he agreed, he stressed that no action
could be taken against the king. Instead, he would try to distract the
king by proffering another potential concubine, the daughter of respected palace nobles." A tentacle pointed, and Purple's young woman
animated: she was the one.

"Oops," Brown murmured, suddenly seeing what was coming.

"Tan's sharper than I thought," Purple muttered. "He saw me coming with the brother ploy."

"So he approached the other woman," the translation continued,
and the young man did just that with Purple's young woman. "He
suggested to her that the king found her interesting, but hesitated to
approach her because he did not wish to offend his friend the noble.
If, on the other hand, she were to approach the king, she might find
a warm reception, and excellent benefits from his favor. She, taken
by surprise, agreed to consider the matter. However, her father overheard, and—"

"Objection!" Brown called. "Neither the girl nor her father is being
addressed."

"Sustained," the Game Computer said.

"As the brother left the girl," the Hectare translation continued, "he
saw her father in an adjacent chamber, separated by only a hanging
rug, and realized that the man had been listening to their conversation. That made him nervous, for he knew the father to be a man
set in his ways, and there was no telling what he might do if he
thought his daughter was about to compromise herself with the king
and ruin her value on the marriage market."

Brown was worried. The Hectare, supposedly not comfortable with human conventions, was addressing them very well. That had to be Tan's input; he probably was serving the Hectare as loyally as Brown was serving Purple, lest his own hide suffer.

"This I can handle," Purple murmured. Brown was relieved, because her mind was blank on this one; she realized that she was not good at devious ploys. "I'll throw him a curve that will scotch this ploy."

Purple spoke to the stage. "I address the father." The man straightened up behind the rug. "What he overheard amazed him, but his reaction was not anger but gratification. He had felt subtly alienated from the king recently, and now understood why: the king was developing another kind of interest. But if his daughter were to attract the king's interest, the father would be right back in the king's favor. Since the daughter seemed to have no good prospects for marriage, this was an excellent alternative prospect. Meanwhile, this development provided him with a sinister private satisfaction. He was privy to certain secrets of the palace, and knew that the fiancé of the girl whose brother was trying to save her from the king was not the sterling character he seemed. He led a double life, and had had a mistress of lower class whom he had dearly loved—until the king had taken her as a passing concubine, and she had dumped him, the friend."

"Objection!" Tan said.

"I am not addressing any other character," Purple said. "I am merely describing the father's thoughts, which cover his knowledge of palace intrigues and affect his course of action."

"Overruled," the Game Computer said.

Purple smiled, and continued. "The father knew that the friend had of course been unable to protest, but nursed an abiding grudge against the king for that episode, though the king had been unaware of his interest in the girl. The friend's present engagement was a matter of expedience; his heart was not in it, though he said nothing to her brother about that. When the king's interest in his fiancée developed, the friend realized that the king might do him an unwitting favor to match the unwitting injury before, by breaking up a liaison he had concluded he did not desire. But now the king was about to ruin even that, if the brother's ploy was effective, and leave him stuck. He realized that it was pointless to allow events to take their own course;

if he was going to settle with the king for the prior injury, it had better be now." Purple smiled. "Such were the thoughts of the father. Of course he intended to protect the king against any such attack, and resolved to watch the young man closely."

Brown had to admit that Purple was a cunning character; he had figured out how to address two characters at the same time, defending his own and renewing the attack on his opponent's.

There was a pause while Tan and the Hectare consulted; this one had them in trouble. Then the Hectare squeaked. "I address the friend. So he considered killing the king, but naturally did not care to do it openly. Casting about for some subtle means, such as poisoning, he went to the storage region of the palace, where the king's special favorite dates were kept for him alone. But as he navigated the tortuous passages, he encountered another person: the girl's mother. He realized that though her father might approve a liaison between daughter and king, the mother would not. Indeed she would be so set against such dishonor that she might do virtually anything to prevent it. He realized that he did not need to do anything; the woman would do it for him. So he took another passage, and left her to go her way. It seemed that he could not lose: if the woman took out the king, his vengeance would be complete and he would be blameless. If she did not, the king would do him the favor of taking his fiancée off his hands."

It was Purple's turn again. "It's learning," he muttered with grudging respect. "It's going along with me, but diverting it. This may get complicated."

"But the mother won't have the nerve to kill anyone," Brown said.

"Sure enough." He faced the stage. "I address the mother. She did indeed have murder on her mind, to protect her daughter, but her encounter with the friend made her realize that she could hardly sneak in unobserved and poison the dates. Also, the closer she got to the storage room, the more appalling the notion of killing anyone became, especially the king, who was a good friend of her husband's. She simply couldn't do it. She would have to talk to her daughter, and persuade her not to do this thing, to save herself for some nice young man who was sure to come along eventually. So the mother set her vial of poison in a niche out of sight, and walked on by the storeroom, relieved that she had found a better way."

Purple took a breath. "However, it occurred to her in a moment that the vial wasn't safe there; a cleaning wench might find it, and ask awkward questions, and if they tested it on an animal they would soon know its nature. So she turned about and went to recover it, despite her nervousness about possibly getting caught with it. But to her surprise and dismay she discovered it gone. It had been only a few minutes, and there was no one else in the passage. She realized that only one person could have taken it: the young man she had encountered and walked with briefly. He must have watched her, and then gone to recover the vial the moment she was gone. Was he going to use it himself?"

Purple had turned it back on the Hectare. The mother was innocent, but the friend still had motive and opportunity—and poison now. The finale was approaching, and Purple's situation was good.

But Tan had evidently been pondering ploys, and came up with a good one for the Hectare. "I address the daughter," the Hectare squeaked. The daughter turned to face him, her proud breasts prominent above her tiny waist, the sparkle of her necklaces calling attention to her frontal assets. Her skirt bands matched the color of her jewelry, providing her an artistic unity that further enhanced her sex appeal. Even her bare toes showing beneath her skirt contributed, suggesting that her legs were similarly innocent of covering all the way up under the skirt. Brown found herself desiring the girl, despite everything; the humanoid robot had come alive in the play, and become for her the highborn daughter of a Cretan noble. Such a girl could readily be loved.

"This young woman has been misunderstood by all," the translator continued. "The brother thought to persuade her to attract the notice of the king, and she seemed to be interested. Her father was glad for that prospect, while her mother was horrified. But in truth she had no intention of indulging with the king—or any man."

Brown felt a chill of apprehension. Purple would keep her secret as long as she supported him, but she had to deal with Tan, who surely also knew her secret. Was he going to throw in lesbianism to mess her up, so that the Hectare could gain the advantage over Purple? If she lost her concentration now, the play might be done before she could regain it. She tried to steel herself.

"For you see she distrusted men. It seemed to her that they inevitably took unfair advantage of women, and the king was the worst of all, because he had most power. Now her friend's brother wanted her to distract the king, so that his sister could remain with her fiancé. But that fiancé was false, having secret affairs and no real respect for the woman he was to marry. If she were to distract the king, the fiancé would find another way to get rid of the fiancée. And her own father, instead of protesting the prospect of her liaison with the king, was in favor of it, because it would lend him additional status. Thus all the men were hopelessly corrupt. Only her mother supported her." As the translator spoke, the named players animated and posed, the three men looking villainous, the mother looking noble.

But maybe he was going another route, Brown thought. Distrust of men was not the same as love of women. Brown herself did not hate men; she had great affection and respect for a number, beginning with the Adept Stile. She just didn't care to have sex with them, any more than the men would care to have it with each other.

"So she, realizing that her mother lacked the gumption to do the job, and not trusting any man to do it, realized that she would probably have to do it herself. She hated the king and wanted him dead, because of his power over women and the possibility of his deciding to take her as a lover. Now was the time to kill him, because she had seen her friend's fiancé go to the storerooms, and take the poison—"

"Objection!" Brown cried. "It has been established that only two people were in those halls at the time. There is no way a third could have been there."

"Sustained," the Game Computer said.

"She had seen him go there, and saw her mother emerge without the poison, so she knew he had taken it."

"Objection! She couldn't know that. He might have—"

"Sustained. A third sustained objection will terminate the turn."

"Why are you objecting?" Purple inquired quietly. "The Hectare is framing his own character."

"I don't trust that," she said. "Whatever he's doing, I want to stop it."

Purple shrugged. "Paranoia is good, in such a contest."

Brown felt pleased, then condemned herself for it. She didn't want Purple's favor! She just had to win this game for him, and go her own way.

"She knew he *could* have taken it," the Hectare said through the translator, after a pause for consultation. If it was annoyed, it didn't show it. "Later she went herself to check, and found no poison, so she believed he had taken it. He was in a position to poison the dates."

Now even Purple was perplexed. "The Hectare *can't* be throwing the game! They play to win, always."

"That meant that he could be framed," the Hectare continued. Suddenly Brown appreciated the point: the buildup of the seeming guilt of a character determined to be innocent. Ouch! "So she could steal the poison from him, use it on the dates, and accuse him of the crime. In this manner she could get away with murdering the king, and another bad man would pay the penalty. It would be a double victory."

"Brother," Purple muttered. "This will be hard to refute. It's him or her, and we don't have room to show much more about him." For the first time he looked uncomfortable; in fact downright nervous. Brown would have enjoyed the sight, if her own situation had not been on the line too.

She appreciated the problem. How could they explain away that motive, or put the young man into a situation that would make it obvious he was the guilty one? Any new wrinkle they might try could be turned around as another ploy in the frame: he looked guilty but wasn't. The Hectare was playing with increasing competence and finesse, catching on rapidly to the nuances of the human condition.

They needed to get the girl out of the palace, far away at the critical time. But they couldn't, because she was one of the suspects; she *had* had opportunity to place the poison. Now she had motive, too; they could not undo that. At this stage, the jury was likely to rule against the girl. They couldn't even give her an alibi, such as a love tryst at the critical time with her brother, because Tan and the Hectare had cleverly shut off that option by making her distrust men.

Then Brown saw the answer. It was painful for her, but it would do the job. "She was with her girlfriend at the time," she said. "You know how to play it."

Purple looked at her. "We made a deal. I need your golems on my side. They won't be, if I break that deal."

"There won't be any deal, if you lose your hand," she pointed out, amazed to hear herself arguing this case.

He nodded. "Play now, talk later. Maybe it will work."

"Nothing else will," she said.

He faced the stage. "I address the daughter," he said, and the actress faced him, as lovely as before. "She had motive to kill the king, and to frame her friend's fiancé, getting rid of two bad men. She had intent. She had the courage to do it. But something happened at the critical time." He paused for effect, and the play paused with him.

"As it has been established, she was a most attractive figure of a woman, but she had a grudge against men. That did not mean that she had no romantic life. She cared very much about her gender. So she went to her friend, and told her of the perfidy of men, especially what she knew about both the king and the fiancé. Her friend was not really surprised; she had tried to blind herself to the infidelities of her fiancé, but had known he was no good. She had no better opinion of the king. The two women agreed that no man was to be trusted. Their dialogue became more animated and intimate, as they discovered in each other a deep current of compatibility. This became physical, and in the end they loved each other. Because this was their first such experience, it was slow, with many hesitations. As a result, their encounter lasted several hours—the very time that the poisoning of the dates occurred."

"Objection!" Tan cried. "The exact time can not be specified. Any of the suspects could have done it."

"Sustained."

"The time the poisoning was believed to have occurred," Purple said. "The reason the two women did not perfectly alibi each other was that they did not want to admit openly what they had been doing. So they allowed themselves to be considered suspects. But it seems likely that they had no care for poisoning, on that night."

"But women don't—" Tan said. Then he looked at Brown, and knew that his Hectare's case was lost. The only truly viable remaining suspect was the fiancé.

The Hectare spoke, through the translator. "I yield the contest. No fault of my second." Then it departed.

Tan stared at Brown, scowling. Then he shrugged, realizing that it was better to leave well enough alone. The Hectare knew that Tan had tried his best, but their team had been outplayed. He would suffer no consequence if he kept his mouth shut. He followed the Hectare out.

Brown felt weak with relief. Tan wasn't going to blow the whistle on her! He knew that there was nothing to be gained by it, as she was already cooperating, however reluctantly.

"Well, you came through," Purple said. "I'm off the hook, and so are you. I don't think we need that talk. I'll take you back to your hideout now."

Brown looked around. "But Tsetse—she got bored and went out. I can't leave her here."

Purple was magnanimous in the flush of victory. "She'll be at the commons, relaxing. I'll authorize passes out for you and her, and you can have a golem carry you back when you find her." He raised his voice, addressing the command net. "By order of Purple: release Brown and Tsetse on their request, this day." Then to her. "Okay?"

She nodded. "Thank you."

"I don't like you, you don't like me. But you treated us fairly when you were on top, and I'm treating you fairly now. Just you honor our deal, and maybe we'll never meet again."

She nodded again. He left the room, which had reverted to the contemporary type.

"It was a very nice set," she said aloud.

"Thank you," the Game Computer replied.

"I wish this were Crete."

"So do I."

She left the chamber, wondering about that. The Game Computer was acting more and more like a living thing. It was of course a self-willed machine, but highly programmed; self-will did not mean freedom. Did it now have consciousness and personal desire? What was it trying to do, with its subversion of the normal game grid that had served so well for so long? She hesitated to guess.

She walked to the commons, looking for Tsetse. She had hoped the figure would be back by the time the game concluded, and had been relieved when Purple had not concerned himself with the matter. Now she just wanted to find the figure and get it home before the real Tsetse returned. If she did not, they could all be in a great deal of trouble. If Purple caught on that she had used him to gain admittance for an enemy of the Hectare . . .

10

Seed

Lysander had suffered a whirlwind change of situation, at the time of the invasion and again when he had fled the city with Echo, the cyborg woman whose other self was a harpy. He had quit Alyc when she turned out to be a Hectare agent, and gone with Jod'e, until the Tan Adept had used his Evil Eye to make her his love slave. Lysander was a Hectare agent himself, but his necessary association with the natives enabled him to relate to their concerns. Alyc's identity as an agent had been a distressing surprise, and he had reacted as any loyal native would, dumping her. Jod'e's conversion had been an uglier shock; he had really come to appreciate her qualities, physical and intellectual, in their brief association. But Echo—

Echo was beautiful, with her slender body and brown fluff of hair. But her body was of inanimate substance; only her brain was human. Alyc had been full human, and Jod'e android, so Echo seemed to be one more step away. But on this planet few things were quite what they seemed, and he found he could accept the emulation of life Echo represented, knowing that her loyalty to the old order was absolute. Alyc had been fully alive in body, but a traitor in mind; Echo was true in mind. He had less interest in her harpy form, except that that was the root of her loyalty to Phaze.

She had taken him to a serf boy walking the halls. "Who is this?" he had demanded.

"Who do you think, unbeliever?" the boy had responded. Then Lysander had known it was the weird child Nepe/Flach.

Three serfs walking ahead of them had assumed the likenesses of

Lysander, Echo, and the boy, for the hall monitors to track. Lysander had ducked into a side passage with Echo, and abruptly had found himself standing here under the trees where he had first encountered the harpy Oche, and handled Echo's legs.

"We're out of the city!" he exclaimed, amazed.

"Yes, the Unicorn Adept conjured us free," she said.

"Where do we go from here?"

"Nowhere."

"But I hardly know how to forage, and I have no place to sleep. I can't be much use to anyone, here!"

The harpy appeared, perched on a low branch. "Willst share my nest w' me?" she screeched.

Lysander tried to mask his dismay. "No affront to you, but I'm not sure I care for the elevation, even if my weight doesn't tear your nest out of the tree."

Echo reappeared, her nakedness glorious in comparison. One hand was on the branch, and he realized that she had made a smooth translation because she had contact with it, and could guide herself during the change. "I also have a nether bower you may find more comfortable."

"I'm sure I would," he agreed quickly.

She put her hand to the trunk of the tree, and pulled on the bark. The bark swung out, becoming a panel or door. Now there was a hole in the tree, just about big enough for a man to crawl through. "After you, then," she said, gesturing to it.

"But that's just a cavity!" he protested. "There can't possibly be room inside it for me! The trunk is only a meter thick."

She merely waited, her gesture in place.

Lysander shrugged. He walked to the opening, and discovered that it was the entrance to a chute leading down. Oh. He lifted a leg and put a foot in, then worked the rest of his body through, until only his head was outside. His feet now dangled in the darkness; he had no idea how deep the hole was.

"Drop," Echo said. "You will not be hurt."

Could this be some trap to put him away? But why would they bother to transport him here for that? He had to trust them, because he wanted to achieve their trust. Only when he had it could he learn the most secret details of their plan for resistance—and betray it.

He let go. He fell down—and landed in a moment in a bed of feathers. There was a sliver of light from above, that soon shut off.

Echo was coming down after him. Hastily he rolled to the side so she wouldn't land on top of him.

He was not quite fast enough. She whomped down beside him, knocking him flat in the darkness.

"Well, now," she said. "This is the way I like my men: laid out." She wrapped her arms around him and squeezed close.

"But we've only met!" he said.

"We met months ago. Now hang on while I take your measure."

"Measure?"

"I need to ascertain whether you are truly with us," she said. "Jod'e was supposed to do that, but Tan took her out. I doubt you're ready to love me on such short notice, but we only have a few days, so it will have to be the crash course."

"I don't think I understand."

"The prophecy says—"

"Oh, that! But how can you be sure that refers to me?"

"We can't. But if it does, we want you with us. We think you will be more likely to be with us if you love one of us. That's why Jod'e had to take you from that spy."

"You know about that?"

"The Adepts did. So they sent Jod'e to—"

"She did! But then Tan—"

"Yes. That really messed us up. They had to scratch at the last moment for another girl, and so I was recruited, because at least we'd met before. I don't know anything about the plan to free Phaze, except that you may be vital to it, so I must bind you to it. That I shall do."

"Now, wait! Do you think you can just pass me from woman to woman, and I'll love any I'm near?"

"Yes. Now kiss me."

It seemed she wasn't joking. "Forget it! I liked Alyc, until I learned what she was. I was getting to like Jod'e a lot; if I had any time to reflect, I'd be grieving for her. But you—you're a harpy!"

"And a cyborg. A nice match for your android body with a living brain. You know as well as I do that it is the mind that determines the person. I can make this body do anything your body desires; you won't care that the body isn't alive. So we'll get started."

"We shall *not* get—"

But she cut him off with her kiss. She was expert, and her body was warm and sleek and pulsing with the seemingness of vitality. Indeed it was easy to ignore the mechanics of it; in the dark she was all woman.

Then there was light, expanding from what looked like balls of cotton set against the walls. He saw her—and she was still all woman.

"Look," he said as the kiss broke. "I did like Jod'e. I know that's over. Tan raped her emotion and made her his. But I knew her before that, and I grieve for her loss. I would have stayed with her, perhaps married her in time; we related well. But this business of simply assuming that any woman can take me just by being assigned—doesn't that turn the stomach of even a harpy, a little? Didn't you have other plans for your life, before Jod'e got taken out? How can you go along with this nonsense?"

She gazed at him, her eyes spots of midnight. "Actually, I did like you, Lysander. I enjoyed flirting with you, though I never expected anything to come of it. I was between males. But that's not the point. Our world is at stake, and any personal plans I might have had are vacant. I must love you, and you me, and hope that you are the one who will save Phaze."

"Just like that," he said with irony. "Phaze needs me, so you and I must fall in love. Then I'll decide in favor of your planet, because I'll want to stay with you the rest of my life, even though you are made of plastic."

"You've got it. Meanwhile, we might as well enjoy ourselves. Let's kiss and talk for a while, before we start on the sex."

"I am at a loss to comprehend why you think any of this will occur. I may be of alien origin, but everything I've learned of your culture indicates that this isn't the way love normally occurs."

"There are three reasons. Are you sure you want them recited?"

"Yes." He was intrigued. If he had to pretend to love her in order to get close to the source of the resistance, he would do that. But the role he was playing required that he offer natural resistance to such bread-and-butter romance.

"First, your body is handsome and virile and responds normally to stimuli. I am in this form an attractive woman, similarly responsive. Propinquity will normally cause us to merge, in the absence of counterindications."

'Granted. But there *are* counter—"

"Second, this chamber is sealed. For the next several days, I will be your only companion, and I will be most attentive and obliging to your interests. You will find me very good company indeed—and I trust I will find you the same. Only when the love is firm will we be released."

"So it *is* a trap!"

"A love trap," she agreed. "But a willing one, for me, and I think not just because I love my planet."

She evidently believed in this! "And the third reason?"

"This chamber is suffused with love elixir. It will take perhaps three days to be completely effective, and we have that amount of time available, perhaps more."

"You really think that—" But he broke off, remembering how Tan had changed Jod'e. Magic was operative here, and surely their love potions were effective, though slower than Adept enchantment.

"So you see, we may try to resist it, or we can go along with it. The outcome will be the same, but it will be more pleasant to go along."

"Suppose I just break out now, before any of this can take effect?"

"I hope you don't do that!" she said, alarmed.

"Why not? I prefer to make my own choice whom I may love." This, again, was consistent with his established personality.

"Because if you emerge without me, my sister harpies will tear you apart. Literally. They are guarding this retreat. Please accept my word, they are mean customers, and fully capable of the act. Even if your android body is resistant to the poison of their claws, it can not withstand their massed attack. They intend to keep you in here for the full three days, and to prevent any possible rescue. Since no one else knows where you are—"

"Point made. I think I'm stuck for it."

She sat up. "I can understand your anger, Lysander. But it will pass. I just thought that since our love is inevitable, and thereafter we may be separated, it would be nice to make the most of it in this time we have. It would be a shame to squander the interim by quarreling."

He had one more objection. "But you are a cyborg! The love potion should not affect you."

"I am also a harpy, and my brain is living. The potion will affect

PHAZE DOUBT | 177

these. It is not purely chemical; it is a magical ambience that can affect even a metal robot. Indeed, I am already feeling it; that is why I am pleading for détente between us."

Lysander shrugged. "Whether I will love you I can't say. But your arguments are persuasive. I want to save your planet too; I just didn't care to be cynically coerced into it." That was a half-truth, but it would do. "My anger is fading; let's give love a try." That was true; it seemed that the potion was already having its effect.

"I'm glad." She leaned into him and kissed him. "We are not always free to choose our destinies or our emotions. I think we can make a good couple, and perhaps save the planet. Then neither of us will be sorry that it wasn't natural."

"But how can you be sure I don't just tell you I love you, so that you won't sick the harpies on me?"

"Unless you are immune to magic, there is no chance of that. Jod'e would have brought you to a similar chamber."

"Jod'e would not have needed to."

"When the fate of our world is at stake, the Adepts do not gamble. They chose her for you, and when she was lost, they chose me. I am not as good a choice, but will have to do; there was no one else convenient. Of course Jod'e will betray you to the Hectare, and they will know about the prophecy and the love, and probably that it is me you love. But we shall try to keep you out of their tentacles, until the prophecy is fulfilled." She paused, gazing at him. "Now you may have the pleasure of using a woman you do not yet love, if you wish, or you may wait until you do. I am amenable to your preference. I have told you all that I know about this matter."

She was certainly being candid! "What is your own preference?"

"Oh, I was hot for you when I first met you. Harpies are lusty creatures, being chronically male-starved. I loved it when you handled my legs! But you seemed destined for other things, so I resigned myself. I'd like to discover how many times and in how many ways it can be done in three days, with one man."

"One man?"

"The limitation is male. If I had ten men here—"

"Oh." He considered. He appreciated both her candor and her cynicism; it relieved him of confusion and conscience. He remembered how feminine even the complete robot Sheen had seemed; Echo was interesting despite what he knew of her. "Then let's find out."

She addressed him with a hunger that seemed even more intense than what Alyc had shown, and in a moment they were in the throes of sex, and in another moment beyond them. Her harpy aspect must indeed be hungry for male interaction! She was evidently ready to continue, but his interest faded, so they talked instead. Her attentions to him continued during the dialogue, restoring his interest more rapidly than would otherwise have been the case.

They continued with both sex and history, in stages and bouts and alternations and mixtures, and time passed both rapidly and slowly, simultaneously. It hardly mattered what Echo said; Lysander was increasingly interested merely in listening to her, and in having her listen to him. Their sexmaking became lovemaking, the passion less, the satisfaction more. Being with her was sheer pleasure, of a sort he had not experienced before.

"It is true," he said at last. "I have not loved before, but I do love you."

"And I love you," she said. "It is magical in origin, but I think I could have loved you anyway, had you had any natural interest in me. Soon we can emerge, but let's not hurry."

Lysander was enjoying himself, but something was bothering him increasingly. He did not want there to be a lie between the two of them. He wanted their love to be perfect, and feared it could not be.

"There is something I must tell you," he said.

"That you now believe in love potions? I know it, Lysander."

"That I love you too much to deceive you," he said grimly. "I must tell you the truth, though it destroy your love for me."

"Too late for that. Three days have passed, and I am lost. You can only hurt me, you can not destroy my love."

The gravity of his situation suddenly tormented him. "I can lie to you only if you ask me to. I would prefer to do that, so as not to hurt you."

She gazed at him with understanding. "There really is something bad," she said.

"There really is. Please, tell me to lie. It will spare us both pain."

"Does it affect our mission to save our world?"

"Yes."

"Then you must tell me. Maybe the Adepts had this in mind."

"Maybe they did," he agreed, realizing that if the Adepts had known about Alyc, they might have learned about him too. In that case, it would be pointless to conceal his mission longer. It would be better to come out into the open. Maybe the love potion was distorting his judgment, but it did seem to make sense. "But can we wait a little? Love is new to me, and I want to savor it before it is dashed."

"No, you had better tell me now. I was never one to postpone either the best or the worst."

"I am an agent of the Hectare."

She shook her head. "But if you were, why would you tell me? If I said one word to my sister harpies . . . " She trailed off, her thought evidently bothering her.

"I did not tell you, or anyone else, not even the local Hectare administrators, because it is essential that no one be able to betray my mission. It is my assignment to infiltrate to the heart of the resistance, and then destroy it, so that there is no further threat to Hectare dominance. No coercion could have made me tell. But now I have to tell you, because our love can not be true if what you know of me is false. I am not just an android with a borrowed living brain. I am an android with a Hectare brain."

She stared. "How can it help your mission to reveal this to me?"

"It can not. Now, if you will, assume your harpy form and kill me. I will not resist you."

"Your love makes you do this?"

"Yes." He smiled briefly. "I see now that the Hectare, having no direct knowledge of love, did not condition me against it. But I *am* a Hectare, a bug-eyed monster, in human form. Kill me now, because if you do not, you are unlikely to do it later."

"I love a Hectare?" she asked, dumbfounded.

"You love the form of a human being. I knew you for what you were when love took me; you knew only a lie about me. You are not bound. Do your planet the most good you can. Kill me."

"But if you love me, won't you join my side? Maybe that's what the Adepts want."

"If you love me, will you join the Hectare?"

"I can't do that!" she protested. "My world is my nature! All that I am, even the metal and plastic—I can not be untrue to that!"

"You have answered yourself," he pointed out. "I am Hectare. I must serve my species."

"If I do not kill you, you will betray our last source of resistance to the enemy?"

"Yes. That is my mission."

"You can't want to do that! You would not have told me, if—"

"I don't *want* to do it, any more than you want to love your home world. It is in my nature to do it. Can you love me, knowing my nature and my mission?"

"If I see you about to betray my world, I will try to stop you," she said.

"Is that an answer?"

"I do love you, despite what you have told me. I will not tell anyone, I will only try to stop you, and die if I fail."

"You have no call to keep my secret. You should at least tell the Adepts."

"I think they know. It makes it certain that you are the one the prophecy means. So I must believe that I am helping my world by keeping silent."

Lysander found himself both surprised and unsurprised. If the Adepts truly believed the prophecy, then he could indeed be the one—*because* of what he was. Yet it had to require a great deal of faith on her part to trust in that. "Now we know we are enemies, or that we serve opposite sides. Can we still love each other?"

She stood, gesturing him to do the same, and took his hands in hers. "I will answer, and so will you, together. Then we will know."

"But—"

"Speak only your true feeling, as I speak mine. Are you ready?"

He nodded, not sure what she thought this was going to accomplish.

She squeezed his hands. "When I squeeze again, we'll speak."

Then she squeezed. "Yes," they said together.

Something strange happened then. A ripple seemed to go out from them, causing the air to shimmer, and the walls of the cave. It was as if the color of reality shifted, though color wasn't quite it. But he didn't care. He drew her into him and embraced her. He didn't care how it had come about; his love for her was real and complete.

She melted into him, as passionate as he. "So it is true," she breathed in his ear.

"I don't understand."

"You saw the splash?"

"Do you mean the ripple in the air?"

"That was the splash of truth. It comes only when the emotion is true and strong, and only once for a situation. We spoke our love, and it is true, though we are in Proton form. Phaze is here too, and it manifests. I love you and you love me; there is no doubt."

He found he had to believe. "Then stay with me, and when I do what I have to do, you do what you have to do."

"Yes. But until then, let it be only love between us."

He was satisfied with that.

It seemed a moment later that there was a scratching at the entrance, above. "They are opening the door," Echo said. "I must see what they want."

Lysander looked at his watch. "Five days have passed," he said, startled. "It must be time for us to come out."

She used the root-handholds to hoist herself up. He followed. Soon they were beside the tree. A harpy with a horrendous explosion of hair and feathers about her head hovered near. "Take thy paramour to the Brown Demesnes," she screeched. "The Unicorn Adept has need o' him."

"Thank you, Phoebe," Echo said.

"Ne'er thank a harpy, slut!" the creature screeched. But Lysander had the impression she was pleased.

"We'll dress and start walking. I suppose you know how it stands between us now."

"Aye, Oche! We spied the splash. Then we dispersed our guard."

"I thought you would. Warn us if dragons come."

"Aye!" The harpy flapped heavily away.

"Who was that?" Lysander asked.

"The chief hen of our Flock, Phoebe. She befriended the Robot Adept long ago, before I was hatched. She speaks for him."

"Then we'd better go to the Brown Demesnes! I hope you know the way."

"I do. It will be a fair walk, but we'll be helped if we need it." She climbed back into the tree and disappeared, going for the clothes.

Soon they were on their way, garbed in belted robes and sandals. The jungle looked wild, but Echo knew the paths. When on occasion she was uncertain, she changed to harpy form and flew high, spying out the way. The first time he had seen her in that form he had thought her ugly; now it didn't bother him, though he preferred her cyborg form. During the whole five days of their time in the love nest, he had hardly remembered that her body was inanimate; it had seemed completely alive. That love potion had been strong stuff!

They passed an open range. On the horizon he could see animals grazing: unicorns, surely. Once a huge shape appeared in the sky; Echo drew him quickly under cover. "Dragon," she explained. "We'll be protected, but we don't want to cause a commotion."

He was in good physical condition, but Echo was indefatigable. That was the advantage of a robot body. By the day's end he was glad to rest.

She opened a breast cabinet and brought out food for him. She was able to eat, but didn't bother. There was no shelter here, and the chill of the night was settling in, but this turned out to be no problem. They simply removed their robes, spread them as blankets on the ground, and lay between them. Echo's body turned warm, like a gentle stove, and drove away the chill.

"I am coming to appreciate your qualities," he murmured, caressing her.

"Had we had more time, we could have done this before the love," she said. "But better in reverse order than not at all." Then she embraced him. "However, now that I mention love—"

He tried to remind himself that her body was inanimate, but it was no good. She was all the way alive for him. Evidently he was all the way human for her, similarly. Their knowledge of each other changed nothing.

He was sorry he would have to betray this wonderful dual culture. But he knew he would do it, when the occasion came.

Next day, as they continued their walk toward the southeast, a figure abruptly appeared before them. It was Flach, the Unicorn Adept. "I need him now," he said to Echo. "I thank thee, Echo, for thy service."

"May I not remain with him?" she asked, alarmed.

The boy smiled. "It were unkind to deny thee, considering. Make thy way alone to the Brown Demesnes and watch; an thou see a woman emerge, take human form and go with her. We shall rejoin thee in due course."

"Thank you, Adept," she said. Then, quickly, she kissed Lysander. As the kiss ended, she became the harpy, and flew into the foliage of the nearest great tree.

The boy faced Lysander, and his small face was disturbingly serious. "Thou has fathomed that we know thy nature," he said. "We like thee not, Hectare, but there be none but thee to give us victory, an thou choose. An thou not cooperate completely with me, thou willst ne'er get close to our plot, so it behooves thee to make thy move not early."

So they had indeed known! "And if you nullify me early, your prophecy will be invalidated before it has a chance," he replied. "Even if you can't trust your love spell to change my mind."

"Aye. So we fathom each other. We work together, until the moment."

"Until the moment," Lysander agreed.

"Now will I conjure thee to the Brown Demesnes, and make thee invisible. Keep thy silence, whate'er thou dost see."

"Agreed." It was an interesting situation: he was an enemy agent, and they knew it, and he knew they knew, but it changed nothing. It was analogous in its way to his love with Echo: the facts simply did not affect the situation.

Flach took his hand. With his free hand he made an odd gesture. Then they stood in a wooden room. Manlike figures of all sizes stood against the walls, immobile. That was scarcely surprising, as all of them were fashioned of wood.

Flach squeezed his hand, and became the girl, Nepe. "We have a little while," she said. "Kiss me."

Remembering the boy's caution about silence, Lysander did not reply. But he obeyed the directive. He leaned down and kissed her on the mouth.

She kissed back, with surprising vigor, but hardly with the expertise Echo had. "Do I have it right?" she asked. "Squeeze my right for yes, left for no; I can't see you."

He glanced down at his feet, and saw only the floor. He was invisible, as promised. But what was her concern with kissing? He extended his right hand and squeezed her left upper arm.

"Try it again," she said. But her body was melting, and in a moment there was only a knob at the top with a pair of lips.

He shrugged and kissed those lips. This time they were more competent. He squeezed her right arm.

"Good," the mouth said, as the blob continued to change. "After I talk with Brown, I will form a sheath over your body, and it will cover your head. There will be holes for you to breathe and it will be transparent over your eyes, but if Purp tests with a kiss it better be right. Don't jump if he pinches your ass. Just do whatever you're told, and I will guide you with pressure on the side I want you to turn away from, or behind the legs to make you walk forward. You'll catch on. We'll both be hung if Purp catches on. Now stay clear and wait."

He did that, watching her change further, until she resembled a squat wheeled robot. What was she up to?

There was a light footstep beyond the wooden door. The seeming machine made a whirring noise. The person beyond paused, then fled.

Shortly, a brown-haired woman of about forty opened the door and entered. She glanced around, then walked straight to the Nepe-machine. "Why didst thou return?" she inquired.

"Mach said you did not betray me," Nepe replied, without the benefit of lips. "Though you did recognize me."

"Of course I did not betray you, you darling child!" the woman exclaimed. Obviously she knew with whom she was talking.

"But Purp will make you talk," the form that was Nepe said. "I know how."

Lysander saw by the woman's reaction that something significant had been said. Evidently the Brown Adept had some personal secret, and the child was playing on that. Lysander had come to appreciate how cleverly this seeming juvenile could play on a person's secrets! Maybe it was some embarrassment of the past, or an illicit deed; whatever it was, Purp—that would be the Purple Adept, he realized—had learned it too, and would blackmail the woman. Purple was working for the Hectare, but Lysander had no more respect for him than he did for Tan, because both were traitors to their societies. The Hectare would dispose of such quislings when their usefulness was done; the termination would come without warning or reprieve or regret. The Hectare would also dispose of diehard resistance figures. But some of the intermediate individuals, who had had the sense to yield without turning traitor, like Citizen Blue—these would be treated with greater respect, because they had ability and judgment and could be trusted.

From this odd dialogue Lysander learned that while he had been distracted by Echo, two more opposition Adepts had been captured, Black and Green. Only two remained, the Robot and the Unicorn. Did that mean that Clef and Tania had also been captured? The child did not mention them, which was surely significant.

Now it seemed Nepe was going to use Brown to get back at Purple in some devious way. Lysander was as mystified as Brown about this.

Apparently there was to be a game played between Purple and a Hectare, and Brown was to be there, along with her servant Tsetse. Except that it wouldn't really be Tsetse.

"As thou sayest, dear," Brown agreed, as baffled as Lysander.

Brown was told to hide Tsetse immediately, and make ready for Purple's visit. She left the room.

Immediately Nepe began changing form again. Her changes were not instant, the way her alternate's were, but they were impressive. The machine became a blob, then a pool that spread across the floor like a blanket. A mouth formed in its center. "Pick me up, drape me over you," it said. "Remove your clothes first."

Even if he hadn't had a mission to perform, Lysander would have cooperated just for the continuing adventure of it, he realized as he quickly removed his robe and sandals. They became visible as he set them aide, so he hid them behind a golem. The more he learned of the child Nepe/Flach, the more he appreciated how difficult she/he would be for the Hectare to capture. This was surely the chief figure of the resistance. Yet Nepe acted as if she were only a part of a much larger plot, and it was that plot Lysander had to discover.

He stooped and put his hands to the edges of the blanket. It felt like warm plastic. He lifted, and it came up as a cohesive unit, not disintegrating like jelly. He draped it over his bare shoulders, and it formed a cloak extending down to his waist.

Then the cloak animated, drawing itself close to his body. It wrapped itself about his torso, and extended down, thinning, forming a snug wetsuit. It reached his genital region and tightened about it. Oddly, his member did not react; instead it became numb. There seemed to be an anesthetic quality to Nepe's substance, so that wherever it touched him he felt comfortable and relaxed. That was fortunate, because otherwise the notion of being so completely enclosed by a female, even a juvenile one, could have caused an awkward reaction.

The material at his shoulder humped up and formed a hood. Then it closed over his face. He was able to breathe through his nose and his mouth, but his nostrils and lips were coated with the film of flesh. He felt activity at the top and back of his head, and realized that the cap over his hair was growing hair of its own, extending down to his shoulders. Nepe was transforming his appearance!

There was a squeeze on his right arm. He looked at it, and saw that it was now visible: smooth and white, with silver-tinted nails.

Then he remembered Nepe's instructions: she put pressure on the side from which she wanted him to turn, guiding him in the manner of a horse. He turned, then walked forward as he felt guiding pressure at his backside.

At the side of the chamber a mirror hung on the wall. He went to it and looked at his reflection—and was amazed.

Not only was he visible now—he looked exactly like a beautiful woman! His hair was silvery, his eyes an echoing gray, long-lashed and large. His chest was a bosom, with extremely full and well-formed breasts. His waist was high and small, his hips wide, his legs well fleshed. There was no trace of his penis or testicles; he now had the dainty cleft of maidenhood. He was the image of a creature who, in other circumstances, he would have been glad to embrace.

Except that he was man-sized. As a woman, he was an Amazon. That would make others take unwanted notice.

His flesh-covering quivered. Then the image in the mirror fuzzed and re-formed—smaller. Nepe had done magic of some sort, and made him smaller—no, made him *appear* smaller, for only his reflection had diminished. That meant he would have to avoid contact with others as much as possible, to preserve the illusion.

Nepe—magic? No, that wasn't the way it worked. She must have had a spell provided by Flach, maybe an amulet to be invoked. Amulets didn't have to be like gems or dolls; one could be as small as a single hair, carried in her substance.

His respect for the child increased another notch. She had evidently prepared well for this mission of hers. If she was only a part of a larger plan of resistance, that plan must be formidable!

She guided him back to his original place, and to his clothing. He put on robe and sandals—and as he did so, they changed appearance and became feminine. He realized that he could have masqueraded as a woman much more simply by having his clothing changed and stuffed, but for some reason Nepe wanted him authentic through to the buff.

He stood in the center of the chamber, before the door, and waited. In a few minutes there was the sound of someone approaching, and the door opened.

Brown stood there. She stared at him, evidently astonished. It was a sentiment he could appreciate.

"Thou needs must come—" she started, faltering as her eyes continued to travel over the apparition. Lysander realized that she had sent Tsetse away somewhere, so knew this was someone else, yet could not verify it by sight.

Now his lips felt pressure, and he knew it was time to speak. He said the most neutral thing he could think of, knowing that his voice would ruin the illusion. "Yes, of course, Brown. Whatever you say." And was astonished again, himself. The voice he heard was not his own, but that of a woman. The illusion changed the sound, too!

The Hectare had sadly misjudged the power of magic! Lysander had not even believed in it, when he arrived, and though the Hectare in charge had surely researched it, they could hardly have appreciated its nuances. For the first time, Lysander suffered a twinge of doubt about the certainty of continuing Hectare hegemony here. Magic was a game that could change the rules of any other game!

Brown recovered. "Something has come up. I am to be Purple's second in a game against a Hectare."

The lip pressure came again, so again he spoke the obvious. "A game against a Hectare! But don't they make natives—?" He broke it off deliberately, as he wasn't sure how much Tsetse would know.

"Aye. Needs must we help Purple win. Now come."

He followed her out of the chamber and out of the castle itself. A small airplane waited there, and Citizen Purple was there, in his purple robe. "You can keep your clothing, Brown," he said as they climbed in, "but she's a serf."

Now he understood why Nepe had taken the trouble to fashion a complete illusion. He wormed his way out of the robe and became the gloriously naked serf woman. Brown helped him, and he knew by her fleeting expression that when she touched his real flesh—rather, Nepe's coating of flesh over his—she felt his real size, and knew the nature of the illusion. But of course she would protect the secret. He knew only that Nepe had to get past the Hectare guard devices to fetch something, and that Brown was helping.

The clothing resumed its original appearance as he doffed it. He wadded it up into a ball and wedged it under the seat; he should be able to pick it up on his return. If not—well, Purple probably wouldn't pay attention to it anyway.

They flew to the city, then got a ride to a Citizen transport chamber. Citizen Purple paid no attention to Lysander; evidently he had been so completely fooled that he wasn't challenging anything he didn't have to. If he caught on, Nepe would be done for—and she knew she was depending on a Hectare agent for the success of her ruse. The child had phenomenal nerve!

Purple touched a button. One wall of the chamber became a video screen. It showed Purple himself challenging the particular Hectare he worked with to a game.

Hoo! As an act of foolhardiness, that could hardly be surpassed. But of course Purple hadn't done it; he had been framed. Lysander understood now how apt Nepe was at emulations; she could have made herself resemble Purple and recorded that challenge, and had it sent to the Hectare when she was safely away. She had a grudge against Purple; Lysander hoped she never had a grudge against him!

Purple nodded. "FlachNepe," he said. "I've tangled with that brat before. If I don't kill her, she'll kill me."

Obviously Nepe could do that, any time she chose. But she wasn't attacking Purple, she was using him. His understandable nervousness about the high-stakes game with the Hectare was causing him to be careless, as she had anticipated, and she was pulling a stunt Purple didn't dream of.

But it seemed that Purple had coerced Brown into putting her golems at the disposal of the Hectare invader, and to serve him personally without trying to do him direct harm. Brown had evidently agreed because Purple was blackmailing her—but also because this allowed her to help Nepe. What a devious interaction this was!

They proceeded to the Game Annex, where the Hectare and its second waited. Its second was Tan. That gave Lysander a momentary start, but he realized that it made sense; the Hectare were playing the game by local rules, and needed competent local advice. So the two quislings were on opposite sides in this matter, but united in their support for the invader. Another interesting situation!

The game proceeded. The irrepressible Game Computer discarded their grid choices, as was its wont, and assigned them a competitive play set in ancient Crete, of planet Earth's history. The chamber assumed the likeness of the old stone palace.

Too bad he had been unable to obtain access to the game source code. He could have found out why it aborted the regular grid, and corrected the malfunction. But now that he knew that the Adepts had known his nature, he understood why Blue had given him make-work instead of real work. That malfunction must relate in some way to the Adepts' plotting.

The Hectare selected an actress by picking her up and carrying her away. She was a robot, but she screamed protest and kicked her feet, seeming exactly like a ravished maiden. Lysander thought of Echo, and could believe it. The robots of this planet were extremely sophisticated, emulating human beings almost perfectly.

He would have liked to watch the game, but his lips and legs felt Nepe's pressure. That meant she had somewhere else to go, and he would have to make an excuse. "I don't care to watch this," he said in Tsetse's dulcet voice, and backed away. Brown saw her, and did not protest. No one cared about a serf servant when there was more interesting business afoot. In a moment he was out of the chamber and on his own.

Nepe had achieved the first part of her plan: she had gotten them past the Hectare alerts, that would have stopped them had they not been an authorized part of Purple's party. But what was next?

Guided by her pressure on his legs and backside, he walked down the hall, not to the concourse, but to a service area. When there was no one to observe, he ducked into the machine passages, and caught a rubbish cart to the Hectare district. Nepe was playing a dangerous game!

They came to a particular apartment. Suddenly Lysander realized whose it must be: the Hectare who was playing the game with Purple! Not only was Nepe using Lysander to assume grown human form, and using Purple to get past the alerts, she was raiding the Hectare's den itself, while the game kept it occupied.

They came to a service access panel. Now there was pressure on his hands and on his back: she wanted him to go forward through the panel. But of course he couldn't do that; it was closed, and any attempt by an unauthorized party to force it open would set off a strident alarm. In fact, entry by the wrong party would do the same, even if no force was used. Only the Hectare code would do, here. Which meant that Nepe knew about that, too. The Adepts had done a real job of investigation on him!

Very well. He had to cooperate if he was to get to the root of their plot, even if he facilitated that plot along the way. Nepe's nervy plot had him in thrall too. If he didn't do it, they would find someone else to, or some other way; he knew that the Hectare had seriously underestimated the cunning of the resistance. Which was, of course, why agents like him were assigned. He represented the backup, to make sure that there were no devastating surprises. He had already learned enough to justify that policy.

He tapped in the code pattern. The panel slid open. He stepped into the apartment, setting off no alarm.

Nepe guided him to an antechamber, where a special unit sat on a table. She made him use the Hectare code to open it. Inside, carefully aerated and protected from all shocks of motion or temperature, lay a set of small, intertwined tentacles.

Lysander stared. Oh, no! Only now did he appreciate the full daring of Nepe's mission. This was a Hectare seed!

Lysander's brain had been taken from a living Hectare whose body had suffered irreparable damage. His memories of his prior life had been eliminated, but his knowledge of Hectare custom and culture had remained, so that he would never lose his fundamental identity. He knew the significance of this seed, and knew that Nepe knew it too. The Adepts must have done meticulous research, and acquainted her with exactly what she needed to know.

Human beings reproduced in the fashion of their mammalian kind: the male, when amorously inclined, used his organ of intromission to insert a number—a considerable number—of viable seeds in the receptive chamber of the female. The species was so organized that there was continual interest in this activity, so that such insertions were made even when there was no reasonable prospect for viability. This was what he had done with Alyc, and thought to do with Jod'e, and had done most recently with Echo. He knew that his android body did not produce viable seed; it would never merge with the female seed and form a new living entity. Only with the help of laboratory enhancement could an android produce offspring. Female androids generally served as brood mares for the embryos of living human women who preferred not to interrupt their social schedules by being gravid. Humanoid robot females could do the same, to a lesser extent. How magic affected this he wasn't sure; strange things were happening on the planet, and perhaps strange crossbreeds were occurring. Nepe herself was an example.

Hectare reproduced differently. They were of one sex, but did pair off to breed. Under their mantle of tentacles, normally concealed from exterior view, were their appendages, which were small and immobile tentacles. Periodically one of these would ripen, at which time the Hectare would seek a compatible Hectare with a similarly ripened member. The two would approach each other and if the compatibility persisted, engage in what the human kind would term a sexual encounter. Their two ripe tentacles would twine around each other, and in the ecstasy of the experience, the Hectare would separate and break off the members. The interlocked tentacles, each containing the chromosomal complement of the parent, represented the nucleus of a new Hectare.

But the course of development was not automatic. The Hectare seed had to be planted in the soil of the home planet, the only place where it would grow. It could survive in stasis for a time, originally brief but with the aid of modern technology up to a year, if the proper environment was maintained. That was the purpose of the housing unit: it provided the environment of stasis, so that the seed could be shipped to the home planet for planting. Hectare did not have families; all seeds were treated equivalently in the protected nursery. They sent out roots to gather nutrients, and drew energy from the sun. They also developed their mantles of tentacles to catch insects and other prey, and their eye complexes, that gave them their beauty. In time they achieved the mass and resources to enable them to become mobile. As they did so, they were captured by the nursery caretakers and brought to special chambers for education. In due course they would emerge as adult Hectare, ready to participate in Hectare civilization, and to help extend it to other planets.

What did the human resistance want with a Hectare seed?

The covering of flesh that made him resemble the woman Tsetse rippled and changed. Nepe's main mass was overlaid at his chest and hips; this now drew the thinner sections into itself, forming a single mass at the region of his stomach. As it slid away from his legs and arms he saw nothing: he remained magically invisible, even to himself.

A mouth formed in the bloated belly he now carried. "Lift me to the seed, then carry me away from here swiftly."

Lysander did not like this at all. He was after all Hectare himself, despite the human body and human attributes he had assumed. How far did his mission require him to go? To interfere with a Hectare seed would be to provoke a ferment that could bring about extraordinary mischief.

But if he did not, Nepe would probably turn him in, and his chance to fathom the Adept plot would be gone. She was putting him to the test, and there would be no evasion.

He made his decision. Better to sacrifice one Hectare seed than the mission, because the mission could affect the Hectare dominance of this planet. What was one seed, which might not survive, compared to the planet, which was important in its small fashion to the alliance dominance of the galaxy?

He put his hands on the ball of flesh that was Nepe and heaved it up and over the unit. She weighed about half as much as a grown man, and probably never would get beyond three-quarters manweight, but what a creature she already was! The Hectare, if they but could know it, should be thankful that there was only one of her on the planet. As it was, even that one might be more than they could handle. Two would swamp them!

A pseudopod extended from the mass, depending toward the seed. It touched the seed, and enfolded it, and then retracted, carrying the seed. In a moment he held the ball again, with the Hectare seed hidden inside it.

He moved the glob to the side and down; his arms were tiring. He didn't know whether Nepe wanted to clothe him again, or do something else, and hesitated to inquire. There was probably an aural monitor that would set off an alarm at the sound of his voice. Nepe had spoken, but she might know of the monitor and how to avoid triggering it. She seemed to know everything else, including exactly how to use him to achieve her mission.

There was pressure on one side of his hands, from protoplasm that wrapped around them, so he carried her that way. It was toward the service access panel they had used to enter. He put a foot through, then carefully shifted to bring Nepe through. But the extra weight was awkward, and his shoulder brushed the edge of the opening.

Immediately an alarm sounded. A device in the ceiling spun about, searching for the intrusion; the moment it spotted him, a laser beam or worse would strike. They were in for it now!

Lysander jammed his body through the hole and shoved to the side, to get out of the line of fire. But there wasn't room for them both; Nepe would get tagged. So he heaved her into the darkness beyond like a big bowling ball, rolling her out of danger. Then he tapped the Hectare "At Ease" code on the wall.

The alarm silenced. The Hectare codes overrode all else. But the brief sounding of the alarm would alert the Hectare security force, and there would be a prompt investigation. He had to get far away from here in a hurry!

He closed the access, so that their mode of exit would not be immediately apparent, and let his eyes adjust to the darkness. He knew there was very little time to waste.

Where was Nepe? She had disappeared, and he just had to trust that she would know how to manage; he would only get them both caught if he searched for her.

He would probably get caught anyway! He heard a machine coming his way, and there was nowhere to scramble out of its way. He huddled against the dark metal wall, waiting for whatever offered.

It was a delivery wagon, self-propelled and empty. It evidently did double duty as a cleanup unit, sent automatically when the alarm went off. It came to the dead-end that was Lysander's niche, and flashed a beam directly on him.

And through him! The magic still made him invisible, and the machine didn't see him! It spun around and rolled away. He had assumed that the effect was limited to the perception of living creatures. He had underestimated it again.

How far did this magic extend? His shoulder had set off the alarm, and Brown had felt his real body (as covered by Nepe), so obviously touch was not included. Nepe had told him not to speak, so sound probably was not included either. But could he walk with impunity among the machines, as long as he did not touch them? It was worth trying.

He walked, and the machines ignored him. He made his way down the dark passage, walking between the tracks of the delivery system. It was working!

Then he heard a larger machine coming—and there was no room to get out of the way. If it did not see him, it would run him down. He turned and sprinted for the last alcove, but the machine was too fast; he knew it would overhaul him first.

Then it slowed, and he made it to the alcove and swung himself out of the way. The machine moved past, picking up speed, and in a moment was gone.

Lysander had to pause to think about that. There had been no reason for the machine to slow; it was a level track, and it had the programmed right-of-way. No reason to slow—except to avoid hitting Lysander.

The machine had known he was there, yet given no other indication. What did that mean?

Nepe's father Mach was a self-willed machine. He must have given a directive, that the machines obeyed. To ignore Lysander as if they did not see him, but not to hurt him. So that he could complete his mission for the Adepts. The magic did not after all affect the machines but their orders did.

He felt a shiver. He was sure the Hectare did not know about this. How much else was going on under their noses? If a machine could be instructed to ignore a spy, why couldn't it be instructed to assassinate a Hectare leader?

He was right to pursue his mission, even though it facilitated the opposition. He had to get down to the fundamental ploy of the resistance. The Adepts might let him do that, because they believed they could not win without his help. He was now less certain about that than they were. This planet was deviously dangerous.

He made his way to an exit panel near the concourse. He would have to get out, trusting his spell of invisibility to humans and avoidance by machines to protect him, and try to find Nepe. She still needed his help, for she could not masquerade as Tsetse alone.

He opened the panel and stepped out. He took one step—and a serf blundered into him. Lysander had done the most elementarily foolish thing: he had assumed that other people would automatically avoid collisions. But they couldn't, because Lysander was invisible to them. They were not machines.

"Hey, there's a man here!" the serf exclaimed, groping as he caught his balance. "I can't see him!"

Citizen Tan's voice came over the speaker system. "Hold him! We want him!"

Lysander brought up his hand and pinched the man's neck, making him gasp with pain and let go. But half a dozen others were now closing in. These were serfs who had volunteered to serve in the new order; they wore the identifying arm bands with tentacle pattern that denoted lesser collaborators. They spread their arms, to prevent anyone unseen from passing by them, and more were converging from beyond. Lysander knew he would not be able to fight his way clear of this. All because of his completely stupid mistake!

Then another serf lurched toward him. Lysander got one look at the man's face—before it vanished. The man had turned invisible!

"Duck down, crawl away," a voice beside him said. "Nepe's waiting next intersection. I'll distract them."

Lysander didn't question it. He ducked down just as the first serf of the closing ring made contact. The man might have felt his touch, but immediately contacted the other invisible man and grabbed on to him. "I've got him! I've got him!" he yelled—before his breath whooshed out from what must have been a blow to the solar plexus.

Lysander slid around and between legs, and got clear as the melee proceeded. Who was the other man? He had never seen him before. Yet obviously the man had not only seen Lysander, he had recognized him—and known his mission with Nepe.

He hurried down to the next intersection, getting well clear of the action behind. He skirted a standing guidebot, but felt a thread extending from it. He paused, then touched it with a finger.

It was warm and alive. It was Nepe in disguise.

Now the machine moved, evidently called for duty somewhere else. Lysander followed. They entered the side hall and got out of sight of the pedestrians. Then they ducked into an empty food alcove.

Nepe was already flattening. Lysander heaved her up and draped her thinning body over his shoulders. He stood nervously while she spread out across his body, making it visible; the process was not instantaneous, and if someone came right now—

No one came. Nepe completed the transformation. He did not need to look in any mirror; he saw the breasts and hips. He was a visible woman again.

Guided by her, he walked onto the concourse. There was Brown, looking about. They approached her. There was pressure at his lips. "I'm sorry," he said in Tsetse's voice. "I didn't know your game was through."

"It's all right, Tsetse," Brown said. "We have passes to leave. My golems will carry us back to the castle."

She showed the way to a public exit, where they stood and waited for half an hour. Then a horse appeared, running toward the city. It was a wooden horse—a golem—with a wooden carriage behind.

They boarded the carriage, and the horse set off for home. "Citizen Purple won his game," Brown said. "I was able to assist him, and I think he was pleased. I must say he has treated me better than I expected."

"I'm glad," Lysander said. He did not feel free to say anything else; Purple might have this carriage under observation, as a routine precaution.

They drew up to the Brown Demesnes. "I thank thee for thy company, Tsetse," Brown said, reverting to her Phaze self. "I will need thee not again this day; do as thou willst."

"Thank you, Brown," Lysander said carefully. She knew that her companion was not the real Tsetse, but did she know who it really was?

They entered the castle. Brown went to her room, probably to lie down; she had had a wearing session, he was sure. Nepe guided him to the golem storage room.

There she drew away from him, and formed her natural self, the naked girl. "We can talk now, Lysander," she said. "This castle is secure, when Purp's not here. I just wanted you to get rehearsed for your role, before. You did well."

"Thank you. But what happened to the Hectare seed? You didn't lose it, after all that?"

She patted her abdomen. "No, I have it in here. I never thought I'd be pregnant at age nine!"

She was a Moebite, of course, able to assume any form; she could as readily carry an object inside her in human form as when she was in ball form or machine form. This allowed her to function normally while maintaining a suitable environment for the seed, so as not to let it die. Still, her remark surprised him. He had absorbed enough of human culture to know that human children did not procreate any more than immature Hectare did. "Glad I could be of help, getting you pregnant," he said dryly.

"You aren't finished. We have to take the Hec seed to the West Pole."

"That's where your center of operations is?"

"You don't think I'll tell you," she accused him mischievously. "But I will. The answer is, I don't know where our setup is, and neither does anybody else. All I know is that I have to get a Hec seed to the West Pole, and then I'll see what else I have to do."

"So if I want to find out, I'll have to keep helping you."

"Right. We're making you fulfill the prophecy, even if you don't like it. But you'll get a choice somewhere, I think, if you stay with it."

"You play a nervy game!"

"I've had experience. I can't save the planet alone, so I'm recruiting whatever I need. You helped a lot, especially with the Hec code to null the alarm. Now we can relax, until Tsetse comes back. Then a long walk, so you better rest."

"Why not change to Flach and conjure us there?"

"Two reasons. First, he couldn't carry the seed like this, so it has to be me. Second, Purp's got magic warners out, to spy on any Adept-level magic in Phaze. So the small stuff, like invisibility, is about all that'll pass. So I have to hoof it, and I can't make it by myself in time, so I need you and Echo to help."

"Echo's coming with us?" he asked, his human heart coming alive. The pressure and oddity of events had distracted him, but now he missed her intensely.

"You bet. We make it nice for you, so you'll think about joining our side. Same way as Purp makes it nice for Brown. So he's got her working for him, and I've got you working for me."

"But Brown is still helping you against the Hectare, and I'm still working for the Hectare."

"Yep. You can't get full use out of an enemy. But you do what you can."

"Who was that man who took my place, so I could get away from the serfs? He turned invisible?"

"That was Bane. My father, aka the Robot Adept."

"Oh! He distracted them, then conjured himself clear!"

"No. After Flach conjured you and Echo out, Purp got wise and set up a magic barricade against conjuration and transformation in the dome. That's why Flach couldn't just conjure himself in to steal the Hec seed; I had to do it. He could've overridden Purp's magic, but it would have made a splash, and alerted the Hecs. Tan's got splash-watch, I think. He's been having a lot of fun with Jod'e, but he watches the warners all the time. So we had to do it the hard way. Good thing it worked."

Jod'e—that still hurt, though now he had other love. "You mean your father let himself be captured—to help me escape?" Lysander asked, astonished. "Knowing that I'm an enemy agent?"

"He did that. Just as Green and Black gave themselves up to spring Flach. We need you, 'Sander."

"You have more faith in your prophecy than I do!"

"We know magic better than you do. Now eat something, if you need it; there's some food in a chest in the corner. And sleep; you can dream of Echo. One good night is all we have before it gets rough."

At this point, he believed it.

11

West

Nepe knew it was silly, but she rather liked Lysander. He was an android with a Hectare brain, a spy for the other side, but that was balanced out by the fact that the prophecy made him necessary to the final victory of their planet. She had watched him for alien ways, but he seemed just as human as anyone else, and more so than she herself. When he had first come to the planet he had had affectations, but these had promptly faded; he was a quick study of local custom. Now that the Yellow Adept's love potion had made him love Echo, he was more to be trusted than before. He might think he remained independent, but he had not had occasion to test it. The moment his mission conflicted with his love, he would discover the love's power!

Meanwhile, she had to compose herself. She wished Bane had not given himself up. Now Flach was the only Adept left free, except for Clef and Tania, who had disappeared. Only Mach had known where they went, and he had erased the memory before letting himself be captured. She had depended on her father to support her when she faltered, and now she knew she was on her own. That made her nervous.

What was at the West Pole? Flach had been surprised by the North Pole, with its slowed-down time and the two Adepts there. It would have been worse if the snow demon's daughter hadn't distracted him. Nepe had learned a lot from Icy; when she came to adult status and modeled her flesh, she was going to make it just like that, only warm, and fling it about similarly. The only problem was that there was really no prospective man for her. Oh, she liked 'Corn well enough, but he wasn't a mixedbreed like herself, and so probably wouldn't do for the long haul.

Well, it would all come to nothing if they didn't manage to throw off the yoke of the Hectare. For now, she just had to go one step at a time, and get the three messages taken care off. Flach had gone to the North Pole; now she was taking the Hec seed to the West Pole. Both of these missions had proved to be more complicated than they seemed. She hoped the third one would not prove to be more of a challenge than she could handle. She knew that the fate of the planet hung on her success, and she was nervous about that.

She settled into a puddle and slept.

Next morning the golem party and Tsetse arrived with the wood. Nepe hustled Lysander out; he remained invisible, but of course she could tell where he was, because Flach had made the spell. They slipped out to join the party and take Echo away; Tsetse would enter the castle alone, where she and Brown would sort things out in their own fashion.

Now they were three: Nepe, Lysander, and Echo. While the other two embraced ardently (though it looked as if the woman were pantomiming, because of the man's invisibility), Nepe changed slowly to wolf form. An observer would have found it a strange scene: a child becoming an animal, and a cyborg woman embracing air. But Nepe wanted no observer, because Purple was alert, and must not catch on to this secret mission. She wished there had been some way to recover Lysander's clothes from Purple's plane, to eliminate any trace of what was going on. But it just wasn't possible to catch every detail.

She carried the Hectare seed inside her. She had joked about it, to Lysander, but privately it revolted her; she liked nothing about the Hectare, physically or mentally. They were true bug-eyed monsters, and they were out to despoil the planet and leave it deprived of its resources, especially its magic. All so they could use the Protonite to power their machines, and the wood for their construction, and the flesh of the animals for their larders, and the magic for whatever devices they could work out. They were still consolidating their conquest, but soon the serious ravaging would proceed, and then nothing would stop it. They had left a trail of lemon-squeezed planets behind; they were very efficient at what they called investment and reduction.

Yet Grandpa Blue had explained to her at the outset that the Hectare were only part of the problem. There were dozens of conquerer species out there, forming their galactic alliance, and any of them could have conquered Proton. The Hectare just happened to be the species the lot had fallen on. If they failed, another species would be allowed to try, because the alliance wanted the resources of this exceptional planet put to good use by its definition. Proton had been a low priority acquisition, before the mergence, because the magic was out of reach. But when it became apparent that magic was present and genuine, the priorities abruptly shifted. So if Proton, and especially Phaze, were to be saved, they had to forge a defense that would be effective against all invasions. That was a mighty tall order.

The truth was that Proton's presence in the alien sector of the galaxy made little difference, overall. The human sector was just as bad, for human beings were the greatest exploiters of all. The humans were taking over alien planets in their sector for similar reduction. Once they had squeezed them dry, they would start on the lesser alien planets—just as the aliens would start on the lesser alien planets once the easy pickings were done. The Hectare themselves might in due course be reduced to servant status by some more powerful alien species. It was the predatory chain, unceasing in its hunger for power.

"And so," Grandpa Blue had told her, "we must be either the eaters or the eaten. We can no longer drift in our isolation. If we do not set out to rule the galaxy, we must suffer the exploitation of those who do. Since we lack either the power or the desire to become galactic, our fate is sealed. Unless we find that perfect defense."

"Then we must find it," she had said.

"Unfortunately, it doesn't exist. At least, there is no mechanism to make it feasible. Conquest seems unavoidable."

"But we can't just give up!"

"Hardly that, Nepe! Fortunately there is a prophecy that guides us and suggests that we can craft our mechanism, in time."

"How much time, Grandpa?"

"About seventeen years," he said.

She stared at him. "But it only takes the Hectare two years to denude a planet! If we don't get rid of them within two months, we'll suffer awful harm!"

"True. But the prophecy indicates that we shall need the help of the enemy to succeed. So we shall have to let them get started, and then see what we can do."

"Grandpa, I think there's something you're not telling me!"

"Whatever gave you that notion, cutie?"

Then she was sure. "But when the time comes—"

"Then you will know as much as you need."

Now, remembering, Nepe still did not know the plan. It seemed impossible to forge a seventeen-year weapon in two months. But she believed in Grandpa Blue, who was also the Adept Stile, and in the others who supported him. More recently she had seen how even the Green and Black Adepts, former enemies, supported him too, even to the extent of giving up their freedom to help Flach get away. They could have saved themselves, but hadn't even tried, preferring instead to distract the enemy. Then Bane himself had done the same to protect the spy Lysander, just so he would be able to fulfill the prophecy—if he chose. So she was protecting Lysander too, and also doing this other awful thing, carrying the Hectare seed to the West Pole. They had discovered how the North Pole related, because of the Magic Bomb—but how could the West Pole relate? Well, soon she would find out, she hoped.

Now she was in wolf form, and Lysander and Echo had finished their first passionate reunion, after a separation of a whole day. Nepe was jealous; she hoped some day to love like that. Of course it was because of the Yellow Adept's potion, but it was genuine; the potion merely enhanced what nature would have done in time. Their love was true, whatever else was artificial.

"We must travel," Nepe told them. "But we need more. You two hide while I go summon the others."

Echo stared. Then she understood. "You aren't really a wolf, so you can make your wolf-mouth talk human speech."

"Yes. Don't let Purp or the golems catch you." Then Nepe loped away. She knew that the two would find something to do while they waited, and would hardly miss her. It didn't matter that Lysander was invisible; Echo could feel him, and he could feel her. She would merely close her eyes.

Kurrelgyre's wolf village was not far away. Nepe was familiar with the region, because Flach's mind was with her. Flach had been content to tune out the past two days, lost in the bliss of foolish fond imaginings relating to snow demonesses. But that was wearing off now, as reality seeped in; Icy was not for him, for about three excellent reasons: age, species, and mission. The last was the most important; if he did not help save Phaze, none of the snow demons would survive.

Right, he agreed, her thought clarifying his sentiment. *Bear left*.

She bore left. He knew every bypath here, while she knew only the approximate routes. It would have been easier to give him the body, but both the Hectare seed she carried and the danger of Purple's snooping on their magic ruled that out. Maybe when they got farther into the hinterland, on the way to the West Pole, it would be safe to transform. So she jogged on, though her emulation of a wolf was not nearly as good as his. She was an amoeba assuming the form, whereas he could change into a real wolf, capable of all the lupine things, including (in due course) reproduction.

Maybe Sirel's approaching her time! he thought.

But Sirelmoba, his Promised, was only nine years old, the same as he was. It should be two years yet before her first season. Still, it was better for him to be thinking of her than of Icy, for Sirel would be coming with them to the Pole.

Yes, he agreed, brightening.

They reached the werewolf village. Well before Nepe entered it, the guard wolves were pacing her. But they knew her, and knew why she was here. In a moment Sirelmoba appeared, formally sniffing noses and tails, and politely concealing her distaste for the alien door. No mock-wolf could deceive a true one!

"And three more," Nepe said using human speech because she could not use the wolves' growl-talk effectively.

Old Kurrelgyre assumed human form. "Runners are going for them. They will join thee on the way."

"But we shall be hiding!" she protested.

"No one hides from wolf or bat at night. He will find thee, and will alert the mares when they draw nigh."

He will, Flach assured her.

"If you will cover our trail—"

"Done," Kurrelgyre said. "And good fortune to thee, little bitch."

"Thank you." She appreciated the sentiment; it was a compliment to be called a bitch by a true werewolf.

She turned to go, the young werebitch beside her. The others of the Pack faded to the sides. They would cross and recross the trail, obliterating it, so that no one would be able to trace the route of the two by sight or odor. They would also serve as an early guard, so that nothing would get through to attack the small party while it remained in the local Wolf Demesnes. They would be unobtrusive about it, so that there was no commotion. They did not know the details of her mission any more than she did, but were well aware of its importance.

Sirel and Nepe ran silently. The bitch held her pace back, because Nepe could not match it. Even so, Nepe was getting tired; she would have done better in human form, because she had had a great deal more practice in it, though it was no more natural to her than wolf form.

They reached the place where she had left the ardent couple. Sirel knew it well before Nepe did; her keen nose picked up the foreign scents. "They be not standing guard," she said in growl-talk.

Nepe could understand the growls better than she could make them. "Love potion," she explained.

"Aye, and strong!"

They made just a bit of noise approaching, so that the couple could disengage. Nepe suspected this would be a problem as they traveled; instead of sleeping at night, the two would be wasting their energies in amour. But it couldn't be helped; it was part of the price of the mission.

Sirel blinked as they came in sight of the couple. Her nose made it plain that the man was there, but her eyes couldn't find it. "Flach made him invisible," Nepe explained.

"Should have made him unsmellable," Sirel growled.

"This is the werebitch Sirelmoba," Nepe said, introducing her to the couple. "And the android Lysander, and cyborg Echo," for Sirel's benefit. "We must travel together."

Sirel growled assent, not wholly pleased. She would rather have traveled alone with Nepe—or better yet, with Flach. But she knew that the preference of any of them had little to do with it.

"We go to the West Pole," Nepe said. "We have three days to make it, and we must all get there. If Citizen/Adept Purple catches on, he will try to stop us, and we will have to scatter and rejoin later, but we must keep moving. Sirel and Echo can sustain the pace, but Lysander and I can not, so we will have help. There will be one more member of our party who will not have a problem traveling." But she realized that there could be a different problem there. She hoped they would be too busy traveling for that to manifest.

"The West Pole!" Sirel said, assuming her girl form, which was much like Nepe's human form except that her hair was always dark. Nepe's hair was whatever color she chose when she assumed the form; she had recently worn it neutral brown, and just long enough to cover her ears, so that she did not have to bother to form ears. "But there be naught there!"

"Maybe there will be something by the time we get there," Nepe said, hoping that was the case.

"Well, there is still a portion of the day left," Echo said. "Why don't you folk start walking, and I will spy out the terrain ahead."

"Thank you," Nepe said.

"I'll go with you," Lysander's voice came.

"I think not, handsome man!" Oche the harpy screeched, flapping up into the sky.

"Point made," he agreed ruefully.

"I will range out the same on land," Sirel said. "Not all can be seen from above." She slid into the bush, disappearing in a moment.

Nepe started walking, trying not to limp; her temporary muscle structure was becoming uncomfortable.

"But Nepe, why can't you assume some form that will enable you to travel more readily?" Lysander asked her.

"All my forms are unnatural," she replied. "I would get tired in any, and waste time and energy changing between them."

"But as Flach—"

"The others can change forms without trouble, as many times as they wish," she explained, "because those forms are inherent in their natures. The werewolves are descendants of men and wolves, and the harpies have vulture and human ancestry. There is no significant magic splash when they change. But when Flach changes forms, other than his natural ones of unicorn and boy and maybe wolf, he has to use a new spell each time, and the splash is detectable throughout Phaze. Purple is watching for it, and would be here in a moment. So Flach has to be very limited in his magic. That, along with the problem of carrying the Hec seed—"

"I understand. You have amazing abilities in either aspect, but you have limits too. You are surprisingly candid about them."

"If Purp closes in on us, you'll have to help me get away, or you won't learn what we're up to."

"Yet if you are the only one who knows how to implement the resistance ploy, then if you are stopped, it may be stopped too."

"Unless I am the only one *I know of* who can implement it," she said. "If there are others I don't know about, you will never have a chance to stop them, unless you help me get together with them according to the plan."

"True." He believed that she was the only one, but it could have been set up to give him that impression so that he would stop looking. Even the story of the prophecy could have been concocted to deceive him. It wasn't safe to stop yet. "So I must continue to support the enemy, until the full nature of the resistance is known."

"Meanwhile, you can love Echo," she said. "And maybe by the time you know the whole thing, you won't want to mess it up."

"Maybe by then she will understand that I have to do what I have to do, and will join me in it."

"And maybe even if she does, when the Hec ravage the planet the magic will go, and Oche will die, and then Echo will be nothing but a machine with a dead brain."

It sounded as if someone had struck him in the gut. He stopped moving, and evidently leaned against a tree.

"I'm sorry, 'Sander," she said. "That was a mean thing to say."

"You scored, Nepe." He sounded out of breath. "I think I didn't really believe the power of that potion! I *do* love her, and I couldn't let that happen to her."

"Maybe they'll let you save a bit of Phazite for her, so she can be all right. It's a chip of Protonite that runs her robot body, and that's the same stuff. If you keep enough of that—"

"Why are you telling me this?" he asked, managing to resume his walking. "It's not in your interest to do so."

"Grandpa Blue taught me you can't win a chess game by cheating. You can hide your strategy, but you have to tell your opponent when you put his king in check, and his queen too, if you want to be sure. We gave you a queen, and she's in check."

"That you did, and that she is," he agreed.

"But it's our whole world in check."

"I appreciate your position."

"If you had it to do over, would you go with Echo and take the potion?"

"I didn't know about the potion until I was locked in with it."

"But you didn't really believe in it, so you didn't try to escape. But now you know it works—if you could go back and avoid it—"

He walked for a while, pondering. "Alyc was just a diversion; she and I both knew that. Jod'e could have been real; I'm still sorry about the way Tan got her. I would change *that* if I could! Echo was nobody special. I just went with her because she had a way out, never expecting to love her. But now I have had the experience of loving her, and that is something I would not change. Before I had only my mission; now I have my mission and love, and that has made a dimension in my life that was not there before. So if I had known the whole of it, I would have proceeded exactly as I did. Love is too valuable to bypass."

"I wasn't teasing you," Nepe said. "I just wanted to know. I like a lot of people, and I love my folks, especially Grandpa Blue, but I've never had romantic love. I figure if it's not worth it, now is when you'll know."

"It's worth it," he said. "But I still have my mission. If you fell in love, you would still have yours."

They walked on. Nepe thought about her relation with Troubot, and Flach's with Troubot's other self, Sirelmoba, and knew that these were friendships, not romantic love. She flirted with Alien or 'Corn, but again, she knew this was a far cry from the kind of commitment she had seen in adults. The fact was that there was no person or creature of her generation that was like her: part alien, part human, and on Flach's side, part unicorn and part machine. Or maybe he had the human lineage and she the machine; it was a matter of definition, since their fathers had used each other's bodies. She was also a male/female mergence, which was fine for association with Sirelmoba/Troubot, but not with anyone else. Thus she was a complex creature, and in her fashion unique to the planet; no one else had her variety of affinities or abilities. If she could meet another like her, only different—

But how could she? It would require strenuous effort to make another like her, which was impossible in the face of the Hec conquest, and even then the result would be at least ten years younger than she. So she was alone in her special fashion.

"Why do I have the feeling that despite all your talents," Lysander asked, "you have an emptiness like that of mine before love?"

"Because you know I'm one of a kind!" she snapped. "I'll never have true love!"

"You don't need another like you for love," he protested. "All you need is a suitable companion, and a love potion. I happen to know."

She laughed, feeling better. Maybe he was right.

The harpy returned. She flapped clumsily down until close to the ground, then manifested as Echo. "Which side do the goblins serve now?"

"Ours," Nepe said. "All the creatures are with us, because they'll all die if Phaze is despoiled. But if they don't know the importance of my mission, they may figure it's business as usual."

"Then we had better steer around the goblin camp to our west," Echo said.

They steered around, cutting north. But as they followed a path beside a streamlet, they heard a commotion ahead. There was a crash and a yipe, as of an animal getting snared.

"Sirel!" Nepe exclaimed, as Flach recognized the sound. "She's in trouble!"

They charged forward, and soon were there. Sure enough, the werewolf was caught in a raised net, that had evidently been set to spring up around anyone who stepped where it was hidden across the trail. This was goblin mischief!

The net had formed a bag, that gave Sirel no purchase for escape. It closed into a rope above, that passed over a fork in a medium small tree and back down to the ground. The tree had been tied down, and when released had carried up the net, closing it about the prey. It was a clever enough device, the kind that goblins had been proficient at for centuries. All that was required for release was to untie the knot at ground level.

But the goblins were as fast as their party had been. Five of the tough little creatures charged up from the opposite extension of the path. "Dinner!" one cried exultantly. "Bitch stew!"

"Keep quiet, 'Sander," Nepe warned. "Echo, you talk." She hoped they understood: the goblins must not learn the full nature of this party.

"No you don't!" Echo cried. "That's *my* wolf!"

The squat goblin chief paused, looking at her. "Thy wolf be at thy side," he said.

"Both be mine. Cut the bitch loose, or we shall have a reckoning."

The four other goblins began to move forward, hefting their knobby clubs. "Methinks we shall eat e'en better than we thought," the chief said.

"I will use my talent to hurt you," Echo threatened.

"Ye be Protonite," the chief replied. "No magic." Meanwhile, the four were coming close.

Echo pointed at the chief's head. "Hurt!" she cried.

Something struck the big head. The goblin blinked, but seemed surprised rather than hurt. He brought his club around.

"Hurt!" Echo repeated, pointing to his feet.

Something crunched down on the chief's big toes. This time he reacted more vehemently. "Ooooff!" He danced on one foot, holding the other.

Now Nepe understood what was happening. Invisible Lysander had gotten close, and was striking the goblin at Echo's command. First on the head, which was relatively impervious, then stomping a foot, which wasn't.

"Now cut down my wolf, or it will go hard with you," Echo said.

"Listen, bitch—" the goblin started, and since his kind had no respect for wolves, this was no compliment.

Then his eyes goggled. He squirmed a moment, as if suffering some kind of seizure. Lysander was putting some kind of hold on him.

"Let her go," the chief wheezed.

The four, about to attack Echo, were puzzled. "But Chief—"

"I changed my mind," the chief said, wincing. "We want bitch stew not." He winced again. "We'll hunt for something else."

"Well, *I* want bitch stew!" one of the four said. He took a step forward.

But Nepe, standing quietly, had extended a tendril along the path, making it the same shade of brown as the forest floor. It had reached the goblin's foot and fastened to it. When he took his step, she yanked—and he crashed down on his ugly face.

Echo strode forward herself, brushing past the three surprised goblins. One tried to swing at her, and she touched his shoulder with her hand, seemingly lightly. But there was the force and hardness of metal in that soft-looking hand, and the goblin jumped, bruised.

Echo caught the rope that supported the net. She started to untie it.

"Hey, thou canst not—" the chief started. Then he winced again, and was silent.

Echo completed the job, and the rope separated. She clung to it, so that her weight counterbalanced the smaller weight of the wolf, and let Sirel down gently to the ground. The net fell open, and Sirel got to her feet and scrambled out.

The chief made one more effort to protest, but failed again. They walked past him and on down the path. When they were at a bend, the goblin gave an exclamation and crashed into the brush. They heard feet pounding.

"Let's get away from here!" Nepe said. They ran, and the pounding feet ran after them, gaining. None of them wanted to be close when the goblin chief recovered his composure. He surely had not lost his taste for bitch stew.

A shape loomed ahead. It was a bat. It flew down to the path, and took the form of a boy Nepe's age. "If I'd known thou wast having so much fun, Nepe, I'd have hurried!" he said, running with them.

"Alien!" she exclaimed. "You found us!"

"How could I miss thee? As a wolf thou be laughable!"

They slowed, satisfied that the goblins were not in close pursuit. "Echo, Sirel, 'Sander, this is Alien, the next of our party," Nepe gasped. "The Red Adept's son, and"—she paused, not just for breath—"my boyfriend, when Troubot is not around."

"We've met," Sirel said. Troubot was her other self, in Proton. "But mine accounting be with Flach, an my season come."

Nepe changed the subject. "Some of us can't travel well at night, so we must find a place to camp. We'll have to forage for some food, and maybe Alien can keep watch—"

"So long as I get to sleep by day," Alien agreed.

Echo assumed her harpy form again and flew ahead to scout for a good camping site. The others walked at a relatively sedate pace. "What happened?" Nepe asked Sirel.

Sirel assumed human form again. "I spied the goblin camp, so circled around, and had almost completed the loop. Became I careless then." She flushed in the human fashion; it was most embarrassing, even for a half-grown pup.

Soon Oche returned. "There be fruit trees near," she screeched. "And a field full o' rabbits."

"Excellent!" Nepe said. Her legs were so tired now that she could hardly wait to dissolve into a relaxed puddle.

In the morning, somewhat refreshed, they set off anew. Nepe assumed her human form, with an especially thick mass of hair, and

Alien clung to it and slept. He preferred to hang upside down, but could manage in any position when the need arose. Sirel and Echo, both in human form, walked beside each other, and Lysander brought up the rear, still invisible. At the rate they were going, they would never make it to the West Pole in time, but Nepe wasn't concerned about that. Their rate would change.

Then the last two members of their party intercepted them. A blue heron flew slowly overhead, and immediately Echo turned harpy and flapped up to hail it. The heron followed her down, and manifested as Belle, the purple unicorn with the iridescent mane. There was a healing scar on her rump. From her back a firefly flew, and manifested as Neysa, the black unicorn with white socks.

"Grandam Neysa!" Nepe exclaimed happily, hardly caring about the technicality that she was Flach's grandam.

Now Nepe rode Neysa, and Lysander rode Belle, whom he had met before. Oche perched on Belle's rump, careful not to dig in her claws, and Alien continued to snooze on Nepe's hair. Sirel resumed wolf form and ranged beside them. Their party of seven was complete, and ready to move swiftly.

The two unicorn mares were old, but were ready for this effort; their strength and endurance had been magically enhanced. They set off like fillies, achieving a hard gallop that covered the ground in a manner few other creatures could match. Nepe relaxed; they knew where they were going, and they knew the terrain. There should be no problems.

The unicorns were indeed prepared. They pounded ahead not only through the day, but through the night, pausing only for natural-function breaks. Sirel was unable to maintain the pace; she assumed girl form and joined Nepe on Neysa; the two together weighed about what Lysander did, so the unicorn was not overburdened.

It was not dull, riding for hours without surcease. The unicorns played music to the beat of their hooves, Neysa's harmonica and Belle's bells merging in extemporaneous melodies and harmonies. Along their route the little animals came out to listen and watch, for the sound and sight of traveling unicorns was always special. These mares might be old, but they remained glorious in their motion.

So it was that on the third day, in plenty of time, they approached the West Pole. There was nothing fancy about it; it was just a place on an island. The water had posed a small problem, but four of them had flying forms, and the other three simply swam across. The two unicorns could have taken to the water to spear any creature who threatened the swimmers; perhaps aware of that, the predators had stayed clear. It was also possible that even the predators realized that this was a very special party, on a very special mission that would benefit every creature of Phaze.

But as they came to the Pole, they had an ugly shock. There was a Hectare guarding it. Nepe had been ready to handle a golem; the wooden things were not smart, and simple illusion could do a lot. But a BEM—this was disaster!

Alien was the one who spied it, flying ahead in the predawn darkness, scouting the way as he fed on insects. As 'Corn he had seen the Hectare, when his father turned himself in; 'Corn himself had been beneath notice, and promptly assumed his Phaze identity so as to remain clear of the invader. The Hectare had been cognizant of the fact that operations would be smoother if households were allowed to maintain themselves, so only the dangerous individuals were impounded. Thus Trool, the Red Adept, was prisoner, his Book of Magic mysteriously missing. But his wife, the beautiful vampire woman Suchevane, and son Alien remained at the Red Demesnes. Similar was true elsewhere. The families remained scrupulously inactive—until this present mission with Nepe.

They halted as soon as Alien returned to give the alarm. None of them could afford to be spied in Nepe's company by a Hectare, and Nepe hardly dared show herself in recognizable form. But the Hectare was standing directly *on* the West Pole; there was no way to avoid it.

They took shelter in the lee of a great gnarly blue birch tree and consulted, all taking human forms except Belle, who had none. So she lay and rested in feline form, alert for any intrusion from without, while they focused their lesser human senses on the problem.

"Sander, you know about Hectare," Nepe said. "Maybe now is when you fulfill the prophecy. How do we get to the Pole? Can we lure the BEM away, distract it, or something?"

"You can't do that," Lysander said from seeming air. "No Hectare has any interest in anything local except its assignment, which is obviously in this case to prevent any native from approaching the Pole. I presume that someone told them that the Pole was important, so they covered it."

"Mayhap they espied us coming here, so laid in wait," Sirel said.

"More likely they realized that there was activity at the North Pole, so set guards at all the Poles," Nepe said. "I think Purp made Brown send golems north, but the West Pole is temperate, so a Hec can handle it. But we have to reach that Pole by the end of today, or we fail."

"Fail in what?" Lysander asked.

"If I knew, I wouldn't tell you!" Nepe retorted.

"Now wait, Nepe," Echo protested. "You want his help, but he has to know how his expertise relates if he is to provide it. Maybe between what you know of the mission, and what he knows of the Hectare, you can find a way through."

She was right. Echo was a woman in love, but she had a good human mind. "I apologize, Lysander," Nepe said. "I'll tell you all I know, if you'll tell us all you know that relates."

"It's a deal," he agreed.

"I have three messages, which I must listen to and implement in order, not even listening to the next until the first is done. The first was to go to the North Pole. So Flach went. He got the help of the snow demons, and used his magic to keep them from freezing him or him from melting them, and they took him to the North Pole. Under it was a chamber where the Black and Green Adepts were. They had planted a Magic Bomb which will destroy the planet if we don't stop it. We came back with them, and they gave themselves up to the Hec. My next message was to take a Hec seed to the West Pole, by the end of today, and to bring along whom the wolves sent. I don't know what's there, but maybe another chamber. Maybe that's where the Book of Magic is. So I have to take the seed there, and that's all I know."

"That must be all the Hectare know, too," Lysander said. "If there had been anything there to find, they would have found it. So they posted a guard and are waiting to see what your business here is, if there is any. They are probably guarding all the Poles as a matter of routine precaution, after discovering the activity at the North Pole; they may not know whether any other Poles have activity. So this is probably just a guard, not an administrator. But why haven't they dismantled the Bomb at the North Pole?"

Nepe smiled. "It's not possible. It turned out that it's frozen slow under the Pole. They actually set off the Bomb, but things are so slow there that it'll take six weeks for the blast to get out of the chamber. When it does it'll destroy the planet, and all of us with it. So the Hec will never get to exploit this world, no matter what. Maybe Clef is waiting with the Book of Magic to null the Bomb at the last moment after the Hec give up and go home; I don't know. I just know I have to do what I have to do, or it's all gone."

"The Adepts are playing hard!" Lysander remarked, and the others nodded agreement; this had been news to them too. "But it gives me a notion. There must be a similar chamber below the West Pole, that the Hectare can't enter because it would take them far too long to do so. Similarly, they can't nullify it from outside, because it is what's inside that has to be affected; they might destroy it from outside, but if it contains the spell to nullify the Magic Bomb, that would be disastrous. So they are waiting for you, to see how you approach it."

"But I don't know how to do that!" Nepe protested. "All I can do is drop the Hec seed in, and then listen to my third message."

"So if we do nothing," he said, "your mission will fail, and the planet will be lost. Presumably the nullification process involves the seed, and has to be started today or it will be too late. If your mission fails, so does the Hectare's mission, because in six weeks they will only have established the apparatus to exploit the planet; they can't do the job on any faster schedule. So I can appreciate the beauty of the Adept ploy, and I see that I have to help you succeed, for your side and mine."

"You have the idea," she agreed. "Now tell me how we can get by that Hec. Can we sneak up on it, or charge it and knock it out?"

"Hardly. The Hectare's eyes cover the full hemisphere that is the side of the planet where it stands. Those facets are the lenses for its thousand-plus eyes. Each covers one section of the hemisphere, and nothing is missed. It surely saw Alien fly by, but because bats are a normal part of the night it took no action. You can not approach it without being observed as soon as there is a line of sight, and you can not attack it, because the moment you tried to it would recognize the weapon and use one of its lasers to stop you. That single Hectare guard could simultaneously laser all seven of us, because it would orient several eyes on each and coordinate them with the weapons-tentacles. When it comes to observation and combat, no creature on this planet can match the Hectare."

She had suspected as much, because of the way the Adepts had yielded to the Hectare. The Hectare had their ships threatening the planet, true, but they would not have been eager to destroy it; they wanted to exploit it. So they had to be good on the ground, too. They knew what they were doing, and they were individually sharp. "But there has to be a way!" she said.

"There may be. But it's a gamble—a big one."

"Go on. It can't be worse than the gamble of not getting through."

"It may be. You will have to approach the Hectare under a flag of neutrality and challenge it to a game."

"They are gameoholics!" she exclaimed, seeing it.

"And if it agrees, then you can bargain for the stakes. If you win, it must let you and your party through. But if you lose—"

"My left hand!" she said, feeling the pain of amputation, though she would be able to restore the hand from her body mass.

"And perhaps that of any member of your party who wants to pass with you," he said. "The Hectare like to game, but they like equivalent stakes, too. Since it can stun you and turn you in and gain a commendation for wrapping up the resistance, you will have to offer a lot to balance that out."

"More than my hand?"

"More than your capture, probably. Since it would know that it is wagering its own betrayal of its side . . . "

"More than my capture?" This was more serious than even she had imagined.

"Probably you would have to agree to serve the Hectare loyally, betraying all your former associates."

Worse yet! "I don't think I can do that. I mean, the fate of the planet—"

"Yes. The fate of the planet, because it would terminate your mission and mine. But you have to bargain in good faith, if you expect it to do so. It will match your honor. The Hectare are creatures of honor; it is their specialty. So my advice to you, as a commonsense thing, is not to make that wager, because you stand to lose everything if you lose, while if you win, you gain only the chance to complete the second part of your mission."

"But if I do nothing, and don't complete my mission, we lose anyway!" she protested.

"Unless there is some other mission you don't know about."

"I don't think so," she said, troubled. "No, I have to go on with it. But I'm supposed to take Sirel and Alien with me, so the risk is theirs too." She looked at the werewolf and vampire bat. "What do you two say?"

"We must do it," Sirel said, looking uncomfortable.

"I agree," Alien said, evidently feeling no better.

"Then the three of us will approach the Hectare and bargain," Nepe said. "The rest of you will have to wait for us—if we win. If we lose, you must go back and tell the others to hide from us, because we will be your enemies. You must not delay, because the Hectare will be after you."

Neysa, in human form, nodded. Echo looked doubtful.

"If Nepe loses," Lysander said, "Echo joins me, and the unicorns take off. If Nepe wins, we will wait for her return, and continue helping her."

That seemed reasonable. Lysander was going along with the Hectare wager. This made it easy for Echo to remain with him, without having to betray her culture. "Then you four remain and watch. Lysander can watch without being seen. By the day's end you will know."

"We will know," Echo said grimly.

"I'm not sure what form to take," Nepe said. She hadn't thought of this aspect before, because she had never expected to encounter a Hectare here.

"It will know that this can not be an innocent encounter," Lysander's voice came. "Best to identify yourself clearly, and bargain honestly. If you try to deceive it, it will refuse to listen to anything else you say."

That seemed to make sense. Why would three children come alone to the West Pole? The monster had to know it was important the moment they showed themselves.

"Hold something white aloft as you approach," Lysander said. "The Hectare will know the human parley convention."

"Something white," Nepe said, casting about and finding nothing.

"I have a slip Tsetse gave me," Echo said. She lifted her skirt, took hold of the undergarment, and pulled it quickly down. It was suitably white.

"Thank you," Nepe said. "I hope I can return it."

"That means nothing," Echo said. "You and I will be on the same side either way."

That was true. Nepe nerved herself. "We must do it now; we do not know how long the game will take."

Sirel and Alien stepped forward, retaining human form. Nepe suddenly realized that they made a nice couple, this way; it wasn't evident that they were actually wolf and bat—or, in their Proton identities, robot and human being. Stranger liaisons had occurred; how well she knew!

Nepe took the slip and held it aloft. She walked around the tree and toward the Pole. Sirel and Alien fell into step behind her. The others neither spoke nor moved.

Soon they came into sight of the Hectare. Nepe had seen the creatures before, but this time she felt a special chill, because she knew she was going to have to brace this one directly, and that her freedom and planet were on the line. She had no certainty of winning the game; indeed, she didn't know what game it would be. Suppose they couldn't agree on one? Then the Hectare might simply capture the three, and it would be over.

The Hectare gave no sign. It stood there as they approached, unmoving. But the fact that it had not fired on them was a positive sign.

At last the three stood before the monster. The Hectare, indistinguishable from any other of its kind, loomed above the three children. Its eye facets were greenish, as were its central mass of tentacles, but its lower portion was brownish. It seemed to have no front and no back; it was a bit like a giant toadstool. She understood that the Hectare breathed the air, but this was not apparent; probably they passed it continuously through hidden gills.

"We come to parley," Nepe said. "Do you understand?"

A single tentacle extended, and its end turned up.

"Do you recognize us?" she asked.

Three tentacles extended. The one pointing to Nepe turned up; the ones pointing to the other two turned down.

"Then we shall introduce ourselves," Nepe said. "I am Nepe, whom you are seeking. The boy is Alien, a vampire bat. The girl is Sirel, a werebitch. Both are my friends of long standing."

The tentacle toward Alien made a turning motion. Alien nodded, then assumed his bat form, hovering in place. In a moment he resumed boy form.

The tentacle toward Sirel gestured. She became the young wolf, then reverted.

Now all three tentacles turned up. The Hectare knew them as well as it cared to.

"We must go to the West Pole," Nepe said. "You must let us do this."

The Hectare neither budged nor signaled—which was answer enough.

"I will play a game with you," Nepe said. "If I win, you will let the three of us do what we wish, and will not report our presence here. If you win, we shall join the Hectare and loyally serve your side against our own culture. We prefer not to lose our hands, but we shall be in your power for whatever you decide—if I lose." And there it was: her offer of betrayal, which she would honor if she had to. The notion appalled her, but she believed Lysander: if she did not honestly put her loyalty on the line, she could not expect the Hectare to agree to let them pass, for its loyalty was also on the line. They were wagering for betrayal.

The Hectare did not even pause. The tentacles straightened, then turned up. It had agreed. Lysander was right, so far: they were game-oholics who could not resist an honest challenge, whatever the consequence.

"We must choose the game fairly," Nepe said, her voice sounding controlled though she was fighting to suppress a feeling of terror. She had no commitment from the monster about the nature of the game; she should have put that in her initial statement.

But the tentacle turned up in agreement. It seemed that the thing desired a fair game.

Nepe used her foot to scuff a line in the dirt. She made a second line, and a third. "We have no Game Computer," she said. "But we can place choices, and play the grid. One grid. Agreed?"

The Hectare agreed. It remained a bug-eyed monster, but its responses were so sure and just that she was coming to respect it despite her antipathy to its person and all it stood for. Actions did indeed count more than appearance!

"Is a grid of nine enough?" she asked as she made the cross lines.

Four tentacles extended. "Four on a side?" she asked.

A downturn. "A four-box grid?" she asked, surprised. "Two placements by each?"

The tentacle turned up.

"Okay. That's fair. We can place our choices slantwise, and then choose our columns. Is there an even way to do that?"

The tentacle turned up again. Nepe didn't know what the Hectare had in mind, but was coming to trust it. "I choose the game of marbles," she said, and used her finger to write the word in one corner.

The Hectare extended a tentacle, reaching the ground readily. The tentacles looked short, but stretched. It wrote LASER MARKS-MANSHIP in a box.

She would be lost if she had to compete in that! She knew how to do it, and surely the monster would lend her a weapon, but she knew that all Hectare were perfect shots with such weapons. Suddenly she doubted that her childish game of marbles was a good choice; those tentacles could probably also shoot little glass spheres with perfect accuracy.

She thought a moment, then came up with something that might be impossible for the monster: "Hopscotch," she said, and wrote it in her other box.

Unperturbed, the Hectare wrote POKER in the final box. Was it good at card games, or did it merely enjoy the challenge? Now she was uncertain. A true gameoholic might want a good game more than a victory.

The box was now complete: HOPSCOTCH and POKER on one row, LASER MARKSMANSHIP and MARBLES on the other.

"How can we choose columns?" she asked.

Tentacles pointed to Alien and Sirel. "Face away and throw one of two fingers!" Nepe exclaimed, seeing it. She used the numbers 1 and 2 to mark both the horizontal and vertical columns. "I will take the horizontals, the one if they throw odd, the two if they throw even. You will take the verticals and the same numbers, in your turn. Agreed?"

The tentacle turned up. The Hectare evidently wasn't fussy about the details as long as the choosing was impartial.

"Do it," Nepe said. "This is random, but it always is, really."

The two faced away. "Now!" Nepe cried.

Both lifted hands. Sirel had one finger extended, Alien two. "Odd," Nepe announced. "I choose the number one line. Now throw for the Hectare."

The two threw fingers again. This time Sirel lifted two, and Alien one. "Odd," Nepe said. "So it is column one for the Hectare."

Nepe looked at the grid. Box 1-1 was HOPSCOTCH. She had won her choice!

But she couldn't relax. "Do you know how to play?" she asked the Hectare.

The tentacle extended, first turning up, then down.

"You mean you know generally, but not the variants?"

The tentacle turned up.

"Then here is the way I play it, and if you don't like this variant, we'll try another. Since we both play by the same rules, it will be fair once we agree."

She used the flat of her foot to wipe the dirt smooth, then carefully scuffed the diagram. "This is called Heaven and Earth Hopscotch," she said. "But there's Hell in it too. I'll mark everything so it's clear what I'm talking about."

In due course she had it complete: twelve boxes in a column marked HEAVEN, HELL, EARTH, and numbered 1 through 9.

```
┌─────────────────────────────┐
│          HEAVEN             │
├─────────────────────────────┤
│           HELL              │
├─────────────────────────────┤
│            9                │
├──────────────┬──────────────┤
│      7       │      8       │
├──────────────┴──────────────┤
│            6                │
├──────────────┬──────────────┤
│      4       │      5       │
├──────────────┴──────────────┤
│            3                │
├─────────────────────────────┤
│            2                │
├─────────────────────────────┤
│            1                │
├─────────────────────────────┤
│          EARTH              │
└─────────────────────────────┘
```

Then she glanced at the Hectare. "Can you hop? You have to hop from box to box. One foot, like this." She lifted her left foot and hopped on her right.

The monster considered. Its feet were short, thickened tentacles, with wartlike excrescences that evidently served for traction. They also resembled caterpillar treads, in a way. It hardly seemed that such a creature could hop!

Then it separated its foot tentacle treads into two segments, shifted its mass, hoisted up one segment, and heaved itself up. Its torso rippled grotesquely and the "foot" came up, then landed to the side.

The body tilted as if about to fall, until the other foot came down to catch it.

"That's it," Nepe agreed, impressed. "Only in the game you have to stay on one foot when you land, except in some places. Let me show you."

The tentacle extended, and tilted down.

"You don't want to play?" she asked, concerned. If the BEM changed its mind now, her chance would be gone.

The tentacle made its rotary motion.

"Turn around?"she asked blankly.

It turned around.

"Something else? That turning motion means neither yes nor no?"

It turned up.

She was getting better at interpreting the signals. "You are playing, but not the way I said?"

The tentacle whirled.

Well, she had *thought* she was getting better! What was the creature getting at?

"Maybe it wants to go ahead and play now," Sirel suggested.

The tentacle pointed to Sirel, tilted up.

"You mean I should take my turn, and you'll learn from that?" Nepe asked. "If I explain as I do it?"

The tentacle turned up.

This must be one smart monster! It figured to catch on to the whole set of rules, with one example. That was a chilling signal of its confidence!

Nepe addressed the diagram. "Oops, I forgot the markers! We need one for each of us." She looked around. "A stone, or chip of wood, or a bag of sand—maybe those balls of moss." She went to fetch a selection. "Something that you can throw accurately, so it doesn't bounce or slide away, because if it winds up outside the box or on a line, you lose your turn." She laid the objects out in a line. "Choose one."

The tentacle pointed to her.

"Okay, I'll choose first." She picked up a bit of bark with moss covering it, as though it had sprouted hair.

The Hectare picked up a bit of twisted root, whose rootlets resembled tentacles.

She cleared away the other fragments, then addressed the diagram again. She stepped into the EARTH square. "This is where you start.

You have to stand inside it. Then you toss your marker into Block One." She did so, dropping it into the center of the right side. "Then you hop there, pick it up, and hop back." She did so. "Only in Earth— or later in Heaven—can you stand on both feet and rest. That's the basic game, but it gets more difficult as it goes."

She stood again in the EARTH square and threw her marker into Block Two. Then she hopped to it, picked up the marker, and hopped back. "You keep going until you make a mistake; then it's the other player's turn."

She played to Block Three, then to Block Four, the first of the paired blocks. "Once you pass these two, you can put both feet down as you pass," she said. "But only in Blocks Four and Five, and in Seven and Eight, and only when you're traveling past them. When your marker's there, you have to hop as usual."

She played on, concentrating harder as the tosses got longer. When she aimed for Block Nine, her marker bounced into HELL. "Hell!" she exclaimed. "That means not only does my turn end, I have to start over from the beginning next time. If I had missed anywhere else, I could have picked up next time where I left off." She walked around the diagram, picked up her marker, and set it in a corner of EARTH, showing her place in the game. "Your turn, Hectare."

The Hectare stepped into the EARTH box, hefted its marker on a tentacle, and flipped it into Block One. It lifted its left foot-tentacle-tread, and hopped lumberingly into the box. It extended the tentacle to pick up the marker. Then it hopped back to EARTH, not turning; to it, any direction was forward.

Nepe quickly saw that the creature had unerring aim, but was relatively clumsy on the hopping. She, in contrast, might miss her throw but never her hop. It seemed to be an even game, so far.

The Hectare proceeded smoothly through Block Five, then lost coordination as it tried to put down both treads on the way to Block Six. It had gotten balanced for one, and the attempt to put down two, then return to one was too much; it recovered balance, but one tread nudged over a line.

The Hectare left the marker, stepped out of the diagram, and waited for Nepe to resume her turn. She had not challenged the error; it had acted on its own. She had to respect the creature for being a fair player. Lysander had said that honor was a BEM specialty; evidently it was.

She went quickly through the opening squares, and concentrated intently as she reached the Nine. This time her marker landed in the center. She hopped to it, picked it up, and returned to EARTH.

"This is just the first and easiest course," she said. "Now I must toss my marker into HEAVEN, go there, and use it as the base to play the squares in reverse order."

She tossed her marker, having less trouble with the larger square. Then she hopped to it. When she was in HEAVEN, she picked up her marker and tossed it into Block Nine. She continued to play in that direction.

She made it through, and started on the next sequence: shoving the marker with her lifted foot as she hopped from EARTH to HEAVEN, and from HEAVEN to EARTH.

"Next I have to balance it on one foot," she said. "If I make it through this, the next is balancing it on my head."

But she didn't make it through. She lost it as she picked it up on Block Six and tried to put both feet down on Four and Five; the shock of the contact with the ground jogged it loose. "I'll have to pick up at Block Six next time," she said with regret. "You have to do it right, all the way, before you can go on."

Now the monster took its turn. Starting on the same Block Six, but with a simpler exercise, it proceeded on through the course. It had learned how to hop better, from practice or from watching her, and was much smoother now.

Indeed, it went on past her, having no trouble shoving the marker while hopping. It also was able to balance it on the lifted foot. The rate at which the creature gained skill was disheartening; Nepe was very much afraid she was going to lose. She would not be able to cry foul, because it was her choice of games and the Hectare was playing fair. She would have to betray her society, and perhaps the last hope of saving her world from destructive exploitation.

The Hectare proceeded to the next course. It set the marker on the top of its head. But this was awkward, because its head was composed entirely of eye facets. It evidently did not like having something sitting directly on an eye, understandably, but the facet was glassy, and the marker did not seem to hurt it.

However, that same glassiness posed a problem. When the Hectare hopped, the marker slid, and only with a special effort did the creature retain it. And hopped into a line. Its turn had ended.

Now Nepe's hope revived. She played on from the Six, and with inspired balancing got through. Then she started on the head. Her eyes were not on top, so that did not disturb her; indeed, her wild hair helped hold the marker in place.

To a degree. The Six Block caught her again, because she had to put both feet down on Four and Five, and it changed her orientation. The marker slid off.

The Hectare resumed at Block One, with its marker on its eye facet. It hopped—but again the marker slid off. It was evident that when the monster's sight was obstructed, in however minor a manner, its equilibrium suffered, ruining its concentration.

Nepe stepped up to take her turn. Now she had a real chance, for the monster had not passed her by in its turn!

The Hectare stepped forward, barring her play.

"But it's my turn!" Nepe protested.

The Hectare picked up its marker and dropped it at her feet. Then it walked away from the diagram—and the West Pole.

"It's conceding!" Alien cried. "Thou didst win, Nepe!"

Nepe, amazed, realized that it was so. The Hectare had realized that she had a decisive advantage at this stage. Only it knew how difficult this course was for it. Rather than continue to flub turns, it had yielded the victory.

"It's true?" Nepe asked the Hectare, who had taken a stance a short distance apart from them. "You will let us go to the Pole, and you won't interfere or report us?"

The tentacle extended and turned up. The BEM was one good loser!

"Then I want you to know that you played a good game, and I thought I was going to lose," she said. "I didn't know you would have that trouble with the marker on your head. I would have served you if I had lost, and I am glad to see that you are honoring our deal too."

The tentacle tilted up. That was all. The Hectare watched, but made no other motion.

Nepe was coming to respect the BEMs. They did have honor, as well as intelligence and skill.

"Come on, then!" she exclaimed to her companions. "We're in time after all."

They approached the spot. It was marked by an X on the ground. That was all.

"This be where the curtains crossed, in the old days," Alien said. "My sire spoke o' it."

"But there are no curtains now," Nepe said. "Everything's merged, so there's no line of separation. But it has to be important some way."

She squatted, tracing her fingers through the dirt. The X was actually a ridge, not a mere marking. She took hold of the ridge and pulled.

It came up. The others jumped in to help, and in a moment the lid covering a hole was all the way over and back. Below was darkness.

"But methinks the BEM could have done this," Sirel said. "Why did it but guard?"

"Because time changes inside," Nepe said. "It may be slower in there, which makes it dangerous for anyone who doesn't belong." She stared down into the mysterious region. "And maybe for us too. But either we have to go in—or just drop the seed in."

"Alien and I would have been asked to come with thee not," Sirel said, "an there be not reason. Needs must we go in, come what may."

That seemed to be the case. "Then we shall do it," Nepe said. She put her foot to the hole—and found a barrier. It would not go down.

"But I think not in this form," she said after a moment. "Maybe it is barred to human beings and aliens."

Sirel assumed her bitch form. She extended a paw, and it passed the barrier without impediment.

Alien became the bat, and flew down into the hole. He neither slowed nor fell; indeed, he bounced back out so suddenly Nepe was surprised. He resumed human form. "It be fast in there!" he exclaimed. "When I went down, it were the two of you who froze, responding to me not."

"Fast!" Nepe exclaimed. "That may explain much!"

"It be not deep," Alien continued. "I fathomed it with mine ears, and it turns below and makes a slanting tunnel a wolf could walk."

She changed her structure, forcing the Hectare seed out. She held it in her hand, protecting it. Then she turned the body over to Flach. He would have to take it from here, for only magic could relate properly to this.

12

Weva

Flach held the seed. "Methinks I be best off in bat form, with Alien," he said. "Canst carry the seed, Sirel?"

The bitch lifted her nose, and took the seed gently from his hand. Then Flach became a bat. "We go together!" he called in the bat language to Alien. "Cling to Sirel, and let her go in. An we spy danger, we can guide her clear."

They lit on the wolf's back. Then Sirel stepped into the hole. She dropped only a short distance before landing firmly at the tunnel floor.

Now Flach's ears confirmed what Alien's had perceived. This was a curving passage, spiraling down below the Pole. Above, in the lighted hole, motes of dust hung motionless. They were living much faster now. He should have realized that it would not be identical to the situation at the North Pole. What point, slowing down, when they had so little time to forge the weapon against the invader?

Reassured by their contact, Sirel walked on down the tunnel.

Several loops down it broadened into a chamber, where there was light: at first dim glows from fungi, then brighter glows from lamps. As Sirel stood at the edge, there was a growl, coming from darkness beyond the chamber.

"Who dost thou be?" the growl demanded. Flach could understand it because of his years with the wolves.

But Sirel couldn't answer, because she was holding the seed in her mouth. So Flach changed forms and assumed his wolf form, Barelmosi. "We be three, coming as directed to the West Pole," he growled.

"Who dost thou be?" the growl repeated.

"I be Barelmosi, also known as the Unicorn Adept. With me are Sirelmoba, who be my Promised bitch, and Alien, o' the vampire bats. Now, in fairness, tell us who thou dost be, and what thou dost demand o' us."

The other came in view. It was an animal head: a man with the head of the wolf. "I be but a servant o' our cause: to save Phaze from being ravished. Hast brought the seed?"

"Aye."

"Give it here, and follow."

Flach assuming human form, reached to take the seed from Sirel's mouth, and carried it to the wolfman. The wolfman took it and turned to walk into the gloom at the far end of the chamber. They followed, Alien assuming human form, Sirel retaining bitch form. Flach wasn't certain what was coming, and knew the other two were as nervous as he.

Soon they arrived at a deeper, brighter chamber, where a group of animal heads stood. Prominent among them was an elephant head. "Eli!" Flach exclaimed. Then he had a second thought. "Or be it thee? Thou dost look older."

"We be all older," Eli said. He used the language of the animal heads, which was a mixture of those sounds common to most of them; Flach understood it because he had learned a number of animal languages when he mastered the animal forms. Eli had helped his father Mach train in table tennis, before Flach's birth, for an important game with his other self; the elephant head held the paddle with his trunk, and played marvelously well. Flach had come to know him in the past year, and liked him. "We be ten years in this den, preparing for thee."

"But I saw thee nigh three months ago!" Flach protested. "With my sire, the Rovot Adept. Dost not remember?"

"I remember. But much o' a month ago in thy time, we descended to this realm and fashioned o' it the Pole Demesnes, that we might train thee and make the decoys. That be ten years, our time, and aye, we be older."

"But thou must get out, then, before thou dost age too far!" Flach exclaimed, horrified. "Thou and thy companions!"

"Nay, Adept, not so! Our lives be as long as e'er, in our terms; we feel not the loss. We have been constructively busy, and now the region be nice for thee and thy companions. For thou must remain with us a time."

"But came I here only to deliver the Hec seed! Needs must I do one more errand before I rest, to save the planet."

"Aye. But this be part o' thine errand. Thou must be trained here, three years."

"Three years!" Flach exclaimed. "But the Magic Bomb will ravage the planet within six weeks! Five weeks." For a week had passed since he had stood at the North Pole with wonderful Icy. Ah, the demoness—

Don't get distracted! Nepe snapped.

"Three years our time," Eli clarified. "One week, outside. We be at gross velocity: an hundred and forty-four times norm. Well we know the outside limit!"

Flach looked at his companions, appalled. But as he did so he realized that their presence here was part of the plan, whose nature he did not understand. Certainly he had no reason to distrust Eli.

"I must trust thine information," he said. "We be at thy service."

"First must we take thy companions to the laboratory," the elephant head said.

"The laboratory?" Flach asked, upset again. "That be a science notion!"

"Aye, lad! We have rovots and computers here and the rest o' science, but the wolf and bat must needs be fresh for our purpose."

"*What* purpose?" Flach demanded. "I can suffer no ill to my friends!"

"Nor shall there be ill to any," Eli reassured him. "We but need tokens from their bodies, that we may craft what be needful."

"Tokens?"

"We may not tell thee more now," Eli said. "For thou must go out again amidst the enemy, and the secret be not secure there. But thou shallst see they be not harmed. Now do the two o' you come w' me, while Flach takes his leisure at thine apartment. The wolf will show thee there, Adept."

Sirel assumed girl form. "It be all right, my Promised," she said to Flach. "We knew we came not here for naught. We will see thee presently."

Flach watched them go with dismay. This was not at all what he had expected.

The wolf head guided him down another tunnel to a chamber that turned out to be very much like a Proton room. There was a video screen and a bed and a machine for dialing food. "I thank thee," he said shortly to the wolf head, dismissing the creature. He felt like a prisoner.

Alone, he turned on the screen. It did not have any input from outside, unsurprisingly; the time barrier stopped that. It did have an assortment of canned entertainments and educational programs.

He turned it off, lay on the bed, and pondered. The North Pole must have been a similar warren, that he had never before his trip there known of or suspected; the elders were good at keeping secrets when they wanted to. That had been slow time, so if the Green and Black Adepts had gone there at the same time the animal heads came here, it would have seemed like only a few minutes, perhaps, though a month passed outside. Meanwhile, here, it had been ten years! Plenty of time of get it in shape for company.

But what were they going to do with fresh "tokens" from Sirel and Alien, and the Hectare seed? He had hoped to have the answer to prior riddles once he got here, but instead he was encountering only greater mysteries.

Disgruntled, he lay there for a time, and then he slept.

He woke as Sirel and Alien returned, both in human form. "See, we be fine!" she exclaimed. "It were but a bit o' tissue from each, and we be done." She changed to wolf form, and back, so that he could see she hadn't changed.

"But we be captive here, for three years," he reminded her.

"Whate'er it takes to free our realm," she said brightly. She looked around. "This be like Proton!" She became Troubot, in straight machine form. "Exactly like Proton," the robot said from a speaker grille.

Alien became his Proton self, 'Corn, fully human. "Yes, it is true." He returned to his Phaze self. "But methinks I prefer to sleep hanging from a rafter." He reached up, took hold of a convenient plank, and became the bat. He flipped neatly over and caught the wood with his feet.

"And thee?" Flach asked Sirelmoba. "Dost thou be similarly satisfied?"

"Aye," she said. "Because I be with thee."

His bad mood eased. It could indeed have been worse.

She joined him in the bed for the night, evidently feeling naughty, because in neither her machine nor wolf aspects did she use a bed.

She tickled him, and the rest of his bad mood dissipated. She wasn't exactly Icy, but she was his Promised, and in due course that would be far more significant than anything he had done with the demoness.

The three of them were kept so busy they hardly had time to be bored. They were subjected to a full program of education in all the things of Proton and Phaze, but especially in music. This amazed Flach again. He liked music, for in his unicorn form he was a natural musician, with the sound of the recorder. But why were they all being trained to be expert in different instruments?

"There must be reason," Alien said philosophically, and Sirel agreed. Indeed, the two, who had not associated with each other much before, were turning out to be surprisingly compatible. Flach was the odd one out.

So, increasingly, for the classes, he turned the body over to Nepe, who was more patient about such things. That had another advantage: it attracted Alien's attention, for he had always been sweet on Nepe. Thus Nepe was the center of attention, because Sirel's other self Troubot liked her too.

One of the things they learned in detail was the scientific nature of Proton. For this all three of them assumed their Proton identities, because it was mind-bendingly complex in some aspects.

Proton seemed like a planet orbiting a star, but it was not. Not exactly, anyway. It was a black hole companion to the star, far smaller and denser than it seemed. The light from the star touched its shell and whipped around it to depart at right angles, leading to strange optical effects. The globe rotated on an axis pointed to the star, so that the South Pole should have been unbearably hot and the North Pole unbearably cold. They were hot and cold, respectively, but not to the degree they might have been, because of the bending of the light; the south got less and the north more than otherwise. The hemispheres of day and night were east and west, clearly demarked at the North and South Poles, where the line of their contrast actually crossed. That was what Flach had seen as a shadow over half the North Pole. That shadow slowly turned counterclockwise, with the clockwise rotation of the globe. At the South Pole the shadow would seem to turn clockwise. There was a complex explanation for just how the light of the sun appeared to be coming from above the equator when actually it was whipping around the tiny black hole inside the planetary shell, but they didn't pay much attention to this. After all, magic made all kinds of illusions seem real. So at night they looked at the stars, not caring what devious route their glitters took. There was a chamber whose ceiling was one-way invisible, so that they could see the day and night skies, though no creature on the surface could see down into the Pole Demesnes. That was enough.

But a greater anomaly was the orientation of the two sides of it. Most planets, being round, had lands and seas extending all the way around, continuously. Thus they had no west or east poles. Proton had such Poles—because they were the limits of the original curtain between its aspects. Beyond those Poles was Phaze, the other side of the planet. But this other side had not been apparent, because it was in the realm of magic. Proton and Phaze were similar geographically, and in their fundamental natures, but the laws by which things operated differed. Yet they remained connected, with the happenings and creatures of one tending to form alignment with the happenings and creatures of the other, as interpreted by their natural laws. Between the two had been the curtain, which few folk could cross. That curtain had wandered in seemingly curvaceous fashion across the planet, from East Pole to West Pole. But when a person crossed it, he crossed to the equivalent nexus on the other half of the planet. This had been the only effective connection between the universes of science and magic, for three hundred years.

When the Adept Clef merged the frames, he had in effect caused the magic hemisphere to slide around the planet to overlap the science hemisphere. Because they were fundamentally similar, they had been compatible, and the sets of selves had become individual folk with alternate natures. But this had changed the face of the planet. With its two sides merged, it lacked anything on the far hemisphere. Now there was nothing there.

That was why there was no reference to the far side of the planet. No one could go there, for anyone who stepped over the edge would fall into the black hole and never return. A short distance beyond the four Poles, the world ended. The old fear of Earthly navigators that they might sail off the edge of the flat world and be lost was valid here. Only on the doubled shell that was the residential continent with its peripheral waters was life possible.

The plan to save the planet (half-planet shell) was simple in essence, if not in detail. It was to slide the doubled shell around to the far side of the black hole, which was in the fantasy universe. Actually this wasn't exactly a physical thing, because the shell already rotated around the black hole, making day and night feasible in their fashion. It was in relation to the aspects of the hole, which transcended normal physics. When the sides had been separate, the curtain had served as the crossing point from science to magic. Now there was no such avenue; a bit of the magic frame was caught within the science frame, so was accessible by other creatures of the science universe. That was the problem with the Hectare. But if the shell could be slid around to the fantasy frame, then it would be accessible by the creatures of the fantasy universe—and not by those of the science one. There might be horrendous magical menaces out there, but in the three hundred years the two sides of the planet had been parallel, the only exterior contact had been from the science side, so the magic universe seemed like a better bet.

But the playing of the Platinum Flute that had merged the shells would not be enough to slide them both around. It was a general rule of magic that a particular spell worked only once for a particular person; only creatures who had evolved with alternate forms could change them repeatedly. The merger spell had been used, and would not work again, even if that were the one needed. What was needed was a slide spell, of such power as to move half a world—and the device to summon such magic and control it did not exist. Neither did any person or creature with the ability to play it.

However, it had been ascertained that such a device could be crafted, in time, and that was being done. And a creature could be generated to play it—and that was being done. So the years necessary for each were being spent under the Poles. Only the proper elements were needed, at the right time—and this was what Nepe and Flach were coordinating.

"But why are *we* being trained to play music?" Nepe demanded.

"Two reasons," the bear head in charge of the class growled. The three children had learned to understand all the animals well enough, as time passed. "First, there is a need for decoys, in case the Hectare catch on; they must not know which person or creature is the one who will play. Similar iridium flutes are being crafted, only one of which is magic, so that if any are destroyed, they will be decoys. Second, you may be needed to accompany the player, for it will be a complex tune. Your flutes may not be magic, but if they help support and guide the true flute, they are essential. You must play well enough to enable the true one to play perfectly, for the fate of the frames depends on this."

Now they understood, and continued their practice with greater enthusiasm. The three, playing lovely iridium flutes together, generated quite pretty and intricate melodies. Nepe and Flach knew that they were not as good as Grandpa Stile or Blue, and certainly not close to the Adept Clef, but they could make the animal heads pause in whatever they were doing, to listen until the melody ended.

So the time passed, and they did not find it dull. The animal head children joined them in the classes, eager to learn about the outside realm they had never known. For a self-sustaining community had come here, complete families, giving up their lives on the surface. All to accomplish the plan to free Phaze from alien exploitation. It was apparent, if there had ever been doubt, that there was an enormous and dedicated complement involved, with Flach and Nepe only one little part. But if they failed, the entire effort would come to nothing.

Suddenly, it seemed, they were older. Sirel came into her first season. Flach would have been satisfied to wait indefinitely for it, so as to remain her Promised, but it was not to be. "I need you, Barel," she said, and though he remained young—about eleven in human terms—he knew it was true. Indeed, her readiness was acting on him, making him mature, at least when in wolf form, rapidly.

They went into a private section of the "park"—a region of honeycombed tunnels where edible plants grew magically in twilight—and there as wolves accomplished in a moment what endless prior experimentation had not approached. Suddenly they were Wolf and Bitch, adults by the standard of that society, and their Promise was fulfilled. Never again would there be this between them; like brother and sister, they had only familial interest in each other, and their shared experience.

They assumed their human forms again, and found themselves still children. But now they knew that their innocence of childhood was over, and that stage by stage, inevitably, they would discard their fancies of youth and assume increasingly those of the adult state.

"Yet still we be friends," Sirel reminded him wistfully.

"Aye," he agreed. "Forever friends." And he discovered that the thing he had feared was not actually a loss, but a portal; behind were the things of childhood, and ahead were the things of the adult state.

If, for example, he were to travel again with the lovely demoness Icy, and she teased him with her luscious body again, wrapping her legs around him as she pretended to instruct him on the delights of his far future, he would have a potent response! But perhaps more likely, and more important, he could now orient on adult relationships, seeking that one who would share his future in the way his dam shared his sire's. It was a dawning but exciting prospect.

Sirel evidently was having a similar realization. Their friendship had not suffered, it had merely changed its nature. They now understood each other and themselves and their culture in a more significant way.

Suddenly, it seemed, their tenure here was done. Three years had passed, and it was time to return to the normal realm. Flach had grown so accustomed to this society that he almost regretted it; there had been comfort in living with the animal heads, and he had made friends with the animal head children. But he had not forgotten his mission.

"Remember," Eli warned him. "Outside it be but a week past. Thou willst have to hear thy third message, and do what it directs, whate'er it be; we know not."

"But Sirel and Alien—what o' them?" he asked.

"The main part o' their missions were accomplished at the outset," Eli said. "But an thy message tell thee to keep them with thee, then that must they do. An it be other, then they be free for their own devices—until thou dost need them at the end."

"We would participate further in thy mission," Sirel said, "an we can. But too would we remain with each other." For after Sirel had achieved her maturity and abated the Promise, her interest in Alien had changed. The two had been friends; slowly they became more than friends. They could not relate intimately in their animal forms, but could in the human form, and it looked very like a rare wolf-bat romance. That could bring trouble with their subcultures, but after the robot-unicorn liaison that had generated Flach, acceptance might be easier.

"An I have a choice, will I keep ye two with me," Flach said.

"And gi'en that choice, will we remain with thee," Alien said.

So it was agreed. The three embraced, and made their preparations for departure. They bid farewell to the animal head children they had known so well for three years, and packed supplies, and of course their three iridium flutes.

They left by the same spiral passage they had arrived by; it was the only avenue to the regular realm. The Hectare stood guard as it had three years before, standing off the Pole. Eli had assured them that it was the same one; the animals had kept watch. That meant that the deal should hold. Indeed, as the three emerged and walked past, the creature took no seeming notice. But after they cleared the Pole and shut its lid, it moved across and stood over it again. That was signal enough.

They walked back to where the unicorns and semi-human companions had waited. They were there; the firefly was first to spy the approaching party and alert the others.

"But these are older!" Echo exclaimed.

"Three years older," Flach agreed. "Time be changed, under the West Pole, as it be under the North Pole, only it accelerates. We have lived and grown."

"It must be," Lysander said, from his invisibility. "No one else has come, and the BEM has kept faith. In fact, it showed us the flag of truce and challenged us to a game; it had figured out where you came from. We declined, but we did talk to it, under that truce; we told it the stories of Phaze, and it told us the stories of the galaxy."

"It be an honorable creature," Flach agreed. "This guard duty must be boring for it, so once it lost the game, it took advantage of the situation to do something interesting."

"Must needs we kill them, when we win?" Alien asked. "Methinks we could get along, an they be not in a position to despoil our world."

"If you win, they will capitulate gracefully," Lysander said. "But unless you have something exceedingly special, that I can not stop, you will lose."

"The more I learn o' the Adepts' plan, the more certain I become that there be something special," Flach said. "But exactly what it be, I know not."

"Maybe it is time for your third message," Echo said.

"Aye. I hope I insult none here an I take that message alone; I know not whe'er it be secret from some or all but me."

"Go by thyself," Alien said. "Tell us what thou dost deem proper."

Flach walked toward the ocean, sat in a hollow, and brought out the message capsule. It said, TAKE WEST POLE'S PRODUCT TO SOUTH POLE, WHEN.

He pondered that. He had gone to the North Pole, it turned out, to bring the Green and Black Adepts out at the proper moment; otherwise, in that slow time, they would not have emerged when they were supposed to, and the Magic Bomb would have been set wrong. So though the message had seemed inadequate, it had turned out to be all he had needed to know. The second message had told him to take the Hectare seed to the West Pole, and to go with those with him and four the wolves sent. Those with him—actually with Nepe—had been Lysander and Echo; the wolves had sent Sirel, Alien, and the two unicorns. Evidently the word had been spread before, for them to be ready for the call. It had all been set up, somehow, so that Flach and Nepe fell naturally into the pattern. Even the use of the enemy agent, Lysander, had turned out perfectly, suggesting that the prophecy had known very well what was to happen.

But they had just left the West Pole, and the only product they had was the decoy flutes. That didn't seem to be enough. Those flutes could have been delivered by other means; they were useful only as decoys. Take decoys to the South Pole? That suggested that the action would be somewhere else. Yet it seemed most likely that the action would be with Flach, the only loose Adept, and Lysander, the person of the prophecy. How could they be elsewhere?

And it said WHEN. What did that mean? Not now? If so, how would he know when? He was baffled.

It's a riddle, Nepe thought. *How would that distressingly gorgeous ice maiden unriddle it?*

Icy? She would instantly fathom the manner some seemingly unrelated factor factored in, and suddenly everything would make sense. She would point out the obvious, that Grandpa Stile/Blue had said it would take seventeen years to forge the counterweapon, and that time was accelerated under the West Pole so that one week outside was three years inside, so that seventeen years inside would fit within six weeks outside, and—but of course that wouldn't match, because in only another four weeks the Magic Bomb would emerge from slow time and destroy the planet.

To which objection she would say—

That if one Pole was slow, and another fast, who could say what might be under the other two? Maybe slower—or faster. In which case those seventeen years could be accommodated!

But if one was faster, why wasn't the whole thing done there? It didn't seem to make much sense to set up at the wrong Pole!

Because different things have to be done at different rates, Nepe thought, speaking for the imagined demoness. *Like a recipe: it only works when the slow and the fast ingredients are mixed at the right moment.*

It did seem to be making sense. But why hadn't they been allowed to remain under the West Pole until the device was ready?

Because we're part of the recipe, Nepe thought. *We're the icing, that has to wait for the cake to bake.*

Well, maybe. So what were they to do meanwhile, since they didn't know when the rest of it would be ready?

Wait for a signal. And that seemed to be it. They would know in the Pole community when their product was ready; they could send someone out to let Flach know.

Flach returned to the others. "I think I needs must wait here until I receive notice from those under the Pole that things be ready. Then will I have to make a very difficult trip. The rest of you may prefer to go home now."

"Forget it, Flach," Echo said. "We didn't wait here for you to come out just to desert you when you did. We'll go with you until it seems we're not supposed to."

He looked at each of the others, including the spot where Lysander stood. The Hec agent would want to remain, certainly! All were certain; they had probably discussed this among themselves.

"Then I thank all of you," he said. "We must wait here for word from under the Pole, if the Hectare guard allows."

"The deal with the BEM had no time limit," Lysander said. "Had you lost, you would have been permanently captive. You won, so you have permanent access. You three, not the rest of us. But you may entertain the guard while you wait, if you wish."

So they entertained the guard, and themselves, by playing assorted games that were not for stakes. They played cards, and the monster learned quickly and well; it was able to remember every card played, and quickly calculate the changing ratios and odds, so that its advantage increased. Nepe played it several games of jacks, after they made the pieces out of local materials, and its eyes were so sure and its tentacles so dextrous that it quickly became unbeatable. They played guessing games, but its lack of local cultural knowledge handicapped it, just as Flach's lack of knowledge about Hectare conventions made some supposedly simple riddles impervious to his comprehension. But overall, they were all having fun, and the time passed quickly. In fact, Flach was getting to like the BEM, despite everything.

* * *

In this manner three weeks passed. Flach was getting worried; there was barely one week remaining of the grace period before the Magic Bomb erupted. Had he misjudged the situation? Was he supposed to go back inside the caves after all? Yet Eli had not told him that.

Then a creature emerged from the Pole cavern. It was a bat— which was odd, because there were no straight bats in that refuge. There was a bat-headed man, but if that man sired a child it would be another animal head, not a full animal.

Alien assumed bat form and flew to meet the other. They had an inaudible dialogue. Then they came together to join the gaming group.

Alien resumed boy form. Beside him, the other bat became a rather pretty red-haired girl of their own age. "This be Weva," Alien said. "She comes to tell Flach to come inside for a day."

Astonished, Flach stared at her. "Thou wast hiding in there, and we saw thee not?" But as he said it, he knew it could not be; she could have been only three years old when they left the cave. If she had hidden, it would have been arranged by her parents. Was she a throwback, one who had turned out a vampire bat instead of a bat head, her two forms separate instead of properly merged in the animal head way? That might account for it; now they used her as a messenger.

"I was kept apart," Weva said. "By the time I was of age to school, thou was gone. But now I be thine age, and glad to meet thee at last. Willst come with me?"

"For a day? Dost mean here, or there?"

"A day here," she said. "Four and a half months there."

"What o' my friends?"

"Only thou must come," she said firmly. "Can they wait not one day for thee?"

"Aye, we can," Sirel said, tugging at Alien's arm to draw his attention away from Weva. She was frankly jealous, evidently realizing that his interest in her had been in the absence of a girl of his own species. Now one had shown up.

"This summons needs must be answered," Flach said. "I will go with thee, and return in a day, outside time." The Hectare was with the group, listening, but unconcerned; their truce covered everything, and only when they departed the Pole permanently would it end. Then, of course, the BEM would report, and the chase would be on. But they had been careful not to mention the next mission to it.

Weva resumed bat form, and Flach followed her to the Pole. She flew down into it, and he jumped in after her.

Inside, he stood for a moment, letting his eyes adjust. Then he started walking down the spiral tunnel.

In a moment there was a growl of a wolf. Flach looked, his eyes adjusting. It was a full wolf, a nearly grown bitch, but not Sirel, who remained outside. He used his magic to assume wolf form, because he had learned that the splash of magic did not extend outside the caves; the time differential seemed to damp it out so that the Purple Adept would not be able to pick it up. "Who dost thou be?" he growled, for he had known of no werewolf here either.

"Thou dost know me not?" she inquired archly.

"I have seen thee ne'er before," he replied, irritated. "Methought none but animal heads came to these caves."

"Thou thought correctly," she growled, amused.

She was teasing him, but not in a way he could quite fathom. He walked on down the spiral with her, not deigning to comment further. Eli would surely explain why these creatures had been hidden from him and Alien and Sirel, who would have been as interested as he in their presence.

"I must leave thee now, but the rovot will guide thee," Weva said.

"Rovot?" he asked, surprised again. But she was gone.

Well, there were robots here; they took care of most of the menial chores and new construction. He turned the body over to Nepe, who hardened it into the aspect of a humanoid robot.

They came to the first nether chamber. There stood the other robot, and it was not a maintenance machine, but a humanoid specimen, of masculine gender. This was another surprise, because there had been no such machine in evidence in the three years they had lived here, and they thought they had come to know every member of the community. Obviously they had missed a lot.

"Who are you?" Nepe asked.

"I have a name," the robot said. "But that is an approximation for convenience, and need not be employed."

Which was a typical robot answer. "Are you self-willed?"

"I am."

"Why didn't I see you before?"

"That answer will be known in due course."

Another robotoid response! Nepe walked on with it, toward the chamber where Eli normally stayed.

"I must separate from you now," the robot said. "But a man will await you."

The robot departed down a side tunnel. Nepe walked on, taking the opportunity to shift to her straight human form—and soon encountered a boy.

She stopped and stared. This was a full, complete, man-headed human being! Which was absolutely unlikely, here.

"Who are you?" she asked gamely.

"I am called Beman, but that tells only part of my story," the young man said.

Nepe studied him frankly. He was a handsome youth, about her own age, with curly reddish hair and eyes that seemed almost to echo that color. She would have liked him better if less perplexed about his appearance here, though.

"How did you come here?" she asked.

"I was made here," he replied.

"Oh—you're an android!"

"Not exactly." Like the others, he seemed amused.

"How many of you are there in this game?" she demanded suspiciously.

"As many as there are in yours."

She walked with him, not satisfied with this answer. Something odd was going on, and evidently Eli and the animal heads were in on it. But what was the point, when they knew she had a mission to save the planet?

"I must leave you now," Beman said. "But there will be one to make everything clear."

"Thanks just oodles," she said sarcastically.

Beman walked away, taking a side passage. Nepe pondered, then returned the body to Flach, who could change forms more readily than she could.

Flach, in his normal boy form, walked on to Eli's cave. He would have the answer soon, or else!

But as he entered the elephant head's cave, he came to a shocked stop. Within it stood not Eli, but a BEM—a complete Hectare!

How could the enemy be here, deep in the time-protected caves under the North Pole? Had the BEM they had gamed with betrayed them after all? No, that couldn't be; Flach had come to know one and a half BEMs, in the guard and Lysander, and he believed in their sense of honor. Besides, this was something he had never seen before: a small BEM, only about two-thirds the apparent mass of the grown ones. A grown one would not have fit in the entrance hole.

How had a young BEM come here, when only adults had invested the planet? How could the animal heads have tolerated it? And how could it have happened recently, since Flach and his companions had been watching the entrance for a sign?

Then it came clear. "The Hec seed!" he exclaimed.

The monster slid a tentacle across a screenlike surface. Where it touched, a line appeared. It wrote an answer in script: YOU BROUGHT ME, FLACH.

"But why do we need a BEM?"

I DO NOT KNOW.

"They raised thee here from seed, somehow, though Hectare cannot grow away from their native planet?" But obviously it was so. "Thou dost be what I were supposed to—thou dost be the West Pole's product?"

SO IT SEEMS.

"But the vamp girl, Weva, said I had to be inside for a day—which be four months here. That be not what—"

Flach broke off. Something so truly amazing was breaking across his mind that his mouth fell open.

Nepe filled it in for him, as flabbergasted as he. *The werewolf, the vampire—WErewolf, VAmpire—WEVA. They are the same! And Beman must be BEM and ANdroid. They are all the same!*

"Just as we are," Flach agreed, awed. "Male, female, robot, animal—where we're unicorn, they're—"

I THINK NOW YOU KNOW ME, the Hectare wrote.

"Change with me," Flach said. He became a wolf.

The Hectare became a wolf.

"But you're a bitch!" Flach growled.

"Aye," she growled, and assumed the girl form.

Flach became a bat. The other became a female bat. "An thou desirest a male, needs must I turn straight human," she said in bat talk.

Flach became Nepe. The other became Beman.

"And one of your forms is a BEM!" Nepe breathed. "Who could have believed it!"

"It was done in the laboratory," Beman said. "As I understand you were, before you merged with Flach. Can we be friends?"

"We'd better be!" Nepe exclaimed. "We don't want to be enemies!"

"Especially since you must teach me magic," Beman said.

Nepe turned over to Flach. "Magic!" he exclaimed.

Weva appeared. "Please?"

"That's what the four months is for?"

"Aye, Flach. Eli says it needs must be, but only thou be Adept. He says I can learn, but there be none but thee to teach me."

That was surely true! Anyone could learn magic, but most folk had only slight talent for it, while those who became Adept had great talent. It wasn't safe for ordinary folk to try too much, because the Adepts quickly cut down anything that seemed like potential competition in their specialties. But a person with aptitude, tutored by an Adept, could learn relatively rapidly. Flach himself had been close to Adept level by age four, but that had been his secret, and Grandpa Stile's. If she had the ability to learn, he could teach her a lot in four months.

"But thou dost be part BEM!" he protested.

"Aye, Flach. But three parts human, as be thou."

Through her werewolf, vampire, and android components, he realized; each of those was one part human, one part other. His own human heritage stemmed from his unicorn dam and his two human grandparents. Because he had more human shares than any other, he regarded himself as human, despite his title of Unicorn Adept, but he could assume any of the aspects of his lineage. The same would be true for Weva. "Aye," he agreed.

"I thank thee for thine understanding," she said, and kissed him.

It was a supposedly innocuous gesture, but it electrified him. The revelation of her nature was still amazing him, on a lower level of his consciousness: she was an aspect of a creature like himself, with his own potential. But superficially she was a pretty girl, much like Sirel. It had been a year since Sirel had come to her maturity, and brought him to his, in their wolf forms, but the knowledge of the change in their status still thrilled and appalled him. He was ready to relate to a girl—to a woman on the adult level, but there had been none to relate to. Now, suddenly, there was, and she was much more than he had dreamed possible. Perhaps her kiss was innocent for her, but it was not for him.

"Aye," he repeated.

* * *

He taught her magic. She was quick to learn. They found that what Weva could do, Beman could not, though he was her male aspect. Weva derived from cells taken from Sirel—which accounted for her similarity to Sirel, making her a person he could like, without having to give her up the moment it got serious—and Alien. These were creatures of Phaze, the magic realm, and magic was in them. But Beman derived from human, robot, and Hectare elements, which were scientific, and they related well to the things of science and not to the things of magic. The animal heads had evidently taken care to educate Beman in Proton speech, to clarify the distinction.

Nepe was curious about the way Beman could assume a full robot form instantly; her robot forms were all emulations, without her flesh actually becoming metal, but his seemed to be genuine metal. But he could assume only the humanoid robot form, while she could adopt any form she chose. The two compared notes, and discussed things of science, while Flach and Weva tuned out, bored. It seemed that Flach and Weva were the naturally sexed forms, while Nepe and Beman were emulations from neuter stock. The rule of no true male-female composite was being maintained.

But mostly it was Flach because of the need to cover the magic. Weva learned to conjure, and to fashion animate clouds, and to assume forms that were not in her ancestry. Thus she could become a machine that was not a humanoid robot, though her other self could not. She had to use a different spell each time, but she built up a collection of spells for such purpose, just as Flach had done in the past. Her new forms were not as realistic or functional as his, but in time they would become so. She was, after all, only twelve years old, and new to this.

Betweentimes, they talked, their dialogues becoming more intimate as their knowledge of each other progressed. "I be glad indeed that thou hast come on the scene," Flach said. "But what I fathom not is why thou didst have to have a BEM component. The BEMs be our enemies."

"I be part BEM," she agreed. "But I be not thy enemy, Flach, and ne'er can be. I serve this planet and this culture, and if it be not freed, then will I perish with it and thee."

"That I know. Yet what can a BEM do that we o'erwise could not? I think this be not part o' the prophecy."

"Nay, it be part o' thy sire's plan, and thy grandsire's plan," she said. "And that we shall fathom not till thou dost convey me to the South Pole."

"Aye. Would I could show thee Proton on the way there, but I dare not. Needs must we go direct, when we go."

They also played the flutes. She had been trained in music, as had the three of them, and had her own iridium flute. She was good with it, too—better, in fact, than he. "Well, I had more time," she said. "From age three on, did I train with it, though not by choice. But I think it be more than that."

"More than training?" he asked. This business of the flutes still perplexed him. Why should they all have to play them, when not one of them could touch the expertise of the Adept Clef? "Be thine the magic flute?"

"Nay, I can play thine as well as mine." She exchanged flutes with him, and they verified that they were the same.

"Then what?" he asked, covertly annoyed at being outskilled.

"It be my BEM component," she explained. "The BEMs be apt in coordination, because o' their many tentacles and eyes. Beman's BEM aspect can play best o' all."

"That would I like to hear," Flach said, intrigued.

The BEM appeared. The sight no longer startled Flach; he had become familiar with it, and his interaction with the guard outside had prepared him. Beman was no monster to him, in any form.

The BEM lifted the flute and fastened an air hose to it, so that the stream of air passed across the mouthpiece and caused a sustained note. Then it applied tentacles to the holes and keys, and played.

The sound was phenomenal. Flach had heard his Grandfather Stile play, and knew that on all the planet only one was better. That was the Adept Clef, whose sound was magical, figuratively and literally. In unicorn form, with his recorder horn, Flach could play very well, because it was natural to that form. The recorder was a form of the flute, with a mellower sound, and this gave him an advantage when, in human form, he played the flute. He played it very well. Thus it had been a surprise when Weva had turned out to be better, since she had no unicorn component. But now he understood that her BEM component was indeed the source of that talent. The BEM might be doing a mathematical translation, and not have any particular feeling for the spirit of the music, but its technical expertise was superlative. Weva, with animal and human components, supplied the feeling the

BEM might lack, and so even her relatively clumsy human fingers had marvelous skill.

Flach took his own flute and joined in, after a few bars, playing extemporaneous counterpoint. The music was beautiful, but he had to stop soon, because the magic was gathering. The BEM had no magical power, and its music was merely sound, but Flach could summon magic when he played, and it was dangerous to do that without turning it to some particular task.

Weva reappeared in mid note. "Teach me that!" she exclaimed.

He had assumed she realized how he used music. He realized that there was more to cover. They got to work on it.

In all too brief a span, their "day" was done, and it was time to go back out into the ordinary realm and make the journey to the South Pole. There, they hoped, the mystery of their mission would be clarified at last.

13

South

Lysander remained uncertain whether he was doing the right thing. So far he seemed to be forwarding the cause of the enemy more than that of the Hectare. Yet what else was he to do? The members of the planetary resistance knew his mission, and allowed him along only so long as he was useful to them. If he balked, they would drop him. If he turned them in, the secret plan they were implementing would never be discovered, for they themselves did not know it.

So he went along, knowing that the cunning child Nepe/Flach was using him. But he had one saving hope: that the prophecy they believed in was valid, and that only he could in the end give the natives their victory. That meant that their effort would fail without his participation and cooperation, which they could not in the end buy. Their magic had been effective in causing him to love Echo, but that love would not make him abandon his mission. So he retained the trump card, and eventually they would have to give him the chance to play it.

Unless this whole business of the prophecy was a lie, to make him cooperate. Yet that seemed unlikely, because their entire framework was marvelously consistent; everything they had told him had turned out to be true. Even the matter of the spell of invisibility: why make your enemy invisible, giving him enhanced power to snoop on you, unless you really need him? Why make one of your own partisans love him, unless you expect him to join your side.

Actually, the invisibility was wearing off now. He could see himself, translucent. So he now wore clothes, and smeared dirt on his extremities, making himself completely visible; it was better than the halfway state. It remained impressive enough, as magic: a single quick spell lasting for two weeks before beginning to weaken. He had no doubt that Flach could have changed him into a toad with similar longevity.

He stroked Echo as she lay beside him, sleeping. Her body was a machine powered by a pellet of Protonite, but her brain was living human, and it did need sleep. When it slept, the rest of her system shut down, and she was responsive only to significant physical shocks. His touch meant nothing to her now. In addition, his love for her was artificial, brought about by magic. But it was authentic. The magic had somehow reached into whatever senses his android body had, and his Hectare brain, and made those connections that natural love would have, and done them more securely than nature would have. A person who was killed by artificial means was just as dead as one who died of natural causes; similarly, his love was just as thorough.

It was interesting, though, that the love spell was not wearing off the way the invisibility spell was. Perhaps they were different kinds of spells. But it was possible that the spell was wearing off—only to be replaced at the same rate by natural love. He might be able to work his way out of love if he tried, by magnifying any doubts that seeped in. But he didn't care to try; there was no reason, when he enjoyed the emotion so much.

Would he have to give her up, when the time to implement his mission came? He was very much afraid he would. He felt grief for the action he knew he would take, betraying her along with the rest. But his discipline as a Hectare required it, and in this respect their effort of making him love a native woman had been wasted. It would not make a traitor of him. He did love her, but he loved honor more, for that was inherent in his Hectare nature. Never in all the history of the Hectare species had one of them betrayed its agreement on even the slightest matter. The protocols of honor were refined to a degree virtually incomprehensible to other species. Thus the Hectare guard, having made a deal with the enemy, honored it in letter and spirit, absolutely. True, it was betraying its species in the process— but had it won the wager, it would have helped its side similarly significantly. The protocols allowed for this; as long as the wager was fair, and the stakes equivalent, it was legitimate.

Lysander's mind reflected on the name, Hectare. This was actually a translation of a concept obscure to aliens. There was a human geographic measure termed the "meter," which was about one man's pace. In two dimensions, this became a square meter. One hundred square meters were an "are," and a hundred ares constituted a "hektare" or "hect-are," or ten thousand square meters. One BEM eye facet could track approximately one square meter at a distance, and the full eye complex could track, individually, approximately ten thousand such units. The massive brain could integrate that information and coordinate response, limited only by physical factors. Since there were not ten thousand tentacles capable of firing ten thousand laser beams simultaneously, this was a limit; with computer assistance, such coordination was feasible, and a BEM in a spaceship could indeed fire at ten thousand enemies and score on each. So the name seemed appropriate as an indication of the capacity of the species. The natives of this planet had seen only a fraction of the BEM potential. That was why the guard had no concern about the visitors to the West Pole; it was aware that they might lack the protocols of honor, but it could laser all of them well before any one of them could pull the trigger on a hand weapon. Lysander had spoken truly, as he had to, when he advised them that gaming was the only way past this guard.

There was a stir, and the bat and wolf appeared. They preferred to forage at night, and perhaps more; it was obvious that the two were quite taken with each other in their human forms. They were each twelve now, having aged three years under the Pole, and had evidently come to know each other well there. Flach, once interested in Sirel, seemed to be so no longer, though she was blossoming into an attractive young woman. They no longer spoke of their Promise.

Meanwhile, the two old unicorn mares grazed nearby, taking turns napping as they did. He had apologized to Belle for his part in her branding; had she not tried to help him escape, the first time, she would not have suffered that. But Flach had made minor magic and smoothed out that brand, and Lysander suspected that the Robot Adept had managed to eliminate the record of the brand number from the planetary listing, before sacrificing himself to help Lysander again. The Hectare was formidable, but so was the enemy, in its devious way. Which, once again, was vindication of the importance of Lysander's own mission: to discover just how formidable the enemy was. The Hectare, long experienced in alien relations (i.e., conquest), knew better than to assume that a quick capitulation was final.

These were all enemy creatures, here by the Pole, yet he found them compatible. It would be a pleasure to be a part of their magical society. Perhaps this, too, was an aspect of their plan: to instill in him a sense of their values and pleasures, so that he would identify with them and choose to join them. But as with the love, it was only partly effective: it gave him desire, but would not subvert his loyalty to his mission.

It was a shame that all this would have to be destroyed, in the interests of the larger initiatives of the galaxy. But it was not his business to consider shame, only his mission.

Lysander relaxed and slept.

Abruptly the lid lifted and two bats flew out. They came to land beside the little group playing a game of poker with the Hectare. The BEM had a pile of pebbles: its winnings for the session. It was an infallible player, understanding all the odds and values; only an adverse fall of the cards could reverse it on occasion. Sirel, playing as Troubot, could remember and figure as accurately as the BEM did, but lacked the finesse to bluff well. The Hectare was matchless at this type of game, as Lysander had tried to warn them. But of course they were not playing for genuine stakes, just the sheer challenge of it. In this the wolf and bat and harpy were one with the BEM: they were enamored of challenge. It was a satisfactory foursome.

Flach and the girl Weva replaced the bats. They looked slightly older than before, because they had aged more than four months in that one day.

"Needs must we travel," Flach said. "Canst complete the game soon?"

"Aye," Alien said. "We know the outcome already. Methinks Bem could hold the deck's weakest hand, and bluff to victory anyway."

Flach faced the Hectare. "Our sojourn here be done," he said. "We thank thee for honoring our deal, and on the morrow thou mayst report us an thou choosest."

The monster extended a tentacle, turning the tip down. It would not report them. Lysander knew that some might assume that was because such a report would bring difficulties to the Hectare, because obviously it should have reported them at the outset. But when a Hectare made a deal, it honored the deal, to the last degree. As far as this one was concerned, they had never been here. Meanwhile, it had turned a dull guarding stint into great entertainment. Its situation was akin to Lysander's own: in the performance of his mission he had had a month of the delights of love.

"Were we not enemies, Bem, we could be friends," Sirel said, laying down her cards.

The tentacle extended, tip up. Sirel extended her little finger and touched the tip. For a moment finger and tentacle curled together, linking. Then she turned and walked away.

That seemed to cover it. They walked to their campsite and cleaned it up. They had kept it largely clear, in case Purple or some other Hectare showed up, forcing them to hide in a hurry.

The two unicorns trotted in. Lysander and Echo mounted. Flach assumed unicorn form himself, and had Sirel mount him, while Weva resumed bat form. Alien also took bat form. It was now a party of three unicorns, three human beings, and two bats, as far as an observer was concerned.

What had happened in Flach's second stint under the Pole, and why was the bat girl Weva now joining their party? Where were they going? Lysander hoped to find out soon. Time was getting short, as he understood it; the enemy plan had to manifest soon, if it was going to.

They rode east, and forged across the water to the mainland, the two bats scouting the way. This time the unicorns swam, following Flach's lead, leaving their riders in place. They reached the shore and resumed trotting, not pausing to shake themselves dry.

Flach sounded his horn, speaking to the others in horn talk. Abruptly they veered to the south. So it was not to be a return to the city. But where *were* they going?

The unicorns picked up speed, running with that same endurance as before. There must have been more magic to enhance them.

Then, in a forest glade, the Unicorn Adept drew to a halt. Sirel dismounted, and Flach appeared in human form. "It be far where we go," he said. "We can make it not in time afoot. Thus will I conjure us—and bring upon us the awareness o' Purple. O' this party, four will be decoys, conjured away in due course for Purple to pursue. I tell none where we go, so that they can tell not our plans when they be captured. Any who be captured must cooperate fully with the captors, so they be not tortured. Methinks the BEMs have no interest in cruelty, merely in securing the planet, and Purple has desire for power, not pain. So make no heroics."

He paused, then nodded to Weva, who assumed her girl form. She produced a shining metal flute and began to play it. She was good; in fact she was excellent. Her tune was eerie, but strikingly beautiful. Lysander marveled at this; how had she carried the instrument while in bat form? The thing surely outweighed the bat body, as it was fashioned of silver—no, platinum, or iridium, to match the flutes Alien and Sirel had obtained under the Pole. The famed Platinum Flute had merged the frames—but what was the purpose of these iridium flutes? The metal was hardly plentiful, even in the elfin mines; it must have taken great effort to mine it and refine it and fashion it into these instruments. Certainly those flutes were a key to the major ploy of the resistance.

The air around them seemed to intensify. Lysander was reminded of the ripple he had seen when he had realized his love for Echo, the magical splash of Phaze. He understood that some Adepts used music to somehow summon magic. But how could a vampire bat girl not yet thirteen years old do this? She was no Adept!

There was also the mystery of Weva's appearance. Alien and Sirel had said little about their stay under the Pole, but he had gathered that there was a community of animal-headed human beings there, who had taught things like flute playing. There must be some other creatures too, such as vampire bats. Had Flach brought this party all the way here to pick up one bat girl? If so, then she had to be vital to the Adepts' plan. But so far he was unable to make sense of it.

Flach gestured. The ambience caught them and wrenched them as a group, as if a huge invisible hand was sweeping up people and unicorns together. The surroundings changed.

Lysander blinked. This was not the first time Flach had conjured him from place to place, but the power of the present case seemed to be of a different order. He looked around, and saw a huge range of mountains rising nearby, their slopes purple.

The Purple Mountains! The boy had transported them halfway across the continent!

Flach resumed unicorn form, and Weva returned to bat form. The two led the way on toward the mountains, and the others followed without question. This time they were not trotting, they were galloping, racing as if desperate.

Theoretically, the Purple Adept would spy the massive conjuration, and zero in on them, summoning whatever help he needed to make them captive. Maybe he would alert the Hectare, who would orient a spy beam from an orbiting ship, and stun them from afar. It hardly mattered where on the planet they were; the Hectare could reach them, once their location and nature were known. But would the focus be on the place they had left, or the place they arrived? If the former, there would be no threat, for they could have gone anywhere. They seemed actually to have proceeded southeast. What was there here near the Purple Adept's home that was important?

A light flashed behind. Lysander looked back. He had his answer: that was a satellite beam, probing the spot where they had landed after the conjuration. Purple was alert, and was able to locate the point of arrival, and was notifying the Hectare. It had taken only about five minutes for them to zero in on the spot.

But in that five minutes the unicorns had covered a fair stretch of ground, moving as no horse could. They were perhaps three kilometers from their landing, and in this forested terrain that was enough. The beam would not be able to spot them.

But the beam was only the start. Now there was the sound of an aircraft, that must have taken off from the closest airport the moment the notice was received. The thing appeared in the sky, flying from east to west, passing on out of sight in a moment. They were broadening the search, trying to canvas the region around the point identified by the beam. They would be taking pictures, checking for any sign of the fugitives. The pictures would be checked by computer, and in minutes their verdict would be in.

"Flach, they'll spot us," Lysander called. "Maybe you don't know what technology can do, but—"

The unicorn pulled up. Sirel slid off, and Flach reappeared. "Off, you two," he said.

Lysander and Echo dismounted with alacrity as Weva resumed girl form and began playing her flute. The music was transcendentally beautiful. Maybe this was her purpose here: she was highly trained on the instrument, and could use it to summon the powerful magic Flach required for his heavy-duty conjurations.

"Farewell, Belle," Flach said sadly. "Farewell, Grandam Neysa. May we meet again in better fettle."

The two unicorns sounded their horns, bells, and harmonica together, acknowledging. Then Flach gestured, and with a clap of shimmering force the two were gone.

Weva ceased playing, and the magic ambience faded.

"An I may ask, where be they now?" Sirel asked, evidently as impressed as Lysander was.

"Nigh the Red Demesnes, running toward the East Pole," Flach replied. "They be first decoys, to lead the pursuit astray. Thou and Alien be second decoys."

"Then let me bid thee bye now," Sirel said. She approached Flach, and embraced him. "Thou wast my Promised, and ne'er will I forget thee though I see thy taste for bats be similar to mine." She kissed him.

Similar to his. Lysander realized that she meant that she was finding love with one of the vampires, and that Flach was too. It seemed an accurate observation. But it was impossible to tell for sure where the young man's heart was; Weva could be merely a business associate.

"Ne'er ano'er like thee, for me," Flach said. "I would have left thee not, an the choice had been mine."

"Aye," she agreed. "But all must grow and change. We be not four years old fore'er."

"Alas, we be not," he agreed. They separated, and Lysander saw tears on both their faces. Whatever these two had been to each other, it had been important. Their separation seemed amicable, and with a certain mutual regret, though both did have other prospects.

"Now needs must we cross the mountains," Flach said. "I will carry Lysander; others may use natural forms."

"I can climb by myself," Lysander said.

"We be in a hurry," Flach told him, and became the unicorn.

Lysander mounted, knowing better than to argue the case further. Sirel turned wolf, and the two bats reappeared. Echo became Oche the harpy.

The unicorn leaped forward, so that Lysander had to hang on. The two bats flew ahead, the harpy following more clumsily but still moving well enough. The wolf disappeared into the brush. In a moment this looked like a party of two: man and steed.

They reached the base of the mountain range. Flach galloped up the slope, dodging around trees and thick brush. The pace was amazing; Lysander realized that the boy must have enhanced his strength magically, because no natural unicorn should be able to move at this velocity with a rider. Indeed they were in a hurry!

A bat flashed ahead, evidently returning from some exploration.

The unicorn turned to follow it into a depression cut by a mountain rill; the bed was dry now, and easier to traverse than the thickly wooded main slope. They plowed on through the saplings and slushy spots.

Lysander noticed that steam rose from the wet spots when the unicorn's hooves touched them. Occasionally a spark was struck from a rock as a hoof hit it. Those hooves were burning hot! That must mean that the unicorn was dissipating excess heat through the hooves, rather than by sweating, for the hide was dry. Certainly there was plenty of heat being generated, because of the breakneck pace of this climb. Indeed, now he saw a thin flicker at the animal's nostrils, that resembled the jet of a blowtorch. This creature could breathe fire, when exercised!

They climbed to a narrow pass and started down the south side. It looked as though there were a path to the side, but Flach didn't seek it; he followed the guidance of the bats, finding natural openings instead. Lysander realized that the path might be watched, so it had to be cross country.

Through the foliage of the trees he saw down the mountainside, south. It opened into a dull, bare, slightly rolling plain which looked as hot as the unicorn's hooves and breath. Could that be where they were going? What could be there?

It was odd that there were no great stirrings of wild creatures here, as they charged through. No harpies, no tusked boars, no aggressive serpents. Lysander had understood that there could be real danger for someone who came carelessly through the wilderness. But he realized that this was not just anyone; this was the Unicorn Adept, and he had magic that could probably pulverize any creature. Also, all of Phaze might know the nature if not the detail of his mission, and give him clearance to pursue it. For Lysander alone this trip would be dangerous, but it wasn't that way in this company.

Another Hectare aircraft zoomed by. The search of this vicinity was resuming. That meant that they had caught the unicorns and discovered the ruse, and were now picking up where the prior search had left off. The two mares had bought them perhaps two hours, and the party had made excellent use of the time. Lysander would not have believed the progress they had made, if he had not participated in it.

They continued on down, evidently trying to get beyond the

mountains. Indeed this seemed wise, because now the range began to rumble and shake. The Purple Mountains were, after all, the Purple Adept's home range, and he had greater power here than elsewhere. No wonder Flach wanted to get past this region quickly! Lysander had thought this trip safe; he had forgotten about the pursuit.

Geysers of steam issued from the opening cracks. Rocks rolled down slopes. The mountains were coming alive, geologically, and soon they would be deadly. The moment the Purple Adept figured out the exact position of the intruders, things would get difficult indeed.

Flach sounded a single short note. Immediately the others came in close. The unicorn stopped, and Lysander slid to the ground. It was a relief; the bareback ride was chafing and fatiguing.

Flach reappeared. "Decoys," he said.

Weva turned girl again, with her flute, and played her eerie, lovely melody. The other bat and the wolf became human and stood there, holding hands. The magic gathered.

Flach gestured, and the two were gone. "Where—?" the harpy screeched.

"To the Brown Demesnes," Flach replied. "But this be not enough; the ships will watch here also. Thou must come with me, Oche; Lysander goes with Weva."

Lysander realized that Weva had not stopped playing her flute when the conjuration was complete, this time. The magic was still being summoned, and fairly crackled in the air around them. He walked over to stand beside the bat girl. They must be getting close to their destination.

Suddenly the scene changed. Lysander discovered himself standing on the plain he had seen before, with the red-haired girl standing beside him.

"He conjured us here?" he asked, though the answer was obvious. "Why? Where are we going?"

"To the South Pole," she said, "Get a move on thee, man; it be far." She started walking south.

"Far? It must be thousands of miles! We can't walk there!"

"Mayhap we can ride a dragon, then," she said. "Yon creature winds us now."

Lysander looked. She was right: a dragon was sniffing in their direction. This hot region was the dragon's natural breeding ground, it seemed. There wasn't usually much prey here, but it was comfortable for the creatures as a resting area, and they could readily fly over the mountains for their hunting. However, they surely would snap up any creatures foolish enough to enter dragon country.

Suddenly it occurred to him that his usefulness to the planetary resistance effort might be over, and that he had been sent out here to die. The bat girl was hardly in danger; she could change form and fly away after verifying his death. Yet why should Flach have gone to such trouble to bring him this far, if that was the case? It would have been easier to dump him elsewhere.

"There be one!" Weva said. "Hurry!"

"What?" But she was already hurrying to the side.

He ran after her. She stopped at a small knob in the sand. "Pull it up. Quick!"

Lysander took hold of the knob and hauled on it. It was heavy, but it did come up, and with it a section of the ground. It was another trapdoor entrance to a tunnel or a cave!

"But it may be changed time!" he protested.

"Wouldst face the dragon instead?" she demanded as she scrambled down.

The dragon seemed quite ready to try the case; it was half running, half flying toward them, jets of smoke issuing from its snoot.

Lysander jumped down into the hole. His feet landed on a sloping surface, and he sat down. The surface leveled out quickly, and he was able to reach out and haul the lid closed before the dragon arrived.

There was light farther down. He crawled through to it, and found Weva there, in a chamber similar to the one he had shared with Echo, opening a chest. "We be in luck," she said. "They left food."

"*Who* left food? I thought there was nothing but dragons here!"

"Goblins, belike, or mayhap trolls. When they travel, they like rest stops, so they space them through. Methinks they will mind not our borrowing it."

He could hear the dragon snuffling above, looking for the vanished prey. It was apt to be a while before it was safe to emerge. They might as well eat.

She handed him a chunk of dark bread, and bit into a similar chunk herself. "I would know thee better, Lysan," she said.

She abbreviated his name the same way Flach/Nepe did. Suddenly he had a suspicion. Nepe could assume any form; was she up to something? Had he been deceived about whom he traveled with? Yet what would be the point? It seemed best to play it straight.

"I am curious about you, too, Weva," he said. "I shall be happy to trade information while we wait and eat."

"Aye, fair," she agreed. "I be more than I may seem to thee. But before I reveal that, I would play with thee."

"Play with me? A game? I know a number, as I am a gamesman."

She laughed. "Nay, 'Sander! I mean as Echo does." She shrugged out of her simple robe, showing a figure that was slender but aesthetically appealing. She was young, but woman rather than child. "Only go slowly, and explain, for I have done this not before."

She had caught him entirely by surprise. "Then I have to say that such play is not so direct," he said. "I have a commitment to Echo, and I love her, and have neither desire nor intent to have any similar relationship with any other woman. I'm sure that in due course you will be able to find a suitable vampire bat boy, after this crisis is over, if the planet survives."

"I be not exactly a bat girl," she said. Suddenly there was a wolf bitch in her place.

Not Nepe—but Flach, magically changing to his other forms! But to what point? "I don't understand."

"I be a creature o' the West Pole," Weva said, reappearing. "All my life, nigh thirteen years, I be 'mongst the animal heads. They be good folk, but none can assume full man form. So I would try it with a full man."

"I'm not a man!" Lysander protested. "I'm an android, with an alien brain." If this was a variant of Flach/Nepe, this was no news; if it really was a girl of the Pole, the news would not hurt at this stage.

"Aye," Flach said. "But thou dost be more human than I."

"I think not. My brain is Hectare."

"Then see this." Suddenly there was a Hectare in her place.

Lysander gaped. The thing was genuine! He knew the details of the species and this was true in every particular.

"Illusion!" he exclaimed. "You are fooling me with illusion!"

The Hectare extended a tentacle. Lysander touched it, expecting to feel a human finger instead. But it was real, unless the illusion extended also to touch.

This was a challenge. He remembered how he had tried to verify Jod'e, in the early game. How could he verify this?

By the codes. The patterns were inherent; Hectare used them to communicate in the planted stage, before they developed sonics. A tentacle could tap the ground, communicating with other rooted individuals, exchanging information.

He tapped the floor with a knuckle and a heel, in the GREETING, STRANGER pattern.

Two tentacles tapped in response: ACKNOWLEDGMENT, STRANGER.

It was a valid response!

The tentacle tapped again. YES, I AM GENUINE. I AM THE SEED YOU BROUGHT FROM THE CITY.

Suddenly it fell into place. They had grown a Hectare hybrid! They had merged it with bat, wolf, and human stock, all of which had been brought to the Pole.

"I believe you," he said, awed. "But what is the point?"

Weva the girl reappeared. "I have told thee much about me. Dost not feel thou shouldst respond in the manner I asked?"

"I will tell you all you wish to know about me. But as I said, my love is elsewhere."

"That can I change." She brought out her flute, played it briefly, and gestured. "Now that love be gone."

"Of course it isn't!" he exclaimed. "You can't just—"

But he had to stop, for he realized it was true. He no longer cared particularly for Echo.

"You have a potion?" he asked. "A null-love potion?"

"Nay, merely mine Adept magic skill. Wouldst prefer I make thee love me?" She lifted her flute.

"No! Please!" He realized that he was in the presence of a creature who could twist him any way it chose, and it frightened him. "I see you have power, but I ask you not to use it on me further. Just tell me what you want of me."

She nodded. "I see we understand each other. I would convert thee to our cause—the cause o' Phaze—for I be a creature o' Phaze. But Flach tells me the prophecy would be invalidated then, so this may not be. I ask thee only this: e'en as I spare thee humiliation and loss o' forced love, though I could do these without stopping the prophecy, so must thou consider carefully whe'er thy side be the correct one."

"I am a Hectare agent. I must fulfill my mission."

"Yet there may be ways and ways to see thy mission. Canst keep thy mind open to that extent?"

"I can try. But—"

"Then let us go from here; it be time." She pulled her robe back up and crawled toward the entrance.

He crawled after her, his mind whirling. This creature—part bat, part wolf, part human, part Hectare—was indeed something special! Thirteen years in the making, but only a little over a month in his time. He had helped Nepe get the Hectare seed, never dreaming how it would be used! Now Weva combined the Hectare intellectual power with the human imagination and the Adept magic. She was surely the tool the Adepts intended to use against the Hectare investment. But how could she change anything? And how was Lysander needed to complete it?

Thirteen—and she had tempted him sexually, just to demonstrate her power, it seemed. She had convinced him; there was no way he could oppose her directly. He had demurred mainly on instinct, in effect capitulating and begging for mercy. Now in his mind's eye he saw her slender body nested in the open robe, her nascent but well-formed breasts. It would have been easy to, as she put it, play with her, despite his relation with Echo.

Echo! Weva had deprived him of his love for Echo—and now there was a void. He was out of love!

Weva pushed up the lid. There was a roar, as the watching dragon spied the motion and charged.

"Begone, beast," Weva said crossly.

The noise cut off. Weva drew herself out of the hole. Amazed, Lysander followed.

The dragon was lumbering away, having lost interest in them. Weva had changed its mind with a mere two words and no music! But if she could do that, why hadn't she done it before?

Because she had wanted to make her little demonstration to him. The supposed need to hide from the dragon had been a pretext. Now that he knew exactly where he stood, she could get about her business of going where she was going.

What would she have done, if he had agreed to play with her? Probably she would have done it, being genuinely curious and perhaps without scruple. Though that was odd, because of her Hectare component.

"But it is still a long way to the South Pole!" he said. "We'll need transport."

"Aye. It be nigh."

Coming toward them was a huge manlike figure. Its heavy tread shook the ground. It seemed to be made of tree trunks and cables.

"That's a wooden golem!" Lysander protested. "The Brown Adept now serves the Hectare!"

"Aye. But she has spot control not. She sends them out on their missions, and knows not what they do till they return."

"But they do her will! That thing will haul us right back to the Brown Demesnes! And you can't interfere with Adept magic without signaling our location."

"Aye. I dare not use my power. But illusion be lesser magic, making no splash, as be emotion control."

As the monster golem came close, Weva signaled it by waving her arms. It bore down on them.

"What be thy name, golem?" she asked as it loomed close and halted.

"Franken," it said, though it did not breathe.

"Well, Franken, what thou seekst be at the South Pole," Weva said to it. "Carry us swiftly there."

"Aye, Brown," it said.

What?

The golem reached down with a giant wood hand and closed it gently around Weva. It lifted her up over its shoulder and set her in a storage box mounted on its back. Then it reached for Lysander and did the same for him.

They rode standing in the box, whose sides came a bit above waist level on Lysander. There were handholds. Evidently this was a standard setup for transporting human beings. Their heads could see over the wood bole that was the golem's head. The thing was now striding south at a horrendous rate; it was almost like flying.

"But you neither look nor sound anything like Brown!" he whispered.

"To it I do, and that be what counts. Thou needst whisper not; it hears only when addressed."

"But you've never even met Brown! You can't—"

"Dost love me still, Lysander?" she asked.

Startled by the change in her voice, he looked at her. She was

Echo! The sound and look were identical. Had he not known that there was no way it could be true, he would have been sure it was her.

"Point made," he said. "And you probably don't resemble Echo to the golem, just to me."

"Aye."

"You miss on only one thing: Echo is Protonite. She speaks as I do."

"Oops!" she exclaimed, chagrined. Then: "Do you still love me, Lysander?" This time the emulation was perfect. Weva was a very quick study!

"No I don't, as you know, Weva," he said. "You took that from me. Are you going to give it back?"

"And play my game with you, to wile the time as we travel?" she inquired. She still resembled Echo exactly, her brown fluffy hair blown back by the breeze of their swift travel, her breasts shaking under the robe with the rocking of each big golem tread.

That made him pause. Maybe he should leave well enough alone, lest this provocative woman/child entertain herself at the cost of his future with Echo.

But that thought opened others. There would be no future at all, if his mission succeeded. The Magic Bomb would destroy the planet. So what was the point of being true to Echo? She would be better off if he were untrue to her—and to his mission. And he—he was objective now, no longer blinded by a potion-inspired love. Did he really want that love back? He could function better without it.

If he did not take back that love, he could do as he wished with Weva. She was young, but the way of this planet made physical age of little account; a robot was adult from the moment of its creation, unless otherwise programmed, and the creatures of Phaze let nature be their guide. If a female was mature enough to desire sex, she could indulge as she chose, requiring only an amenable male. That was probably seldom a problem. So Weva's notion of playing with him was valid on her terms. She could do it in the semblance of Echo, or Jod'e, or Alyc, or in her own; she would have control of the situation regardless. If the planet was soon to be destroyed anyway, why not enjoy the time remaining?

Yet Echo had shared the love potion, and her love had not been nullified. She was a good creature; he could appreciate her qualities with clear vision now. He would never of his own choice have taken up with a woman who could turn harpy, and whose body even in her human state was fashioned of metal and plastic, but his experience had shown him better. He had been in love with a good woman, who had returned his love; it had been an excellent state. She had the mind of a harpy in the body of a robot; he had the mind of an alien creature in the body of an android. They were a good match, and he would be satisfied to let it stand.

"Give me back my love, but do not play your game with me," he said.

Weva's natural likeness reappeared. "Thou canst gain from that only if thy mission fails," she pointed out.

"And if it fails, I will be a criminal in the new order," he agreed. "I have no future here, either way. But until then, I choose to live honorably."

"I fathom that not!"

"You have a Hectare component. Surely you understand honor."

"Nay, that were not in my syllabus."

That was interesting. Apparently this Hectare protocol did not manifest full-blown. Perhaps it had to be evoked by contact with other Hectare as the individual developed. He did not remember how his own honor had developed; it seemed always to have been part of him. He was learning something about his own nature, by seeing the effect of an alien upbringing on her. "I'm not surprised. Your whole life must have been taken with learning to play the flute and becoming Adept and integrating your several components and preparing for whatever it is you will do to try to save your planet. There would have been no time for such subtleties as the concept of honor."

"Aye. Teach me of honor."

She had taken him by surprise again. "You want to take time with a subtle concept that can only inhibit your immediate benefit as it inhibits mine?"

"Aye, Lysan. My thirst be to know what I know not. An thou dost prefer not to play with me, teach me instead."

"All right. Give me back my love for Echo."

"I can not."

"What?"

"Magic works but once in Phaze, an it be not inherent. I nulled the potion, but it be a far cry greater to null the null, and I fear it would be not the same."

"But what will I do, when I am with Echo again?"

"I know not, and care not. Teach me honor."

It was, he saw, a thing she needed to learn! She had carelessly changed his life in a way she could not reverse. An honorable person would not have done that.

He was Hectare. She was Hectare, in a sense. It was proper to provide what her alien tutoring had lacked. That might even have an effect on his mission, if he could make her appreciate her Hectare heritage.

"Then listen, child," he said grimly. He started in.

The golem marched tirelessly south, through the day and night. Lysander talked, and slept, and talked again, with hardly a murmur from Weva, but she was listening and learning. He was surprised by the amount he knew of the subject, but realized that he had been thinking about it because of the awkwardness of his own position as an enemy of Phaze that a prophecy claimed could help save the planet. It was not that the definition was complicated, but that the nuances were. Weva wanted example after example, of what was honorable in a theoretical situation, and what was not, and why. She seemed fascinated by the subject, and he realized that he was abating a lack she had not before been aware of. She *was* Hectare, in this respect, and becoming more so as she absorbed the lesson.

"But how canst thou call it integrity, an thou dost prevaricate?" she asked.

"My loyalty is to my mission, in a hostile camp," he explained. "I must complete it, and if telling the truth to an enemy would endanger it, then I must lie. However, in all things not related to my mission, I tell the truth. And when I make a deal, I honor it, even with the enemy."

"Mayhap I fathom that," she said.

Meanwhile it grew hotter as they neared the Pole. The dragons had long since been left behind; perhaps they could handle the heat, but it was too far from their hunting range. There was just a sea of baking sand. Weva took off her cloak and fashioned it into a canopy to shade them from the sun; that, and the air rushing by, cooled them almost enough. But they needed water, so she risked a small conjuration to fetch a jug of it for him, and assumed the form of a humanoid robot herself, so that she didn't need to drink. Throughout, she continued to listen to his discourse on honor, and to question it. Evidently the Hectare component intended to get this quite straight, and to live by it in future.

There was something odd on the horizon. Weva, as the robot, saw it before he did, and inquired. "Be there a storm, here? Flach said naught o' that."

Lysander considered, fearing that it was a sandstorm, then realized what it was. "We are approaching the South Pole. There is an anomaly that would show up here, and perhaps also at the North Pole if a snowstorm doesn't obscure it. That is the night."

"But it be near noon!" she protested.

"Time for a small planetary physics lesson. The light comes to this planet from its sun, as is the case elsewhere, but it makes a right-angle turn, and—"

"Because o' the black hole," she said. "Phaze be but a shell round the hole, and the light be bent. Now I fathom it!"

"Black hole?" he asked blankly.

"Thou didst not know?"

He realized that she probably *did* know what she was talking about. "You mean what we take as a planet is something else? You say a shell—?"

"Aye. Half shell, now that the frames be merged. Canst not see it from space?"

"It looks just like a planet, from space."

"Aye, a planet with only one side! Saw thou not the missing half?"

He tried to visualize what he had seen during his approach to the planet, but his normally clear memory let him down. He had no picture of the far side of Proton/Phaze. Probably he had seen only the near side, and not questioned it. That might be the case with all travelers; the effect that turned the light at right angles might also deceive the eye about what else was seen or not seen. This place was stranger than it seemed, and that was saying much.

Weva guided the golem to the edge of the night, sparing them the further ravage of the sun. They walked in shadow, and it was a relief. They had no trouble seeing ahead, because of the sunlight just to the side.

Lysander glanced up, cautiously. The sun was glaringly bright in its sphere, but stars twinkled in the adjacent sphere. There was no hint of the mechanism by which the light was bent; it was either full day or full night.

They came to the South Pole. It was a simple marking on the ground, across which the shadow fell: the shadow of night. That would rotate counterclockwise, always covering half the Pole as it did half the planet—or half the shell.

They dismounted. "Thank thee, Franken," Weva said, donning her robe again. "What thou seekst be beneath the Pole, but it be protected by magic, so thou must wait for it to emerge."

The golem stepped into the light and became immobile. It would wait until the end of the world, quite likely. Weva brushed off the Pole, and there was a small spiral stake. It had evidently been taller once, but broken off. She pulled, and it came up, revealing another chamber below.

"Is it safe to go in there?" Lysander asked. "If time is changed—"

"Aye, time be much changed, but needs must we go in." She paused. "I apologize to thee, 'Sander, for taking thy love, and will make amend an I be able. I acted before I fathomed honor, but after learning from thee, I know it be in my nature. Thou didst give me as much as I took from thee."

"Echo will be here?" That would put him on the spot.

"Aye, they took another route. We went apart so that they could decoy pursuit from me. Mayhap Flach can help thee."

"No. Say nothing. I'll play it through as seems best."

"There will be time, for it be magnified greatly here. To others it may seem but one day before the end, but we shall have nigh five years."

"Five years! One day is five years?"

"Aye, almost. So hurry not."

He nodded. Then he followed her down into the hole.

He was not aware of any time change, but did not question that it was happening, because he had seen how Flach and Sirel and Alien had aged in one week under the West Pole, and how Flach had aged again in a mere day. Weva had come into existence and become a dominant young woman in a bit over a month. Now she told him that time was much further accelerated here at the South Pole, and he had to believe her. The Adepts had needed something like this, to give them time to forge their weapon.

"Hello, Weva!" a voice called. It was Flach, looking another notch taller and older. "Methought to worry lest thou be lost."

"Nay, Flach, merely distracted," she said. "How long hast thou been here?"

"Six months."

"So thou didst come two and a half hours before me," she said. "Thou couldst have waited."

"Nay, I wanted to meet the elves." Flach glanced at Lysander. "Didst enjoy thy session with her?"

"Yes, actually," Lysander said.

"I drew from him all I desired," Weva said. "Now do I know all about honor."

Lysander had the satisfaction of seeing Flach startled. "Honor?"

"Aye. What didst think I meant?"

"Me feared for him," Flach admitted. "When I spent time with Icy the demoness, she—but that be long ago. Be he ready to work with us?"

Weva shrugged. "Ask him."

"No," Lysander answered. "You know I represent the other side."

"Then needs we must tell thee the whole o' our plan," Flach said, seemingly unperturbed. "I will bring thee to Chief Oresmite o' the Iridium Elves."

Iridium Elves! That explained the flutes. But what were they doing under the South Pole? The elves normally mined under the mountain ranges. "There is iridium here?"

"Nay," Flach said as he led the way. "But their expertise were needed, so they came with the Adepts Clef and Tania."

"The Adept Clef!" Lysander exclaimed. "So this is where he came!"

"Aye. But he be with us no longer."

"What happened to him?" Lysander was concerned. He had liked the Adept, with his beautiful and evocative music, and he had liked Tania, who were merely beautiful.

"They died o' age. It were a hundred and fifty years ago they came here."

"A hundred and fifty years!" But he realized it was true. The two must have come here before the Hectare came, anticipating the investment. The accelerated time scale—he did a quick calculation, and realized from the hints they had dropped that the ratio was about 1,728 to one, or 12 cubed, just as it was 144 to one under the West Pole. The East Pole was probably a mere 12 to one, and the North was the opposite, slowed by one of those factors. There was indeed a pattern to the Poles!

"Their descendants be here now," Flach said. "They have ne'er seen the outside."

Lysander thought of the couple he had met so recently. They had not died in untimely fashion, so he did not need to mourn them, yet they were gone. Did it matter that they had lived their full lives, perhaps quite satisfactory ones, and had done what they did voluntarily, to save their planet from alien occupation? They were still suddenly dead, and there was a hurting in his mind where they had been.

They came to a pleasant chamber wherein sat an old elf whose beard was the color of iridium. Behind him was a bank of indicators whose nature he recognized: this was a large computer. Yet the other walls of the chamber were rounded stone. Obviously high technology existed here, but the elves did not care about appearances. Or perhaps to them rounded stone was the proper appearance.

"Sir, this be Weva, mine analogue," Flach said respectfully, and Weva made a little bow. "And Lysander, o' the prophecy." Lysander nodded.

Flach turned to the two of them. "This be Chief Oresmite o' the Iridium Elves, who governs here. I leave thee here with him, Lysander, while I take Weva to introduce to the local community. Any deal thou dost make with him be binding on us all."

Flach took Weva's hand and led her from the chamber. She went without protest, like a docile maiden. Lysander was privately amused; she was anything but that!

Oresmite wasted no time. "Have a chair, Lysander. I know thy nature, so I will tell thee mine. I be the last surviving elf in these Demesnes to have known the Adepts Clef and Tania personally; today their great-great-great-great-grandchildren be with us, those o' the sixth generation of descent, though in thy frame little more than a month has passed. Our life here be not ill, merely accelerated. Hast questions before we proceed to business?"

"Yes," Lysander said, still relating with difficulty to the time change. He had no reason to doubt it, but also had had no evidence of its reality, here. "How could they have descendents, if there were no others of their kind?"

The old elf smiled. He was in every sense a man, but only about half Lysander's height. "Others came with them, several families, to establish the community. They be closely inbred, and eager to gain fresh blood; I must warn thee that thou willst be a target for their damsels."

"But my body is android! I can not reproduce."

"Aye. But the urge for fresh blood takes little note o' that. Since thou be already committed—"

"There's a problem there. May I speak in confidence?"

"Aye. We be here to come to an understanding."

"Is Echo the cyborg here?"

"Aye. She has waited impatiently for thee, despite being pursued by the local males."

"Weva is a creature of extraordinary skills. She nulled my love for Echo, and now I fear my meeting with Echo. If there are other women pursuing me, for whatever reason, I fear for our relationship."

Oresmite stroked his beard. "So Weva truly be Adept?"

"I believe so. Certainly her incidental magic was potent."

"And she made a play for thee?"

"Yes. I talked her out of it."

"Why?"

"It would not have been fair to Echo."

"But an thou hadst no further love for Echo—"

"It was, as I explained to Weva, a matter of honor."

The elf gazed at him for a moment, evidently pondering. "Tell me aught o' honor."

"That would take all day! It did take a day, and a night, to explain it to Weva. It's no simple concept."

"I be not a nascent girl. Give me one sentence."

"Honor is integrity with a moral dimension."

"And so it were not proper for thee to dally with another, when one who loves thee waited on thy return," Oresmite said. "E'en in the absence o' love and presence o' one who could compel thee. E'en with the planet ending in a day."

"Yes."

"How canst thou feel thus, and thou an agent for the enemy?"

"My brain is Hectare, and Hectare are honorable. I have an assigned mission, which I shall complete to the best of my ability. My relationship with Echo is incidental to that, despite the intent of the Adepts, so my honor applies separately to her."

"Then surely can we deal. But first I offer thee this notion: wouldst thou find it fair an Echo be also nulled o' her love for thee?"

Lysander snapped his fingers. "Yes! I never thought of that! It would make us even."

"Then let me do this now." The elf turned to the bank of equipment behind him. "Mischief, contact Weva, and suggest that she offer to do for Echo what she did for Lysander."

"Aye, Chief," the computer replied through a grille.

"Mischief?" Lysander inquired.

"It be a machine with an elfin humor."

"Thank you, Chief. When I talk with Echo, and have her leave to separate, I will not have a problem with the local maidens."

"Now come we nigh our business," the elf said. "Thou knowest the prophecy?"

"It suggests that only the cooperation of an enemy agent can enable the planet to free itself from the Hectare investment. It does not specify who the individual might be, but there is a strong likelihood that I am the one."

"Aye. An thou be not the one, we be lost, for there be none other here. But we need to guess not, for we can have the answer." He turned again to the computer. "Mischief, be he the one?"

"Aye, Chief."

"Now wait!" Lysander protested. "How can that machine know such a thing?"

"Answer, Mischief," the Chief said.

"I be what thou didst know as the Game Computer," the grille said. " 'Cept that I ne'er met thee, Lysander; I were gone ere thou didst come to the planet. Before I left, I was in touch with the Oracle, who knew the prophecy, and it gave me information that enabled me to know thee when I encountered thee. I verified it with the Book o' Magic, which be my current reference."

"The Game Computer!" Lysander exclaimed. "The one that stopped functioning when the frames merged!"

"Aye, Bem brain. We knew o' trouble coming when the mergence occurred, and set about dealing with it then. The formerly deserted Pole caverns were occupied and stable communities established barely before the invader came. A lesser machine was put in my place, unable to handle the complete complexity o' the games, but assisted at need by the Oracle, and I came here to fathom the technical aspect o' the effort."

That explained a lot! A concerted planetary effort had been made from the outset of the planet's vulnerability, so that the investment could be nullified before the planet was reduced to trash. It was impressive, but probably futile; the power of the Hectare was over-welming.

"What identifies me as the one of the prophecy?"

"Thine honor."

"Then you know that I will *not* help your side, regardless of any inducements you may proffer."

"Nay, not so," Oresmite said. "The prophecy shows thou mayst do it, an thou choose."

"Honor dictates my choice."

"Aye. So must we deal."

"We can not deal."

The Chief leaned forward persuasively. "We need thy help now. An we wait longer, all be lost regardless. Willst not yield the accuracy o' the prophecy so far?"

"So far," Lysander said grudgingly. "But not only do I have no intention of helping you in the key moment, I have no certainty that I can. I assure you that if I went back to my people now and asked them to depart the planet, they would not heed. I have no authority; I am only a special agent of a type routinely employed."

"But an thou couldst help us, and thou decided to at the last moment, would it be not ironic an thou hadst let the moment pass and could not? What be best for thou is to keep thine options open, so that an thou dost change thy mind, it will count until the end."

"Keep my options open," Lysander agreed. "Is that possible?"

"Aye. Mischief needs thine input now, for calculations that be beyond it o'erwise. An thou help it now, thou canst prevent them from being used on our behalf until thou dost decide."

"How can I be sure they would not be used without my choice?"

"The honor o' Mischief."

"A machine with honor? Or do you mean it is programmed for it?"

"Aye. Dost think we lack this?"

"You serve the interest of your planet, and this is integral to it. I can trust you only to do what you must to save it."

"But an thou hadst access to the programming o' the machine? Thou canst verify that we have touched it not, lacking in such expertise."

"If you let me modify the programming, then I can be sure of the security of the data."

"We will let thee do what thou choosest, and thou willst be welcome in these Demesnes meanwhile."

Lysander nodded. "Then I can tackle the problem."

"Give us an hour to access the sealed panels—"

"No need. I can verify the status and programming from a keyboard."

"A keyboard?"

"You really have no experience with computers!" Lysander exclaimed. "All your dealings have been verbal!"

"Aye. We be Phaze folk."

"You know I could completely ruin your system?"

"An thou choose to help us not, there be no difference; all will be destroyed."

True enough. "Where is the keyboard?"

"Mischief, tell him."

A light flashed. A panel slid open. There was a standard work station access, with keyboard and screen and accessories.

Lysander sat down before it and began typing. In a moment he was lost in the intricacies of the very type of work for which he had been trained.

"Lysander?"

He looked up from the screen, blinking. It was Echo.

For a moment he was at a loss. "I—I should have sought you," he said. "To explain—"

"Weva explained. I accepted her offer."

"That seems best. But I want you to know I did not seek—"

"I know. But we both know that love potion was a contrivance, intended to influence you. That failed, and there was no further purpose. Now we are both free of what was perhaps an imperfect association."

"Perhaps." He looked at her. He still found her beautiful. "But I found no fault with it. I never loved before, and was happier in that state than now. If it was imperfect, it remained good enough for me."

"For me also," she said. "It was a nice time. But now it is over, and—"

"Does it have to be over?"

She shrugged. "What is the point, without love?"

"What was pleasurable in love, may be so also without it. We do not need to break off our association—"

"Oh. Sex without obligation. Forget it."

"I didn't mean—"

But she was already sweeping out of the chamber. She had misunderstood him, but perhaps not completely. He *had* been thinking of sex—but also of the association. It would have been nice to discover whether their compatibility had been wholly the product of the love potion, or had a natural underpinning. Perhaps, if they had given it a chance . . .

Well, she wasn't interested, and that might be answer enough. He had loved her, and through her the culture of the planet. But she was, in her Phaze aspect, a harpy, and they were not known for sweetness. If the potion had reversed that portion of her nature, and the nullification had restored it, it was pointless to speculate further.

Too bad Jod'e had been taken by the Tan Adept! There had been no love magic there, and she was a most intriguing woman. In fact too bad that Alyc had been an enemy agent. Though he was also one, he no longer respected her, but if even she could have been here . . .

He put such thoughts from his mind. The intrigue of the challenge that had defeated the computer was here for him, and he intended to lose himself in it.

It wasn't long before he ascertained the nature of the problem: they hoped to slide the merged frames as a unit around the black hole to the fantasy side. For the distortion in the vicinity of the black hole was not just physical, so that light bent at a right angle; it represented a tangential connection between the science and the magic frames themselves. When the shell had been a perfect sphere, the curtain had transported some people from the science hemisphere to the magic hemisphere and back; now the two were melded and could not be separated without destroying the whole. But they might be moved together, like a tectonic plate, if there was a sufficient shove.

That shove was to be provided by the explosion of the Magic Bomb. If conditions were right, it would move the frames into the magic realm, and there would be nothing remaining in the science realm except an apparent black hole, unapproachable by any ordinary means. If the conditions where wrong, it would simply break up the shell, and the fragments would fall into the hole. In either case, the apparent planet would be gone from the science universe. But in only one case would it move intact to the magic universe.

If it moved intact, science and magic would work here. But away from this shell, only magic would work. Perhaps there would be exploitive creatures who came to take advantage of the unique qualities of science, or to steal the Phazite that powered the magic locally. But there had been no sign of such intrusion in the three preceding centuries. All the colonization, both animal and plant, had been from the science realm, crossing over. So it seemed likely that the inhabitants would be left alone. That was what they wanted.

If it slid around intact, the Hectare would be brought with it. But they would be cut off from their home planet and their section of the galaxy. They might be able to retain control, but that would be pointless, because they had not taken over the planet for themselves, but as part of the reorganization of this sector of the galaxy. They would do the practical thing, and yield power to the local authorities, trusting them to act in a practical way. To find ways to use the special abilities of the Hectare. It could be a richer society than it had been, because of that infusion of new talent.

It was a good plan. It should work. If the shell could be rotated intact.

The problem was that there was a virtually infinite number of connections to be made, to channel the stresses of the push correctly. A path had to be charted for every atom individually. Any that were not charted would go astray, and not make it to the magic realm. Any that were inaccurately charted would interfere with their neighbors that were on course. There would be overlapping and friction. In effect, there would be sand in the gears, and the whole thing would be brought to a halt. That would be disaster. There was only one chance, when the Magic Bomb took effect; it had to be done exactly right, or all was lost.

The Game Computer was a fine machine, but it simply wasn't up to this calculation. It had been working on it for a hundred and fifty years, and was less than halfway through. It had a scant five years to go, by local time, and it wasn't nearly enough. The paths had to be at least ninety-nine per cent charted and correct, or there would be destruction. The Book of Magic could not assist in this, because this was basically a science problem.

There was a way to speed it up, he saw. What was required was an algorithm: a set of rules for solving each case in a finite number of steps. A way to reduce the parameters so that the Game Computer—Mischief—could handle the simplified problem in the time allowed. A good algorithm could enhance effective calculation velocity a thousandfold. Even an indifferent one could speed things up thirtyfold, which was what was required.

Mischief was not advanced enough to devise such an algorithm. But Lysander, with his Hectare brain and training, could. Oh, it would be a challenge, and it might take him months to complete it, but he had that time. He could, indeed, save the frames.

And he could secure Mischief against any other intrusion. It hardly mattered; the untrained elves could barely comprehend the mathematics even if he gave a course in it. It was his decision.

His mind was already coming to grips with the problem, for this was the nature of the Hectare brain. He had to solve it, for his own satisfaction, even if that solution were never used. Since he could do so without risking his mission, he would indulge himself.

There was however one detail he had to find out about. The calculations could be made, and the courses set—but a connection had to be made between the two. There had to be a mechanism to tell the atoms where to go, in effect. The elves surely had something in mind, but it wasn't evident in the computer.

He got up. His shoulders were aching; he had concentrated so hard he had been hunching over. "Where is the Chief?" he asked Mischief.

"On the way, Lysan."

Indeed, in a moment Chief Oresmite appeared. "Thou has need o' me?"

"I can solve your problem. But I need to know the mode of communication between the—"

"The flutes."

"The iridium flutes? But mere sound will not—"

"They use music to marshal magic."

"Oh. Yes. But only two folk play them, and it would take a hundred to—"

"Nay, two suffice. The harmonics and the beats, guided by the Hectare aspect, will bear the signals."

"Chief, it isn't physically possible for just two to—"

"They will play the flutes only for practice. The true melody will be in their minds, guided by Mischief—an thou allow it. The iridium flutes be mere decoys; the ultimate flute be in Weva's fancy."

Lysander nodded. "Now I understand. I will key the pattern of solutions in to music, so that it will work—if I allow it."

"An thou wish to talk to any, in the interim, any will talk to thee. If not, not. We trust in thee, and in the prophecy."

"You have a lot of trust, Chief," he said wryly.

14

Duet

The time passed seemingly swiftly, though this bore no relation to the ratio beyond the Pole. Lysander worked hard on the algorithm, using Mischief to make supplementary calculations. It was an irony, he thought, that he finally had complete access to this computer, as he had wanted at the outset, but wasn't bothering with either games or machine consciousness. Instead he was working out a program that would defeat his purpose in being on this planet (shell). But what a glorious challenge it was!

He could not work all the time; even his Hectare brain could handle only so much at one sitting, and then he had to take time off. The community was eager to entertain him. There were indeed a number of human men and women, and to his eye there was a certain resemblance between some of the women and Tania, their long-gone ancestor. He dated them, and they were barely restrained in their eagerness to get him into a breeding mode, though he told them plainly that he was infertile. "Aye, but mayhap with magic . . ." one suggested as she seduced him.

He thought about that. Magic did phenomenal things, here. It was responsible for Flach/Nepe and Weva/Beman. (He had grown quite interested in Weva, until she teasingly showed him her other aspect: she too was a male/female composite. That turned him off, as perhaps she intended.) Surely it could make a full man of an android, if properly applied.

"Aye, 'Sander, it could," Nepe replied when he asked her. She had grown into a charming young woman, her charms no accident, because of course her amoebic flesh could be shaped to any form she chose. She showed a certain physical interest in him, but he thought of Flach, present as her alternate self, and did not reciprocate. It was obvious that however much those two composites played around, it was each other they were destined for. Whether it would be Flach-Weva or Beman-Nepe wasn't certain; so far both male versions seemed more interested in relating to the eager young females of the colony than to their opposite numbers, while the females were more reserved. It was an interesting situation.

"If Phaze survives?" he asked.

She smiled teasingly. "Aye."

And of course there would be little point, if it did not, for he could sire no offspring, fertile or not. This made him think about his position, as perhaps Nepe had intended. The choices were simple. Either he held to his mission, and torpedoed the plan by refusing to release the computed figures, and the worlds of Proton and Phaze perished, along with the Hectare who were here. It was already too late to warn them; in less than a day they would not be able to evacuate. So they were doomed. Or he could cooperate with the enemy, and save the frames, and render the Hectare into subservient status. He would incidentally save himself, too.

But his mission was clear. It was not his place to judge its merit. It was his place to fulfill it without question. His judgment was confined to questions of compromise necessary in order to facilitate his mission, as when he helped Nepe fetch the Hectare seed. That had indeed enabled him to discover the Adepts' plan, so carefully implemented here by Clef and Tania and Mischief and the elves. Now he had simply to act to complete his mission—and he could do that by inaction.

So he set the matter aside and sought his date for the evening. She was as eagerly obliging as always. But the truth was, with the number of eligibles limited to about six, the matter was becoming a bit dull. He was also tired of walking in the subterranean park, where stalagmites formed a forest of trunks in many colors, and in watching reruns of the community's store of video shows. Life was healthy here, as all things physically necessary to survival were provided, but emotionally stultifying. Many of the natives spent a great deal of time sleeping or gaming, but sleep was not for him, beyond the minimum required for survival, and gaming was now his vocation instead of his avocation.

It was no better for the elves, who on the surface had mined iridium and fashioned it into assorted artifacts. Deprived of their natural way of existence, they reacted in much the fashion of the human beings, sleeping, gaming, socializing, and fighting. Chief Oresmite was at times hard put to it to keep the peace.

There were some human-elf liaisons, not because of any natural affinity, but because of sheer boredom with the limits of their own populations. Lysander had not understood this well at first, but in time the relative unfamiliarity of the elf maidens became appealing, and he found himself dating them too. Such liaisons were officially discouraged, but privately tolerated; they were better than violence.

The whole community existed to support Mischief and the effort to save Phaze. But most of its work had been done before the four newcomers had arrived. Only if there was a cave-in in a tunnel or some other emergency was there actual need for human or elfin action. It was apparent that those who had settled here had made a considerable sacrifice. All longed for the time when they would be freed to live again on the surface—or die.

"The truth be," an elf lass confided to him once, as she showed him what elves knew about fundamental interaction that human beings did not, "that I care not o'ermuch which it be, just so long as the dullness be done." That seemed to be a general sentiment. They knew his position, but were not pushing him to save Phaze.

He avoided Echo, and she avoided him. But after a year desperation brought them together. "I told you I wasn't interested in sex without obligation," she said. "I have changed my mind."

"It was better when we were in love," he said. "If there were another potion, I would take it with you."

"So would I. But there isn't. Such potions work only once, for a given couple. We would have to do it the hard way."

"The hard way?"

"By falling in love naturally."

"You mean that's possible? I thought—"

"So did I. But others say that though it is harder, after a potion and nulling, it can be accomplished. It has to be worked at. I know you wouldn't be interested in that."

"I thought *you* wouldn't be interested!" he said.

She gazed at him. "I wasn't interested in being your mistress. Then. Now it doesn't matter. Anything's better than this boredom."

"Are the two incompatible?"

"Love and sex? They weren't before."

"Let's consider it a challenge."

"A challenge," she agreed.

It turned out to be worth it. They could handle the sex readily enough, for they had had a lot of practice in their original month in love, but the love was slower. After a month there was only a flicker of emotion. After six there was some. After two years it was significant. After three it was assuming the aspect of a shadow of their former feeling.

"I think we are right for each other after all," he said. "I have not been bored since we undertook this challenge."

"Nor I," she agreed. "Now I am glad we lost the unnatural love, because we are proving what is real."

They kissed, quite satisfied. It seemed that love was most valuable when it was a struggle to achieve.

Four years after his arrival, Lysander was able to announce that the algorithmic computations were complete. "The figures, if invoked, will do the job," he said.

Oresmite's delight was restrained. "Then we must deal."

"My position is unchanged."

"But thou hast had opportunity to consider. Be it a victory for the Hectare an all be destroyed?"

"They would not consider it so."

"But it be a victory for us, an it be saved."

"Agreed."

"So one side can win, and the other can only lose."

"Yes. But this is logic. My mission is not subject to that."

"Suppose it were possible at least to save most Hectare and some natives, by warning them now?"

"It isn't. It would take several days to organize for a disciplined withdrawal, and only one day remained when I came here. Had I known the nature of the ploy sooner, I would have warned the Hectare."

"Aye. We told thee little, until thou wast here. Yet there be a way."

"Something you didn't tell me?"

"Aye. I be thine enemy, remember."

Lysander laughed. "I had almost forgotten! What is this secret?"

"We can, by special magic, transport some o' the acceleration to the surface o' the shell. It would deplete the effect at the Poles, but provide perhaps a week at the cities."

"They could get away!" Lysander exclaimed.

"Aye."

"But there's a catch."

"Perceptive o' thee to fathom that."

"You won't let it happen."

"Aye. Why facilitate the benefit o' mine enemy?"

"And I, lacking your expertise in magic, can not do it without your cooperation."

"Aye, no more than I can gain thy figures from Mischief."

"Then what is the point? It changes nothing. I will not save your frames, and you will not save the BEMs. Our positions are consistent."

"The point be that we have chips to bargain. An the Hectare had a choice, would they not choose to exit Proton?"

"Yes, of course! But you aren't going to give them that choice."

"Here be my challenge: play me a game. An thou dost win, I will provide magic to save the Hectare and those they choose to take with them, and thou and Echo. That be a half victory, but better than naught. An I win, thou dost release those figures."

"But the stakes aren't even!" Lysander protested, guiltily intrigued. "You aren't offering victory against victory, but half against whole."

"True. But our victory be not complete loss for the Hectare or thee. We will treat them fairly, and put thee in charge o' integrating them into the society. We can use their skills. And we will make a spell to make thou fertile—"

"I'm with Echo. She can't conceive."

"An we do the magic, she can. Remember Nepe; she be child o' machine."

Lysander considered. It was true: the full victory for the natives would be only half a loss for the Hectare, while the full loss of the natives would be half a Hectare win. The stakes were fair. But did he have the authority to make such a deal?

"Be the Hectare not gamesmen?" Oresmite inquired. "Would they not let the game decide, an the stakes be even?"

"Yes, they would. But I can't—"

"An the leader be incapacitated, who has authority?"

"The next in command. But—"

"An the leader be away or distracted, and the next in command learns aught that must needs be decided instantly, what then?"

"The next in command must act."

"Does the authority for this matter then not devolve on thee, the only Hectare to know its nature in time to act?"

"Well, there is Weva—"

"Woulds't have her make the decision?"

"No! She's on your side!"

"Then methinks it must be thee, unless my logic be in error."

Lysander realized that the cunning old elf had him. He had been maneuvered into a position where the authority was his; a Hectare court would agree. He might lack the authority simply to decide the fate of the frames, but as a player in a game of decision—a case could be made.

"Agreed. But it must be a fair game."

"Aye. We shall decide together. Or wouldst prefer to have Mischief decide?"

"No!" Then Lysander had to laugh. "No, we shall come to our own agreement. Only when both are satisfied will it be set."

"Aye." Oresmite smiled. "We have time."

There followed several days of negotiations. Oresmite, being old and small, would not commit to any brute physical contests. Lysander, wary of the elf's lifetime experience rejected those that were culturally oriented. Intellectual games like chess or go were tempting, but Lysander wasn't sure how much the elf might have played these to wile away the time, and Oresmite was nervous about Lysander's analytic Hectare brain.

"Methinks we require a new game, ne'er before played," the Chief remarked at last.

"Yes. So that neither experience nor special aptitude is likely to count."

They brought the others in on it. The challenge: create a new, fair, playable but unplayed game whose outcome could not be certain.

The boredom evaporated as elves and human beings got to work. Proposals were made, analyzed, and rejected.

The key, as it turned out, came from an elf child. He had been listening to the stories of the history of magic before Phaze, when it had existed back on Earth. "Why not Merlin and the Witch?" he asked.

This was an episode recorded by T. H. White in a book titled *Sword in the Stone* but later excluded from a larger compendium, perhaps because it revealed too much about magic. Merlin had fought the witch by form changing, each trying to assume the form of a creature that could demolish the other. Merlin, sorely pressed, had won by becoming a germ that infected and killed the witch's monster.

"But I can't change forms!" Lysander protested.

"Nor can I, neither any elf," Oresmite replied. "But we can in illusion."

The illusion chamber was normally used to generate lovely vistas similar to those of the outside world, so as to lessen the claustrophobic restrictions of the caves. But it could be turned to any fancy. A person had only to take his place at one of the focal points and imagine something, and it was animated in the chamber. There were regular puppet shows, the puppets illusory but realistic, because complete living detail wasn't expected in such creatures. Few could imagine sufficient detail to make an image seem truly realistic.

But if animals could be represented crudely, puppet-fashion, as pieces in a game, then it might be feasible. He could imagine a tiger, chasing the elf's antelope. Only the elf would then imagine a dragon, and turn on the tiger. Then—

"But we'd just both wind up with the biggest, most ferocious monsters, and it would be a stalemate," Lysander said. "Or as germs, trying to infect the other. I don't think it would work as well as it did centuries ago on Earth."

"Aye," the Chief agreed. "It were a nice notion, but impractical."

"Not necessarily," Beman said. "Appropriately restrictive rules could make a fair game of it."

"Agreed," Nepe said. "Scientific rules applied to the magic. To prevent stalemates."

"Then work it out," Lysander said, intrigued by the notion of being able to change forms, if only in imagination. It was as close to magic as he could get, on his own. "If we like it, we'll play it."

They retired with a committee of elves to work it out. Next day they returned with the proposal for "Animals." Oresmite and Lysander reviewed it and liked it. They had their game.

The Chief took the key position at one end of the chamber, and Lysander the one at the other end. At the sides sat elves and human beings holding pictures of assorted animals ranging from ladybugs to fire-breathing dragons. The animals were paired, with one of each kind at each side of the chamber. One side represented Lysander's animals, the other the Chief's, and they were even.

Each player had an iridium coin. They flipped them together. Lysander's bounced, flipped, and settled down with the picture of an equine tail showing. The Chief's coin spun and rolled, finally falling with a donkey's head in view. The two did not match, which meant the result was odd rather than even, and that meant by prior agreement that Oresmite chose the first animal.

The Chief glanced at his pictures. One glowed, and its figure jumped off the paper to take its place in the chamber beside the pictures. It was a donkey, appropriately.

Lysander looked at his pictures. He focused on the unicorn, and it left its paper and hit the chamber floor running. It charged the donkey, its horn lowering to point forward.

The onus was on him, as predator, to dispatch the prey within one minute, or forfeit the game.

The donkey took off, running fleetly. The illusion expanded to fill in the surrounding terrain: a grassy plain, bordered by mountain ranges to north and south. It was a miniature of the frame of Phaze, with the seas at east and west and the dread Lattice at the center: the network of deep crevices in which demons lived. The animals were bounded by these natural features, and could not go beyond them. But there was plenty of room to maneuver.

The unicorn was faster than the donkey, and its horn was capable of making a lethal thrust. In thirty seconds Lysander had almost closed the gap. The donkey dodged, but so did the unicorn; the imagination that made the creatures go was limited by their natural abilities. The Chief had to act.

He did. The donkey became a tiger, whose paws skidded as it turned to face the unicorn.

Lysander veered aside. The tiger was trouble. True, the unicorn could spear the feline with the horn—but the tiger knew how to avoid horns, and if the first thrust didn't score, the tiger would pounce and bite. The prey had become the predator.

Now the tiger had one minute to bring down the unicorn, or forfeit. The onus had shifted.

Lysander elected to remain with the unicorn, because there was an advantage in avoiding change. An animal could be used only once; then its sign was taken down, and it was retired. If one side used up all its animals, and the other saved a number, that other side would have a significant advantage in the end game. That player would be able to use a fleet animal to catch the other, then shift to a killer animal for the finale.

The unicorn took off. The tiger leaped after, but already the unicorn was at speed. The tiger put forth its best effort, and gained, but it was evident that it would be unable to close the gap within a minute, if at all. Tigers were good for the short run, but not for the long, while unicorns could run all day if they had to. The Chief had to change forms again, or lose by default. That onus was a deadly thing!

The tiger became a flying dragon. The onus was still on the Chief, because it belonged to the last form change, but the minute started fresh from the moment of that change. Lysander had gained a long-range advantage, because he was on his first animal while the Chief was on his third, but that dragon could finish the game in the short range.

Indeed, in a moment the dragon was looming overhead and orienting its snoot for a fiery blast. He had to change!

He changed to a salamander, and stared up at the dragon. The dragon did a doubletake and popped into a blind eel. The eel fell to the ground and wriggled desperately away. The Chief had been caught by surprise and made an error; he should have continued his attack, because though a magic salamander was immune to fire, it wasn't immune to teeth. The Chief had confused it with a basilisk, whose stare could kill; the Chief had taken the handiest way to stop the meeting of the eyes by adopting an eyeless form.

Lysander scrambled after the eel, who wasn't well suited to motion on land. The eel heard the noise and hastily became a hawk, who flew away without looking back.

Lysander had definitely come out ahead in this encounter. The Chief had used two more forms to his one, and still had the onus. And—Lysander had done it on a bluff, for this was neither basilisk nor magic salamander, but an ordinary one, harmless to anything larger than a fly.

As the Chief was about to realize. The hawk was coming back, and it would make short work of the salamander. One snap of its beak—

Lysander burrowed down into the grass, trying to hide. If he could remain clear for another thirty seconds—

The hawk came to the ground, and changed. Lysander couldn't

see the change, but he knew it had occurred, because a bird on land did not make that slithering sound. That was either a lizard, or—

The head of a snake loomed over him. It struck down—as Lysander became a mongoose.

He spun about to face the snake. It was a simple black racer, not venomous to man but deadly enough to a salamander. But the mongoose was able to kill even the most deadly snakes. Lysander had the onus now. He dived in—

The snake became a wolf. The wolf's jaws snapped at the mongoose—

Lysander became a giant serpent. The serpent's jaws opened to take in the wolf.

The wolf became a bear. A bear was a lot tougher animal than many supposed; it could handle just about any other animal its size, and anything smaller. It swiped at the serpent's head.

Lysander became a rhinoceros. He swung his nose-horn viciously at the bear—who became a monstrous roc, a bird capable of catching up a rhino in its talons and carrying it away. Indeed, those talons closed on the rhino's body, and the great wings spread. In a moment he would be lifted up. He could be carried high and dropped; any fall over five or six feet might kill him.

But he didn't change. He let the bird haul him into the air. The roc carried him over a nearby rocky region, and let him go.

But as he fell, he became a sparrow. Of course he had nothing to fear from being dropped! Not as long as he could change to another flying form. Now the Chief had used up his largest and second largest flying forms—the roc and the dragon—and would not be able to use them again. Lysander had both those forms in reserve. He was still gaining.

But it would be foolish to let any opportunity pass. He needed to try for the quick victory, lest the Chief catch him first. He remembered seeing chess games where one player had pieces all over the board, but the other had the victory because of the position. Pieces were only part of it.

The sparrow looped and flew in at the roc. The roc's beak snapped down, but the sparrow was swifter at close quarters, and got by. It came up against the roc's fur-feathered leg—and became a cobra. By the definition of the game, a poisonous bite affected any other creature, even another of its kind, if it scored well. Lysander opened his mouth and struck at the flesh of the leg.

The roc became a gnat and zipped away; the cobra's jaws snapped on nothing. And now he was in trouble, for he was in the air and falling.

He became a hawk. The Chief's hawk had been used before, and it could not return, and there were few other birds that could catch a hawk. But the onus was on Lysander; he had to do the catching, and this was no form for gnat-hunting!

He pondered. The Chief would surely outwait him if he didn't find a quick way to catch that gnat. A toad could do it—but the gnat would be flying high up, out of reach of a landbound creature. This was a problem!

Then he had it. He became not a dragon, but a dragonfly. Dragonflies hunted smaller insects on the wing, and were strong flyers and efficient predators. He looped around and spied the gnat, who hadn't gone far. Indeed, a gnat couldn't get far in a few seconds, compared to a dragonfly.

He revved up his four wings and zoomed in for the kill. But the gnat became a toad in midair, its mouth opening. Lysander realized that though the toad would fall to the ground, it would get the dragonfly first, and win; the fall didn't matter.

Caught by surprise, he found his mind blank. The toad's sticky tongue came out, rooted at the front, catapulting toward him. He would be caught before he—

In desperation he became another toad; he couldn't think of anything else.

The two toads collided in the air, and fell together.

Lysander still had the onus. He had only seconds: should he assume a form to crunch the other toad, or wait for the Chief to change, so the Chief would be committed, and Lysander could immediately counter the form? The latter seemed better.

But the Chief seemed to have the same idea. They continued to fall. What would happen if they both splatted into the ground? They were playing a game of chicken!

Probably if they both perished, it would be declared a draw, and they would have to play another game. Lysander was ahead in this game; he didn't want to start another.

That decided him. So what if he went splat immediately after; he should grasp the victory first.

He became a weasel, which was more than enough to dispose of even the illest-tasting toad. He twisted around in the air and snapped at—

The Chief became a hippopotamous—and he was just above the weasel! He would land and squash the weasel flat! He would die himself—but *after* the weasel. This was the strategy of suicide.

Lysander became a horsefly and zoomed away. Such a change would not have been safe while the toad remained, but no hippo could nab a fly in the air.

And the Chief became a dragonfly, borrowing from Lysander's prior strategy, and winged swiftly after him. The onus was on the Chief, but he was playing with greater savvy now. Lysander was on the run—or in flight, in this case.

He didn't want to waste a good predatory form that would be immediately countered; he wanted to force the Chief to use up more of his forms, until he was starved for variety at the end and subject to a power play. He saw water below, and had a notion. He plunged toward it, the dragonfly gaining but not yet in range.

He plunged in, becoming a fish.

The Chief plunged after, becoming a pelican.

Trouble! Lysander became an alligator just as the pelican's beak closed on the fish. The beak closed instead on the hide of the alligator.

Lysander whipped his toothy snout around to snap up the bird, and the bird became a giant sea serpent whose much larger toothy snout whipped around to snap up the alligator. Lysander was having trouble matching change for change, and couldn't think of a good rejoinder on the spot, so became an elephant.

The sea serpent stared. An elephant?

But the water was not deep, and the elephant was only halfway submerged. It wrapped its trunk around the head of the serpent, tying its jaws closed, and pushed the head under the water. Drowning was as good as being bitten to death. Lysander had found a good predator form after all.

The serpent became a fish and slid away. Lysander waited, knowing that no fish could hurt him here; the water was too shallow for any really big one. Nothing much could hurt an elephant. But the Chief had the onus, and would have to try.

Then he spied something sliding through the water. It wasn't a fish, but more like an eel.

Oops—an electric eel! Again by definition, the shock would stun any other creature. Lysander became a frog and leaped out of the water.

So it went, change and counterchange, and the assortment of animals was depleted on both sides. But Lysander's strategy of forcing the Chief to change more often was paying off, and it came to the point where Lysander had several top predators left and the Chief was reduced to his next to last form: a sheep. Lysander became a roc and pounced on the sheep, forcing the Chief to take his last form: a mouse.

Lysander became a dragon, and inhaled. He would send a blast of fire that burned out the entire region, the mouse with it.

But the mouse, astonishingly, did not flee. Instead it jumped onto the dragon's nose and clung there.

Lysander shook his head, trying either to toss the mouse into his mouth, or fling it to the ground where it could be scorched before it fled. Another creature it could hide from, but the fire of the dragon would seek it out regardless. But the mouse refused to be dislodged; it dug its tiny claws into the snout and hung on.

This was a problem Lysander had never anticipated. His forelegs were too short to reach his snout. He tried to whip his tail about to wipe the mouse off, but it only stung his nostrils sharply. He tried to roll and squish the mouse against the ground, but it was in the declivity between eyes and nostrils. He could not dislodge that mouse!

He blew out fire. But his snout was insulated so that its own flesh would not be destroyed by the heat, and that protected the mouse too.

If he changed form again, the mouse would get away; he had no specific mouse-catching forms left, having labored to save the largest predators instead. If he hadn't used up his weasel—

Maybe he could bounce fire back on his nose. It would hurt his own flesh, but it would fry the mouse, and that was what counted.

He put his nostrils against a rock and blew out fire. It bounced, but to the side. He tried again, and missed again. He needed a rock with a hollow, that would cup and reflect the fire—

Suddenly a gong sounded. The minute was up, and he had not destroyed the mouse. Since the onus was his, he lost by default.

The game was over, and Chief Oresmite had won.

Lysander had tried his hardest to win, and thought he had the win assured, until that last astonishing ploy. He had been fairly beaten, and now was obliged to give the figures to the enemy. Yet, somehow, he was relieved.

Only later did it occur to him that he had blundered crucially. He had been a roc when the Chief was a sheep; the Chief had become a mouse. Lysander's blunder had been in changing to the dragon. All he had had to do was maintain roc form and fly away, and the Chief, stuck with the onus, would have lost in one minute.

Flach and Weva stood before Mischief, and lifted their flutes. They played, and Lysander remembered the magic, figurative and literal, of Clef's music. Flach was good, because of his unicorn heritage, but Weva was better, because of her Hectare heritage. That, of course, was why she had been brought into existence. Only a Hectare mind, trained also in magic, could handle the figures Lysander's algorithm had produced.

The magic came, much stronger than before, almost tangible. The two set aside their flutes, but the music continued, generated by their minds.

Mischief began to run the figures on a screen. It was a massive array: thousands of numbers jammed together. But Weva's eyes were on them, and they were being fed through to her mind, and changing the music. No human mind could have done it, but hers could, with the support of her companion.

The world began to change, as the paths for each atom of matter were defined, and the push from the Magic Bomb began. The merged frames would slide around the black hole, nothing changing within them, but everything changing beyond them. Like a cover on a piece of equipment, turning without altering its shape or nature; it was the nature of the universe that was changing instead.

There was a shudder. Dust sifted down. Elves and human beings glanced around alike in alarm. This had the feel of an incipient earthquake, and they were underground.

The shuddering intensified. Cracks appeared in the stone.

"It's going wrong!" someone cried.

The computer screen went blank. Then the single word ERROR flashed, blinking.

"We kept faith with thee!" an elf cried at Lysander. "Thou didst promise true figures!"

"My figures are true!" Lysander replied. "The error must be somewhere else!"

"Cease playing!" Oresmite rapped, and the music halted. "There be error somewhere, but Lysander has honor; he would not cheat on this."

"Then he made a mistake!" Flach said.

"I made no mistake," Lysander said. "Every figure checked. It must be in the translation."

"Nay, none there," Weva said. "We play true!"

"If we resume not soon, the detonation of the Magic Bomb will destroy us regardless," Flach pointed out. "Now be the time; the paths must be set."

"The time factor!" Echo said. "We're accelerated, but how does it relate to the rest of the frames?"

"We allow for that," Weva said. "Our music relates."

"The Poles!" Lysander said. "Their times are different. Do you allow for that?"

"Yes, o' course," she said. "Twelvefold for the East Pole, a hundred and forty-four for the West Pole. I were made there; I would forget my home region not."

"And the North Pole? The one that's slower than normal time?" Weva looked stricken. "Slower! I adjusted for faster!"

"Can you correct for that?"

"Aye. Now." She lifted her flute again, and Flach quickly joined her.

"Rerun the figures, Mischief!" Lysander said. "The error is being corrected."

The figures reappeared on the screen.

They resumed playing, and in a moment set aside the flutes and continued. This time there was no shuddering; the magic intensified, and there was a feeling of something colossal shifting, but it was smooth. It was working.

Yet there was in the background an almost imperceptible disharmony, a keening as of something not quite right. The error had caused them to start over, slightly delayed; did that make a difference? If so, it could be cumulative, and . . .

Lysander did not care to finish that thought. He had been an agent for the other side, but he had made a deal, and now was bound to see it through. He would not care for the irony of having his original side win through default. Not after he had resigned himself to the prospect of living, and of love with Echo.

The eerie trace of wrongness did not fade; it got worse. Lysander knew what was happening: the delay occasioned by the failure to zero in the North Pole correctly *had* thrown the timing off slightly, and that imbalance was recycling and building. If it expanded logarithmically, as such things could, they could still get dumped, and all would have been for nothing.

Echo was near him. He caught her hand and squeezed it to let her know that whatever happened, he was glad for their association. Then an elf girl caught his free hand, and someone else caught Echo's free hand. The impulse spread, and soon everyone in the chamber was linked, including Flach and Weva and Chief Oresmite. The music went on, through all their heads and all the frames, translating the figures to reality, carrying them all on the wave of force that was the detonation of the Magic Bomb.

That Bomb had been confined by the slowed time at the North Pole. That had been a bad Pole on which to err!

The linked hands provided comfort, but the wrongness worsened. Lysander felt as if his guts were being removed and convoluted topologically and strung through the electrical conduits of his brain. He didn't dare vomit, because he didn't want the contents of his stomach suffusing his brain. He suspected that the others were experiencing similar distortions. If the frames didn't complete their journey soon—

The music stopped. They were there!

There was a silence. Then the Chief looked around. "We remain alive," he said. "That means it is successful. But perhaps not entirely. We must proceed cautiously."

"The timing," Weva said. "I couldn't quite compensate. I think things are all right, but some detail may have changed."

The group let go of hands. Lysander brought Echo into him. "Just so long as *you* are not changed!" he said.

Her eyes were round. "I fear I be. I—"

"Check your body," he suggested. All around them others were similarly concerned. No one seemed quite certain what had happened, but knew that something fundamental was not the same.

"Well, it be metal and plastic, o' course, as always. I'll show thee." She opened her robe and touched the place where her left breast was latched. "Uh-oh."

"You look fine!" he said. "I don't care if your latch is broken."

"There be no latch."

"Well, whatever. I have accepted the local way, and you are part of it."

She closed her robe. "E'en an I be not exactly the creature thou hast known?"

He experienced an unpleasant chill. "Are you trying to say that your emotion has changed? That now the crisis is past, you don't—"

She put her finger across his lips. "Nay, Lysan! I love thee yet! I would spend my life with thee! But an I be other—"

He swept her in and kissed her. "My emotion didn't change either. I love you too, and no potion is responsible. But I think we have work to do outside."

"Aye," she breathed, seeming relieved.

The others had come to a similar conclusion. They were forging toward an exit.

But when the hatch was opened, a stormy swirl of air rushed in, blowing back the elves.

"Must be a dust storm," Lysander said.

"But it's wet!" an elf protested.

So it was. "Then it's safe to go out there," Lysander said. "I'll do it."

The elves gave way for him, and he scrambled through the tunnel and thrust his body up through the hole. There was a storm raging, all right; warm rain plastered his robe to his body in a moment.

Echo emerged after him. "This be not the heat o' the South Pole!" she said.

"But it's warm enough. Drop your robe and come on; we can handle this."

She did. He took her hand, and forged on, trying to gain a point of perspective.

Then a rift opened in the clouds. The sun shone down, directly south of the Pole.

Lysander froze. *South?*

Beside him, Echo was similarly amazed. "Be the magic gone?" she asked. "The sunlight bends not?"

Flach and Weva came up behind them. "Now I see what happened," Weva said. "That imbalance—the shell got twisted! The South Pole is now the West Pole!"

"That's why the storm," Flach agreed. "The temperature patterns changed; it has to get resettled."

"A quarter turn!" Lysander said. "We're lucky it wasn't worse."

"It was worse," Weva said. "We have changed similarly."

Lysander looked at her. "No you haven't."

She smiled. "You are an idiot, 'Sander."

"Is there something I've overlooked?"

Echo touched his shoulder. "Aye, because thou be not affected, mayhap, having an alternate self not. Watch me change forms."

Then she assumed her Phaze-harpy form, and flew a short distance into the air.

Her body was shining metal, and her feathers plastic. "Now do you understand?" she called.

"You're a robot harpy—a cyborg!" he exclaimed.

"I am Echo." She descended to the ground, and returned to human form. "And I be Oche. Now dost recant thy pledge to love me?"

Suddenly the change in language penetrated. Echo had been talking in the Phaze dialect! The cyborg harpy talked in Proton dialect. They *had* changed!

"But you said you still loved me!" he said, stunned.

"Aye, Lysan. I be Echo's living aspect, and I love thee as she does. It were always I who loved thee, but I said naught, lest I revolt thee. Now I would be with thee, but I will leave thee an thou ask."

"But if the harpy body is now inanimate—"

"This human form be alive," she said. "I offer it thee, with my love, an thou desire either."

Nepe appeared. "Methinks thou be wisest to accept, Lysan," she said.

He turned his head to look at her. "You are Flach," he said.

"Aye. But I were always both, as be Weva and Beman. It be a big adjustment, but we shall do it, as we did mergence before." She—he—smiled impishly. "Methinks those in the cities have big adjustments to make too!"

Weva became Beman. "Yes, I be Weva," he—she—said. "Needs must we all adjust. But it be especially important for thee, Lysan, because thou willst have to coordinate the integration o' the Hectare into the new order. The faster we can all come to terms with ourselves, the better off we shall be."

Lysander turned to Oche. "I always knew you were both," he said.

"I knew the harpy watched everything. I knew she was the brain in your machine, just as you knew a living Hectare was the brain in my laboratory-generated body. What has changed is only a detail. I love the whole of you. If you love me—"

"Aye," she said. Then she stepped into him, and they embraced. "But I think thy body be human now too, Lysan."

"All the way human? But that would mean—"

"That we can have a family," she finished.

He realized that his future was likely to be even more busy than his past. But there was no time now to ponder the implications; they had to organize for the reorganization of the frames.

Epilog

They gathered beside the wooden castle of the Brown Demesnes. Tsetse looked out a window and spied them. "Brown—there's an army outside! But a moment ago it was just open fields!"

"Mayhap it be Franken returning," Brown said. "His step can shake the ground. He were on errand, returning the Book o' Magic to the Red Adept."

"No, I mean there really are people out there," Tsetse insisted. "And animals, and everything."

"Methought I felt a conjuration," Brown said. Because her selves were the same, and Tsetse had only one self, the two of them had not been affected by the exchange of identities. It had taken a while to get used to the quarter turn the compass had taken, making the sun now rise and set at the North and South Poles instead of the East and West ones, but the climate of her region had changed only slightly. She considered herself well off in most respects, now that the alien conquest had been reversed.

But whatever could have caused this sudden gathering? She gazed out, and spied wolves, unicorns, elves, demons, animal heads, BEMs, and of course human folk. It seemed to be some kind of celebration, for the folk were brightly garbed and there appeared to be picnic sheets spread out.

"Needs must we go out and see," Brown decided, speaking positively though she was perplexed and a bit nervous.

"Maybe I should stay in," Tsetse said.

Brown came to a decision. "Nay, friend. I love thee and will deny thee not. An thou lovest me, come face the world with me."

"If you're sure—"

"I know only that I will live a lie no longer, come what may." She took the woman by the hand, kissed her, and led her to the front portal.

Outside, the gathering was organized almost like an army, with contingents spread in a large semicircle, and a small group centered, facing the castle entrance. As Brown walked out, the visitors came to attention, silently.

At the head of the assembly was Purple, whether Citizen or Adept she would not know until he spoke—and then she would remain in doubt, because of the reversals. This was another surprise; she had thought him imprisoned again. Just behind him stood the woman Alyc, the one who had dated Lysander but then worked for the enemy. Evidently she had found another companion. Brown stopped before Purple, Tsetse beside her.

Purple spoke. "Thou knowest my life be forfeit, for that I twice betrayed my culture. Thou must believe I bespeak thee truth now. I yield naught to none, except to thee, for that thou didst treat me kindly. Know, Adept, that the specter I held o'er thee were but a phantom; others differ but judge thee not for it, as thou dost not judge them. An thou accept it not from thy friends, accept it from thine enemy: it be no barrier for thee."

She stared at him. There was only one subject he could be addressing. Had he come to shame her openly, before them all?

Purple stepped forward. He caught Tsetse's timid hand. "My purpose in sending thee to the Brown Demesnes were malevolent," he told her. "I sought to blackmail her, that she would serve the Hectare. But it were a lie. None begrudge Brown her way or thee thine. I now renounce any power I had o'er thee, Tsetse, and wish thee well." He turned to Brown. "Deep do I regret repaying thy kindness with malice, and using a lie to savage thee. Thou didst deserve it not."

He turned in place and walked away. Alyc followed.

"Wait!" Brown cried. "What did they promise thee, to make thee speak so?"

He paused. "That need concern thee not. Be assured I bespoke thee the truth."

"It does concern me!" she insisted. "I know thou dost do naught for naught. What—?"

"A clean and painless death," he said, and resumed his walking.

"Nay!" she cried, hurrying after him. "I wished this not on thee!

We made a deal, and I agreed nor to seek harm to thee neither to be silent an I learned o' harm coming."

"This be not o' thy making," he said gruffly, still walking. "In any event, the deal be off; it were in power only while the Hectare governed. Concern thyself not farther on this matter."

But she could not let it go. "An they brought thee here for a public execution, I tolerate it not! I forgive thee aught thou intended, and thank thee for bringing me a companion. Thou must not die!"

"I ask this not o' thee," Purple said, pausing again. "I came only to spare myself a life confined, under geis. An the truth purchase me that, I be satisfied."

Brown looked to the side. There was the Blue Adept and the Lady Blue. "Stile! I beg thee, an our friendship mean aught, let not this horror be!"

Stile lifted his hands. "Thou be pardoned, Purple, at Brown's behest. An thou do no further evil, we spare thee death and confinement, and they paramour too. Get thee gone from our sight." He was evidently somewhat disgusted—but only somewhat. He had never been a vengeful man, when there were reasonable alternatives. He turned to the Hectare standing behind him. "Do thou input it to thy net: he to be watched but not molested."

The BEM extended one small tentacle, its tip tilted up.

Slowly Purple turned. "Lady, thou be more generous to me than I were to thee. I thank thee for what I expected not." Then he turned again and walked away, and no one challenged him. No one except Alyc, who tackled him and embraced him. He put an arm around her. He had always had an eye for young women, and she was reputed to be a most passionate one.

Now Brown saw the Tan Adept, with the vampire Jod'e beside him. Tan had used his power to fascinate the lovely bat woman, who was blameless. Brown opened her mouth.

"And Tan, pardoned," Blue said before Brown could speak.

The BEM made another note.

"I thank thee, O my lady!" Jod'e exclaimed.

Tan walked away, with Jod'e. Brown had to admit that they did make a decent couple. With a bat wife, Tan would not again betray the interests of Phaze.

Another couple came forward. It was Lysander, who had turned out to be another enemy spy, but who had in the end chosen to help save Phaze, and his companion Echo or Oche. "When you took

Tsetse to Hardom to help Purple play his game with the Hectare, I was the one you took, in the guise of Tsetse. I apologize for deceiving you in this manner."

Brown was amazed. "Thou? A man?" But she realized that it was possible. She had known that the person was larger than Tsetse, and of course she hadn't verified for gender.

"Yes. The prophecy indicated that my cooperation was required if the planet shell was to be saved. Thus I was integral to Phaze Doubt, and Nepe brought me to help her fetch the key element of the counterploy."

Phaze Doubt. She realized that that would have been their name for the project to save Phaze. "The key element?"

An attractive young woman of about seventeen stepped up. "I was the one he fetched, in the form of a BEM seed," she said. "I am known currently as Weva, though with the reversal this is approximate. I want to thank you, Adept, for enabling me to come into existence, and to help save Phaze."

So this was the new BEM Adept, whose music had indeed saved Phaze! Without her, all would have been lost. "I be glad, now, it happened," Brown said.

"My companion Flach sends his regrets, and those of the Robot Adept; they are occupied at the moment in conjuring the last snow demons to the western reaches, where it is now suitably cold. I offered to help, but Flach preferred to handle it himself."

Brown looked at her. "Thou dost disagree?"

Weva smiled wryly. "Not really. I think he has to bid farewell to a certain snow demoness before he can get serious about me."

Brown laughed. "Methinks I heard about Icy! Believe me, he had his future not with her!"

"True. But I think I will remind him of it several times before I let him settle down to his future with me. Meanwhile, I am glad to meet you, who were instrumental in my genesis. I had no parents, really, but I always thought that someone like you—" She shrugged. "A foolish notion, of course."

"A mother figure?" Brown asked, amazed.

"I should not have mentioned it," Weva said quickly, flushing. "Now I realize that I had no right to cast you as—"

"Nay, girl, I be not affronted!" Brown exclaimed. "Gladly would I have had a child like thee, an it been possible without—"

A tear showed at the girl's eye. "Then—?"

"May I hug thee, Weva?"

"Oh, yes!" Weva opened her arms and embraced her.

"Thou must visit me," Brown said. "Thou and thy young—" She hesitated. "Flach and Nepe be similarly reversed?"

"Yes. We are working it out. For now, we agree that he is male and I female. In time I'm sure the ambiguity will be resolved."

"Surely it will," Brown agreed. It occurred to her that there could be another reason that Weva chose to identify with her, Brown. That sexual ambiguity . . .

Now a unicorn stepped forward. It was Neysa. She assumed her woman form, actually that of Nessie the Moebite emulating hers. "I be last," she said, " 'cause my burden be most onerous."

"Thou?" Brown asked, astonished. "Thou hast been always my best friend, Neysa!"

"Aye. That be why my pain be most, that I betrayed thee in thine hour o' need."

"What? Thou didst ne'er—"

"Nay, I did! When thou didst tell me what I somehow had ne'er fathomed before, and sought my support."

"Thou gavest it, Neysa. Thou didst—"

"I said thy shame would not be known. I, who loved outside my species, and had not the courage to confess it, and who condemned my filly when she did have the courage—how could I have condemned thee for loving in other manner! I were a hypocrite when I hurt thee, Brown, and deep be my grief thereof." There had been one tear at Weva's eye; there was a stream at Neysa's eyes. "It were not thy shame, O truest friend, it were mine."

Brown opened her mouth to protest, but was frozen. For from the mare radiated the splash of truth. It caused the air to shimmer, and the ground to ripple, and the sky to shift color. It crossed the assembled folk, and from them radiated echoing splashes, their ripples crisscrossing. That backwash intersected the spot where Brown and Tsetse stood, and suddenly Brown felt the great current of support from all the gathering. They knew—and they accepted her way, as she accepted theirs.

Brown embraced Neysa. "There be no shame," she said. Now it was true. The last doubt of Phaze had been resolved.

Author's
Note

This is the second Author's Note in this series of no-note novels. Don't froth at the mouth; you read this novel for better or worse.

One of the criticisms of my Author's Notes has been that a novel should stand on its own and not need to be explained separately. I suspect that such critics read neither the novels nor the notes with much comprehension, because normally my notes discuss not the novels, but my life and times during the writing of the novels, or they may give credits to particular readers who suggested notions used in the novels. Well, muster your ire, because this time I shall discuss the novel.

Two names were borrowed from those of readers who wrote to me, though the characters surely bear little resemblance to the originals: Alyc and Jod'e. Another went the other way: Icy turned up in real life as a reviewer in an amateur magazine, *Fosfax*.

I was accused of doing a poor presentation of a lesbian, in the second Adept novel, *Blue Adept*. It must have been poor, because I had no lesbian character there, or in any of my novels. Apparently some readers assumed that a woman who hated men had to be a lesbian; I don't see it that way. But in this novel I do have a lesbian, and any of that persuasion may now chastise me for doing it wrong. Certainly homosexuality is not one of my stronger subjects, but I felt that it wasn't fair to exclude a sizable segment of the human population—about ten per cent—from representation in my fiction. Do I think that such folk are misguided, and that appropriate therapy will show them the error of their ways? No. No more than therapy would turn me gay. I would resent anyone, however well intentioned, trying to reverse my sexual orientation, so I follow the Golden Rule and leave the gay community alone. No, I don't exclude them from friendship, and yes, I wouldn't want my daughter to marry one. Fair enough?

There were several problems in the course of the writing of this novel. For example, in the interest of developing new games for the game sections, I subscribed to *World Game Review*—and then didn't use it. The novel led me in other directions than I expected. This sort of thing happens to writers. Sometimes characters take over their roles, too, and enlarge their parts, as Icy the demon chief's daughter did. She was supposed to be a bit part, but she played me for a sucker with that sweater. You know, the one with the mountain contours.

I had intended to present the Master Game Grid layout here, so that interested readers could see exactly how every game was derived from the assorted grids and subgrids. But when I checked, I discovered no Master Grid. Oops! Two things, actually three, had happened. Years back I had worked out the full grid, and spent three hours one morning perfecting its details—then made an error on the computer that wiped out everything. I was never able to re-create it as I had had it. I can get very upset by such things, and I labor to see that they happen only once. Then I changed from CP/M to MS-DOS, and got everything set up—and a hard disk crash took it out. Later I changed computers, and my old one glitched. In sum, I couldn't get anything that might have been salvaged. I was dependent on prior printouts. But I had also moved to a new house, and my back papers were buried somewhere in the refuse, where we are slowly cleaning up a decade's worth of neglect. Eventually we'll find those printouts, under a pile of other manuscripts. But I had a novel to do *now*. Which meant I had to do it without the Master Grid. Aarrgh!

Ah, now you understand. I faked it. This will be no news for reviewers, who have been privy to the fact that I faked any ability as a writer from the outset of my career. But I am sorry that I was unable to provide the Master Grid; it was my pride.

I try to benefit from anything that happens. Sometimes it's a struggle. I received a letter from a reader, Ben Mays, who said that his play group would be putting on a show in my county at such and such a date. I hate to take time off from writing to sleep, let alone for anything else, but I do have an interest in drama. I acted in college, and while I'm sure I was not a great actor, it benefited me by helping me to abolish stage fright and teaching me how to make myself heard by an audience when there was no mike. I support the arts, and acting is one of them. So I made myself go to the play.

It was a disaster. Oh, the play was all right, I'm sure; it was *Red Fox/Second Hanging*, and was of the kind where stage and costuming are minimal. In fact there were only three actors, all male, covering perhaps a dozen parts. They changed parts almost in midsentence, going from scene to scene without pause. It started as a dialogue with the audience and worked seemingly by accident into the content of the play, but was actually highly integrated. It was a story of backwoods Kentucky, corruption and law enforcement and odd histories. The whole thing was the kind that you don't see on mass market television, and yes, I think it's great that small groups maintain the tradition and bring this sort of art to communities like ours. Attendance was free, even.

So what's my gripe? Well, I was dead center in the audience, and the acoustics were such that the sound came at me from left and right, overlapped and garbled, and I could barely make out one word in ten. It was like watching TV with the sound turned down, or with interference that made the sound unintelligible: you can't get much of the sense of it, but do have a glimpse of what you are missing. I suffered about two hours of that, thinking how I could have been home working on this novel instead. What a waste! Others heard it, and there was a standing ovation at the conclusion, which I didn't join, because it would have been hypocrisy; I don't do something just to conform. If only I hadn't been stuck in that dead spot.

After the play I located Ben Mays and explained why I couldn't say anything about the play. He said that that is a problem in some theaters, and wondered why I hadn't moved to a better spot. Well, I should have, but I hadn't realized how big a difference location can make; I might have made a scene by moving, only to be in a worse spot. He also said that they had it on video cassette. Oh, okay. He sent me the catalog, and I ordered that and some records and audio tapes while I was at it. As I said, I support such enterprise, and one good way to support it is to buy their productions.

At this writing I haven't listened to any of it, because I have to assemble my new record and cassette tape players and I was determined to finish this novel before taking a break for anything else. But the material has had an effect on me, because one of the records, *Heartdance*, put out by a group called Song of the Wood, has a beautiful wraparound cover painting showing monstrous stone musical instruments cracking and being overgrown at a shoreline, as if some giant left them there millennia ago, and a girl dancing at the top of the fifty-foot-high hammered dulcimer. Beyond is a bucolic countryside, a village hamlet, and a distant castle on a hill. That picture fascinates me. In fact it set my fevered brain working, and I may use that as the setting for a future novel. Girl tunes in to the music of the ancient gods and dances to it, there at their ruins, and life stirs in the great old instruments that none alive can play, and—

But I don't mean to bore you. My point is that via this devious channel I did gain something of value to me: a compelling picture and an idea. However, I did try to use the experience of attending the play in this novel. When Purple played the game of the Cretan mystery with the BEM, that was really an unstructured play. Of course it didn't resemble the play I had seen, because I hadn't heard it, but it was what came out after the experience slopped around in my cranium for a while. So if you liked that scene, then you can say I benefited, and if you didn't like it, you can say I didn't.

When I got into that scene, I had a real headache working out the devious ploys and counterploys. I set it in ancient Crete because that is one of the aspects of ancient history that fascinate me. You may have noticed that I sneak bits of history into my novels, because my love is for the far future and far past; only the present bores me. Fine; I completed the scene and moved on. Then when I came through on my editing sweep, I got into trouble again.

You see, there are two pillars at the main gate to the great Palace at Knossos. One is round in cross section, the other square. I called the round one a cylinder, but what's a square one? It took me forty-five minutes to run that down (an ornery writer just doesn't know when to quit), and then I couldn't use the word. It's a right parallelepipedon (or you can leave off the last two letters). Technically, a polyhedron with right-angled parallelograms as faces. That is, a figure with four rectangular sides and two square ends. If all six sides were squares, it would be called a cube. Why couldn't they have had a simple four-letter word for a stretched-out cube? I decided on "block-shaped" and I do feel like a blockhead for wasting so much time on it. I mean, what idiot would spend three quarters of an hour editing a single word? Sigh; the worst of it is that I know that next time such a thing occurs, I'll do it again.

Yet in the course of that spot research I ascertained that the fabled land of Atlantis was in fact Crete (I looked in the book that showed the square columns, you see), destroyed by the eruption of Thera about 3,500 years ago. Those of you who have spent your lives searching for Atlantis may now relax; my forty-five minutes has serendipitously solved your problem. No, don't thank me; I do this sort of thing routinely for my readers.

Thus the troubled course of this novel, which is typical for me. Those who believe that great works of literature spring full-formed form the head of the author and that lesser ilk requires even less effort will want nothing to do with me, because I struggle and sweat over even indifferent material, as in this case. Most real writers do. But how I love that struggle!

This is the conclusion of the seven-novel Adept triology. To forestall the screams of outrage by fans of the series who never want it to end, and the sighs of relief by critics who never wanted it to start, let me explain that I regard some series as open, meaning they can continue as long as the market tolerates them, and some as closed, meaning that when their tales are told they are allowed to retire. This series is the latter type. This does not mean that I am abandoning fantasy, just that I am making way for a new series, Mode, whose framework is such that the whole of the Proton/Phaze frames can be considered a subset of it. That means in turn that should I some day suffer an irresistible urge to write another Adept novel, I could do so in the Mode context. That's neither a promise, fans, nor a threat, critics; merely a clarification I hope allows each of you to relax. This series has been phased out. Of course I have been wrong before, when I thought it was complete as a three-novel set; like a tropical tree, a series can sometimes regenerate from the roots. But I think it's done.